# TALES OF THE APT

## Volume III
## For Love of Distant Shores

# Tales of the Apt
# (NewCon Press)

Spoils of War (2016)
A Time for Grief (2017)
For Love of Distant Shores (2018)
Tales of the Apt 4 (2018) (forthcoming)

# The Shadows of the Apt
# (Tor UK)

Empire in Black and Gold (2008)
Dragonfly Falling (2009)
Blood of the Mantis (2009)
Salute the Dark (2010)
The Scarab Path (2010)
The Sea Watch (2011)
Heirs of the Blade (2011)
The Air War (2012)
War Master's Gate (2013)
Seal of the Worm (2014)

# TALES OF THE APT

## Volume III
## For Love of Distant Shores

Adrian Tchaikovsky

NewCon Press
England

First edition, published in the UK April 2018 by
NewCon Press
41, Wheatsheaf Road,
Alconbury Weston,
Cambs,
PE28 4LF

NCP146 Hardback
NCP147 Softback

10 9 8 7 6 5 4 3 2 1

ISBN: 978-1-910935-70-5 (hardback)
ISBN: 978-1-910935-71-2 (softback)

Cover art by Jon Sullivan
Editorial meddling by Ian Whates
Interior layout by Storm Constantine
Cover layout by Ian Whates

# Contents:

# Cities of Silver

*Being an account of Doctor Ludweg Phinagler's expedition to Lake Limnia, and what he found there, as told by his amanuensis, Fosse.*

Suffice to say, we had a good many reasons to leave Collegium just then, and I will not bore you with them, save that the good Doctor had just finished a terrible spat with Master Dormer of the Modern History faculty, with all the name-calling and bad reviews that entailed. As Master Dormer was a noted member of the Prowess Forum, and last seen stalking the halls of the College, blade in hand, demanding the Doctor's head, my employer thought it prudent to bring forward a piece of research he had been mulling over for some time. For myself, I confess to certain debts in respect of games of chance that had robbed the Collegiate streets of their customary appeal. I felt myself ready to travel again.

We made Helleron easily enough by airship, there to meet the artificer Jons Collier, whose work would be integral to our study. The Doctor himself swore he had sent messengers ahead whom our own passage had outstripped, and that he would have words with the Guild when we returned to Collegium, but certainly Master Collier was neither expecting nor pleased to see us. He had anticipated his invention being tested in the calm, blue waters of Lake Sideriti, north of Collegium. The prospect of roughing it on the moribund shores of Lake Limnia failed to enthuse him.

If Dr Phinagler, my employer, is good at any one thing, then it is his ability to bring people round to his point of view. By his usual combination of rhetoric, flattery and vague promises in respect of College funds, that I have often thought should be taught as an advanced class, he won Collier over.

A sketch of Jons Collier: a Beetle-kinden man of medium height, more slender and well turned out than most, bespectacled and of a neat and efficient manner, if seeming slightly agitated and/or exasperated at all times. This last may be an effect of his association with my employer.

Transporting Collier, his experiment and ourselves to Lake Limnia was another forbidding hurdle readily overcome. The keen student will appreciate that Limnia is deep within Imperial territories, where travel is closely regulated. However, the Doctor located a Consortium factora – a house of the Empire's mercantile arm, for the ignorant – and, as per his usual luck, found a factor whose caravan would be making a stop there.

The Doctor spent an evening wining and dining Lieutenant Hermon, the factor involved, and the two of them were soon boon companions, with Hermon promising to take us to Jerez, Limnia's only town, and the Doctor agreeing to credit Hermon in the eventual paper and generally tell people back at the College how very helpful the Empire was being. It may be that the Doctor might have slightly exaggerated his level of influence within the Assembly.

Master Collier was less delighted, and I suspect he harboured more concerns about Imperial policy than my employer, but he accepted with bad grace that we were hardly likely to get to Limnia any other way.

A sketch of Lieutenant Hermon of the Consortium: a stocky Wasp-kinden, both shorter and portlier than most of his kin, but as pasty as they all are. He wears a long coat to travel, dyed a faded black and yellow down the right side. His face is somewhat baggy, with pouchy eyes and a broken-veined nose telling of a rather dissolute lifestyle,

His sergeant, te Sander by name, was a more welcoming sight. A sketch: a strapping, strong-jawed man of my kinden, broad-shouldered and with a ready, pleasant smile. His skin – paler than Lowlander Flies – has many mementos of his military past, and he discussed them in detail with me over the course of several evenings while our respective superiors were sampling the Empire's brandy.

Hermon's caravan was comprised of three automotives, plus the fourth that the Doctor had persuaded Jons Collier to hire for our own equipment. Two of the Imperial wagons were stocked with goods

Hermon had purchased in Helleron – swords, crossbow bolts and machine parts made more cheaply, and to a more exacting standard, than in the Empire. The third carried a less happy cargo in the form of some three dozen men and women of various kinden, crammed in so that they must mostly stand at all times. The Doctor assured us that these wretches were criminals either exported from Helleron or being repatriated to the Empire after an escape. Master Collier did opine that merely wanting to leave the Empire was probably a criminal offence in and of itself, but not within Lt. Hermon's earshot.

In addition to the dozen regular soldiers under Hermon's command, there were half as many in full-face helms who discouraged any further investigation of the prisoners, and te Sander told me they were Slave Corps – said with a curl of the lip that told me he did not approve either. He pointed out that there were no Fly-kinden in the cage, and said that our own kinden were well provided for in the Empire, and that I would see for myself should I visit him in Capitas, an offer which he took pains to make as attractive as possible.

Our journey was of several tendays, with Hermon calling at various garrisons along the way. At each, he arranged for us to be found bed and board of a uniform and decent quality – such is the difference between travelling with the Empire's blessing and without, as any who intend to journey there should note. Had I space I would pen a gazetteer, for the sight of so many disparate cities beneath a single flag would be of interest to many, but alas... Another time, perhaps.

I can confidently say that Jerez, Lake Limnia, is the least welcoming place that I, a seasoned traveller, have ever beheld,

For one thing, it was raining. You may feel it harsh of me to hold that against the place, but believe me when I say that it rained *all the time* we were there, or at least, when not in active deluge the precipitation was just stopping or about to start. Even Dr. Phinagler, Master of the Geography faculty, was unable to explain how this could be so.

The community itself was an extended shanty town of slumping, ill-constructed shacks, merging without warning with the lake's reed-stubbled shallows that were cluttered with rafts and houseboats of dubious buoyancy. The one solid building was the Imperial garrison, and this was canted at a slight but noticeable angle because Jerez offered no foundations firmer than semiliquid mud.

Of the locals, who were stretch-limbed, pallid, sharp-featured creatures of a universally sly and sinister demeanour, the less said the better. For the record, they are known as Skater-kinden, and possess an Art to walk on water. Given the quality and quantity of the weather I am mildly surprised that they could not use the same to fly.

I will confess to one of my rare unprofessional moments on seeing this dismal vista. I found myself in my allotted rooms at the garrison feeling despairingly that I should have gone into accountancy as my mother had urged. I considered that – not for the last time – my association with the Doctor would be the death of me, possibly of pneumonia. Thankfully, te Sander came and cheered me up a little by saying that, of all the Empire's conquests, Jerez was the one that the Emperor would give back if he could. Sensing my delicate state, he was thoughtful enough to console me into the small hours.

Master Collier and my employer had the next of their arguments that morning, albeit in hushed tones so that our hosts did not overhear. It turned out that, whilst in his cups, the good Doctor had set our project before Lt. Hermon, and the lieutenant, similarly merry, had become quite enthused by the idea and pledged the Empire's assistance. Jons Collier was not keen on any further Imperial involvement, and the two conducted a fiercely whispered ideological debate that Dr. Phinagler won by the simple rhetorical device of pointing out that it was a done deal, and that backing out now would likely see us arrested as spies. Collier – though he made some unfounded predictions about my employer's likely eventual fate vis-a-vis digging a hole no Art would suffice to climb out of – accepted this logic. For myself, though I had some sympathy with Master Collier's stance, I found myself not averse to further Imperial interference – solely, of course, for the added ease and efficiency in respect of our project.

Some days later found us out on the lake on an enormous raft Hermon had commandeered from the locals. It had a sort of house at one end but, most importantly, a hole in the centre some five yards across. The walkway around it was another four yards wide and more, giving some idea of the scale of the vessel. Needless to say, the whole was slick with moss and weed, and appeared at all times to be on the cusp of disintegrating into its component parts. However, it bore the three of us, Hermon, te Sander and a couple of Hermon's men without complaint, along with a crew of half a dozen locals.

Apparently, the raft's design, so apt for our purpose, was to aid fishing, which I imagine is most of what there is to do in Jerez. The central hole, throwing a pool of sunlight onto the lake below, draws the smaller waterlife and concentrates it there, especially with the aid of a little bait thrown on the waters. This was explained to us by the raft's master, a gangling Skater called Scarvy. He is hardly worth a sketch but picture a grimy little man, not much past Fly-kinden size, with a long nose, chin and ears, and greasy hair down past his shoulders, then give him longer arms and legs than a tall man would know what to do with. He wore a padded tunic, stained with fish guts and worse. At first he was resentful about becoming Hermon's menial, but the Doctor practised upon him as his crew sculled us out onto the lake, and the prospect of what we intended quite hit a chord with the disreputable creature.

Specifically, Scarvy thought we were mad. He took pains to tell us that the lake was full of terrible, dangerous beasts that could destroy boats larger than his and pluck the crew from the water. More, he swore that the lake harboured worse terrors than this, though he did not specify save for vague references to unaccountable lights and sounds out on the water. All this was not said as an attempt to dissuade us – indeed he had the crew rowing all the harder for it. Scarvy, epitomising the meanness of spirit that Jerez must breed into its denizens, wanted to see what would happen to us.

At this point there was another argument between Master Collier and the Doctor which I recall well enough to set down in fair detail.

"You can't possibly be considering going ahead with this," was Collier's opening foray. "You've heard what he said. We're going to get killed." He had plainly been affected by Scarvy's tales.

"What? That there are large animals in the lake?" the Doctor retorted. "That is as expected. It is a large lake. That some are predatory? To be otherwise would be unnatural. We need a test in the wild, Jons. Little dunks in the pool at Helleron prove nothing save that it is watertight – a prerequisite, I grant you, but no more than that. If your invention is to be the great aid to research that you hope, it must be tested."

"And the other business? The man's strange lights and sounds?" enquired Collier.

"Stuff," declared Doctor Phinagler, with all that esteemed confidence he was noted for. I, however, who knew him better than most, was well aware that he can wheel that confidence out whether it is justified or not. More, I knew full well that the good Doctor's academic interests do more than flirt with the controversial. He is inveterately one of those men of study who believe that there is a Great Mystery to be uncovered behind each thing we know, always on the trail of some elder secret from the Bad Old Days: lost kinden, cryptic species, or some trace of an ancient and unknown civilisation. This was what starts so many of the disagreements he has with his peers.

I had the uncomfortable suspicion that the sort of tall tale Scarvy was mouthing had been the lure that had brought the Doctor to Lake Limnia in the first place.

This is probably the time to explain just what project my employer had devised with Jons Collier. I shall describe for you Collier's device, as Hermon's men drew the tarpaulin off it. That should satisfy both narrative and academic requirements.

It was a sphere, with circular windows of thick glass set into each quarter and an opening underneath. The construction was brass and bronze-shod steel, and all treated and caulked against the water. From its top, like the leaves of a radish, sprouted a bundle of ribbed leather rubes about a strong cable.

"Well I'm not going down in it," I recall Collier insisting.

"Of course you're not. I need you up here to manage the pump and winch," came the Doctor's reply, for this was the balance of the device – a strong engine to control the sphere's ascent and descent, and a set of mechanical lungs to freshen the air within.

Collier looked caught between relief and offence that he had already been written out of testing his own invention. Relief won out. "Why then, I salute your courage, but, Founder's Mark, I don't give much for your chances."

Doctor Phinagler waved his concerns away with a gesture suggesting that he would still magnanimously share credit with Collier despite his naysaying. "Fosse, if you're ready?"

I suspect my demeanour verged upon the unprofessional again, for just a moment. I certainly went so far as to ask, "Must I, Doctor?"

"You are my amanuensis, are you not? Well then, I may wish to dictate something."

Te Sander started forwards, and I truly believe that he would have tried to intervene on my behalf. It was to save him from his superior's displeasure – not to mention the withering force of the Doctor's scathing oratory – that I stepped forward to take my place.

Besides, I have always prided myself on my professionalism.

And Dr. Phinagler himself? Was he not daunted, you ask? I assure you that, whilst he remains a man of more many and varied flaws than I can, in all conscience, expose, cowardice is not one of them. Indeed, his blind faith in his own correctness is something often remarked on by his peers.

"Just a brief test dive, to start with, I think," he informed Collier. "Haul us up after ten minutes or so, eh?"

I will confess to mouthing the word 'five;' rather urgently at Master Collier, in a moment of weakness, but one problem with being Fly-kinden is that one is seldom on eye level with most people.

Conditions were cramped inside the sphere, and although Collier had included a ring of seats inside the circumference, the curve of the walls forced us both into a conspiratorial forward lean at all times. The Doctor kept shifting his place, seeking elusive comfort, even as Collier and Hermon started to hoist, and, as he is not a small man, the sphere swayed alarmingly as they manhandled it over the fishing hole. We had gained ingress via the opening in the sphere's underside, and soon the view through this changed from wildly-swinging deck to the dark water beneath.

I suggested that this aperture should perhaps be sealed before we progressed, but on enquiry of Jons Collier, it transpired that it was intended to remain open.

"The air within will keep the water out," Collier's distant voice assured us.

The Doctor seemed reassured by this. For myself, I had a number of tremulous and unscientific thoughts, and it was all I could do to stop my wings manifesting themselves – our kinden's natural reaction to peril.

The sphere began to descend. I could feel the faint breeze of the air pump and hear the grinding of the winch. The water crowded at the hole below us, lapping in an exploratory manner about the aperture's inner edge.

To my amazement – also my relief – whilst the water on the outside of the sphere swiftly occluded the round windows, the level beneath us climbed only so high as to make the Doctor draw up his feet to avoid wetting his sandals.

The light swiftly dimmed, leaving us in muddy gloom – the shadow of the raft combining with Limnia's natural murkiness to throw us into eclipse. Undaunted, the Doctor opened a panel in the sphere's upper reaches, letting in a cold, greenish illumination. The Doctor explained that any flame-based illumination would compete with us for the same goodness in the air that we ourselves would need to live, and so Collier had harvested the organs of fireflies in order to gift us with light.

Through all this we were still descending, but soon we came to a halt, suspended in the dark. The view out of the windows was not an inspiring one, being just the dour water with flecks of organic matter catching in our light. When we were stationary, though, the luminescence attracted a scattering of fish and other small water creatures to gawp in on us, and I was uncomfortably aware that it might just as easily call up the sort of predatory giants that Scarvy had referred to.

Even as I thought this, the Doctor was directing my attention to beneath our feet. I had briefly forgotten that we had an additional unglazed window there by default.

"Look at that beauty," the Doctor said, and I looked.

It was hard to make out – a shadow passing deep beneath us, not picked out by our light so much as silhouetted there: the long teardrop shape of a water scorpion gliding through the abyss, hooked arms held close to the beaked head, and its long stalked tail behind. How large, I could not say, but greater than our little sphere of a certainty. You must bear in mind that Lake Limnia is truly huge – one can see water to the horizon from any bank. It is like a little freshwater ocean.

As we were to discover, all manner of surprises were hidden within it.

Soon after, the sphere jerked and we began to ascend. I confess I did indicate by my manner that I was glad of it, and the Doctor reprimanded me for my lack of a true scholar's love of investigation.

Jons Collier was in much better spirits on seeing that we had not drowned, suffocated or been devoured, and he and the Doctor were quickly discussing the technical aspects of the experiment. Another descent was soon arranged for the next day, and I was instructed to write up a report of the morning's activities.

It was while I was writing up my notes back at the garrison that I found the Doctor standing over me with one of his speculative looks. The expression, very familiar to me, was one of a man who has found a place to push, and is wondering just how much of the world he will break open when he inevitably tries it.

"I don't think the lieutenant has grasped it," he remarked to me. "Collier has, I suspect, but he's keeping his thoughts to himself." He leant over my shoulder and tapped a finger on the page. "Silhouetted against *what*, eh? Tomorrow, we're going deeper. Collier's fairly sure the sphere will stand it." He gave me a smile intended to be reassuring, "Do you know, nobody has even worked out how deep Lake Limnia is?"

The next day we were greeted by a regatta.

The news had spread swiftly that a Collegiate Master was about some piece of lunacy on the lake, and when our huge raft put out, we found ourselves escorted by a flotilla of all manner of lopsided and unlovely boats, rafts and other floating objects not worthy of any civilized label. It seemed that every outsider in Jerez had hired some locals to paddle them out to watch our experiment, and a fair number of the locals themselves had come to join them. Although I am writing with the benefit of bitter hindsight, I like to believe that I felt some stirrings of suspicion, even then. Perhaps I am wrong, and perhaps that lurking, sinister people had no part in what happened next, but I am convinced otherwise, and I will say that a shudder passed through me, seeing them all hunched and angular and watching us.

Doctor Phinagler took the attention in good humour, waving to his audience, and wanting to make some manner of speech, save that nothing had been brought that might have allowed his voice to carry so far. Jons Collier, in contrast, was plainly embarrassed by it all.

At last the Doctor and I re-embarked, settling ourselves in the close confines of Collier's sphere as best we could. The Doctor's instructions this time had been, "Take it down as far as we have cable, and leave us there for at least half an hour."

I took one yearning look out of the portholes at the daylight, and the people, and te Sander especially, whose own expression was a particularly fetching one of worry for my wellbeing, a look that certainly seldom graced the Doctor's face. Then we were in motion, lurching in jolting stages towards the water, and then beneath it. Once again, the air within contrived to keep the water out, as though they had come to some manner of gentleman's agreement that might be broken at any moment by the wrong word. Once again our firefly-organ lamps gave out their odd luminescence, drawing the little insects and fish of the lake to come and goggle at us. This time, though, the winch did not stop, and we plunged downwards into an utter pitch.

The Doctor appeared to be counting, and at some point significant only to him he covered the lamps once more, and I thought we should be left in complete and utter darkness that even my eyes could not pierce.

Yet we were not. It seems as astonishing to me now as it did then, my post-facto knowledge replacing the initial novelty as the source of my wonder. When the lamps were sealed up, I quickly detected a cool, pale radiance coming from *outside* that our own light had served to hide.

I locked eyes with the Doctor. There are rare moments when we share a discovery in such a fashion, just he and I, and I genuinely appreciate the privilege of being his amanuensis. It is only a shame that they are few and far between and so often followed by prolonged periods of extreme peril. This was to be no exception.

"Look below," he told me, indicating the open aperture beneath, where the water lapped – a little higher now that we had gone deeper.

The sight that greeted me will remain to my dying day among the most awe-inspiring and beautiful from all my many travels.

Below us, through the murk of the water, was the source of that radiance, and I saw there a great swelling curve of silver – and then more, a whole conglomeration of them, as though a family of moons had somehow been trapped in the depths of Lake Limnia. Distance and scale were impossible to measure, but they must have been vast, and I had the sense of shadows within them, not simply grand bubbles of light, but things as intricate as living creatures.

"What am I looking at, Doctor?" I asked.

"I have not the faintest idea," quoth the man of learning.

Then a shadow passed between them and us. For a moment I thought that it was the water scorpion again, but those grasping arms were absent. Instead I beheld the grand oval of an enormous beetle that sculled across the face of the silver light. The pale luminosity leached all colour from it, but I could see the patterns of its shell, a light band edging the darker shade of its thorax and elytra.

The Doctor made a slight sound of consternation. I understood later that he had made a better estimation of just how large the creature was. Still, what happened next was unprecedented.

We had lost sight of the monster for a moment, as its path took it beyond our narrow window, but a moment later it was back, coursing below us, far closer, and actually turned on its back so that its great dark eyes could scrutinise us. I, who had been foolishly thinking how lucky we were that the scorpion was not about, was given a harsh lesson in natural history by the sight of enormous sickle-shaped mandibles, far larger than would be needed to scissor even a man of the Doctor's proportions in half with a single twitch. The breadth of their gape threatened the diving sphere itself.

The creature was interested in us. The second pass was inexplicable otherwise. Even though our lights were out it was drawn to us, for all that we would be wretchedly inadequate morsels for its undoubted appetite.

Then it was gone again, and I ventured to ask, "Doctor, what signal did you arrange, with Master Collier, should we wish to be drawn up *earlier*?" I recall clearly that the question was couched in just such calm tones, and no other.

It was plain from the look on my employer's face that this was a detail neither he nor Collier had considered.

A moment later I saw a great rounded bulk occlude the windows on one side, and then it had brushed us, the slightest of contacts, and we were swinging and spinning in a great slow-motion dance through the water.

*Let them notice that!* Surely Collier and the others up above would feel the motion through the cable and know something was amiss. The Doctor and I were clinging desperately to the seats to avoid being thrown out of the central aperture, and as the sphere revolved I had momentary glimpses of the great black bulk of the beetle on its way back, coasting sedately towards us with its jaws agape.

Then the winch above started its work and we lurched into a sudden ascent that nearly pitched both of us into the water. The beetle picked up speed with flicks of its paddle legs, but our abrupt motion had misled it, and its curved and armoured back passed beneath us close enough to reach a foot down and touch. My eyes met the Doctor's with sudden elation. We were free of it!

The next moment we were most certainly not, as the beetle had turned with remarkable speed and shouldered into us, one hooked leg scrabbling at the side of the sphere. I fell from my seat, and was half into the lake before the Doctor and my wings had hauled me out, and the world around us was wheeling madly. Up above, I could only guess at the chaos that was being enacted – the raft was not exactly sturdy, nor was the winch so strongly bolted to the deck to survive much additional strain.

I could see some segments of the beetle's underside in one window. The creature was vertical beside us, scrabbling to hook a limb on our round hull, its head out of sight above, and more of the rest of it similarly unseen below. We were still ascending, though, and I dared to hope that it would lose hold and fall back into the depths from which it came. I had not considered what that fearsomely-armed head might be doing.

Then it happened: without warning our upward motion died away and we were descending again, almost ridiculously smoothly, leaving the beetle behind with our sudden change of direction. We dropped back into the silver abyss, and it seemed to me that each second we descended faster and faster.

"Why are they letting us down?" I asked the Doctor, and he turned an expressionless face to me.

"They are not," he said. "It has severed the cable."

By then the water had touched my toes, and I saw to my horror that the level was rising up the inside of the sphere – and intuited with an unwanted clarity that there must be air escaping from the ravaged tubes above us. And what would that matter, came my next thought, when we were dropping into the void, all contact with the sunlit world cut from us?

Then, and just as I would have sworn the worst had already happened, the beetle came back for us.

I saw it rush out of the silvery light, a swift-sculling shadow diving for us, and I thought that it was going to ram the sphere. Instead, at the last moment, those great jaws gaped, and an instant later it had us, the entire sphere within its mandibles. Almost immediately I heard a whole orchestra of groans and creaks as the insect's strength began to crush inches of solid metal. One point of its mandibles forced itself through the wall by the Doctor's head, and our spherical space became abruptly oblate. And all this time the beast was swimming down, towards the light.

It took no care with us, and in moments our conveyance was on its side, and the air's inclination to keep the water out vanished almost immediately, so that a roomful of lake washed over us with a force like a hammer blow. I was thrown against the sphere's side, my head bouncing from the window, and I remember little more.

I awoke to light.

There is much philosophical speculation as to whether some figment of our selves survives death in some way. Many of the Inapt people have very colourful legends about ghosts and other worlds and the continuation of spirits and essences and such credulous business. Still I confess that, waking into that omnidirectional pale radiance, I felt that I had travelled to another world, one where such stuff as gross matter was but a memory. Perhaps, I considered, those Inapt sages were right about this one thing.

Then I heard a groan, and saw that, lain next to me, was Doctor Ludweg Phinagler, and abruptly I found I was uncharitably hoping that I was not dead after all, if only because spending some post-life existence of unspecified length with the Doctor would seem to be a poor consequence of having been his employee in life. The final nail in the coffin of Inapt belief was knocked in by the fact that beside us was the ruin of Jons Collier's diving sphere. Certainly no Inapt afterlife would allow you to bring your machines with you.

I stood somewhat shakily and regarded the wrecked device, for it was an easier thing to understand than our surroundings. I saw plainly where the beetle's jaws had deformed it, where the brass casing had split, the steel ruptured. A little more force, I felt, would have sufficed to crack the entire contrivance open like an egg.

"So where are we now?" I mused. "This is no beetle's gullet, but what is it?" The light came from all around, and it had been blinding in the moments after opening my eyes, but now I had adjusted and I found that we were in a room of unusual angles. The walls and floor were all of a substance unfamiliar to me – not stone nor wood nor metal, but a pale, gauzy, translucent material that gave very slightly at the touch but nonetheless seemed remarkably strong, as though someone had learned to freeze cloth in place.

The light seemed to come from tiny fragments trapped within the substance of our surroundings, and beyond the confines of our prison – for that was the sense I was increasingly given of the space – I could see suggestions of other chambers.

"Fosse?" came the Doctor's voice, and I turned to find him sitting up.

Moments later, he had exhausted the limited range of exploration available to him, marvelling at the fabric of our new quarters but noting, as I had, that we were in a chamber that had somehow admitted the diving sphere, and yet had no doors whatsoever.

My kinden have a particular horror of being trapped. We are so used, through our wings and our small size, to being able to come and go as we please, that the wonder of that place's construction wore off almost immediately and left me only with a gnawing dread. I sat on the wreck of Collier's sphere, arms about my knees, while the Doctor pottered in a circle about the confines of our cell, nothing daunted, even whistling to himself a little. The instant annoyance of that tuneless and arrhythmic sound went no small way towards keeping me sane.

Then he stopped – walking and whistling both – quite suddenly, and in a hushed voice called me over.

I dropped down to where he was, but could see nothing more than another span of that pale wall. The Doctor guided me, shifting me left and right until I saw. At a certain angle, the wall became almost transparent, as through some trick in the weave, and I found myself looking out at our captors.

There were three of them, and the most remarkable thing was how familiar they seemed, for they were Beetle-kinden. All men, and all taller than the Doctor, I saw an elder and two youngers, broad-framed, strong but also run to fat. Although their race was unmistakable, their skin had a weird, pallid shade, the colour I imagine a Wasp might be after a day drowned in the lake. Compared to the Doctor's own pleasant rich brown, it was a unnerving sight.

They were dressed in robes, but of a cut and style I had never seen before: blue-grey silk rolling in sumptuous folds over their bulky bodies, and starched-looking epaulettes or pauldrons to fill out their shoulders, making them seem bigger still. The eldest had the most elaborate clothes, appearing every bit as grand as a magnate of Helleron, all gold edging and jewellery at his wrists and neck and fingers. He carried a staff that seemed made of something not unlike the walls, pearly-white and artificial. His two friends had some manner of tool or weapon scabbarded at their belts. Based on my usual luck I was already putting money on their being weapons.

We saw the older man's lips move and he gestured at us, and the Doctor murmured that they could surely see in a good deal easier than we could see out. A moment later a new figure had come into view, a hunched little monstrosity only a little larger than I and seeming something like the Skater-kinden up above, if only because its limbs were so oddly proportioned – legs very long and the arms, though short, held weirdly elbows-out. He had a moon-round face as pale as his masters' and short-cropped hair, and he wore a sort of smock that made me think of artificers. This prodigal creature approached the wall and ran some little device in a straight line, from the floor up to as high as he could reach, and in the wake of that the wall simply peeled back like fruit rind.

The Doctor and I backed up quickly, and the three Beetles swept into the room. I saw, without surprise, that the two younger men had their devices in hand – short metallic rods that were linked to their belts by a length of cord.

"Travellers," said the older man, regarding us with the coldest eyes I ever saw, "Welcome to Scolaris." Never was there less welcome in a man's voice.

It is to be said, however, that my employer is not the most astute man when it comes to picking up these little social nuances. This same faculty, I believe, accounts for both his ability to strike up an instant rapport with otherwise hostile strangers, and his inability to stay amongst colleagues and friends for more than a tenday without offending someone.

Additionally, although he is a geographer by specialty, he is a remarkably knowledgeable artificer, and often's the time I have wondered just how the world might have fared if he had shown a practical interest in that field to match his grasp of theory.

He strode towards the three men as though they were nothing, heedless of the wand that one of them raised, and examined the wall of our cell, which was now hanging like a curtain.

"Why this is most remarkable!" he exclaimed, oblivious to the eyes of all upon him. "It is silk indeed, and yet a moment ago I'd have sworn this was a solid wall." And, glancing about him, "but it all must be silk then. How is it held so?" There was such enthusiastic wonder in his voice, and frank admiration, that only a heart of stone would have denied him.

However, our chief captor seemed stone through and through. "Our secrets are not for outsiders," he snapped. A sketch of him here is appropriate, I think: though big, he was baggy, age drawing the bulk of him into sagging curves. His mouth was very wide, and seemed almost lipless, and the downturn at each corner presaged a poor temper. His eyes, each sitting in a web of wrinkles, were like slightly misted glass, so that I wondered how well he saw. His hands were knotted, short-fingered and arthritic. Despite all these signs of age he stood very straight.

"I have it. This entire room is akin to a tent, held suspended. The tensions between the ropes hold the walls straight and there must be – no, there's more than that – some chemistry at work? Some manner of treatment to stiffen the fabric...? How is that possible?"

"Very easily possible, for the learnéd," said the old man, but his voice had thawed, perhaps just a little. "I take it, from your erudition, that you are the master of this device, and no mere subject?" A twitch of his staff indicated Collier's sphere.

The Doctor glanced up, bright eyed. "Indeed, indeed, a remarkable experiment with, it would seem, rather unforeseen results." If he was not engaged in a polite discussion with his peers in a Collegiate drawing room, one would never have known it from his manner. "Doctor Ludweg Phinagler of Collegium, at your service."

"My name is Wellgrind," croaked the old man. "Master Wellgrind, and you have fallen into my domain."

I dared to speak. "We're within the lake, aren't we?"

I received a withering and contemptuous stare from all concerned, even from my own employer. For him, it was that the question was needless. He had already assimilated this fact and walked away from it. For the others, I was made to feel that my very existence was surplus to requirements and might be extinguished at any moment.

"I take it you are a man of learning," Wellgrind stated to the Doctor.

"Amongst my own people I am reckoned something of a prodigy," he confessed mildly. I felt that his claim was somewhat disingenuous, missing the opportunity of using a number of other adjectives favoured in Collegium, but the company had already made it plain to me that my views were not invited.

"Curious," said Wellgrind. "We ourselves hold no ideal higher than knowledge of the world and its workings, but we had not thought the same to be true of your Empire. We had thought that our first intruder

24

from that realm would be a warrior of some nature."

"Excuse me," replied the Doctor, greatly put out, "but it is not *my* Empire."

"Please." Wellgrind waved the objection away, looking as though the conversation had begun to bore him. "Do not think that we have no spies above the water. We are well informed of what manner of savages dwell on the shores of our domain."

Which was interesting in and of itself, and I had a sinking feeling, so to speak, as I considered all those locals who had come to watch our second dive. How many of them, I wondered, had secret, submarine paymasters? I should have known the Skater-kinden were a pack of shiftless and untrustworthy villains.

"Ah, well, I won't deny I was able to wrangle some Imperial help," the Doctor came back, with precisely the sort of dry, conversational tone that Wellgrind was using, "but in truth my home is very far indeed from yours. I come from the city of Collegium, and there a scholar such as myself is honoured above all things. The quest for knowledge is what has brought me here, and not any Imperial policy."

"And are you happy in your discoveries?" Wellgrind asked with a mirthless grin. He plainly intended the words as a taunt, to indicate to the Doctor that curiosity had led him fatally astray when it led him to Lake Limnia. Of course, as I noted, the Doctor is often poor at picking up such hints.

"I'm ecstatic!" my employer exclaimed. "What man of learning would not be? To think that such an advanced civilisation was flourishing unseen here – and with such a technology." He ran his hands over the curious fabric of the walls. "An architecture of silk, and a chemistry that must conceive of and enact things that Collegium has not dreamt of! The necessity of your surroundings here has plainly guided you on so very different a path to that which we have taken. I cannot imagine the untold histories behind it."

In all the world there are few things purer and more innocent than the enthusiasm of Doctor Phinagler.

I saw it work on Wellgrind, who plainly wanted to be menacing and tyrannical, but who was yet a man of letters and could not help but recognise something of a kindred spirit in the Doctor. "Perhaps you are something a little more than this Empire might send, at that," he conceded reluctantly. "Yet no doubt you have some knowledge of them, and would be prepared to speak of them, and of your own people...?"

"Hmm? Oh, of course." If the Doctor was very blasé about turning agent for the lake-kinden, I could hardly blame him. If I had the Empire as a neighbour on all sides, I would want to know as much as possible about it, too. Beyond that, it seemed unlikely that Wellgrind and his fellows would mount an invasion of Collegium. Perhaps, I mused, they might even end up sending students to the College, once my employer had infected them with his tales of its virtues. It is notable that the Doctor becomes a more fervent supporter of Collegiate policy the further away he actually travels from the city. Whilst there, he finds rather more to complain about.

"Then perhaps we should retire to more comfortable surroundings," Wellgrind suggested. "You would no doubt find some refreshment welcome, after such a tumultuous journey." He turned to sweep out, his two aides flanking him.

"Very kind," the Doctor agreed. "Come on, Fosse."

There was an awkward pause. "Alas," Wellgrind said at last, "the invitation was not extended to your slave. I cannot think that she would enlighten our conversation, and besides, if we are to speak of our sciences and our study, these are not matters to rattle in empty heads."

The word 'slave', that seemed to have rather easily bypassed the Doctor's notice, lodged quite securely in mine. It is our Lowlands' proud boast that Beetles, even the Helleren, do not hold slaves, having been the slaves of the Moths so long before. Here in the depths of Limnia, it would appear that matters had fallen out rather differently.

"But..." The Doctor made vague gestures in my direction. "I may wish to dictate something."

I, for my part, was attempting to lock eyes with him and transmit, by some Art hitherto undiscovered, the full length and importance of our association vis a vis not abandoning me to the mercies of strange aquatic Beetle-kinden. I think it was the eye-level problem that thwarted me, once again.

"One of our research assistants will record your every word," Wellgrind promised, again injecting a suggestion of menace that hit square on the mark with me but was lost entirely on the Doctor. "As for your slave, we will house her with our own subjects."

That, at least, sounded magnanimous, though there was something in his tone that did not match quite with the words. So, I thought, these Beetles think themselves absolute rulers, like little Emperors. Well, we will see precisely what their subjects think of that. I was firmly, and correctly, of the opinion that we two were in a great deal of trouble, and further, that if either of us was going to extricate us, it would not be my employer.

"I'll sort something out, Fosse, never you worry," were the Doctor's parting words to me, over his shoulder, as he left with Wellgrind and one of the two younger lake-Beetles.

The remaining Beetle regarded me as a cleaner might look at a stain, and then gestured, and the hunchbacked little man I had seen before hopped into view on his long legs, bowing unctuously.

"You heard Master Wellgrind, Stammers. Get her out of here. I wish to examine their conveyance," he said, and was already walking past me towards Colliers' sphere, fumbling at his belt for some manner of toolstrip.

Stammers, barely a foot taller than I, bowed and lurched as though he were on springs, and was abruptly right next to me. The moment the Beetle's back was turned, the menial's ingratiating smile decayed on his face, leaving as nasty a leer as I have ever beheld.

"Well now, ain't you a pretty little piece of flotsam," he hissed, hunching lower to put his face very close to mine.

"Good day to you, my name is Fosse of Collegium, a student of the Great College," I told him, trying the Doctor's trick. Apparently

Stammers did not have the same high opinion of learning as his masters, or possibly he simply had a low opinion of me in particular. A moment later one of his hands, small but with a grip like a vice, was about my wrist, and he was dragging me after him.

I stopped almost immediately, and for a moment he was physically hauling me along by my arm. I could not help it. The sight was breath-taking. For a moment I shared every jot of the Doctor's childish wonder.

Beyond our cell there was a hall, with the same weirdly-angled walls, and open entirely along one side, and beyond that...

It seemed another world, a world to itself. We were, I think, close against one side of it – for they would not have moved the bulk of the sphere further than they had need to – and I was looking into the very heart of what they called Scolaris. I saw a vast space about me, and it was cluttered with hundreds of chambers constructed as our cell had been. Each was held in place and shape by cables and tethers, so that what might once have been loose bags of fabric were pulled into taut, flat-walled shapes by ingenious use of tension and counter-tension, linked to each other and to the inside of the far distant dome in a complex webwork of architecture that must have taken three score mathematicians years to calculate. Cut a single tether, I felt, and the entire spanning assembly would simply spring out of existence. Reason suggested that there would be considerable redundancy built in by any sane architect, but reason was not in session just then, as I gazed out into that busy constellation of chambers. It all seemed so fragile, and yet so vast. Though the silver light was omnipresent, my eyesight was not sufficient to see the end of it.

Those chambers whose walls allowed me a glimpse within showed shadowy forms busily at work, likewise the tubular tunnels connecting proximate suspended halls. I saw some few fliers making somewhat laborious progress in the distance – too far for me to determine kinden save to be sure that no Fly ever handled the air so poorly.

The next yank from Stammers almost pulled my arm off, and I turned my wondering face to him, to find nothing but an expression of petty annoyance greeting me on features as devoid of poetry as a stone. My own kinden are small, but we are broad-minded and great-hearted, more alive to the beauties of the world than most others. In Stammers I saw a man far smaller than his physical stature, and so I pitied him.

Unfortunately, my pity was just one more thing entirely lost on him, and he hauled me onwards, dragging me onto a narrow bridge between hanging chambers, railed only by the near-invisible gossamer strands that were holding it aloft. Had Stammers not had such control of my arm I might just have taken flight right then, for I saw immediately how a good pair of wings would make anyone a master of the place. I could not have carried Stammers with me physically any more than I could mentally, however, and so my feet remained on the ground. This turned out to be important later.

I consider myself to be a personable sort of woman, but try as I might I cannot match the Doctor's effortless way with – frequently hostile – strangers. I did my best to make small talk with Stammers as the deformed creature hauled me over bridges and through suggestively intestinal circular tunnels, but he had taken an instant dislike to me which, I felt, was just a subset of his more general dislike for everything in the world except his vaunted masters.

"So, what manner of kinden are you then?" I tried.

"A bigger kinden than you, you little freak," came the reply.

"And what is the position you hold here?"

"Oh I do what my masters tell me. I help them with their experiments. I clean up their little messes. And I handle their subjects, oh yes I do."

I was having my doubts about the terminology used in Scolaris, for Stammers seemed like nobody's idea of a majordomo.

"You are an artificer, then?" cued by his smock, from which an assortment of hard-to-identify tools was hung.

"Oh no, oh the masters would whip me if I claimed it. Just a lowly assistant me, but if I'm very, very good, maybe they'll let me play artificer with a pretty-faced little freak like you, eh?"

By this time I will confess that my usual sunny personality had started to show a few clouds. "And what sort of a stupid name is Stammers anyway?"

At that he stopped – we were in a descending passageway where the stiffened fabric underfoot had been woven rough to provide purchase, and just about to enter into a new chamber. Stammers' mean, pinched face glowered at me, and I knew I had struck a nerve. "Oh the masters" – and ever that reverential tone over that word - "give many names, little freak. You'd better hope you never earn one. Maybe I'll suggest they call you stumpy, or gimpy, or lefty, eh?"

His meaning was not entirely clear, but no more pleasant for all that.

As we had moved resolutely downwards throughout our journey, the quality of our surroundings had begun to acquire a more slipshod feel to it, and the lights were less frequent, the overall conditions gloomier and the very fabric of our surroundings seeming dirtier. The chamber that we entered was awkwardly slanted, so that both Stammers and I progressed as though walking along the side of a hill. But I saw figures ahead that instantly seemed to make sense of everything I had seen here so far, and I leapt to a conclusion in exactly the way that the College masters caution students not to.

There were two of them and they were Spiders, and to my ignorant eyes the hunched figures with them seemed merely servants or escorts. Spider-kinden were common enough in Collegium for me to know their ways a little, and each one of them seemed at the least a minor lord or lady of their convoluted body politic, walking through our Beetle streets as though it was the height of our good fortune that they deigned to honour us with their presence. I knew they ruled vast lands across the sea to the south, and had dozens of other kinden as loyal and willing subjects to their will, such was their charm and mastery of the human mind. Everything fell into place in that moment. Of course cold-mouthed Wellgrind did not rule this place: here were the masters that Stammers spoke of. They stood, the pair of them, slender and pale, he silver- and she gold-haired, and I tried to pull ahead of Stammers to approach them, earnest to make a good impression on the true rulers of Scolaris.

"Lord and Lady, I present the compliments of my city of Collegium!" I announced. "I present myself Fosse, ambassador and scholar, at your service!"

There was a terrible silence. I have, in the past, said the wrong thing in the wrong company, but never to that degree.

I looked again at the two Spiders. They were wearing only shifts that left their limbs bare, and they seemed slighter than others of their kinden I had seen. Or perhaps it was that they did not hold themselves with the customary arrogance and mastery I was used to. Perhaps it was that they stood turned in upon themselves, every line of their body shielding themselves against the world.

Mostly, though, it was that they did not meet my eyes. I have never before known a Spider-kinden who would not look into anyone's face boldly, even a criminal trading gazes with a sentencing judge, This man and woman were cowed and humbled, retaining the fair seeming of their kinden but with all the power and majesty stripped from them.

They were prisoners too, and the hunched, Stammers-like creatures with them were guards.

"More subjects, is it?" Stammers demanded, and his fellows nodded. They had the same peculiarity of limb as he, the same rounded back and moon face, but seemed to me less objectionable of feature and manner, though perhaps that was merely through my more casual acquaintance with them. I had the horrifying revelation that perhaps this kinden had arisen through repeated pairings between Wellgrind's Beetles and the Skater-kinden above, a thought so repulsive in every particular that it turned my stomach.

"Toss 'em in." And then Stammers was hauling me towards the lowest end of the room, and I realised that the far wall was, in fact, further than I had thought, and that there was another chamber beneath us, slightly offset for ease of access, and that it was occupied.

The two Spiders had been brought with me, and moments later they were pushed unceremoniously over the edge, the man crying out but the woman staying resolutely silent. I was already thinking what I would do – take flight, evade the guards, go… where? For I was lost in this dreadful sunken place, and at the mercy of its inhabitants.

The dregs of a plan started to come together in my head, belatedly. No fool would drop me into a pit to keep me safe if they thought I could fly. I must therefore hide my ability, and make the most advantage of deploying my wings when the opportunity presented itself.

Not calling on them instantly, as I was shoved over that abyss, required a fearsome effort of willpower, and I am afraid I was sufficiently unprofessional so as to scream a little on the way down – adding verisimilitude to my deception. I could only hope the landing beneath was soft enough to warrant casting people down onto it whom my captors might later have a use for. As it happened, though, I found myself caught by a pair of strong yet slender arms.

The silver light was tightly rationed down here, and the walls curved steeply out from the opening above, then in towards the sagging centre of the floor where the bulk of the residents were clustered – less a room than a bag, a sack to keep people in. The fabric gave slightly even beneath my small weight, explaining how those above could throw people down here so blithely.

It was the Spider-kinden man who had caught me. The expression on his face was stark, nameless – my eyes, keen even in this gloom, could not identify it. He set me down gently.

There were perhaps around a score and a half of Spider-kinden here, men and women, most young but some of middle years – and that was a tell-tale too because Spiders where I come from have arts and cosmetics enough to look young even if they walk with a cane. The bulk of them were simply sitting in a despondent mob, many seeming to be hurt or simply half-starved. They spared me not a glance.

The man who had caught me, and the woman he had been thrown in with, seemed to retain a little more spirit, probably just because they were newly arrived. I studied them, and after a while I felt as though I was intruding on something private. They were fair and well-formed as Spiders always are, but so stripped of the expected self-assurance that I was horrified and yet unable not to look. Their natural grace had become something fleeting and furtive, the slave's agility that teaches how to roll with a blow. The magnetic Art and force of personality that was wont to demand, *Look at me*, now cringed back with, *Overlook me, master, please*. It was as though I saw Spider-kinden naked for the first time. It was as though I saw them anatomised on a slab. I felt profoundly ashamed and guilty, and yet fascinated.

"Good day to you, my name is Fosse of Collegium, a student of the Great College," I said faintly. Where before, Stammers' hostility had turned aside the words, here it was the apathy of the majority. Only the two who had preceded me down here were paying me any heed at all.

"This is how the Beetles treat their subjects, is it?" I threw in, as though I was the great cosmopolitan traveller who had seen all manner of accommodation in my time.

"No," the man said very quietly. "This is." He reached out and snagged the arm of one of the more introverted Spiders. I say 'arm', but in truth there was little left of it – some manner of corrosion had eaten away all the flesh below the elbow, but the bones were bizarrely attached and still together, coated with a verdigris-like patina. What was worse was the skin just about the elbow, where some neat hand had marked off various demarcations and lines, with careful numerical annotations beside them. This was no accident, no carelessness in a laboratory. Some painstaking artificer had been at work, with measurements and scrutiny.

In one of those sudden-reversal moments that seem to attend so many of my travels, I redefined the local use of the word "subjects" with special reference to Master Wellgrind and his fellows' love of science.

"I am Tarn," said the Spider-kinden man. "This is my sister, Ilve. You have plainly come from somewhere far away. I am sorry that you have come to this place."

"She is just some experiment," came a cracked voice from the pack. "Some creature from the vats and the tables."

"Did you not hear how she addressed us?" Ilve returned sadly – everything she did was laced with profound melancholy, beyond even a slave or subject's lot. "How very far from here you must have come from, to speak such words."

"Then she is mad," scoffed the doubter.

"I am neither mad, nor grown in a vat," I announced, as grandly as I could manage. "And I do come from far, far away, from the upper world, and not this lake at all." Because it was still their home, I left out a number of choice adjectives. "I am come here with my employer, Doctor Phinagler, as an embassy to your city. Where I come from, there are no slaves, nor 'subjects' such as you have become. Even the meekest and poorest may walk the streets in safety, and nobody goes hungry or without a roof over their heads." Or that was the idea, anyway. I will not say that Collegium has quite achieved all of this, but we certainly intend to. We are working on it.

If I was expecting instant revolution and the institution of voting as soon as I had finished speaking, I was to be disappointed. The bulk of them were still ignoring me, and Tarn and Ilve looked at me only with sympathy, but not with any hope. Into the silence was dropped a single mocking grunt, though, far too deep to come from any Spider throat.

My attention was drawn to a figure hunched at the very edge of the floor, where it curved up to become the wall. He sat in the darkest spot in the room, and filled it. I saw impossibly broad shoulders and eyes that glittered in a small, round head.

Tarn put out a hand to restrain me but I was already approaching cautiously, rounding the group of apathetic Spiders to get a better look. This, I was to discover, was Donarvan, and he is worth a sketch for his very appearance.

When standing, I suspected he would be seven feet tall, twice my height, and the breadth of his shoulders perhaps all of four feet. His arms were huge to match, the hands looking each big enough to crush my ribs. His waist, by contrast, was far narrower, the torso making an exaggerated triangle, and his legs were, if not slender, then strong like a dancer's rather than a weight-lifter's. His head really did seem almost comically small, joined to those massive shoulders with very little neck. Round, hairless, almost noseless, with a lipless gash of a mouth, only his eyes seemed human. His skin was the colour of bronze after it has lost its shine.

I saw at once that he was like a Scorpion-kinden, and guessed his totem from that – the same beast we had seen pass beneath us on our first dive. He lacked that people's snaggling fangs, and their thumb and finger claws, but his Art had given him more terrible weapons than that. From over each set of knuckles arched a great hook, extending his reach by most of a foot. My imagination helpfully supplied an image of those long arms snapping out, the inward turned point of that hook catching me over the shoulder, driving deep into my flesh and then drawing me towards that bleakly murderous visage.

"Fosse, you mustn't," Tarn cautioned, and indeed I was keeping my distance, save that the room was so cramped, and his arms so long, that this was more difficult than you might think.

"Scoff all you want," I said, to the Water-scorpion, and to all of them. "I'm to be nobody's experiment." I was going to say something about the Doctor rescuing me, but even as I thought it I decided that there was such a thing as stretching the truth beyond all credulity. Even then, I heard voices above, though, and one of them very familiar – oh, I can tell you, I felt ashamed to have doubted him then. Here was Doctor Phinagler himself, and he had come to rescue me after all, having smoothed things over with our captors, No doubt we would be back on the surface, no doubt, no doubt…

Faces peered over the lip, looking down on us from the room above. Two were fishbelly pale, and one was dark.

"And here you see the holding pen for our experimental subjects," I heard Wellgrind's loathsome voice. "These are in readiness for my house's next studies, or are being studied following the minor, less disruptive procedures. The ready supply of them is limited, of course, but knowledge must be advanced. I, for one, will endure the hardship of fewer slaves to ease my bodily comforts, if it advances the cause of science."

The Doctor looked down – his expression was hard to make out, with the bulk of the light behind him, but I did my best to meet his eyes. He saw me there, sure enough, and glanced sidelong at Wellgrind. I think he said something, too quiet to hear. I am sure he registered some complaint.

When he looked back at me, I made out a helpless, awkward expression on his face – one very familiar from Collegiate society, which in many ways is mimicking old Inapt customs it does not truly understand. It was an expression that denoted that he wanted to say or do something, and yet to do so would be terribly impolite, and the social impasse had defeated him.

I wanted to call out to him. No, I wanted to *cry* out to him. The same social strictures had seized on me, however, and I would give nobody the satisfaction. What self-destructive mores we do surround ourselves with.

The heads withdrew. The voices receded.

I could sense Tarn and Ilve's eyes on me, their useless, wasted sympathy that they should better spare for themselves. As far as I was concerned, I was getting *out*. My options had narrowed to the point where any next step in the plan was purely theoretical. *Out of here* was its own reward.

Then the big Scorpion chuckled, quiet and yet hugely amused, and I rounded on him. "That's funny, is it, where you come from? What a primitive sense of humour you do have!"

"Fosse, no –" started Tarn, but I wanted to take my frustration out on someone, and the giant looked like the only one I would get a rise out of.

"I don't see the rest of you doing anything," I snapped at them. "And you – there you are, so much cursed bigger than me, and all hooks and claws, and are you any better off? So laughing at me's the only joy you're likely to get –" My next words were lost in a kind of a squeak as he stood up.

More than seven feet, I decided. In fact, he was probably not far from just reaching up and hauling himself out. I had expected a kind of savage stoop, with those hooks dragging on the ground, but he stood very straight, making his bizarre physique almost a caricature of a strong man. He wore only a loincloth of what looked like fishskin. The anatomist voyeur in me was thrilling even as the rest of me froze in fear.

"I am very hungry," he said, almost a whisper, but a purring bass whisper that thrummed the very weave of the walls.

I made some sort of interrogatory noise.

"Do you think, having got me down here, they will be calling me up for their experiments?" he murmured, taking one step forwards, so that if I had wanted to evade his reach I would have had to push myself against the very far wall of our sagging prison. "This is the experiment, right here."

Tarn and Ilve had gone very quiet and still, prey in the presence of a predator. I made my noise again.

"The Beetle-kinden believe that my people eat human flesh – by choice, by necessity, the details vary. It is one of the ways they know they are more civilised than we. So here I am, unfed for days, and penned with their *subjects*, of whom they have a sufficiency. And I am very, very hungry."

"And do you…?" I could not stop myself asking, cursing the scholar in myself. "Eat human flesh, I mean."

"We await the results of their experiment," the Water-scorpion growled, still oh-so-softly, though the deep smooth rumble of his voice turned my insides to water – and yet, at the same time and despite everything, something in me responded in a very different way. Power and control is always attractive, and given the company, his was the only game in town just then. You may be shocked, but I learned then that a man so very keenly perfected for violence, and who is fully aware of it, has a destructive allure to him that goes beyond kinden.

"I'm getting out of here," I told them all.

Tarn and Ilve's impotent empathy only increased at my declaration, and the Scorpion's thin smile broadened without ever getting more amused. I looked from one to the other.

"Why are you still here, if you know what they're going to do to you? I never met a Spider yet that couldn't climb."

"The walls are slick, near the mouth," Ilve told me. "This isn't the first time I've been in one of these." Hidden tragedy beat behind the words. "There is no escape. Our masters know what they are about."

"Are we observed, right now?" I squinted at each of the walls, trying to see shapes through them, and in doing so almost walked into the Scorpion, who gazed down at me curiously.

"I don't think so," Tarn said. "I don't think they care enough. This isn't somewhere you put someone you're that interested in. They'll just check up on us every so often, take some away, bring some back. See if…" His gaze strayed to the Scorpion.

"You'd get out of here, if you could, wouldn't you?" I asked the question of the whole room, but the bulk of the Spiders just huddled away from me, turning their backs.

"The masters would be angry," one of them muttered.

"What could happen to you that would be worse than staying here?" I demanded.

At that, some faces did turn towards me, and several had been disfigured, their natural fair features twisted and warped by some experiment, or simply by proximity to whatever studies the Beetles were carrying out. In their gaze I saw that, at the hands of a cruel and Apt people, 'worst' could mean a great many very bad things indeed. They were broken, I thought. They had been here too long, and had lived under the rule of Wellgrind and his people all their lives. And yet…

"You seem different," I noted, looking at Tarn and Ilve. "Where are you from?"

Tarn glanced around him. "There are some places within the water where a few of us can live free, caves where we can hide, little bubbles we have built for nobody but ourselves. Scolaris and the other cities are grand, but the lake is vaster still."

"But they caught you," I finished for him.

"They caught her," he said, indicating Ilve. "They caught her and took her as a slave, and a subject. And I could not abide living free and knowing that. So I came after her." His voice shook at the very thought of it. It was so plain that he was only one step above the lifeless sitting-dead around us, as far as being in awe of the Beetles went, that the sheer unspoken courage of what he had attempted touched my heart, for all it had failed. I reached out and gripped his hand, remembering his arms about me as he had caught me. It was strange to find such bravery and such kindness in such a man, in such a place.

"I'm getting out," I told him. "Come with me."

He shook his head, and I called for my wings, letting them carry me a foot off the ground for a moment before touching down once again. In the wake of that, though the mass of dispirited Spiders did not change, something had. The air had a spark in it. It spoke of hope.

"And can you carry me?" he asked wryly, but I was getting a bit fed up with all this doomsaying talk.

"You're Spiders," I told him. "Make me a cursed *rope*. We're sitting in an entire city of spun silk. Do you really need me to spell things out for you?"

He stared at me. His despairing expression vanished, leaving his face blank as an egg.

I had not watched this particular Spider-kinden Art in use before, as it has little practical value in polite society – outside the bedroom in any event – and so it was fascinating to see their hands move, the strands stringing from fingertip to fingertip as the siblings worked together. A twined cable of silk took form swiftly between them, twisting and writhing as they formed it. I took up the end, expecting it to stick to my fingers, but it was already dry, and felt as solid and substantial as rope.

Soon I was ready to fly. The Spiders had formed the line with one clubbed end that would remain adhesive, because the architecture of Scolaris was notably short of handy projections to tie anything to. Armed with this lifeline, I took to the air and carefully manoeuvred up into the room above. Which was still tenanted.

I touched down and found myself looking straight at Stammers and one of his fellows, who had been sitting up here quite silently doing who knows what, save that their expressions of surprise showed they had not been eavesdropping. I think if I had been a more fearsome specimen then one of them would have run for help, ruining everything. As it was, they decided to stuff me back in the bottle by main force, and rushed for me, Stammers on the ground and his friend with a short airborne hop, his own Art wings glimmering briefly. *These* then had been the flying kinden I had seen briefly, dotting the open spaces of Scolaris. In the exhilaration of my own plan I had almost forgotten that I did not own the only pair of wings in the city.

I made a determined bid to jam the glued end of the rope on the floor, as this was the only way that I would get reinforcements, but Stammers' friend was on me too quickly, bowling me over in a tangle of limbs. Stammers, a moment behind, grabbed me by my collar and shook me hard enough to make my teeth rattle. "Treacherous little freak, ain't you," he spat. "Now you get taught a fine lesson, before you go back down."

I pushed out at him furiously, and stuck the rope to his smock. For a moment he stared at me, and I stared at him, and his friend stared at both of us, and then I gave the line a yank and shouted "Pull!"

Tarn or Ilve had been ready, and the resulting yank had Stammers halfway to the pit before anyone could react, and me along with him. He let me go quickly enough after that, though, and was frantically trying to get his smock off, whilst his friend got in his way by hauling him back from the pit's edge, and the Spiders below continued, I surmised, to actually climb up the rope, whether in desperation or because they had misunderstood my circumstances. I was left entirely to my own devices and I could have had it away into Scolaris at any time. It was my own basic decency that held me there, rather than any knowledge that I would be utterly helpless and without resource in the city, and I rolled up my sleeves and descended on Stammers and company with the intention of enacting violence on them. I never had the chance.

There was a moment when the pulling from the pit stopped, and with a cry of triumph Stammers had his smock half-off. A moment later he, and his friend, were gone. The ensuing tug had been sufficiently powerful to haul them both off their feet and over the edge in a moment.

I took to the air, but the screams were already starting – and they finished moments later, because the Water-scorpion was brutally efficient. When I got there, the mob of listless Spiders had finally been persuaded to move, and the centre of the floor below was given over to a display of sheer dismemberment. Those Art-grown hooks had torn both of our jailers bodily apart.

The big man himself was crouching over the sectioned bodies and I had no wish to know why.

With his eyes wide and his face transfigured with fear, Tarn was holding the rope aloft. I dipped down and took it without landing, hurling myself up again and over the lip. The sticky end was sticky for different reasons now, and considerably less adhesive, but I managed to get it fixed, and braced myself against it too, and Tarn and Ilve shimmied up it and were with me a moment later.

He embraced me instantly. He did not have so many words – none of his aquatic kinden seemed to have that gorgeous love of language our landbound Spiders do – but he made up for it with the spontaneity of his gestures. *You did it!* he was saying, and *How brave you are!* and all manner of thanks, and I will admit to hugging him right back.

Ilve had sat down, seeming exhausted just by climbing out, and none of us were ready for the rope pulling taut once more. There was a moment when we all leapt to the same conclusion, and I flurried over to the lip of the pit to see the Water-scorpion testing the line. Our eyes met.

"What now, little one?" I heard his soft voice murmur. "No gratitude for disposing of your enemies?" There was a little blood at the corner of his mouth, but that might just have splashed there. "Is my experiment so much to your liking that you will leave me here with my hunger?"

"He's dangerous," Tarn stated, helping Ilve up. "There's no telling what he might do."

Even looking down at the man from a safe distance sent a little shiver through me. He had exactly the poise and grace of a deadly predatory animal, a mantis or a hunting spider – terrifying and beautiful all in one, and nothing to divide the two impressions.

"Perhaps dangerous is what we need," I said quietly. "Brace the rope." To my surprise the two Spiders did as I said without argument, despite Tarn's plain misgivings. Even having lived beyond the city, they came from a long line of the subservient. I wondered what catastrophe had sufficed to bring their once-proud kinden low, or whether they had always been this shadow of their other kin.

It took all our combined strength to get the Water-scorpion out of the pit, and us waiting for a change of the guard at any time. When he stood there, though, fierce and free, I felt as though I had indeed released a caged beast, hungry and savage, out onto the street. It was a feeling of equal parts elation and helplessness.

He crouched down before me, which still didn't bring his head down to my level. I was acutely aware of being within the arc of his massive arms.

"I am Donarvan, little one, and you are a strange and bold creature to visit our depths." Not a word of thanks, note, but I don't think he had such niceties in him. The compliment was all, and genuine, and I felt my heart flutter. His voice was deep enough to resonate within my chest.

"I need to rescue Doctor Phinagler," I announced.

"If you mean your friend, he didn't need rescuing, it seemed to me. It looked as though he was fitting right in," Donarvan reasoned. "You need to leave this city, if it can be done, before this is discovered."

"He's right," came Tarn's voice from behind me. "If we are fleet and nimble, there may be a way out, and so a way back in to save your friend. For now, though, our only chance is to exit Scolaris and hope we leave no trail.

"What about you?" I crouched by the edge, looking down into the dim recess beyond. "Come on, time to trust to your feet."

The dispirited huddle beneath did not move. Not a single face tilted up towards us.

"I'll leave the rope," I told them, but without any conviction in my voice.

Tarn had his arm about Ilve, and I didn't like that much. It was difficult to say that there was something concrete wrong with her – she did not cough or wheeze, and her skin was not ashen, nor her eyes sunken – and yet plainly there was. That all-consuming melancholia seemed to weigh on her worse than a plague.

"We go down," Donarvan announced. "It's the only way."

"What's down?" I asked him.

"The lower reaches, no place for a fragile little creature such as you," he told me, crouching down to not-quite-my-level again. "The failed experiments, the leaked poisons, the stale air, the scavengers and the discarded bodies, and yet, if we are to break from here, that is the one place the eyes of the Beetles will not look too carefully. They do not like to see evidence of their own failures."

"And we can get there?"

"It's always easy to go down, little one," he told me. "It's the reverse that's the trick."

We were well made for stealth, all four of us. My kinden are light and silent by nature, gliding through the world without a ripple, and Tarn and Ilve had the furtive care of those born of a long line of slaves. Donarvan moved like a hunting beast, a killer shadow. I had expected no less of him.

We moved down three levels before I had my moment of doubt, and it was swift but savage work. Tarn would pad ahead of us, in the hope that, if spotted, he would be taken as just one more slave about his business – and several times this is exactly what happened, with the little hunchbacks – Boatman-kinden I was told – restricting themselves to pushing him aside or kicking him and suspecting nothing amiss. I was given to understand that they themselves occupied some uneasy position between the Beetle-kinden masters and the Spider-kinden slaves, and that the reason they were more than mere chattels was that they could help in the masters' scientific work. Aptitude, therefore, was the key. For all the cruelties, it was plain that the Beetle-kinden of Lake Limnia were an advanced lot in their narrow way. I only hoped that this was not proving too seductive to my employer, although I would have some truth of that sooner than I had anticipated.

Twice, Tarn returned to say that the way was blocked – some sentry on watch to keep out prying eyes, and most likely because the greater Beetle scholars were all very jealous of their discoveries, and constantly tried to spy on one another.

Donarvan dealt with the obstruction both times, managing the grisly duty and stowing the bodies without a single sound out of place, and with barely a suggestion of blood. I was terrified of him in those moments – when he came back to us as though nothing had happened, the way ahead prepared for us and not a word spoken. It was not that murder was second nature, but as though it had no meaning to him. He killed as a predator killed, and would have no more understood guilt or morality than a tarantula.

We descended in fits and starts, hiding while Tarn searched out a way downwards, then quickly scurrying down slanting bridges, or sliding through tunnels that were surely meant more for disposal than as a means of travel. Much of the time we were 'outside', or the nearest to outside that one could get in Scolaris – creeping like parasites across the face of the city's many linked compartments, exposed to the cluttered void, sometimes almost pressed between that place's great organs and its silver skin. The light down here was of a poorer and poorer quality, and the air was harsh on the lungs, acrid with chemicals. I could hear fluid slosh and ripple from not so very far below us.

We had just taken a brief space within again, virtually falling from one chamber to another, and then exited to the increasingly hostile miasma without, when I heard a familiar voice. It was the Doctor's, of course, and I soon worked out that he, and his interlocutor, were inside the very chamber we were walking atop. The others froze, and retreated to where their shadows would not fall on those within, their footsteps not dimple the ceiling. I, however, crouched there and put my ear to the smoothly-woven material. I could hear some low-voiced man – Wellgrind, I thought – explaining some matter that sounded technical, and then the Doctor replied in a manner that suggested praise, and then, "but suppose that..." and some complication I was unable to catch.

The others were urgently gesturing at me, but I knew that I could not go, not then. Doctor Phinagler was *right there*. I could not abandon him without some attempt to bring him out with us.

I hissed my intentions at the others, but I did not get close enough to really make myself clear, for fear they would prevent me. Instead I flew back to the opening we had just emerged from and headed inside, navigating via my kinden's characteristically immaculate sense of direction until I found a tube that opened, perhaps for ventilation, into a large, bulbous chamber from which the Doctor's voice came.

What I saw down there was not pleasing to any of the senses, and at last I appreciated that the difference between the rulers of Scolaris and their Beetle kin of the Lowlands was something more fundamental than any quirk of appearance.

Much of the chamber below me was taken up with vats formed, as was everything else, from that silk-like material, but presumably treated in order to bear their roiling contents. Their gaping mouths were suspended from the ceiling by silken scaffolding, with their gut-like bodies bulging out on the floor. The fumes that arose from them made my eyes and nose smart.

Beyond them, I could see what I took to be tables, although again they were strung in midair, held in rigid position by the crossbracing of their cables. I could see a few cringing Spider-kinden there, attending to some menial tasks, and a couple of the Boatmen were fussing about some manner of machines – although they seemed quite unlike any device of Collegium or Helleron. I saw little in the way of gears or moving parts, but instead the devices seemed weirdly intestinal, like little models of the city around us, with the work being performed somehow by a precisely calibrated mixing of chemicals. Some of the artifacts gave off a crackling, humming sound, with sharp flashes of light racing along thin lines strung between them.

"The very force of life," Wellgrind's voice was saying, in a conversational tone. "Here, it is a simple enough demonstration, fit only for novice students, but I imagine it is new to you. Let me show you."

I let myself down from the vent and crouched between the vats, edging closer and yet desperate to retain my concealment. I saw Wellgrind's broad back as he supervised one of his hunched little familiars in preparing something on a hanging table, and with a lurch of my stomach I identified a Spider-kinden body. Corpse it most definitely was, for sections of it had been laid open or removed entire, enough to obscure any detail of age or gender.

"Now, behold," Wellgrind instructed, and I saw none other than my employer step in – with a pronounced reluctance in his tread, but step in he did, nonetheless. A moment later the humming sound intensified, and the corpse began to move. It was all I could do to prevent myself crying out in shock.

The limbs twitched, and a shudder passed through its spine, as though it was trying to sit up. One hand clutched at the table, and I had a horror that the dead thing was still being made to feel pain even beyond the merciful point of extinction. Another spasm showed me its head – the top of which was missing, the brain hollowed out entire, and yet it moved.

"I, ah, remarkable," came the Doctor's strained voice.

"I am well aware that you have nothing of the sort, above," Wellgrind observed. "Do not doubt that we keep a careful eye on your Empire."

"As my presence here demonstrates, yes," the Doctor confirmed.

"Here, I'll show you something more – no mere prentice's trick, but some true science. Let me set the matter in motion." At Wellgrind's gesture the cadaver was removed and a further device lowered from above, as impenetrable in purpose as the rest. Whatever this was for, it was plain that Master Wellgrind would require some time to prepare it, and so I shuffled as close as I could to the heels of my employer and hissed at him until he glanced back. I saw his eyes widen, and then he was looking resolutely straight ahead again, eyes apparently focused on

Wellgrind. However, he contrived to shuffle back until I was almost at his feet so that I could speak as low as I might, and be heard by him and him only. It was the same piece of business we first practised on our trip to the Spiderlands, and we knew it well.

"I'm very glad to see you well," he murmured from the corner of his mouth.

I wanted to pick him up on that, given our last encounter, but the opportunity would be wasted at the volumes I was enforced to speak at. Instead I told him, "Doctor, you must come with me. I'm getting out of the city."

"Yes, that might be for the best," he agreed softly. "You run along, indeed."

"You come with me."

His eyes remained fixed on Wellgrind. "I'm not entirely sure that will be possible. Master Wellgrind is a powerful man here, and I do rather seem to have his attention. I'm really not sure he's ready to let me go just yet."

"Doctor, he's crazy. He's a monster. They all are."

"Now now, generalisations help nobody," he returned. "And you have not seen what I have seen. Their chemical sciences are so vastly far in advance of our own – to build all this, to treat their materials in so many ways, a wealth of understanding born of necessity. There is so much that might be learned from them, and they are respecters of knowledge. They see in me an equal. If you had only seen their machines, their refineries... all the world of mechanics contrived by the admixture of compounds..."

"Doctor, what I have *seen* is slaves and torture and a madman playing with dead bodies," I got out as forcefully as I dared. "Whether there are Beetle-kinden here untouched by such grotesquery I cannot say, but Wellgrind and his peers are no respecters of anything wholesome."

He glanced back at me briefly, and I saw the flash of misery on his face. He knew, full well he knew, that what I said was true, and that he had fallen into a nest of horrors. "It is rather like riding a wasp, Fosse," he said, and I saw that Wellgrind seemed to be reaching some manner of conclusion. "Staying on is hard, but infinitely preferable to falling off and into the way of its sting."

"Doctor, I think it's like riding a scorpion that'll kill you off any cursed time it likes!"

"Nonetheless, I don't think I'm in a position to say my goodbyes just yet. I fear Wellgrind is rather possessive, and I am his novelty for today. Tomorrow, who can say? For now, I will feel better knowing that you have contrived some exit. You take what chances you can, Fosse."

And I believed him. When we are in the vice together, he does sometimes come through with a certain greatness of spirit. I watched as he strode towards Wellgrind, clapping his hands together loudly and requesting in a hearty voice to be shown what the man was about. Under cover of that I made my exit and returned to the others.

They no doubt made all manner of unfounded assumptions about the feckless nature of my employer, but nothing was said, and so we progressed downwards until we were crouching above a festering soup of acrid, bitter water that formed the bilges of Scolaris. It was murky, with a rainbow sheen upon it that made me feel unclean just to see, and things moved there, weird, lopsided insects that sculled and hopped and crawled. Many just floated, quite dead, and I saw at least one Spider-kinden corpse, part-eaten. A great stilt-legged water-skater, bigger than I was, drifted over the oily surface towards us, but one look at Donarvan warned it off.

I opined that I was not going into that, no matter what the alternative. The eyes of my companions were already searching the near wall of the city, though, and at last Tarn pointed something out to the others.

"What is it?" I asked. They seemed to have some trick of seeing more through the effluent water than I could.

"The acids have eaten away at the bubble," he explained. "There is a hole there that the slaves have not been set to fix yet."

"A hole into the lake?" I demanded.

"Even so."

I wanted to ask why the air hadn't escaped, but I remembered Colliers' sphere. So long as the rupture was on the inward-curving underside, as here, the lighter air would not readily displace – at least not so swiftly that a repair in a day or so would not deal with the problem. I stared at the fetid soup, imagining its poisons mingling with the lake's clear waters, seeping out in a filthy cloud.

"We must go," Donarvan stated, "if we are going at all. They will be hunting us already, and the scholar-lords take errant slaves very seriously."

"But I..." For I had not considered one salient point. "I may have to stay. No doubt you all have Art to breathe water like this air, but I cannot. My kinden has never needed to."

Tarn was about to say something comforting, but Donarvan immediately saw an opportunity for mischief, if such a juggernaut of death can be said to deal in mere mischief. A moment later he had snatched me up – uncommonly fast for such a big man – and was literally bounding out into the vile waters, and then swimming with legs and one arm, holding me effortlessly out of the water. I had my wings with me by this time, and was frantically trying to wrench myself from his grip, but I had not a fraction of the strength that would have required.

Then he had paused near the vast, upwards-arching wall, treading water, and I knew we had reached the hole. He looked up at me, showing sharp teeth when he grinned. Tarn and Ilve were splashing closer – I remembered they had never trusted Donarvan from the start – but they would not get to me in time.

He forced me down into that water and I screamed. After that I screamed some more, my voice sounding unnaturally loud in my ears. My eyes, which had screwed shut in panic, were at last persuaded to open again, and I beheld a remarkable thing.

My legs and arms were wet, and I could feel a faint stinging wherever that water touched my flesh. My head and torso were bone dry and, looking down, I seemed to be wearing some enveloping garment of silver that made a bulky sketch of my contours. Donarvan was similarly costumed, head and body, and he was already pulling me through the water with powerful strokes, heading down. I could feel a strong force trying to drag me back towards the surface, and I realised that I was wearing a coat of air. Past me, I could see Tarn and Ilve on their way – he assisting her – and they had their own external lung in just such a fashion. This, I saw, was the Art of the Lake-kinden – of all of them, no doubt. This had allowed them to live in the waters since time immemorial.

Then a shadow passed over me, brief but with a sense of immense size, and a moment later we were out of Scolaris entirely. I looked back to see a blank wall of tarnished mercury, seeming almost flat it was so grand, but curving away as it receded upwards.

Abruptly Donarvan had dragged me close to his face, and I thought for a moment he intended to bite, but instead he touched our envelopes, and spoke low through our common air so that I could hear him.

"Well, little one, have you ever been more out of your element than now?" he asked me. There was a gauging look in his eyes, though, searching my face for weaknesses such as fear, and impulsively I planted a chaste little kiss on his lipless mouth.

"Thank you for rescuing me," I told him. "But where now? Surely the waters around Scolaris are still the domain of its masters? Have you some lair nearby?"

"A lair?" His smile at that was almost human. "Do not be so swift to follow where I might travel, little one – but look, our fellow travellers have some destination in mind."

Indeed, Tarn was gesturing at us, the two Spiders already striking out strongly away from the great dome of Scolaris. Donarvan hooked me with his claw and swam after them. All three were enviably free in the water, assisted by some Art that no kinden familiar to me ever knew. I myself failed abjectly at swimming, and my wings simply foundered when I deployed them. Besides, the air jacket kept yanking me irresistibly upwards, and though to break into clear air and daylight was something

I fervently wished, I could not abandon the Doctor. I even toyed with the idea of seeking out te Sander and his superiors, leading an Imperial task force to scour the lake, but the technical difficulties would have been insuperable, even if they believed me, and the timescales would have seen the Doctor vivisected long before.

We travelled through near darkness for some time, and I began to fret about the freshness of the air within my little cocoon, when I saw a silver shape ahead. For a moment I thought the Spiders had led us full circle and I was seeing Scolaris gleaming in the distance, but soon I realised that our destination, though similar in construction, was closer and far smaller than I realised. A single bubble, tethered to the stem of some vastly attenuated water weed, which descended into darkness beneath us and ascended into grey water above. When we reached it, I saw that the bladder's skin was a weave of silk – not the hard and artificial stuff of Scolaris, but something that looked spider-woven and natural.

Tarn confirmed it to me: this little refuge had been spun by a water spider, the totem of his kinden, and Scolaris and its sister cities had been made in mimicry of such construction, back before the Beetle-kinden shouldered their way to ascendancy.

"Why are we here?" I demanded.

"To take on fresh air, for one," he explained. "And to take stock. They will be hunting us. Myself and Ilve at least. They have ways of tracking us in the water – specially trained beasts to sniff us out, and Apt devices that can scent us, somehow. But there are ways..." He regarded Donarvan warily. "No doubt you have some place to go, Scorpion."

"Why, I rather thought I'd see what happened next," Donarvan told him easily, crouching in the centre of the bubble like a gargoyle – there was not room for him to stand. "You will take her to the Mother, of course."

The two Spiders stiffened at the mention. Ilve made to say something angry, but lost her breath just as she tried, and sagged back. Donarvan chuckled a little.

"Did you think she was such a great secret? I know of her, and don't think the Beetles don't either. I couldn't tell you where to find her just now, it's true, but to give that name to the leader of the pitiful remnants of your kinden who live free? Common knowledge."

"And you think we'll lead you to her?" Tarn challenged him.

"You think I'm a spy for the Beetles?"

"I know your kind work with them, sometimes."

"And the circumstances you found me in? And the numbers of their people I have killed for you, that we could get this far?" Donarvan enquired, ever so politely and with a deep undercurrent of menace.

Ilve had been scrabbling at the concave surface of the bubble, digging into the web, and now she produced some little bundle with an expression of desperate triumph. When she opened it, a strange, rancid smell leaked out into our close air.

"Someone has left us a gift," she said, and was going to expound when some will to speak went out of her. She looked thin and unwell, and I wondered for a moment if she had some plague that the Beetles wanted spread to the rest of her kinden.

"Let me." Tarn took it from her, and I saw that it was a container made of stone, with some sort of unguent within it. Swiftly and surely Tarn smeared Ilve with it, and then himself, so that they both ended up stinking of its sour, rotten reek. In our confined quarters the experience was somewhat overwhelming.

"This will throw their devices and their animals off our trail," the Spider explained, stowing the half-empty pot, and webbing over its hiding place with his Art. "Now..." He regarded Donarvan unhappily, but it was plain that he would not be able to stop the Scorpion following wherever he wanted to go, especially with Ilve's strength, or at least her determination, so visibly flagging.

"Let us go," he decided, at last.

As we had proved that a lucky and determined slave – albeit one assisted by a huge murderer – could escape Scolaris, and as my comrades were equipped for the basic necessities of aquatic survival, I was privately wondering that the Beetle cities did not just disintegrate as their masters' treatment drove out the slaves that they depended on. Collegiate political theory (or one of them) surely held that a system driven by such cruelty would inevitably end in revolution or transformation into something more egalitarian.

However, on our trip through the dark waters, with me now clinging along Donarvan's back, sharing our doubled envelope, I had to revise my opinion of just how carefree a life in the open lake might be. We spent a surprising amount of our time hiding, and I was able to witness a number of different predators for which I would have barely been an appetiser – fish, dragonfly nymphs, even a leech longer than my body that made me wonder if there was some loathsome kinden somewhere below us that had taken it as their totem. The most fear was generated by a great diving beetle – though only a little fellow compared to the giant that snagged our sphere – but that was because it was thought to be a spy for the Beetle-kinden back in the city.

All in all I had the distinct impression that life as a savage within Limnia was to find oneself constantly on the menu. And of course, should the Spiders protect themselves from the wild world by crafting their own bubble cities, as they could surely do, then they could not hide from the Beetles. I began to see how this unpleasant, vitriolic society had come to be.

At the last, I saw something vast looming ahead – not the pale of a city wall, but rock, the very foundations of the lake, and there we entered an aperture so narrow that Donarvan had to wriggle to get through. Shortly after, we had ascended a twisting passage and found ourselves in the air. It was a cave.

Caves, in fact – a series of fissures and chambers that had, I felt sure, a number of ways in and out. It was not unlike the old warrens back at Merro, where I still had living family, and the resemblance, however trivial, gave me some heart.

We were accosted within minutes of our arrival, if accosted is the word. A half-dozen Spider-kinden turned up, bearing knives and spears, and kept their distance down the tunnel. Donarvan could have broken them all into pieces, I had no doubt, but he was being uncharacteristically respectful and standing at the back.

Tarn introduced us, skating over the precise details of my provenance. "We seek refuge," he told them.

"All that we can provide," a woman with a spear told him, which sounded innocuous enough to me, but Tarn took it poorly.

"What do you mean? They have not...?"

"The last in before you had not masked their scent. We are already preparing to move. They are coming here. The Mother has foreseen it."

We had come so far, and the news seemed to devastate Tarn. His concern was plainly for Ilve, who had folded to her knees again, staring down at the floor. "Have we no time?" he asked weakly.

"Who can say? Stay if you wish. Perhaps the Mother will speak with you. She is determined to see all safe before she leaves."

We headed inwards, until we came to a larger cavern, dripping with water, which had plainly been the lodgings for a fair number of people until very recently. Even now, there were many Spider-kinden gathering some few meagre possessions – mostly woven or hand-carved, clothes, blankets, some poor tools. I saw men and women and children, whole families disassembling all that circumstances had left them of their lives. Here, Tarn let Ilve lie down, and she curled into a ball.

"Tarn," I found my voice at last. "You can't live like this, surely. Is this all you have?" It was not tactful, but the misery I was witnessing had driven tact from me.

The look he turned on me had more dignity than I expected. "This is what we have. This is what they have left us. Most of my people have less – they live within the cities, and serve their masters in whatever capacity is required – menials, assistants, whores or the subjects of their experiments. They are safe from the lake there, and the price of that safety is their birthright."

"Tarn... where I come from, your kinden do pretty well," I observed. "In fact they tend to be the ones owning slaves and telling people what to do – although not so much with the mad experiments, it's true."

"Then I am happy for them," was all he said to that – and I could tell he was sincere. "It is like a story, Ilve," he murmured to his sister. "Another world that turned out differently, where our people are free. Perhaps that is enough, that knowledge."

"Tarn, listen to me. Come up. We'll get Doctor Phinagler back somehow and all go up to the surface – why not all of your people, even? I mean, yes, you'd be in the middle of the Empire, and they're not slack on the slave-taking front, but even so…" But my voice tailed off because a curious look had come over his face, and he was shaking his head in little, jerky movements.

"*Up there?*" he whispered. "We cannot go *up there*. I have seen that place, when I have gone to gather air. It is terrible. We *cannot.*"

"It's not all like Jerez." I had misunderstood him.

"It's empty, all above, and it burns, and it freezes, and there is *nothing* all around." He was shaking, "We cannot live there. It would destroy us." Indeed the very thought of it seemed to have unmanned him beyond all sense of proportion – it was not a mere rational consideration of the difficulties involved, the heat of the sun, the night's cold, the novelty of what must seem the great open space all around. I saw something deeper, an irrational terror that he was fighting back.

Miserably, I wondered if this, too, was the work of the Beetles, whether they had, by artifice or selective breeding, shaped their slaves to fear that most evident of escapes – or perhaps they, too, were afflicted by such fears, and simply living in this water, generation on generation, had instilled these patterns in every mind.

Ilve let out a curious choked sound, not a moan, not a whimper, not quite a sob.

"Is she ill? Or poisoned?" I pressed.

"They made her their subject," Tarn said. "They knew that she had lived free, and the thought was like acid in their minds that she might have known even a moment's joy. So they put a venom in her mind that ate her joy, and darkened her thoughts. Now there is nothing left but sadness, and she loses the will to move, to speak, to be herself in any way. Soon, perhaps, she will not care enough even to breathe. I have seen it before."

I looked into his face carefully throughout this, searching for any sign that he was speaking metaphorically, and found none.

"I would have been next," Tarn said, so softly I had to lean forwards to hear. "She knew I would not leave her. It shows the depth of her love for me that she could stir herself to escape with us, against all the efforts of the venom."

"I'm sorry," I told him.

He shrugged, kneeling by his sister's side.

Donarvan had remained silent and still all this while, but now I saw his stance change subtly, as someone new arrived. I knew without needing to be told that this was the one they referred to as Mother.

A sketch: she was, I suppose, a study in what Spiders would look like denied their place in the world, their Art and their craft. She looked older than any Spider I have ever seen, her face lined, her hair grey, tied back out of practicality and not fashion. She was small, too – all these Water Spider-kinden seemed to be smaller than I recalled their land-bound kin to be, or at least less imposing. The Mother stood very straight, though, and had a composure and focus that her younger wards lacked, and I think that was the real tragedy. I could see, in her, the ruin of her people's past glories, a sense that once they really had been lords and ladies, as were the Spiders I knew.

Tarn was obviously going nowhere without Ilve, who was just as obviously going nowhere at all, and although the hurried departures were continuing all around us, there seemed just as many Spiders – I realised then that these caves must extend deeper than I had thought, given how many were suffering this tragedy of displacement.

"You are from the surface world," the Mother remarked.

I nodded, wordlessly. Ilve made another sound, weaker than before.

"I remember, when I was young, I used to hide at the meniscus and watch the boats, such a strange, unreal world on the other side of the mirror." She knelt down beside Tarn, one hand resting gently on Ilve's shoulder. "How do you like our home?" she asked me.

The question robbed me of words. She seemed so calm, with her world ending all around her – no, with her world ended, long ago, and whatever her people had made of themselves devolved into lives as vermin or as slaves.

"How did it come to this?" I asked her, a question of infinite degree and yet she seemed to know what I meant.

"This? This is the far end of justice," I was told distantly, as her real attention was on Ilve. "Once we ruled in our cities of silver, and made *them* our slaves, our clever, clever slaves, that would work at all our tasks so that we could waste our lives in admiring our own reflections. When they uncovered their secrets, all their tools and tricks and devices, we did not see, we did not understand. All the prescience in the world, wasted, because the threat was something so inimical to prophecy. That is the story we tell, that once we were great, and cruel, even as they are great and cruel. Then they cast us off, the slaves breaking their bonds of silk – cast us off and cast us down and put us in the place we had made for them." She looked directly at me, her eyes shocking in their matter-of-fact steadiness. "Or at least, so we tell it."

Donarvan made a rumbling sound in his chest from behind and above me. "What use are histories if all they preserve are your defeats?"

"Perhaps we tell the story to remember that slaves need not stay slaves. Perhaps it is that we know we deserve our fate, that we brought it on ourselves. Perhaps simply to comfort ourselves, that we were not always thus. What of you, Scorpion? What do your people tell?"

"We have no histories," he answered gruffly, "We do not live in the past. We are only the Now."

"Then you have no future, either," she reproached him, and for once he had nothing to say.

Then there was some commotion from nearby, echoing weirdly from the tunnel walls, and I knew we had stayed too long.

I called for Tarn, but he was holding to his sister, head bowed. Only when the Mother touched him on the shoulder did he look up. I could hear screams now, and a strange harsh crackling sound.

"She is gone," the Mother told him simply, "and you must go too."

Tears were running down the Spider-kinden man's face, but he nodded. "Come then, Mother," he said.

But she just shook her head. "This moment, I have foreseen. This is the end, for me. There will be other Mothers."

Then the invaders appeared from a tunnel across the cavern from us.

I saw a scattering of the hunched little Boatman-kinden, and each carrying some serious-looking sort of crossbow, but behind them strode three armoured forms that, from their bulk, could only be the Beetles themselves. I was surprised that they had come to do their own dirty work but they seemed to be taking no chances. Their shells covered them from head to toe – not steel but a pearlescent substance no doubt just as hard. Their helms were featureless, without even an eyeslit, but they strode forward surely enough.

"Go," instructed the Mother, and she approached them with her arms wide.

I tugged at Tarn's arm, and at last he came to himself, and he, Donarvan and I were heading for the nearest exit, the last to evacuate. I cast a look behind me as we went, and I saw the Mother face them down, those armoured fiends. For a moment, just a moment, there was all the fierce Art of a Spider-kinden in her, beating them back, cowing them with the force of her personality. Then one of them reached forwards with a slender staff he held, and I heard a sharp crack, though he had barely touched her, and her body convulsed and was thrown aside as if by an invisible hand.

After that we were running – or they ran, and I half-flew to keep up with them. We kept crossing paths with other fleeing Spiders, and soon it was apparent that the Beetles had sent men in at several entrances, though not all, and nobody was sure which way was clear. Everything was a confused, panicky mess, and we darted one way and then the other, seeking egress, until at last we pushed into a cavern that was submerged at one end, and there we found the enemy.

There were three of the Boatmen and a single Beetle, standing like an articulated statue or an automaton, still in water to his ankles. He also held one of those innocuous-looking staffs, seeming all of silvery metal, and linked to his belt by some manner of cord.

"We go through," Donarvan snarled, and then he was hurtling forwards, arms flung out with the great hooks of his Art directed at the enemy, and to my surprise Tarn followed him. To my greater surprise, so did I.

We had a moment where they had not seen us, and we closed much of the distance. Then the Boatmen were trying to bring their crossbows to bear, but Donarvan was huge and very fast indeed, and they lost their nerve. One got a shot off, that went far wide, and then the Scorpion's first swipe caught him up and flung him against the cave wall. The other two scattered before him, long legs skittering them out of the way. Tarn dashed past to the water, turning chest-deep to reach back for me.

Donarvan had gone for the Beetle-kinden, and I saw one great barbed fist rake into that armour, staggering the man without breaching his shell. Then the lance jabbed out – a pitiful, weak thrust that would barely have broken the skin, had the weapon been a spear.

I heard that same crack, and saw a blue flash from the staff, and then Donarvan was knocked flat, and possibly dead. I cried out and my wings flung me over to him, because I was not thinking. I heard Tarn call after me, but by then it was too late.

The staff jerked round for me, the Beetle seeing my approach as an attack. Only my nimbleness in the air saved me from the Mother's fate. Instead I dipped beneath it, low enough to skim the water, and then one of the Boatman-kinden grappled me from the air, dragging me down.

I had a brief glimpse of Tarn staring after me, aghast, but he did the sensible thing. Before they could take him, he fled into the water, and I wished him better luck than I.

Then the Beetle was ordering the retreat, abruptly. The two Boatmen had me between them, dragging me into the water in a jacket of air, just as I had arrived. I did not realise, then, why my captors had suddenly decided to make their exit – certainly I knew it was not for any great importance attached to me.

They had me out into the open water swiftly, giving less the sense of cruel invaders so much as fugitives themselves, and at the last I thought I saw their reason. In the cave mouth we had exited from, even as I was yanked swiftly through the water by the Boatmen, I saw a figure loom. Donarvan without a doubt, having survived the Beetle's wand and looking little the worse for wear. And they were scared of him. Despite my precarious position, it gave me some hope.

Then a vast darkness coursed over us, and I thought at first that the Beetle-kinden had called up one of his insect namesakes as protection or transport. A moment later, however, I had identified the curved and streamlined form as a vessel of sorts – a great teardrop shape with two sculling legs and a sort of open cagework where I was stowed, and to which my captors held fast. The entire construction felt as hard as steel, but it was of the same artificial materials as everything else the Beetles made – not wood nor bone nor shell nor hardened silk, but some man-made amalgamation of all of those. Still, it made a swift and energetic progress through the water, and I am only glad the vessel made sufficient speed that they had me back in Scolaris before my jacket of air became a stifling tomb.

The next you can probably predict, for I was most certainly bound for the cruel durance of these aquatic Beetles, who bore me all manner of ill will as thwarted jailers always must their truant charges. First, though, I was brought before Wellgrind himself. It was apparent that I had made just that much of a nuisance of myself.

The old, pallid Beetle stared at me, and I half expected the Doctor to be there as well – as though I was some naughty child being paraded before her parents. Instead, Wellgrind just had a pair of younger Beetle men to flank him, and a look of cool loathing on his wrinkled face.

"You, land-slave, have put me to some considerable trouble." He sighed, surely the put-upon scholar called from his researches by trifles.

"I have been deprived of some valuable research subjects on your account, and regaining you will hardly make up the loss. Whilst your vivisection may provide a novel challenge to our anatomists, I myself do not subscribe to those theories that suggest those that dwell above are materially different enough to our own slaves as to warrant such study."

I was waiting for the deaths of Stammers and his fellow Boatman to be added to my account, but Wellgrind was already turning away, having spent quite enough of his valuable time on me, and I realised that his fallen servants were further beneath his notice than even his slaves.

I made just such a comment to my escorts as they led me away – holding tight to me with their pincering little hands. The three of them – so many to subdue one poor girl – said nothing, stony-faced and bleak, until they had found me a bubble of silk suspended taut from the wall of what was plainly a laboratory. They unseamed this with a wand, and thrust me inside, and sealed up the membrane behind me. There would be no airborne escape this time, I saw.

One of them remained behind, then, and I assumed it was to gloat, or to guard, but after the others had departed, this Boatman – Boat*woman* as I learned – leant close in. She was as moon-faced and hunched as the others, her torso showing precious little delineation of breast or waist, but her voice was unmistakably feminine, when she spoke.

"You should not have come, overworlder," she told me, somewhat muffled through the veil. "You aided an escape, and there is nothing that incenses the masters more than lost slaves. It enrages them beyond all reason, as you saw."

I had seen nothing of the sort, but I realised that simply being dressed down in person by Wellgrind was evidence of the great trouble I had apparently put them to.

"I would do it again," I declared nobly. "Where I am from, there is no slavery."

I was fishing for a reaction, but caught something unexpected. "That must be grand," she said sadly, almost too soft to hear. "It makes a fine story."

"It is no mere story," I protested. "Just ascend to the surface and you shall find it." I did not complicate the issue with the amount of west and southward travel also necessary. I saw there would be no point in it. The mere mention of the surface had frozen her, just as it had terrified Tarn before. Of all the horrors, that was the true tragedy of the place, that all who dwelt there were slaves of their own making, in the end, each mind effortlessly forging its own chains.

Then she started back, taking a long-legged step away, and I saw newcomers approaching. This time there were a good half-a-dozen of the Boatmen, and a Beetle man too, and in their midst a very familiar figure indeed.

"Doctor!" I could not help but cry, and he nodded and managed a weak smile and half a wave as he was brought over to examine me.

"Well there you are," came his muted voice, and I saw that he had looked better. Certainly he had a few bruises, and for a moment I just thought that he'd had an experiment blow up on him – not for the first time. Then he was being led past my bubble cell and into the next, a cramped prospect for him. He managed an apologetic grimace for me as they sealed him in.

"No longer flavour of the month then, Doctor?" I asked him somewhat tartly, as I still felt aggrieved at his abandoning me before.

He turned a reproving eye on me. "Unfortunately, your own exit was somewhat to blame. When they found you gone, I'm afraid that they rather felt that I was involved, or at least responsible, as your keeper. They are an enlightened lot, in some ways, but in others they have a very narrow view of the world." He shook his head, genuinely regretful. "They have a science here that we cannot guess at, just as a lot of our clockwork and steam power would no doubt baffle them. If they could bring themselves to meet in peace with our people – even with the Empire, perhaps – then what advances might we not make together. Alas, they view all who are not of their cities with the utmost suspicion – and a vexing condescension for that matter. They would be almost as slow to learn from an outsider as they would be to teach, they hold their superiority so highly. And, as you have had cause to know, their attitude towards other kinden is less than pleasant. Above all things they are concerned with maintaining their control over their underlings, and pile cruelty upon cruelty on them, thus fomenting more discontent. I believe they probably had their Apt revolution close on ours, but matters have gone very differently here, as you see. The confining nature of the lake, some inbred insularity in the minds of all here... still, it is a sobering thought." He raised his eyebrows philosophically, as though he were not, in fact, imprisoned and under some dreadful sentence, no doubt. "For all that, they *are* my people – I can see us in them, and we might so easily have gone the same way, had we wished to wreak a greater revenge on those who had been our masters."

"Doctor," I interrupted, because sometimes he does need help focusing. "I can't help noticing that we are prisoners, and of a people whose primary diversion is vivisection. Please tell me that you have a plan."

"I have half a plan," he told me, a flick of his eyes searching out any listeners and finding none. "However, you will appreciate that it does not take these walls to imprison us while Scolaris remains a greater prison. We are a great ways underwater. I can only hope that the locals have constructed some manner of submersible conveyance that we might borrow, for without that I fear we might be somewhat out of options."

My eyes lit up, I am sure. "As to that, Doctor, it so happens I was brought back to the city in just such a device, and I had some look at its workings." In fact my memory was running ahead of itself, skipping over some crucial details along the way, but I was too keen on escaping to think things through.

"Why then," the Doctor mused, "we may have outstayed our welcome. I propose we leave."

I am not engaged as an advisor to my employer, of course, but Doctor Phinagler's frequent rash enthusiasms have taught me to add a dash of caution to the mix. I briefly outlined the obstacles: namely that we were within a city hostile to our kinden, surrounded by sadists and their creatures, and all of this parcel of joys sunk within the bowels of a lake populated by ravenous beasts. And, more immediately, we were incarcerated snugly in cells.

"Nothing will ever get done if we allow ourselves to be cowed by the enormity of the task," the Doctor lectured me. "Instead, we break it down, as you must surely have been taught, into manageable segments. Firstly:" and he produced from within his robes a curious pale wand.

It would be unfair to claim that the Doctor is particularly light-fingered, or that he has larcenous tendencies. However, he is a man led by the nose by his whims and obsessions, under the influence of which he tends to divide the moveable goods of the world not into categories of 'mine' and 'theirs' but into 'those things I am interested in' and 'everything else'. I do not know whether anyone but myself has ever considered just how lucky the world is that his interests are so self-involved and esoteric. He would have made a terrifying merchant magnate, still more so a statesman.

The device was the mirror of those that our captors had employed to seal us up, and before I could argue for a greater interval of planning, he had sliced open his own cell, and we were committed to the venture. He freed me, and we were at large within one of Wellgrind's laboratories.

There were no half-complete experiments or remnants left lying about, for which I would have been more thankful had I not suspected that the decks had been cleared for the next subjects, meaning us.

"We're going to have a hard time getting anywhere in this place without being seen," I decided.

"I would say impossible," corrected the Doctor. "I won't play you false, Fosse, we're in something of a pickle. However, a little improvisation may grease the wheels." Of course, he had been shown more of these workshops than I, and his recent conduct had led me to underestimate him again. I was pleasantly surprised when he uncovered a sort of compartment wherein protective clothing had been stowed.

"I hope you see what I intend," he prompted, and waggled his eyebrows in a vexing manner. After a pregnant pause, he added, "You should say, 'I have a hunch'."

The gift of humour, I have often found, is oft misplaced amongst the Beetle-kinden.

So it was that we disguised ourselves as best we could. I put on a smock too large for me, just as well, for a second such garment was wedged between my shoulder blades to better approximate the uncomfortable posture of the Boatman-kinden. I am a fine mimic, so I was able to make something of their long-legged gait, my hands clutched in close to my chest like a miser in a play. Of my natural fair looks, which would never be taken for the pallid idiot-visages of the locals, a sort of mask was found, to cover my nose and mouth, presumably intended to ward off fumes rather than for day-wear, and a sort of baggy cap to hold my hair. The Doctor himself had procured a sort of suit of armour – not the impenetrable-looking plate of the Spider-hunters, but something plainly intended to help with dangerous lab-work. It was of a thick leathery material that no doubt had arisen in some chemical vat somewhere, gleaming black, and reinforced with plates of what were recognisably common chitin – and even this tiny piece of familiar craftwork made me unbearably homesick. I was privately swearing that I would never leave Collegium again, if allowed to return.

Doctor Phinagler took up broad goggles and a mask similar to mine. Thankfully, land and lake Beetles both tended to rotund frames and fugitive hairlines, and little enough of him otherwise was visible that I hoped the rather marked difference in skin tones would be written off as the grime of the labs, given that he was plainly attired as one of those lowly sort who actually had to *work*.

"How is your memory for where these contraptions were docked?" he enquired.

My sense of direction is, as noted, impeccable, whereas his is mostly non-existent. So it was that, with me leading, we crept from the workshop. I was somewhat surprised that we found no guards immediately, but it seemed that Wellgrind had great faith in his ability to hold prisoners secure.

There followed a painstaking and throat-tightening performance, as we made our way through the least-used byways of Scolaris that I could secure, forever avoiding the locals without looking as though we were avoiding them. We were certainly spotted on a minute to minute basis, but the Boatmen and the Spider slaves paid us little mind as our makeshift disguises held, which at the time I put down entirely to my acting ability. The Doctor, unused to the cumbersome protective gear he wore, progressed by blundering, stumbling and bouncing off the walls, so that I thought any moment we might be unmasked, but then again, Beetles are not the most agile of kinden at the best of times, so perhaps this was a frequent sight in Scolaris.

Eventually, I began to feel that we were having too easy a time of it, and the Doctor explained in a low voice that we were protected in some ways by not having left Wellgrind's estate. The various aquatic magnates of the lake were all fierce rivals, and to cross from the domain of one to another would be a gruelling task even for a local, but those already within would be accorded the benefit of the doubt. Besides, the lesser kinden were not encouraged to question their betters, and even the least of the Beetles apparently had power of life or death over the rest. That being so, there was little incentive for some nosy Boatman to denounce the Doctor for being drunk and disorderly.

Then, and sooner than I had thought, we descended to a chamber that was half-submerged, finding three separate conveyances moored there, just as I recalled. Except that by then I was beginning to think that my famous sense of direction had miscarried, and even now I wonder if we did not simply stumble on a completely different marina by way of the sort of mad luck the Doctor is so often subject to.

We surveyed our chariots, and the shortcomings in our plan were immediately clear. So obvious was the difficulty, and so totally had it been overlooked, that the two of us spent some time staring at the machines, looking for a solution that was simply not there.

"Fosse," said the Doctor after a while, "when they carried you on these machines, how did they get you inside?"

"Well Doctor, I have to admit that they did not." I padded over to the water's edge. "There is some Art they have, you see, that when they enter the water, the air seems to stick to them…" And I thrust my arm in, with some vague idea that the coats of air might not have been Art at all, but some weird property of the water itself. Needless to say, it did not work for me.

"So they just popped you on top, in that sort of cage thing, did they?" The Doctor was being rigorous in exhausting the possibilities, "that, I cannot help noticing, is entirely open to the water. Which we cannot breathe."

I confirmed concisely that this was the case.

"Well, this is not optimal," the Doctor remarked.

At that point, the others arrived. Because Beetles are, as noted, not stealthy, we heard them approach, but they were coming along our trail, and we had nowhere else to go but the water. We were at bay.

There were a good dozen of the Boatman-kinden, armed with short hooked pikes, and a few with big, double-strung crossbows, and in their midst a trio of the Water Beetles – perhaps even the same trio that had first greeted us. The flanking two were in that all-over pearly mail that I remembered so unfondly, but their leader was Wellgrind, in his fine and outlandishly-styled robes. His broad face, with its long gash of a mouth and pouchy, vice-riddled eyes, had a new expression on it, which sat there awkwardly. I realised that he was amused.

"Look at you, what a paragon of ineffectual invention," he addressed the Doctor. "What do you think you look like?" When the Doctor made vague gestures of comparison between himself and his hosts, the old man shook his head almost merrily. "Oh, no, you surely do not think so? Believe me, had I not decided on this little experiment, this test of your resourcefulness, then you would have been set upon the moment you stepped from your cell. Why, you make such a grotesque assault upon the senses the very slaves would probably have attacked you out of superstitious fear. My, my, my, no, what a ludicrous show you make."

Wrenching off goggles and mask, the Doctor revealed a highly put-upon expression. "I take offence at this treatment."

Wellgrind shook his head, almost fond. "Ah, I had high hopes, Ludweg, that you might prove something special. Your understanding of our ways seemed so genuine. It is a shame that you have failed me like this."

"I would submit that our difference of opinion arose only after you decided to imprison me," the Doctor said heatedly.

"Ah no," Wellgrind said. "Alas no, your shortcomings are more deeply rooted than that, and no point denying it. I do not know what manner of bizarre latitude your people allow within their cities, what curious laxness of discipline, what perverse ways of dealing with their slaves, but it is plain that there is a kernel of wrong-headedness at the very centre of your culture. Even the Empire of the Wasp-kinden, from our studies, is not quite so deformed in its beliefs. I have only to look upon your concern for your own slave to know that something has gone drastically wrong in your culture. I am willing to bet that you have never beaten the creature in her life. I will not deny that this sentiment does not arise occasionally within my own people, but we are swift to excise such weakness. We must be men of science, after all, and such mawkish ways of thinking will only cloud our judgment. The slaves must be kept in their place. It is the way of the world."

"We have no slaves, where we come from," I announced. Nobody paid me the blindest bit of notice, but I soldiered on nonetheless. "But you, you have nothing but. I see it plain now. Your Spiders are kept as slaves, and as scared and beaten as slaves can be, to keep them down. Your Boatman are slaves still, taught to hold you in awe as though you were something more than human. And you, you yourself, Master Wellgrind, are a slave of the first order."

At that, I had buried a hook into him deep enough to bite, and he was forced to acknowledge my existence. Doctor Phinagler was making frantic gestures to get me to shut up, but I kept on despite him.

"You are slaves because you are helpless without your slaves. You are reliant on them for all things, even the construction of this city itself.

You must keep them terrified of you, for if they realised for a moment how weak you are, they would destroy you – and so you are a slave to your own fear. You care so much when a slave escapes because you fret night and day about your hold over them – no doubt you wake from nightmares where a single slave dares tell you 'no'."

The wonder of it was, a brief twitch of his face told me that I had hit the spot exactly with those last words – and it was not news to him. He was self-aware enough that he knew all of this, the teetering foundations his society was based on, lurching from generation to generation in a constant cycle of oppression – riding the Wasp, as the Doctor has said, because no matter how bad it is, to fall off would be worse.

"You are prisoners and slaves, all of you. You are your own jailers," I told them all. "And you sit in your little bubble cities, in your little bubble lake, of no more consequence to the world than a fish in a tank."

Wellgrind's mouth was working. I saw a little foam of spittle at the corners and wondered for a moment if apoplexy would carry him off before he could order our demise. In the end, though, he did not have the words to riposte. I had broken all records for insolence in Scolaris. Nobody had spoken to one of these Beetle-kinden so in living memory.

"Gah!" he got out, at last, but the Boatmen took this as an order and advanced on us, leaving us to choose between the points of their pikes and the dark water beyond.

"We will have words about which of us is best placed to engage in high-level diplomacy," the Doctor observed tightly, as the lake lapped at our heels.

"Enough words," came a new voice – unexpected enough that I did not recognise it at first, and then something was amongst the enemy.

I had not seen him properly at work, before. His murders had been for the most part out of sight. He was a big man, this Donarvan, and yet how swiftly, how elegantly he moved. Mantis-kinden would take notes on grace, and Wasps on ferocity, and for sheer natural armament, his landbound kin could not have matched him.

Dripping with water still – surely he had only emerged moments before our arrival, having dealt with whatever watch was posted in the lake without – he struck and struck, each blow driving his Art-grown hooks into a foe and then flinging the luckless, ruptured victim aside – the little Boatmen seeming mere toys to him. They died mostly trying to get out of his appalling reach.

One of the armoured Beetles had a staff such as they had stung him with before, but Donarvan was ready for that– he closed swiftly and had his foe's weapon-arm in his huge hands, lashing it about so that I saw the elbow twist entirely the wrong way, the armour plates bending out of shape, and then the staff itself smashed into the helm of the other Beetle warrior hard enough that both weapon and mail shattered. There was a percussive flash and crack, as of strange energies unexpectedly released, and the blow's recipient was flung all the way across the chamber into the water, where he surfaced face down and lifeless. The man that Donarvan held, with his broken arm, was tossed aside with contempt.

That left Wellgrind.

I expected rhetoric. No College Master in the world would  have failed to take the opportunity for a scathing decrial of his enemy, and a eulogy for the virtues of Collegiate philosophy. Surely Wellgrind had courage in his convictions, and would quell this insurrection with an angry word?

But it seemed that he had no courage at all. He had crumpled to the ground, though not a blow had struck him, crawling backwards on arse and elbows away from the menace of Donarvan. All I had levelled at him was shown true in that moment, and I remembered how frightened his kin had been of the Water Scorpion before, and how Tarn had hinted that the Beetles even came to arrangements with the man's kinden. Here was no whipped slave, no brainwashed lackey. Here was freedom personified – and if it was freedom from morality as well as chains, well, in that moment I felt my heart leap all the more.

Danger is always attractive, in a man, after all. In moderation.

With one stride, Donarvan had struck, but his hook simply snagged the Beetle's fine robe, hauling the man to his feet and then a foot further.

Even then, some more of the Boatmen were crowding at the entrance, armed and fretting, but Wellgrind's mere presence made a more than ample disincentive for rash action.

There was a scuffle, then, from one side, and I saw that a Boatman had been silently aiming one of those ugly crossbows at Donarvan, but a lithe figure had pounced on him and was now wrestling furiously – Tarn, of course. I was already in motion then, snatching up a fallen pike and taking to the air with it, but even as I descended, point first, I felt a twinge in my heart that he, too, had so overcome his nature as to come after me. Or perhaps vengeance for his sister had moved him, but I preferred the former.

I am no great fighter but I too can be inspired, and it was clear that the Boatman was getting the better of the squabble. So it was that the wretch got the business end of the pike in him with all the force my wings could muster, after which I helped Tarn to his feet.

"This is all very dramatic but what now?" came the Doctor's voice.

"This is the creature you wanted rescuing, little one?" Donarvan demanded, still dangling Wellgrind, but nodding towards my employer. "He hardly seems worth my time."

"We need to leave. They'll come at us from the water soon," Tarn snapped out.

Donarvan was backing up, Wellgrind before him like a shield, I saw several crossbows levelled amongst the watchers, but none of them dared risk their master. The dogmatic awe that had been pounded into them now worked to our advantage.

"Get them in," the Scorpion snapped. Tarn nodded and laid hands on me, pausing a moment, with terrible wheels moving behind his eyes. Then he set me in the water up to my neck and I felt the jacket of air form about my body.

The Doctor, who did not know what to expect, submitted to the same treatment rather less willingly, but eventually we were both bobbing there, watching to see what Donarvan would do.

What he did was throw Wellgrind. The old and sagging Beetle made a surprisingly fine missile and struck into the ranks of his followers very satisfactorily. In the confusion, the three of us made to go.

I counted, though, and stayed because there should have been four, and the other two stayed for me, so we saw it all.

Tarn had no intention of fleeing. He had come to that decision by the time he had readied us for the water, and perhaps my example of spear-work had set him on the course. As we retreated into the water, he was running. He had another of the Boatmen's pikes.

They were helping Wellgrind to his feet, the old man's mouth open to issue a command. It never came. Tarn was already upon them. He had been moving even as Donarvan flung the Beetle away.

I saw the pike-head ram home, scarcely slowed by the heavy artificial fabric of Wellgrind's robe, however ornamented. In that moment I knew how it must have felt to be a Moth-kinden lord in Collegium – Pathis as was – when the first crossbow bolt struck home amongst their people. It was a gesture, a symbol, more than it was an attack. It was the slave turning on the master. Whether he had learned such desperate courage from me, or from Donarvan, or from the dark depths of his own despair, I could not say.

Word would spread, of that I was sure. Even in trying to keep this act quiet, the Beetles would ensure that Tarn's infamy grew. The slaves would hear that one of their own had drunk the blood of their masters. Fear would temper, as the story grew, into something harder.

They killed him, of course. In a frenzy they killed Tarn, set about him with weapons and the butts of crossbows, with their crabbed little fists and their overlarge feet, and all the while Wellgrind was squealing like a child, his artificer's hands flapping madly at the bulging, red-slick mound where his insides had spilt under his robe – a breakage that I hoped no artifice could mend.

Then crossbow bolts began lashing the water, and Donarvan grabbed the Doctor and me, and kicked out into the lake.

I thought there would be some cave, some temporary shelter. I thought that he would be afraid, as they were all afraid, a prisoner of Lake

Limnia. Donarvan was a man who scoffed at barriers and boundaries, though. He had been taken once by the Beetles, because of that utter lack of fear and respect. Now he shouldered aside the very edges of his world. He brought us up, swimming swift and sure despite the burden that was all we were. Though our air grew stale, and I confess I felt a little unprofessional panic towards the end, we broke the surface unexpectedly, into the blessed, blessed rain of Limnia above.

It was night – we would have seen the growing light otherwise. There was, of course, no sign of the raft, the Empire, Jons Collier. Even Jerez was absent – Limnia is huge, after all, and the Skater-kinden can only despoil one small part of its shore at any given time.

We made the water's edge with Donarvan's help, and the three of us lay there for some while, soaking wet and getting no drier, exhausted mentally and physically. I think the Doctor went to sleep – he always did have the knack, no matter what. For myself, I huddled close to Donarvan, feeling the hard contours of his muscles, leaching at the warmth of him. His arm, when he curled it about me, was as large as my whole body.

In the morning he was gone, slipped back into the lake that was his domain. He had stayed beneath the stars with me, though, and I think he had done so to show that not all the denizens of Limnia were afraid of the open sky.

We found Jerez after some stumbling along the lakeshore, and turned up cold and hungry and very weary indeed in the Imperial garrison. Our reappearance prompted some general rejoicing. Hermon and te Sander were both glad to see us, but perhaps Jons Collier was most so, if only because he had been held in the garrison cells under suspicion of having something to do with our vanishing. He took the loss of his invention philosophically.

The Doctor and I spoke for some time, in the Imperial infirmary, about precisely what we should say. As far as we knew, the world at large was entirely ignorant about what lay within Limnia – and the ferocity with which the aquatic Beetles guarded their knowledge suggested to us that we should leave the lake's vicinity as swiftly as possible, before any reprisals. We both had the uneasy feeling that the lake's masters would be more than capable of striking into Jerez – even into the Imperial garrison itself.

What could be done, what should be done, or if anything should be done, that was the subject of our talk. The world below was one of subjugation and cruelty, but then the world above was not noticeably lacking in such commodities, whether within the Empire or beyond. Even Doctor Phinagler, who does so see the best in everything (mostly from wilful blindness) was forced to admit to that.

In the end it was decided that the Doctor would present a formal paper to the College, detailing our findings. He really did have very firm intentions on this point. This would be the discovery that made his name and rocked the Collegiate view of the world. We would be a wined and dined talking point for years to come.

Of course, when we did finally return to Collegium – and somewhat delayed for certain other escapades that befell us on the way – the Doctor's enemies within the College turned out to have gained rather more influence than he had expected, and his face was decidedly unwelcome despite his best efforts – he who could talk amiably with bandits, lakemen and Imperial bureaucrats. His hopes of a formal presentation were dashed, and instead certain historical matters concerning debts, unpaid dues and unwise and defamatory comments were given much airing. Only such shameful treatment at the hands of his peers would have reduced him to the level of publishing to the city at large in such a lowly format as this, and it is with a grim heart he acknowledges that, whilst such an imprint may yet provide him with some modicum of funding for his next expedition, it will nonetheless cast a suspect veil over the veracity of what I write here.

Nonetheless, every word is true, and you may go into Lake Limnia and assay the weight of my words for yourself, though of course if you do, you may find the return journey rather more challenging.

# Written in Sand

*Being an account of Doctor Ludweg Phinagler's expedition to the ruins of the Nem desert, and what he found there, as told by his amanuensis, Fosse.*

It is fair to say that, by the end of the war, Doctor Phinagler's stock in Collegium was not riding high. Prior to the outbreak of hostilities with the Empire, my employer had distinguished himself with a number of ventures that, while embarked upon with the genuine and well-meaning intent of broadening the horizons of Collegiate knowledge, had instead brought down upon his head the disbelief of the masses and the disdain of his fellow academics. Not to mention, in some cases, legal action and threats of violence in relation to certain debts, defamations and damage to a priceless prototype diving bell.

These professional matters were compounded by the Doctor's brief flirtation with politics, in which he added his voice to the camp of Helmess Broiler and others in arguing the case for the fundamental reasonableness of the Wasp Empire. Arguments that fell somewhat flat after the Wasps invaded the Lowlands, sponsored Collegium's habitual enemies in Vek, and thereafter brought an army right to the city gates. Whilst it might be argued that, given the low ebb of his general reputation, his support for the pro-Empire faction did it more harm than good, he did make a speech to the Assembly in which he drew unfavourable comparisons between Stenwold Maker – not then confirmed as War Master – and an infestation of boll weevils. Such things are apt to be remembered.

So it was that, after the precipitous retreat of the Imperial Second Army following the equally sudden death of Emperor Alvdan II, the Doctor found a certain amount of hostile attention turned in his direction, and the prospect of an extended sabbatical from Collegium began to exercise a strong attraction. For myself, I will confess that an innocent friendship I had struck up with the husband of Mistress Sorro the grain magnate had been so misconstrued by that worthy as to result in certain threats to the safety of my person. On that basis I overcame my misgivings sufficiently to be in the Doctor's company when he took an airship east along the coast.

I had believed that our destination would include the civilized comfort of Solarno, which was very much the talk of Collegium at the time we left. The shabby tramp dirigible that had been cheap enough for the Doctor's purse instead put in at Merro, Porta Mavralis and then Ostrander, avoiding any such opportunity for enjoyment. Being denuded of funds and somewhat at odds with my family there, our overnight at Merro was a miserable affair, as I shared a windowless chamber fit for one small Beetle with a large Beetle prone to sporadic snoring. Porta Mavralis was worse, with the airfield located outside the city and the Spider-kinden essentially restricting us to lodgings in the machine sheds. Ostrander was the last straw: a filthy village of savages. I was seriously concerned that the Doctor intended to stay there because of some curious edifices that the locals had commandeered and moved into, but the hostility of the resident Ant-kinden sufficed to convince him to move on.

His plan was to be the first Collegiate scholar to arrive in the city of Khanaphes. Word of this place had come to Collegium via the Exalsee, and it was noted for being a city of the Doctor's own kinden, some long-lost relatives separated by the murky gulfs of pre-revolution history. He had a good deal to say about the scholarly attractions of the place, but I confess that by then I was suffering greatly from lack of sleep, and an unprofessional lack of patience with his lecturing. I therefore confess that the page of my notes where I should have set down these things instead displays an unflattering but recognisable caricature of my employer.

As matters turned out, taking any great note of the Doctor's intentions as regards Khanaphes would have been wasted effort, as we did not in the end spend any significant time in study there.

We were waiting in Ostrander under the suspicious eyes of the locals for some time, with our available funds diminishing, when at last the opportunity to continue our journey arose. The Doctor fell in with a handful of artificer-merchants from some new cartel calling itself the Iron Glove. They had a rough and ready demeanour, were fond of drink and gambling, wore armour and bore weapons and in all things comported themselves more like mercenaries than merchants. I cite this as a trait very much in their favour, and they proved the first good company we fell into since leaving Collegium. They were a mix of Solarnese and halfbreeds led by a humorous fellow named Corcoran, heading to Khanaphes to test the waters of the trade there. The Doctor performed his usual trick of inveigling himself into everybody's confidence, a trait that for some reason he never chooses to exercise when he is at home. For myself, I was able to restore some of our modest funds at cards and dice without antagonising our new hosts, so all was well.

So it was that, in their company and aboard a ship of advanced design, we finally made Khanaphes.

At first sight, the city appeared to want for nothing that my employer might have sought. Plainly the place was ancient, a metropolis of heavy stone buildings weathered by the desert wind, and everywhere doodled with tiny pictures the purpose of which was obscure. There was some surprising statuary flanking the river, twin towering white figures remarkable both for the uncertain kinden depicted, and in their state of undress, which was unmitigated by even the Collegiate modesty my readers might be used to. For precisely ten minutes Doctor Phinagler was in raptures about the contribution to scholarship a man such as he could make, with such a venerable city at his disposal. Moreover, and as advertised by rumour, the inhabitants were Beetle-kinden just as might be found upon a Collegiate street, save for their dress and manner which was wholly alien. Here, my employer declared, was a conundrum that would bend to his incisive intellect.

At around that time, with the men of the Iron Glove departing to a dockside haunt where they might stay, we met with the administration of the place. The full complexities of this were never explained to me, suffice to say that, if you can conceive of some pettifogging bureaucratic responsibility then Khanaphes had a minister for it. We were accosted by a robed individual of mature years who enquired as to our origins and purpose and, on hearing the word, 'Collegium', offered to show us to the embassy.

I will confess to some early qualms, but the Doctor was buoyed by one of his optimistic moods, and seemed to assume that they had spontaneously created such an office entirely for him. Sadly, this was not the case. We were taken to a rather pleasing pool-fronted building flanked by statues of haughty Moth-kinden, and there discovered our error.

While we kicked our heels in Ostrander, it seemed that fate had outstripped us. Another Collegiate scholar, one with a fuller purse and more reliable transport, had stolen a march on us and established himself already. This worthy went by the name of Master Kadro, and was known to Doctor Phinagler. Perhaps more saliently, my employer was known to him.

I am ever slow to impute flaws to the character of one of my own kinden. We Flies are, as the world knows, the mildest and most virtuous of folk, law-abiding, industrious and generous of spirit. Alas, there will always be those who echo the vices of larger kinden. So it was with Kadro, who took one look at my employer and declared that he would set himself against any attempt Doctor Phinagler made to 'commit' (Kadro's word) research within Khanaphes. In argument, he had a great deal to say and, it is true, did touch on certain episodes which scholarly opinion has misinterpreted to show my employer in an unflattering light. It was plain to me that mere academic envy prompted all of these hurtful accusations, but Kadro already had the ear of the Khanaphir administration, and those functionaries and flunkies to be found within earshot were plainly taken in by his words.

There followed two days of very cold welcome. Kadro did not have us thrown out onto the street, but he ensured that we would receive no cooperation from the local officials, and it became plain that Khanaphes was a place consisting entirely of closed doors unless one arrived bearing a minister's writ. Every appeal was referred to some unseen 'Masters' whom the ministers purported to consult, but whom my employer declared entirely fictional. This was to become relevant later.

Doctor Phinagler spent our time in Khanaphes in protracted, and sometimes strident, discussion with Kadro over this interdiction, in which endeavours Kadro was supported by his own assistant, a narrow-eyed hysteric and second rate scribbler by the name of Petri Coggen, who was plainly tagging along after her disreputable master because her skills could afford her no better placement.

For myself, already worn down by the journey, the heat, the sand and the unnerving close-mouthed silence of the locals, I found two days of this my limit. Seeking less pugilistic company, I took myself back to the small district around the docks where non-locals might reliably be found.

For once, therefore, I must make an earnest confession. What happened next, and all the sequel, is my fault. I do not know what may have happened had I done my duty and waited patiently at Doctor Phinagler's feet for the end of his exchange of views with Kadro. What did happen, however, was that I found the Wasp-kinden.

I am sure the average Collegiate has an image of the Wasps as a race of intemperate warriors, devoid in equal measures of mercy, humour and tolerance. However, they are human beings such as we, and moreover are never as good at cards and dice as they think they are. So it was that I ended up in the company of some half a dozen burly, drunken men of that kinden, and one woman.

The woman's name was Saveta and her status amongst them was a curious mixture of master and slave. Women within the Empire are, sadly, not greatly valued for their own talents, but at the same time she plainly had a protector who ensured the increasingly drunken soldiers did not turn unwanted attention towards her. When I was able to get her talking, after winning sufficient coinage from the men that I judged a pause in my gaming activities was wise, I discovered she and I were in related professions. She was also a scholar's assistant.

"His name is Brandt," she told me. "Colonel Brandt." She put a stress on the rank, and I understood entirely. History has recorded this period of the Empire as 'The Rise of the Traitor Governors'. Emperor Alvdan II was dead and his throne had been seized by his sister Seda, who was struggling with precisely that Imperial disregard for the sounder sex that I have mentioned. So it was that various parts of the Empire were in arms against the throne, or else the throne was in arms against them. At that time, it was not at all clear how matters would fall out.

The emphasis on this Brandt's title suggested to me that his colonelship was more than a little self-appointed, and his presence so far from the struggle for Imperial power further indicated that he had not done well for himself. What, then, was he after in Khanaphes? This was hardly the place to raise an army to take back his birthright. I had not seen so much as a crossbow amongst the locals.

Saveta explained that Brandt had a more scholarly bent than most in the Empire. He was a man on whose shoulders there rested a not-uncommon chip. It was well known that the kinden that swayed an Empire had been savages of the hills only a few generations back, derided and disregarded by the rest of the world. Brandt did not believe that the origins of his people were so humble, she told me. Brandt believed that the manifest destiny of the Wasp-kinden to rule the world had already been written in the dust of history. He believed that, if one dug deep enough, one would find that they had already been great, and that their conquests, rather than the tyrannical imposition of their power over their neighbours, could be seen simply as their reacquiring a lordship that, in shadowed former ages, had been theirs by right.

We had both had a few jars of the local paint-remover by this time, as the soldiers sang some kind of slurred battle song behind us, and Saveta let go of her decorum enough to sound highly sceptical about this Colonel Brandt's hypothesis. I understood that, having fallen foul of both Empress and some of the other traitor governors, he reckoned he might win his way back to favour with whoever won by presenting them with this sort of archaeological testimonial to their kind's greatness.

I, unfortunately, was similarly unwise in my speech. I declared the entire venture a splendid idea, and why didn't they take my employer along, as he was the foremost Collegiate scholar of times past? I intimated that Brandt's stock could only rise if his discoveries were mouthed about in Collegium, thus impressing the worthies of the College with the superiority of their enemies.

The night deteriorated from there and, in truth, when I awoke in the morning on the hard floor of the small room that Kadro had grudgingly set aside for me, I remembered very little of it. Memory returned with a swoop, however, when a banging at the door resounded through my head, and Petri Coggen, Kadro's aide, ran panicking about the house declaring that the Imperial army had arrived to murder us all.

Such was the contagious nature of her terror that we sent a servant to ask the Imperial army what it wanted. The reply came back that Colonel Brandt awaited the presence of the esteemed Ludweg Phinagler before setting off on his expedition to the Inner Nem.

I did my level best to brief my employer on what might have been said the previous night, but he was already striding outside. Two days of vitriolic back and forth with Kadro had begun to make him feel that his genius was unappreciated, and he was more than happy to bask in a little Imperial estimation. Swiftly I gathered our possessions and hurried after him.

Outside in that little square we saw some two dozen soldiers in the familiar black and yellow banded armour of the Light Airborne (everyone refers to the 'black and gold' but in my experience yellow is yellow) headed up by a squat and balding man, his bare scalp already red with sunburn. Beside him, showing the expected feminine deference, was Saveta, and also a figure in robes of halved Imperial colours, marking him out as an Auxillian – a sort of semi-slave serving in the army. This figure stood with a stiff arrogance that threatened to overshadow bald Brandt's real authority. Within the cowl of his motley I saw the pale eyes and grey face of a Moth. This was Ethiganos, and I pride myself in saying that I didn't like him from the start.

"What do you mean, the Inner Nem?" This from Master Kadro, who had turned up by now, even as the Doctor and Brandt were getting acquainted. "You can't go into the Inner Nem. It's forbidden!"

"The power does not exist that can forbid the Wasp-kinden," Brandt informed him coldly. "Collegium would do well to remember that."

"The Scorpion-kinden will slaughter you if the desert doesn't," Kadro insisted.

"Yes, yes." My employer waved him off. He had very swiftly understood that there was a theatre of study to be pillaged here that Kadro and the Khanaphir ministers had no power to keep him from, and all other considerations were secondary. Also, needless to say, he and Brandt had instantly taken a shine to one another: two men with aims different enough that they would not be jostling elbows over the ruins. That erratic Phinagler charm that I have noted before now, and even complained of, was out in full force.

"Ludweg," Kadro tried, "just come back inside. I'm sure we can work something out," but my employer was having none of it. For my part, I was hungover enough, and fed up enough of Kadro and his squawking assistant, that I wrote off all these protestations as a mere subterfuge intended to preserve Kadro's academic primacy in the region. Only later did I wonder if some genuine concern for our wellbeing had not played a part. By then it was too late, and anyway, both Kadro and Coggen were to meet with bad ends in that city, so it is doubtful that he would have actually done us any good had he persuaded us to stay.

So it was that Doctor Phinagler and I joined Colonel Brandt's expedition to the ruins of the Nem, an occasion that, like so many other escapades I have shared with the Doctor, I wish I could somehow make unhappen.

The Imperials had a conveyance with which to plumb the desert, which had sufficient space to bear the additional burden of one large Beetle academic and his faithful Fly-kinden assistant. I say 'conveyance' because its precise provenance, or even original purpose, was unclear. It was certainly a much re-engineered piece of artifice and not exactly Imperial standard issue. It had six arching legs, which held the body of the contraption a man's height off the ground when it was striding, but folded up to rest the thing's belly in the dust when still; there was a compartment at the front which seated Brandt and Saveta and the coldly impersonal Ethiganos, and also my employer after some considerable fast-talking and squeezing up. The rest of us – meaning the soldiers and I – got to sit out in the blowing sand and the heat, on various attempts at rests bolted onto the vehicle's frame, with the more educated soldiers taking turns to direct the thing's motion. Behind us, the machine bloated out into a bulbous abdomen, its purpose at first unknown. At night, when we stopped, they had tent fabric that spread out from the sides of the machine like tattered wings to give us a little shelter, though precious little privacy.

The rough company of the hardened soldiers was not entirely without merits. I could hear Brandt, self-made colonel, holding forth almost constantly within the passenger compartment about the historical greatness of the ancient Wasp empire that he had hypothesised, and after an hour or so I am not sure that I didn't have the better deal.

The Nem is a great desert that lies between the Exalsee and the Jamail River upon which Khanaphes rests. It is a proper desert, too – much of the machine's abdomen turned out to be laden with casks of water for us, and it was strictly rationed by the chief soldier, a scarred and broad-shouldered man named Sergeant Smer. It was his misfortune that in Collegiate theatre 'Shmer' is a common character name for one who is cuckolded or otherwise gulled by his more perceptive underlings, and his further misfortune that I informed his men of this. He never did find out why they all started slurring his name when addressing him.

The machine, whatever its mechanical merits, strode ably enough out from Khanaphes, through the agricultural hinterland that stretched tediously beyond it, and then into the desert, and for two days we had ourselves for company, and no other. The Doctor weathered the tidal wash of Brandt's rhetoric, and I myself was a sufficiently novel and engaging raconteur that I endeared myself to the soldiers. Then the Scorpions found us.

The Nem is the domain of Scorpion-kinden – a host of tribes that collectively refer to themselves as the Many. This particular band numbered perhaps forty or fifty adults, three dozen animals and an indeterminate number of squabbling, spitting youngsters. They made a very fierce show, riding around us on beasts of their namesakes, and on high-stepping desert beetles, brandishing spears and halberds and whooping. The fully grown amongst them were bigger than the largest of us, chalk-pale and strong-framed, their hands and lower jaws bulked out and barbed by their Art. The soldiers had their blades out and their hands ready to sting, but Brandt was unalarmed. Instead he hailed out the Scorpion leader with a shout of "Chirnemeg!" It appeared this meeting had been planned for.

Chirnemeg was a woman fit to rule Scorpions. Brandt's pate barely reached her armpit, and she was broader across the shoulders than a champion wrestler, bare arms and legs corded with muscle, whilst her torso was quite unabashedly womanly. You could, in short, have lost a man of my kinden in her cleavage, a display both shameless and apparently endlessly magnetic, to judge by the eyes of the Wasps there. She greeted Brandt familiarly, and it was clear a deal had been struck previously, whereby this band would escort us through the desert, avoiding conflict with their brethren. In return, Brandt gave over to them the cargo in the machine's rear section, which turned out to be staves of wood and ingots of steel – common enough commodities anywhere but here. Soon after, we were on the move once more, with the entire Scorpion tribe riding around us in a riotous, boisterous host.

My readers whose paths have not led them much beyond Collegium's gates are no doubt awaiting the tale of betrayal, knives in the darkness, being hunted across the dunes by our erstwhile guides, but in truth our few days with Chirnemeg's people were pleasant and uneventful. The Scorpions were skilled hunters for whom the barren sands were an inexhaustible larder. At night, they had songs and drink, and I could write entire scholarly articles on their trials of wrestling, in which prodigiously muscled youths would contest, all but naked, in fierce tests of strength, skill and flexibility. The Doctor, for his part, found himself much in Chirnemeg's company, most especially after dark and with a jug of the Scorpions' harsh, clear liquor. He was plainly impressed by the acquaintance of such a statuesque matron, easily capable of breaking even a large Beetle in half over her knee. Of that I shall say no more.

You should understand that the Nem was not always the haunt of the Scorpion-kinden alone, or it would have held no attractions for either Brandt or my employer. The dunes are littered with ruins – whole cities that have been scoured of civilized folk by the sands' advance. These are exceedingly ancient, as I understood it, and their makers passed beyond living memory. As the amateur archaeologist will always impute to any gap in their knowledge the most self-serving and outlandish theory they might conceive of, so Colonel Brandt had decided that these fallen cities would show the marks of the lost Wasp empire. The more easily accessible ruins, however, were already the haunts of various squatting Scorpion-kinden tribes, and so Brandt's acquisitive eye had drifted further, into the utterly uninhabited heartland of the desert.

I had assumed that his intentions were entirely well known to his new associates. That misapprehension was corrected after several nights when Chirnemeg burst from the lean-to in which – from the sound – she had been demonstrating Nemean wrestling manoeuvres to the Doctor. It turned out that a chance mention of Brandt's aims from my employer's lips had been the first she had heard of it.

"We do not," she insisted to the colonel, when everyone was sufficiently woken and clothed. "That is not a place we go."

"You agreed –" Brandt started.

"No agreement can take us to the inner Nem," Chirnemeg cut him off. "Only death is there."

When a seven-foot Scorpion clan matron says that, you take notice.

Or you do unless you were Colonel Brandt.

"The very heart," he told her. "The Empire dares anything."

"Then the Empire shall fall," she pronounced.

The soldiers went very quiet at that, and I became concerned that matters might devolve into nationalistic violence. As it was, my employer chose that point to emerge, robes awry, to make peace.

"I think we are rather a long way still from the actual centre of the desert," he remarked, as though the tense silence he stepped out into was the expectant hush of a Collegiate debating chamber. "Of course, if you cannot guide us all the way there, then you can't. I understand the desert has ruins like a flea has fleas, though. Perhaps we could start our investigations at the closest of these forbidden ruins?"

Neither Brandt nor Chirnemeg looked overly happy at this, which therefore recommended it as a fair compromise. Doctor Phinagler spoke on: the erudite scholar to him, the earnest companion to her; eventually it was agreed that the Scorpions would bring us at least to within sight of the Inner Nem and its stone bounty, though that was as far as they would go.

I am not sure what I expected: probably a handful of sand-scoured stones projecting from the dunes, the sort of abraded rubbish that scholars could interpret forever and never be out of work. However, it was not so. When they spoke of the ruined cities of the Nem, cities were what they meant.

"The hand of the Masters is upon them all," Chirnemeg murmured, her voice tinged with bitter fear. "Even the desert dares not touch them."

"The Masters?" I think my employer was thinking of the Assembly of Collegium, where the title was rife.

"Those who built Khanaphes, the great sorcerers," she explained, "the ancient enemies of my kind. The pale ones."

At that, Brandt pricked his sunburned little ears up. "So not the Khanaphir, not like this man." He jabbed a finger at my employer's dark face. "And not your kinden?"

"You have been to the river city there," Chirnemeg pointed out. "I have seen, guarding their river, the images of their Masters."

I remembered those curious and mighty statues on the river gates, that had the features of no kinden I could name. Not Wasps, surely, but Colonel Brandt was a man to start with theories and then find facts to match them. The prospect of the Khanaphir Beetle-kinden ruled over in antiquity by a pale race of Masters was exactly what he wanted to hear.

The ruins themselves were still some way distant when the Scorpions declared they would take us not one footfall more towards them. What broken stone we saw spoke of a grand and sprawling city. Even now, with the sea of sand washed in upon it on all sides, there were stubs and stones of it jutting from a great expanse of the desert, with the roofless maze of broken walls rising in grandeur towards the centre. The style was similar to that we had seen in Khanaphes and, just as there, the grander edifices had been grand indeed. Now they were just echoes of their ancient glories, the sun stretching their shadows across the endless sands.

We parted from our guides, then, and Chirnemeg said she would return in half a tenday's time to guide us back. She did not hold much hope, from her expression. Indeed, she had a murmured conversation with my employer in which she suggested he abandon Brandt to his fate and continue in her company.

What were the Scorpions so frightened of? Once we had left them, Doctor Phinagler told me that these mysterious Masters had apparently laid an interdiction on their fallen places, to keep out the kinden that had ever been their enemy. There were guardians, he told me, or so the Scorpions believed. He and Brandt were properly dismissive of this superstition. Perhaps beasts used the abandoned places as lairs: scorpions or desert spiders, or even centipedes. All these might be dangers, but they were dangers that could be overcome.

Another night and a day, and when the shadows were lengthening once again we came to the outskirts of that blasted metropolis.

We progressed inwards slowly, the machine making heavy going over the broken terrain, stumbling and lurching. The outermost stones, those not buried entire, were mostly worn to nubs by the sand, but their presence, I assumed, had shielded the inner reaches of the place, which were more complete. Neither Brandt nor my employer wished to painstakingly catalogue every least stone chip and potsherd, and by swift agreement they determined to press on towards the centre of the ruin and find somewhere to camp. The soldiers had disembarked and were flanking the labouring machine, assisting it when it became stuck.

For myself, I took the chance to sit beside Saveta up on top of the vehicle. She had a scarf about her face and hair, and her eyes did not look happy.

"What's it like working for Brandt, then?" I asked her.

She shot me a look. "'Working for' is a fine euphemism."

I grimaced: I was aware how things so often worked in the Empire. "I'm guessing you're not family." Wasp men owned their women, wives and daughters, but I reckoned the arrangement with Saveta was of a more traditional nature.

"I'm spared that, thankfully," she confirmed. "He bought me, because I was well read. My father was in the Consortium. He loved books and he indulged me. Then he had debts, and he sold me. At least I have a master who values that much about me. It could have been worse. How is yours?"

I tried to explain to her that being dragged around the most dangerous and outlandish places in the world by an erratic Collegiate scholar was entirely different, but in truth I feel I did not quite convince her.

Sergeant Smer pointed out that the sun was now perilously close to the horizon, its brazen disc already bitten into by the teeth of the ruins. We had advanced some way into the city by then, and the walls that rose on all sides were at least half complete, many of them still bearing the ghosts of their original decoration. Some had panels of those massed little pictures we had noted in Khanaphes, whilst others bore grander scenes: I could make out human forms engaged in activities that time had made unrecognisable to the casual eye.

"Make camp here," Colonel Brandt agreed. "Doctor, would you join me in an initial examination of these tableaux?"

I sat with Saveta, considering that 'tableaux' was not the sort of word one looked for, from an Imperial officer. The soldiers were unfurling our canvas, keen to get some shade up.

"Tracks," Saveta noted. She hopped down in a flurry of wings and I followed. Out there, beyond the marks of our own progress, the sand was disturbed.

"Some beetle or desert ant or something," I suggested. Certainly the individual prints were clawed and fearsome enough.

"Only if they go on two legs," Saveta said softly.

I am no tracker and could not see it, and by the time we had anyone's attention the light was too poor to make much out. Nobody seemed to value Saveta's opinion in the slightest, but I added my voice to hers and Brandt agreed to set a double watch – we had grown lax travelling with Chirnemeg's people.

I remember, as they set up camp, the stark figure of Ethiganos staring up at that thin scar of moon, his back to the rest of us. He was here as another slave-scholar in Brandt's service, some captive from the Empire's recent foray into the Lowlands. He did not act like a slave, though, and he played sufficiently on his people's reputation for learning to avoid being beaten, as any other slave would with his manner. I should have felt sympathetic towards him, as a fellow Lowlander denied liberty, but in truth there was nothing in his manner to suggest that was the situation. I marked him as a man with his own agenda.

Then it grew dark, and we huddled by the automotive, a narrow sliver of moon touching the old stones light as cobweb. There was a silence to that ruin that was not like that of the open desert. Out on the sands, the quiet had been an absence, just us adrift on that great dusty sea. Enclosed by those great dead buildings I felt that I was hearing the quiet of things holding their breath and waiting their moment.

I was right.

I woke to screams. My considerable experience categorised them:

more than a massacre, less than a fight. I heard stingshot, no clang of steel, the sergeant shouting, but the voices of the screamers knew fear as well as pain. I bolted straight up with my wings ablur, half-collapsing the canvas I had forgotten was above.

For a terrifying moment I was snarled in the cloth, with the skirmish going on all around. Then I was loose and in the air, my eyes harvesting the moonlight. We were under attack by giants.

They were huge as Mole Cricket-kinden, the least of them the size of two men. They were a world away from those lumbering, clumsy giants, though. They were sometimes on two legs, sometimes on all fours, bounding along with their knuckles to the ground. They moved as swift as Mantids, rushing forwards to attack the Wasp soldiers and then bounding away into the darkness. We had a fire going, and a handful of torches on posts, but they targeted our lights, dousing them with sand. My eyes could still find them in the moon's fickle light, but the Wasps were blind save when their own stings flashed.

And they were strong! They struck with terrible swiftness, rushing from between the buildings and using no weapons, just the great barbed balls of their fists. I saw a half-dozen soldiers dead already, and not one of our assailants.

Chirnemeg had been right: there were indeed guardians.

I will confess to an absence of useful ideas, confronted with this nightmarish vision. All I could do was find the Doctor, who was crouched in the shadow of the automotive, staring futiley into the dark.

"What is it?" he demanded of me. "What are they?"

"Monsters." I lacked the composure to say anything useful. It seemed very likely that we were going to die or be scattered. I did not think I could fly all the way out of the desert.

Then the night was split apart by a furious white glare, as though someone had lit a spare sun right there in our camp. Instantly the whole battlefield was revealed by an uncompromising light. Saveta stood above us, atop the vehicle, and in her hands was a hissing globe of radiance, a lamp burning some incandescent chemicals.

Smer was shouting, and the Wasp soldiers pulled back to us, reforming, their stings spitting to all sides. The attack had ceased, though: the searing light had banished the creatures like bad dreams, sending them the way of the shadows. I had got no clear look at them, save for one moment, the very instant that the light had flashed to life. I had seen a face. It upset me a great deal.

It was something like a Scorpion-kinden, only more so. The jaws were massively bulked out into a tusked and fanged muzzle, a horror of jutting hook-like teeth. The brow sloped, and every part of it was ridged and reinforced, the skin taut over a lumpy and armoured skull. Without a doubt it had been a face, though, with the common humanity that implied. I had been assuming our attackers were beasts of some kind, their huge, long-limbed frames to resolve themselves into the familiar threats of whip scorpions or harvestmen, perhaps. These beasts had been men, though, or perhaps they had been men once. The sight shook me, and when everyone else spoke about an attack by some kind of desert animal, I did not correct them.

Of our two dozen soldiers, seven were gone. Not just dead, either: the assailants had snatched up every body when they fled, which soured the mood yet further.

"That light was a timely idea," Doctor Phinagler noted.

Brandt frowned. "We have limited supplies of the chemicals," he muttered, but nobody suggested we douse it.

I had assumed that the next morning would see us beat a hasty retreat. Colonel Brandt, however, had other ideas.

"I have decided we will press on to the heart of this tomb of a place, where the structures are most whole," he declaimed to his captive audience. "Sergeant, you will find a more fortified position for us to spend the night, and ensure that we are not caught unawares again."

I was ready for a chorus of disagreement from the soldiers, but that would have been the Collegiate way, not the Imperial. Instead, the soldiers exchanged grim glances but got on with their orders.

I caught up with Saveta and murmured, "This is crazy, surely. Those things will be back tonight."

She gave me an unhappy shrug. "We must hope the light will keep them back."

"The Colonel will not let a few savages stand between him and his destiny," came the sharp tones of Ethiganos, who was somehow right behind us, in that way the Moth-kinden have.

"And you, of course, are deeply concerned with Wasp hereditary destiny," I said sarcastically, mostly to remind him that I had some academic credentials, and could use long words with the best of them.

His narrow, blank eyes fixed me. "You Apt understand nothing of destiny."

"At least we can use a doorknob. Hey, you want to hear a joke, Saveta? Knock knock." I put my hand to my ear, guessing that Collegiate humour was not likely to be on the syllabus for an Imperial slave-scholar. "'Who's there?' you say? The Moth-kinden. All of them."

To my delight she laughed, although Brandt gave her a very suspicious look a moment after that shut her up. Imperial slaves aren't supposed to have much to laugh about, I suppose.

Ethiganos gave me a very unpleasant look of his own, but I reckoned I could take him, if it came to it.

I went on to bother Doctor Phinagler, in the hope that he, at least, might be leery of staying another night in that city of the not-dead-enough.

"What do you think they were?" I asked him, "and don't say just animals."

He made sure the Wasps weren't eavesdropping, then shrugged. "Some kinden unknown to Collegium, perhaps. Or maybe they were animals, though of a manlike frame: some creature of bone and blood, certainly, rather than chitin shell. Like a horse."

"You think they were horses?" I asked him incredulously.

"No, but there are some very ancient carvings in storage at the College – I got a look at 'em the once. They show some kind of beasts that are like horses, but they are attacking people and insects, with teeth like swords and hooves like knives."

"And that's what you think these things were?"

He looked profoundly unhappy. "No. I think they were people once. Whether they still are… I cannot believe it. Living in this place has turned them into beasts."

"You think they built this city?"

Then we came out into a grand square, where a statue had once stood that could have played voyeur at a third storey window. It lay in segments now, broken across the open space and into the shattered columnade of a building opposite. Beyond its great stone corpse we saw a wide pictorial wall with a single scene picked out so grandly that the details were still visible.

"No," Doctor Phinagler answered my query, his eyes wide, "I think we did."

The vast majority of the figures on that wall were recognisably Beetle-kinden, just like the Khanaphir. They were shown bringing bundles and boxes and baskets, bowing and scraping and generally abasing themselves, and all leading towards a single central figure. This was a man of a wholly different kinden – one I recognised from those enigmatic sculptures at the river gate. He was shown twice the size of the toiling underclass that served him, looking down on them with an expression of benign contempt that had survived the ages.

"There!" Brandt exclaimed. "One of the Masters, the lords of this city in its heyday," which seemed unarguable, but then, "Do you not see the Waspish features?"

He sounded a little unsure, and to my eyes they were nothing of the sort. Ethiganos chose that moment to declare that, yes, of course, it could be Brandt's close cousin there on the wall, and then the rest of the Imperial party was following suit like gears in a train, because apparently the chain of command extended to aesthetic matters also.

"How do you want to proceed, Colonel?" Saveta asked him.

He craned his neck, somewhat defeated by the sheer scale of the mural. No amount of charcoal rubbing on scraps of paper would capture this image.

"The interior of the buildings," he decided. "Sergeant Smer, detail some men to set a defensible camp within – defensible and lit – and the rest should start searching. There will be artifacts left here – statues, regalia, perhaps even records." He didn't say 'treasure' but I swear I saw the thought flash through the mind of every soldier. It seemed likely that a certain amount of portable archaeological evidence would not be made available for the Colonel's thesis. "Saveta and Ethiganos will oversee the search," he added, although by that time the damage was done.

"If you don't mind, I'll spend a little time sketching the carvings," Doctor Phinagler offered. Everyone else was far too preoccupied thinking of gold and gems to mind, and to tell the truth I myself was a little put out that the Doctor should choose this point in time to remember his scholarly priorities. However, as the rest were splitting up into squads – Smer, Saveta and Brant taking a third of the soldiers each, and the Moth vanishing off on his own – I decided that my employer needed my keen eyes to watch his back.

"So, not really like a Wasp-kinden then," I observed, once the Imperials were about their business.

Doctor Phinagler made a noncommittal noise. "It's very stylised."

I didn't think so. The smaller figures had very plain Beetle features. "I never saw a Wasp that was twelve feet tall," I pointed out.

"No doubt an artistic convention, to show the prominence of rank," he told me. "Not uncommon for Inapt representations, if you'll recall."

I looked up at that carven likeness as it stared out over my head, cold and regal. Some unsung sculptor had put a great deal of work into that visage. That was not just a very specific kinden being depicted, but an individual. The face was full, ripe with hedonism without sacrificing its arch beauty. I never wanted to see a face like that in life, and this wish would be granted in the worst way possible, as you will see.

Doctor Phinagler worked tirelessly until the sun grew low enough that I had to intervene. Despite his somewhat motley reputation, he is a man of first class scholarly dedication at times, usually the worst possible times. I had already checked on Smer, finding that he had set up in a mostly complete room with the light globe ready and soldiers watching the jagged holes that time had rent in the walls and roof.

"Doctor, we need to go," I said now, watching the sun seem to put an extra burst of speed on as it raced for the horizon.

My employer had approached the mural, and was staring up at the large carved figure, one hand up to touch the stone.

"Doctor," I said, more urgently. "Come on, now."

He looked at me, and for a moment I think he did not know me. Then he blinked, frowned: plainly he was thrown at finding himself where he was. No doubt the desert heat, the strange silence, had worked upon his mind.

"Is it so late already?" he asked, demonstrating that he had fully recovered his facility for stating the obvious.

I opened my mouth, and then shut it again. This was mostly because we were not alone. A thing had just slouched in with the gathering dusk, slope shouldered, spike-knuckled, a beast as big as the carven enthroned figure, but of a wholly different nature, like that man's deformed shadow. Just one of them, we saw, but one would be more than enough to turn us both to paste.

It lifted its face to us, that brutal, sub-human mask. The eyes that caught the last gleam of the dying sun were those of a human being in torment.

For a moment it just crouched there, knuckles in the sand. Its physique was lean and long-limbed, while still appallingly muscular. When it lifted its muzzle to the last rays of the sun there was a strange beauty to it: man or beast, this was a thing that had been perfected for one task. Sadly, that task was killing us.

Abruptly it came to a decision and was pounding towards us as we cowered back against the wall. I clutched at the Doctor's leg, convinced that we were going to be pulped before I could write any of this bizarre venture down.

The creature shied away, skittering to one side and backing off again, snarling and baring its teeth. Doctor Phinagler and I exchanged baffled glances. Then it was back, and when it keened out, there were a dozen voices lifted from nearby to join in. This time it got well within arm's reach of us, advancing at a terrifying pace, the spiked bludgeons of its fists lifted to blot us from the world. And still it held back, face locked not on us, but past and above us. I craned back, and saw that serene stone countenance smiling down on us, and on the creature: distantly benign, inviolable.

The monster cried out, caught between the need to kill and whatever prohibition the carving exercised. It was a human call, too, no matter the throat that made it. There were words in there, slurred and mangled by its tusks.

Then came a more familiar sound: the crack and sizzle of stingshot. Sergeant Smer and a half dozen soldiers came barrelling out, shooting as they went. The gold fire crackled about the monster, which flinched from the flash of it, although the shots themselves seemed barely to warm its hide. Doctor Phinagler grabbed me, preparatory to making a run for it, but then the monster was turning to go for Smer, and in doing so it struck my employer with a thorny elbow.

He was slammed back into the carved wall and I heard the breath go out of him. Even as I was scrabbling after him, though, the whole world tilted away, and abruptly all the fuss and bother of the fight was retreating from us at some speed. A panel at the base of the wall had hinged open, triggered by the beast's stroke or by some unseen catch knocked by the Doctor's flailing limbs, and we were both thrown into sloping darkness.

We landed together – thankfully with me on top, which further knocked the wind from my employer. Above, we could hear fighting, the caterwauling of the creatures and shouted orders from Smer. Around us was a darkness so deep that even my eyes could not penetrate it.

Always resourceful, the Doctor clicked at his steel lighter until a fickle flame sprang up, illuminating a little space of the walls around us, so densely carved with little pictures that there was barely space between them. We stood carefully, and I judged from the echoes that the chamber must be large, a good thirty feet to a side at least.

Then they brought the great lamp up, above, and a silver shaft of light speared down to illuminate us. We could hear the monsters retreating, swearing incomprehensible vengeance, and I hoped none of the soldiers had been badly hurt on our account.

Then someone was calling our names: Saveta.

I hailed her, and she told me, "We need to pull back to the camp before the creatures come back!"

"The Doctor can't fly," I called. "Let down a rope or something."

My employer had advanced further into the buried space, heedless of traps or denizens. The weak radiance of his lighter danced and shuddered across walls that were cracked and sundered. The floor was rocky with fallen masonry.

Then Smer was being lowered down towards us, a flaming torch in one hand, calling for the Doctor to hurry.

My employer did not move, though. He was standing, transfixed, staring into the gloom. There was a shape there; a pedestal or high dais, and upon it, battered by rubble… A supine human form.

At that point, with the tortured howling of the city monsters echoing down to us, prudence overcame curiosity. Smer helped the Doctor up the rope and I followed under my own power. We retreated hastily to the room fortified by the soldiers and took the lamp with us.

The mood amongst our companions was buoyant. We had lost no more of our number to the creatures, and Doctor Phinagler's revelation sparked a great excitement in Brandt. All our scholars had been convinced that the great edifice had once served a living purpose, but now they were speaking animatedly of tombs and mausoleums. I am not sure why historians seem to value the house of a corpse far more than those places it dwelled in when still alive, but it seems to be a fact of the trade.

Plans were made to conduct a thorough search of the place in the morning. Again the word 'treasure' was never quite spoken.

I exchanged a glance with Saveta and she rolled her eyes once she had checked that Brandt would not see her. Looking past her, I surprised Ethiganos's face in an unguarded moment, and the expression thus revealed was avid, eager, almost obscene as it gripped those normally calm features. I am afraid I put this down to my general poor relations with the Inapt, and Moths in particular – they are not the most popular of folk back home after all. In retrospect, I should have thought further on it.

The monstrous creatures came close many times, but the harsh artificial light of our lamp kept them away: we heard their voices and the scrape of their claws, but saw no more than deformed shadows on the walls.

Those voices, though: the Imperial party line was very much that they were beasts, but I heard them speaking to one another in the night. I heard rough words amongst the gutterals and the mumbled diction. Lying awake, I stared at the night sky through the cracks in the ceiling and thought I heard them slur and grunt of duty left undone, and a frustrated loathing for the intruders, meaning us.

Smer argued for conserving the chemical lamp and investigating the tomb by torchlight. A sergeant's arguments don't go very far in the face of a colonel's wishes, though, so we embarked on our scholarly grave-robbing with the best light that Aptitude could create.

I had thought everyone would be mobbing about the cracked sarcophagus at the back, but some sort of residual reverence seemed to hang about it, so that first the wall carvings got a thorough seeing-to. In the gloom of the past evening I had not marked them, but they were not limited to the minute scrawl of pictograms that cluttered every unworn stone of the city. Those were there, yes, in great quantities, but they were an illegible commentary to a dozen grand tableaux like the one on the wall outside. And when I say 'like', they were very like: they were all in celebration of the same man.

Here we saw that hugely-rendered figure receiving tribute from ambassadors of a dozen different kinden, some recognisable and some not. Here he was, armoured in antique fashion, smiting what were plainly Scorpion-kinden with an expression of stern judgment, while Beetle-kinden soldiers rendered in far less detail clustered about his knees. Here he sat in judgment over some incomprehensible trial, or possibly a sporting activity. Everywhere we looked, the stones themselves cried out the greatness of this solitary individual. The masons had poured every last dreg of their craft into cramming us with awe and reverence for he who was presumably interred herein.

The masons had never met a Collegiate, I'd wager. Perhaps this is what the Wasps want. Perhaps every little dictator in the Empire, every magnate of Helleron or Spider Arista, is truly lusting after this lost glory: a time when a powerful man could have the utmost control over the lives and deaths of his underlings. Perhaps, before his death, Emperor Alvdan the Second, mightiest ruler in the known world, cried himself to sleep that even his life should suffer checks and balances, and that when he was gutted by that Mantis slave, nobody would build such a temple of adulation in his memory as we found there. Perhaps they would all be consumed with envy, at the sight. Not me.

For me, hailing from a city where it is we the people who choose who governs, and where we can pluck down any man who seeks to stand above the rest – a city which has known slavery, and has thrown those masters out on their grey and mystic ears – it was all in the most appalling bad taste. I shared a sidelong glance with Doctor Phinagler: the same thoughts were evident on his face.

But Brandt was transported into ecstasies. "Look how our ancestors were worshipped!" he cried out. "At last we have discovered our birthright!" And then his expression twisted with agony, because how was he ever to get any of this *home*?

"Get to work," he told Saveta and Ethiganos. "Rubbings, sketches, anything. We will enter the gates of Capitas in triumph, with what we've found!"

Doctor Phinagler was content at first to follow suit, and for a frankly tedious couple of hours the academics scrubbed and scribbled, and the rest of us kicked our heels while the resting place itself remained a silent, brooding presence at our backs.

For myself, I was greatly taken with one of the carvings that showed the unknown deceased in a grand cityscape – the buildings rendered small to emphasise his importance. He stood before a quailing crowd of less significant people, his hands resting on the bald scalps of creatures that I recognised as our nocturnal assailants. As with every depiction, that stone likeness bore a calm and detached smile, but I reckoned that he was about to loose his pets on the crowd, and that in real life he'd have been smiling just the same as he did so.

Then one of the soldiers discovered another chamber while kicking about against one wall, and let out what I thought was a cry of horror, but which turned out to be avarice.

That there were bodies in that further chamber was no great source of concern to Imperial soldiers. They were dried and withered almost to nothing, anyway, so brittle that the least touch would send hand's breadths of parchment skin flaking away like autumn leaves. They were sitting about the walls of this smaller room, and they were garbed for the sort of war nobody has fought for a thousand years. They had mail of bronze scales, oval shields, spears, and all of it had only been saved from the claws of time by the dry air and the fact that it was liberally ornamented with gold.

Regalia, too, we found there: a sceptre four feet long that seemed to be solid gold set with rubies and spiral patterns; several chains of precious metal inset with turquoise sigils; rings; torcs. It was all laid out on a slab, and the dessicated soldiers had been set to guard it. *Until what?* I wondered. Until their dead master stopped playing dead? Whatever hold the tomb-owner exercised in life had somehow persuaded these stupid Beetles – and I reckoned from their dry faces they had been Beetles – to let themselves be walled up in here with him.

Well, needless to say, that particular force of guards proved no bar to Imperial expansionism. I think that there were barely two dry bones left connected by the time the soldiers had finished, and although Brandt was loud in proclaiming that everything must be preserved for posterity, I'm sure a fair few knickknacks found their way into private pouches: swords, daggers, broaches, things that could be conveniently hidden down a tunic or under a cloak.

Saveta and Doctor Phinagler were both watching this display morosely: more was being lost to scholarship in the acquisition than the display of the mere treasures themselves could ever restore. Beyond them, I saw Ethiganos.

He was still working on the wall carvings, but I saw him peer closely at the tiny pictograms and his lips moved, as if counting or reading. A chill went over me then, to think that whatever secrets were locked within those engraved minutiae were yet known to the Moth-kinden, another people that had once styled themselves as 'masters'.

All of this excitement had taken some time, and it was only late in the day that Brandt decided to turn his attentions to the sarcophagus itself.

The figure carved in white stone that lay atop it was twelve feet long, the same artistic exaggeration – Doctor Phinagler assured me – as could be seen in the wall reliefs. It was also stark naked, its fleshy, powerful physique quite open to scrutiny, save for where the ceiling had come down on it. The head, one shoulder and half the broad chest was buried in broken debris, although none of us had any doubt whose face we would see when we excavated it.

"In this coffin," Brandt eulogised, "lies one of the great kings of the Wasp-kinden." By then we had almost given up rolling our eyes at his obsession. Perhaps the soldiers believed him, but I could see Saveta look from Brandt's own features to the exacting depictions on the walls and draw the obvious and unflattering comparison.

"You want us to start shifting this, sir, open it up?" Smer asked, jabbing a thumb at the rubble.

Brandt laid his hands on the pale marble of the figure – in a somewhat indelicate spot, actually, though he didn't notice. "I…" and for once he seemed uncertain. The weight of ages interred in this chamber had failed to light on him, previously, but now he was at least brushed by it.

Everyone was waiting for him to make his call, except me. I was looking at everyone else. The soldiers didn't care much, save that the uncovering would plainly involve some heavy lifting. Saveta seemed eager enough – perhaps with a conveniently portable body to snatch we could all be off out of here. My employer was also plainly keen to number himself amongst the first to look on that dead visage, and see what time had preserved of the face that beamed down on us from the walls.

Ethiganos was tense as a wire, waiting. His expression was almost feverishly bright, his white eyes wide and staring as though he were using some Moth Art to influence the colonel.

And Saveta piped up, "There's no lid."

"What?" Brandt demanded, and she showed us. There was not even the thinnest line to show where a lid might part from the rest of the block. The supine carved giant might be resting on a slab of solid stone.

But Brandt had already demonstrated his reluctance to let evidence get in the way of his pet theories. "It is just the craft of the ancient stonemasons. If necessary we will split it open with chisels and acids, but I am sure we will find the secret of opening it once we have cleared the debris." And then, "But let us start work tomorrow. We may as well be fresh for it."

The soldiers greeted this suggestion warmly, but not half so much as did Ethiganos.

And so, because I am a naturally suspicious person when circumstances warrant, I stayed awake when the others had bedded down, listening to the snarls and the laments of the city's unseen guardians – off the leash of history, and yet still prevented from driving out the foreign invader.

I almost missed him, even so. He was a sneaky one, that Moth. He crept past the sentries before I noticed he was gone, and then I had to duplicate his feat, which I did mostly by crawling through a gap in the ceiling that no larger kinden could have fit through. Had Ethiganos simply fled into the shattered paths of the city, I would have lost him, but I knew where he must be headed and I descended noiselessly into the tomb to find him there.

He needed no light, of course: it's said to Moth eyes, midnight and midday have little to distinguish them. I needed a little more, but the waxing of the moon sent just enough silver radiance down the shaft that I could see the Moth's shadow as he moved about the walls.

If he had glanced back, he would almost certainly have seen me. He was absorbed in his task, though, muttering to himself, confident in his solitude.

He flitted from panel to panel, reading the inscrutable glyphs there, murmuring his conclusions, then on to the next. He was not simply swotting up to please Brandt, either. Here was a man about a mission.

And at last he strode to the centre of the chamber – with me circling to keep at his back – and he spoke, loud and clear.

"Uncounted ages have passed since the eyes of Teshemes last opened," he declared, and the air shivered at the word – spoken to match the sound of 'Khanaphes' closely enough that I knew he had unearthed the name of this dead place. "And in those many aeons, how the world has turned. Those that were its great masters are forgotten, save in the meagre dreams of the Khanaphir Beetles. Those to whom the mantle was given, to govern in your stead, we are overthrown by our slaves. Where once our wisdom swayed the world, now we are banished to its far places, the forest and the mountaintop, while the ignorant hold court and feast within our halls."

I bristled at that, and very nearly betrayed myself with a fierce rebuttal in true Collegiate style. Thankfully I managed to hold my peace.

"Lost is the rod and the crown of the ancient days," Ethiganos continued strongly, "gone the majesty that you cloaked us in. Our great wonders would be your least curiosities, so diminished are we. Yet we are magicians, still. We are your heirs, your children. And your children call upon you for your patronage, your recognition and your aid. *I* call upon you. I am Ethiganos of Tharn, and I have studied the most ancient of texts, and I have bowed the knee to the unworthy, so that my destiny might lead me here. I call you now, from your long rest. I call your name: Achemalas, He Who Guides the River, Slayer of Ten Thousand in the Sack of Nemeth Arta, Conqueror of Those Who Race The Sun, Eternal Watcher, I call you, I name you."

He stopped, and the echoes of all those long lost titles continued to resound about us, as though the mere sounds had taken on lives of their own. I could see his arms upraised, the sleeves of his robes fallen back. He held the pose as the reverberations died down, waiting, waiting.

Nothing.

"I name you," he repeated. "Achemalas, I name you." His shoulders sagged; his voice died away into a disappointed whisper.

I was of a mind to make myself known then, so I could make fun of him. Some residual caution held me back, and just as well it did, because he was answered.

"Who calls?" It was a great whisper, that voice. It came from everywhere and nowhere, but chiefly from that half-sundered sarcophagus. It was deep and soft, and terrifying in a way that no other voice I ever heard has been. That it was a disembodied voice speaking out of a tomb might have prompted that, of course.

"I am Ethiganos, of the Moth-kinden of Tharn," the Moth gasped out.

"Moth-kinden," the voice murmured, as though it couldn't recall the name but was too polite to say so. "Why are you here?"

"Great Lord Achemalas, Master of the Lands of the Khanaphir!" I saw Ethiganos tremble, even by that poor light. "Your halls are fallen, great one, your servants have deserted you. There are come to your places those who give you no reverence, who steal your treasures, who –"

There was a monstrous grating sound, part stone, part human voice. Whatever spoke, it was as fixated on treasure as the Wasps. "Who dares…?"

"Great Lord, I am of the Inapt," Ethganos declared. "I am a magician, your heir in the ancient ways. Make me your agent, take me as your chiefest servant. Rise up and give me power over these upstarts, Lord!"

Outside, the voices of the guardian monsters were growing more and more agitated, as whatever unpleasantness the Moth was about infected them. I could hear them calling to one another all the way across the city.

There was a sound then, another stone sound. I thought it was the voice, but it was stone for real, this time. First dust, then pebbles, then the grinding crunch of great jagged blocks being displaced.

I saw what I saw. You will not believe it, but I saw him sit up.

I had heard that voice, and my mind had assigned it to the tomb I thought lay within that great pedestal. I think Ethiganos, for all his elder lore, had believed the same. We both started back as the stone began shifting, and if I cried out it was lost within his own exclamation.

The moonlight loved the pale stone of that statue, seeking it out to make it glow in the darkness. So it was I saw the alabaster flex and shift, and then the rubble was falling and sloughing away. Achemalas, Slayer of Ten Thousand, stirred in his millennial slumber, and woke.

He sat up as a mountain might, ponderous and inexorable, the shattered stone sliding from him like scree. I saw his pale face in profile as the concealing stone fell from it, though the gloom spared me from having to look on that condescending smile.

And I knew more, then, than Saveta or Brandt or my employer. I knew that if the carvings exaggerated, it was only by a little. He was the height of two men at least, a great pale giant from the dawn of time.

He did not look on Ethiganos, not yet. That hollow gaze was fixed on ages past, days when this city lived.

"Where are my brothers and sisters?" he cried out, surely to be heard across the city. "Where are my servants to bring me my raiment? Where is the sceptre and the crown, that Teshemes shall know its lord once more?" He made his demands of the air, in the manner of a man whose least whim had been granted the moment it had been expressed.

"They are not here, Great Lord." Ethiganos was brave, at least, to speak into that echo. "The great days of Teshemes and Khanaphes have fallen from us. Sand now hides the floors where once you trod, just as the Apt and the ignorant squat in the seats of the mighty. But we remember, my folk who learned all their arts from yours. Great Lord, give me your blessing!"

For a long moment the pale giant sat, staring at the dark-shrouded wall. Perhaps his lips moved. Perhaps a hundred expressions passed fleetingly across those majestic features. I could not see.

"Gone," intoned that resonant voice, and then, "*Gone?*" His outrage was that of a Helleron merchant told some delicacy is out of stock, only writ large enough to deface the world.

"Great Lord, let me serve you," Ethiganos wheedled. "Lay but your hand on me – imbue me with the power of the days of your greatness."

"What winds have scoured my home and my mind?" In that moment, and only then, did I pity Achemalas. His voice was distilled loss, a creature out of all time and compass, woken in an age when everything it had ever known was dust.

But then it said, "Bring me these intruders that they may be judged," and lost my sympathies entirely.

Ethiganos squirmed. "Master, they have swords and weapons. My little strength will not suffice, unless you give me –"

"Then I will send forth my servants," growled that profound voice. "They have shirked their duty long enough, to suffer to live those who would profane our places.

"Lord, your servants are held back by the intruders' cursed artifice!" Ethiganos said quickly. "But bless me, and I shall open the way for them."

Still staring at the wall, as though all of this was but a dream to him, Achemalas rumbled deep in his chest. "Prove yourself my servant, little Moth-kinden, and there may be a place for you at my feet."

"I will, Great Lord, I will, only…" Ethiganos had half moved to go, but now came back. "Your servants will destroy me, Great Lord. I would not deprive you of what meagre use you might make of me." It was a particularly elegant piece of self-serving equivocation.

"You fear Those Who Race The Sun," and the vast figure chuckled unpleasantly. I saw one vast white arm lift, slow as molten lead, and there was a light. It was greenish in hue, sickly and pale, and he drew with it in the air: a sigil, like the thousand that marched on every wall, but written in that unwholesome fire on nothing. It flared, practically burning itself into the backs of my eyes, and Ethiganos shrieked, stumbling away from the light.

"Now they shall know you, through my mark," Achemalas told him sternly. "Now prove yourself a faithful agent of my will, or I shall rip my mark off you once more."

He swung his legs over the side of his plinth and stood, facing us, and Ethiganos screamed, at what his Moth eyes saw too clearly. For myself, I saw enough to know that whatever Achemalas had once been, he was that no longer but damaged and mad, and I fled, determined to warn them all.

I burst out of the shaft from the tomb almost into the thorned arms of one of the guardians. Only my wings saved me, flinging me into the air beyond its reach. The ruins were crawling with them, the moon betraying their skittering movements everywhere I looked. I pelted inside for our camp, and the sentries opened up on me with their stings the moment I came around the corner. With the monsters close behind, I had a tense moment of Imperial-Collegiate diplomacy in order to convince them that I was, indeed, me, and had already evaded their notice once to make my exit. Then I was into the comfortingly harsh radiance of the chemical lamp, and everyone was awake.

"They're coming!" I yelled, which was probably not the most edifying way to go about things.

"How did you get outside the camp?" Sergeant Smer was demanding, and "Have you riled up the natives, Fosse?" from my employer, and, "It doesn't matter. We have the lamp," from complacent Brandt.

The sounds of the city, the howls and curses and snarling, these were all mounting fiercely, closer and closer and all around us.

"Ethiganos has betrayed us!" I insisted.

"To who? To them?" Brandt demanded. "How?"

"Where is Ethiganos?" Saveta asked.

Then the sentries were shouting, and the monsters of the city came down on us furiously. They blundered into sight, all the twisted and brutal glory of them, then stumbled back from the uncompromising illumination of our lamp. It almost seemed that it was their own hideousness they were hiding from when they reeled back into the darkness. They were scrabbling about above us, too, clustering at the holes in the ceiling, scratching and battering at the stone so that dust rained on us, and yet they would not step into the light.

For myself, I was heading right for the lamp, but the soldiers, who had received a fairly confused version of events, got in my way and dragged me from it.

"It's Ethiganos!" I fairly howled, but I had neglected to mention the rest of the story, and they would not have believed it, and so nobody paid me any attention.

Or perhaps Saveta had absorbed more of it. Certainly she had put herself by the lamp, but neither she nor any of them saw the Moth before he struck, only me.

His face was twisted: of course it was twisted – the glyph of the Masters had been seared there by that greenish fire, darkening one pale eye and locking his expression into a desperate snarl.

He had a shovel, only that, one of the digging tools the soldiers had brought. He struck Saveta with it first, to knock her aside, and then he struck the lamp and shattered it into midnight darkness.

There was one despairing moment when everyone present absorbed what had just happened.

Then Those Who Race The Sun descended on us, our sun having set. It was pitch dark save for a little moonlight coming in from the cracks above, but the guardians of the city could see like Moths. They shied away from the searing flash of the Wasps' stings, but those brief handclaps of illumination could save nobody, any more than the fire of the stings themselves could hurt the creatures' Art-strengthened hides.

There is a time and a place to stand beside one's comrades and fall, entwined in their arms, to be sung of in posterity. That time and place, in my opinion, is in Mantis ballads from five hundred years ago. The real world is too precious to be cast aside for imponderables like honour and glory. When the creatures from above came through, tearing open the ceiling of our little camp as though it were matchwood and not thick stone, my wings flicked me high into the night sky.

Below, the rest were fighting. The Wasps could fly, surely, or most of them, but none of them followed my example. I saw their stings flash as they tried to defend their leader. I heard their cries.

Sobbing for my employer, I fled across the broken rooftops of lost Teshemes until I found a high perch to cower on. I assumed all was lost, that all I could salvage from that terrible place would be my own weak body, if I could survive long enough to rejoin the Scorpions.

I stayed up there, clutched in upon myself, long after the sounds had ceased.

Then the creatures began to emerge from the sundered ruin that we had thought safe. The moon picked them out as hunched, long-limbed shadows, on two legs or four, creeping one by one into the open.

And they were not alone.

The sign of Achemalas was plainly efficacious: I could see Ethiganos quite clearly, in his Auxillian robe, the coat that he had turned so completely. He strode amongst the monsters like a little tyrant, wearing his borrowed authority on his face. I longed for a bow right then, I can tell you. I would have put an arrow right through his good eye, if I could.

Then they brought out the rest: not all of them, but some. Whether by Ethiganos's intervention or the will of the Master, the monsters had taken prisoner those who had not fought them directly. I crept a little closer to see: there was Saveta, stumbling, clutching one arm to her. There was the bald pate of Colonel Brandt, who had apparently not possessed the courage of most of his soldiers. There were a few other

Wasps, who had presumably surrendered when all had been lost, for which I blamed them not at all. There, moreover, was Doctor Phinagler. No warrior he, and that fact had saved his life. Ethiganos was obviously taunting him with something, though I could not hear the words – the Moths always love to have a Beetle at their mercy, presumably because it reminds them of the Bad Old Days. My employer, for his part, was taking it all in good spirit, even addressing his monstrous captors with what appeared to be a vestige of his customary cordiality. Then again, there are few others in the world with the emotional resilience of Doctor Phinagler, a resilience that often far outlasts the ability of others to be resilient towards him.

I crept closer still, hoping to hear some lengthy exposition of future plans from Ethiganos, but the band of them were already moving off, the captives shoved and prodded forwards by a pack of the monsters perhaps a dozen strong.

There was plenty of night yet remaining, and somehow I thought that Those Who Race The Sun would not simply abandon their prisoners come dawn.

I came up with many rescue ideas, all of which were thwarted by my having absolutely no chance of putting them into action. Nonetheless, I shadowed the little prison party as they trudged across the city: apparently Achemalas had somewhere else than his tomb to call a home.

Unfortunately, I am not as good at being stealthy as I sometimes like to think, or perhaps the eyes of the monsters were sharper. There I was, doing my best sneaking from shadow to shadow, while their sight could cut through the night itself. Needless to say I attracted their notice.

The problem was that, despite being so large, they were no slouches in the stealth game themselves. I heard a faint scuffing from nearby, and when I looked round, there was one of the creatures, fists raised to pound me into the dirt.

Well, I got airborne quick, I can tell you, but not quite quick enough. The strike missed me, but the barbs of its hands snagged my clothing and sent me spinning through the air like a ball. I hit the ground hard, rolled, and saw the shadow of a second creature eclipsing the stars above me.

I got out under its armpit, because its spiked hands were already clutching for the more obvious way out. Still it clipped me, and even as I rolled to a bruised halt the pair of them were on me.

They were so fast! Like hunting beetles or spiders, just skittering across the ground like blurred shadows. I made for the sky again, but the air around me was full of their murderous clutching fingers. Instead, I went to earth. In the ruins nearby there was a hole, some collapsed doorway that left just enough room for a Fly to squeak in. Squeak I did, and I lost a sandal to my pursuers, but not a foot.

There was, of course, no light at all down there. The scratchings of my own steel lighter showed me cracked walls, ruined carvings, a single hand from a broken statue lying ghoulishly at my feet. No other way out.

But I was safe, at least. No insane giants were going to come through that little gap.

Except, of course, the bastards could *dig*.

They went at it with a will, shunting aside the debris with all their appalling strength. They were chatting, too, in their guttural voices. They were plainly in high spirits about the prospect of winkling me out.

With nowhere left to flee to, I calmed myself and decided to defend myself the only way I could think of.

Wars are fought with swords but won with minds. That is, if you can believe it, an Ant-kinden proverb. Right then I was racking *my* mind, trying to remember a very particular image. I used my lighter to make a little torch of my cloak, and with a rock as my page and a sharp stone as my stylus, I scratched frantically away.

Then the unwelcome moon shouldered its way into my refuge, let in by the widening of the opening, and the monsters followed it.

I closed my eyes, averted my face and presented my makeshift tablet as boldly as I dared, thrusting an arm out towards them in the full expectation of losing it at the shoulder.

I could hear their harsh breathing, smell the earthy, fierce scent of them. Slowly I opened my eyes to see what I had won.

The lead monster was right there, close enough that I could have poked it in the eye. It was frowning ponderously at my little tablet, on which I had sketched out, as best as I could recall, the sigil that Achmalas had branded onto the Moth's face.

The creature squinted at it, ridged brow furrowed in a burlesque of concentration. The expression on that terrible face was so familiar from shortsighted old scholars at the College that I half expected it to take out a pair of eyeglasses.

It was not sure, I realised. That understanding shook me, because it finally bridged that gap between the horror of their appearance and the fact that they were, despite it, human. They were not supernatural monsters from the myths of the Inapt, conjured up to prey upon their usurpers. They were not ravening animals. They were men.

They were men who had dwelled here, in this dead place, since time immemorial, and they had once known masters – Masters – who had trained them to fear a certain sign. But how long had it been since they had seen that sign? What long ages had passed since the voice of their Masters had brought them to heel? And now, here I was with a surely inaccurate approximation of the glyph that symbolised their slavery, and it had been too long. The pair of them cocked their heads and blinked at it, and were unsure if they were permitted to kill me or not.

I had envisaged them going howling off, baffled and confused, but instead the lead monster sat back on its haunches, huge arms resting on its knees, and stared at me. As I say, they were men: they were not bound by some mystical chains to obey or flee me. They did not know what I was about and so they waited to see what I would do.

All my ideas about commanding them or banishing them with the mighty power of my sigil were quietly buried. I didn't think I wanted to try it, not just then.

"So," I said brightly, and "So," grated the monster.

"You understand me?" I wasn't sure whether it was just echoing my word.

"Understand you, yes." Except it was more like "Unnrstan'yrr" because of the tusks, which crowded out its lips so that it could barely shape words at all.

"You, er…" What does one say to a monster? "You don't seem as disappointed as I'd thought." Rather than make a decision, apparently I was just going to let my mouth flap.

It made an inquisitive grunt. I suspect they had quite an eloquent language of indeterminate noises, given their limitations.

"At not getting to kill me." I was eyeing the exit behind them and wondering how far I could push my luck.

It spoke again, but I didn't catch the meaning. At my frustrated expression, it gave me the words more slowly, as though I had asked for directions in a foreign city.

"Not what we want," it was saying.

"Right," I said doubtfully. "I saw you before. You've killed most of the others, haven't you."

"Is duty."

"Masters say," the other monster put in. its voice was higher – though still very deep – and I wondered if this was a female monster. "When they are gone, protect their city, protect their things. None must come to steal their treasures. Keep their places for them."

I had to have it say all that about three times before I understood, but my ear was becoming more tuned to their gravelly, mashed-together words.

"I suppose even you can't fight the desert," I said without thinking.

The creature nearest me flung up its head and howled mournfully, and the other followed suit. In the confined space the noise was deafening. I heard kindred laments from the city outside.

"Well," I decided. "This will make a fascinating footnote in the College kinden studies journal," and – presenting the sigil boldly throughout – made to push past them to the exit.

They did not move, and I found I was not bold enough to start physically muscling past them. The nearest creature's snaggle-fanged mouth twitched into a grin.

"No, look," I told it reasonably. "I've got the… the thing, the rune, whatever it is. Look, you have to obey me."

"Is that so?"

I virtually had the sigil shoved up its nose at that point. Its deep-socketed little eyes peered at it.

"Is looking like Glyph," the creature declared but, as I was about to try and assert my rights again, "Is not Glyph."

A hand the size of a human torso had abruptly caught me about the body, and I was lifted up to that nightmare visage.

"Is interesting," the monster murmured. "Is close. Is no pain, not to kill you. Is no pain, to touch you."

"Is that how it works?" I asked, a little breathlessly. If it had made a fist, it would have splintered my ribs into my organs, but it held me with a very precise strength. "You obey the thing, or it hurts you?"

"Hurts, yes." The eyes – those human eyes – creased a little more.

"But you, look at you…" I didn't want to remind them how big and strong they were, especially in comparison to me, but it was implicit. "What made you like this?"

"Masters," said the other one. "We fight Masters, long time. Beat us, crush us, take away what we were. We were Spiders of the Sun."

The one that had hold of me hissed angrily. "Is forbidden to say. We are Those Who Race The Sun, now. Sun is forbidden us, by Masters."

"But…" Around us, the midnight city lay in ruins that the desert had lapped against since before the Moths built Collegium. "When is this even supposed to have happened?"

"Do not count," grunted the other one. "Enough to know: beaten, made to kneel, made to know the Glyph. Told to guard their places, guard their things, for when they come back."

I blinked. "I don't think they're coming back." I was thinking, then – mostly about Aptitude and Inaptitude. Why can a Moth not use a crossbow? It is not because their grey fingers cannot grasp the trigger, but because their minds can't. I was imagining such a mental compulsion somehow graven into the brain of these creatures, deep enough to run down the generations, that bound them to their stupid, pointless duty.

"You're slaves," I told them. But of course they were slaves, to speak so about Masters.

The creature that had me gave a great, round-shouldered shrug. "All are slaves of the Masters."

"Is the world," the other creature added resignedly.

"Put me down," I instructed them. They eyed me suspiciously, and I went on, "You have the choice to kill me, do you? I got close enough to your little mark that you don't have to, not close enough that you can't. So make a choice. Kill me or put me down."

They made a sound – not threatening, but inquisitive. *And then what?* they were saying.

"Put me down," I said, "and I shall tell you about Collegium, and how not everyone stays a slave to their masters."

They were called something like Rurat and Meret, the latter of whom was probably female. Despite neither of them wearing a stitch, there was precious little on which to hang a diagnosis of gender. Possibly the males amongst them had an Art to retract their more vulnerable parts until required.

They were an attentive audience; enough so that I wondered just how much they understood what I was saying. Their people had led an isolated and barbaric existence in the ruins, prisoners and guards at the same time. The potted history of Collegium must have seemed a convoluted myth to them.

And yet, with a little of the night still to go, when I finished my speech and made to leave, they left with me. I was not taken like a prisoner, instead, we went side by side. "Take me to your Master," I had requested, and that was what they did.

By the time we arrived there, at that sand-clogged auditorium, the sky was already grey with dawn. I had seen plenty of Those Who Race The Sun by then, creeping about their dead city, crouching on rooftops all elbows and knees, scuttling through the silent streets. As the first signs of the sun clutched at the horizon, though, they were creeping into holes and doorways, folding themselves away into those covered scraps of night that would survive the dawn. They had loved the sun once, Rurat had said. They had borne a rayed banner and called themselves the sun's favourite children. How this lore had transmitted itself over so many generations, I could not say, save that it showed the hold of the Masters had never been absolute. Now, it was a part of their punishment to know only darkness, unless their Masters called on their service.

The ages that we spoke of were remote enough that the records of Collegium bore no trace of them. I could not know how things had really been, between the Masters and their enemies. Perhaps Rurat's ancestors had been the perpetrators of atrocity after atrocity until enslaving them was the only choice. Somehow, I doubted it. The only histories that sing of the kindness and wisdom of slave owners are those they write themselves.

There was an auditorium, as I say, or there had been. I could see the ringed stone benches, but they disappeared into the sand so that only the upper tiers were visible. At one end a grand building sat, which retained most of its walls. The stumps of pillars jutted out like broken teeth, and where statues had stood – no doubt further glorifying the forms and deeds of the Masters – there were now only orphaned feet in white marble.

Here were two dozen of the Sun Spider-kinden, their hulking frames crouched low. The sun was just touching them as I arrived, and they shuddered and cringed from it: the first dawn they had observed for a thousand years. They did not race the sun this once, though: their Master had awoken and had need of them.

In their midst were the prisoners: the Doctor, Saveta, Brandt and a handful of the soldiers. Ethiganos strutted before them, and I could hear his spiteful voice taunting them, though thankfully not his actual words.

Rurat and Meret left me to my own devices then. They crept off and I saw them meet with others of their kind, and speak to them. Soon enough Meret was down there in the sunlight, blinking and shading her face, but grunting and muttering to her fellows.

I had some idea that a wildfire revolution would sweep the ruins in minutes, leaving me the Speaker of a new and monstrous Assembly. I thought Collegiate rationality alone would brush away the cobwebs of a thousand years of superstition. That fond thought lasted precisely until the Master actually appeared.

Those Who Race The Sun were abject instantly. The guards out in the dawn light, and the great host of them that had crawled into their holes and haunts, they let out a gibbering murmur of awe and dread which contained not the least squeak of revolution. They abased themselves, kissed their foreheads to the dust and trembled.

The Master strode out into that early light, the vast bulk of him striped by the long, ragged shadows of the desert city. I saw then, too clearly, what the gloom had half concealed before. I saw what had made Ethiganos scream.

He was twelve feet tall and massive, a colossal weight of muscle, bone and fat on two legs. Thankfully for all concerned, he had been given time to attire himself in a manner befitting a king of ancient times. He had on many-layered robes whose folds recalled, in the very slightest way, the dress of a Collegiate Assembler. These were not the respectable white of the Assembly, though, but every inch embroidered with pictograms, most in black but some picked out in golden thread. The mysterious characters of ancient Khanaphes mustered in great armies across the breadth of his shrouded paunch and chest, running in busy columns down the flowing folds of cloth. When the nascent sunlight gleamed off them, his servants cowered back.

There was gold at his wrists and his ankles and a torc about his neck, all finely worked and richly ornamented. He had not donned a circlet or a crown, though, and the reason was obvious. The falling masonry of his tomb had done more than crack his plinth. Half his head was gone. There is no other way to say it. I had seen his perfect profile, before. Now I saw that single profile was all time had left him. The other side of his face was a smashed ruin, driven in by the blunt hammers of the stone, and then the flesh withered back from the wound, desiccated and dry and dead. I could see the broken bone there, gone brown-yellow and with its jagged points abraded away to a shiny smoothness. I could see the blackened landscape that was the inside of the man's brain, cracked like a dry riverbed. And yet he stood, and the good half of his face looked over the broken ruin of his city and saw something that brought back that imperious smile they had carved on the murals to his glory. What was Teshemes, seen through that one remaining eye? Did he view the green fields and the white roofs and the world as it had been when he slept?

Then he was approaching his servants and their prisoners with a slow, stately tread.

"Who are these, who dare breach the walls of my city?" he demanded, and his voice rolled out, past the buildings and across the vistas of the desert itself.

"Thieves!" The screech of Ethiganos was pathetic in comparison. "Ignorant, unbelieving thieves, Lord Achemalas, who know nothing of your works and your ways. They come to steal away your treasures, Great Lord."

Achemalas stood over the prisoners, the dawn light making him radiant where it touched him, but only highlighting what it could no longer touch. Those Who Race The Sun trembled when they gazed on him. There was something curious about the eyelines of everyone concerned, though. I frowned and peered closer.

"Who speaks for you?" the Master of Teshemes demanded archly.

Nobody felt like owning up. Colonel Brandt seemed abruptly less certain of his entitlement to the rank badge.

"Then you are nothing but thieves, after all," decided Achemalas, even his low murmur carrying clearly to me. "Destroy them all."

"Wait!" From beneath the shadow of the guardians' fists, a voice cried out. "I am leader. I speak."

Not Brandt; Saveta. What loyalty she felt she owed her owner, I cannot say, or whether it was for the soldiers, or perhaps just because it was the right thing to do. She struggled into a standing position, though – they all had their hands behind their backs, secured with chains of gold so heavy they could barely move. "I brought us here."

Achemalas had been turning away, but now he swept back and stared at her. He was not looking at her like a one-eyed man, I realised. He did not cock his head that way, but kept her in the middle of the field of vision he had once known. I was absolutely certain that his broken mind was feeding him madness and illusion from that missing eye.

But the guardians, where were *they* looking? Not into that ruined visage, not abjectly at his feet, but...

"We came because we sought knowledge of our ancestors," Saveta stated boldly. "We came because we had heard of the... splendour of your cities, and we wished to seek our heritage."

For a long time, Achemalas regarded her, or whatever he thought he saw in her place. Then came the whinging voice of Ethiganos again.

"Great Master, she lies. She is nothing but a slave, a slave of slaves. This man brought them here," and he yanked at Brandt's collar, "and this one guided them, this one is the worst of the liars, the most debased of the ignorant." For a moment I assumed that the Moth had known my employer at the College, so familiar was the rhetoric.

An expression passed across Achemalas' face, but there was insufficient face on which to read it. A moment later he had made some gesture at his servants and they killed Brandt. It was swift, that much I will say. It was also appallingly brutal, spattering the others with rags and wet shreds of their leader as the creatures tore and bit and fed. I almost forgot they were human, then.

Ethiganos was piping up again. "Great Master, this is the true enemy!" And he was yanking Doctor Phinagler about once more. "These wretches have usurped your true servants in the wider world. You know my people, Great Lord! We are the Moth-kinden, who learned our craft at your exalted knee. In all the ages when you have slept, we have kept true to your vision of the world. But we have been driven from our power and our haunts by turbulent slaves such as this! Destroy him, Great Lord! Destroy him, and give me your blessing and your recognition, so that I may bring ruination to his people!"

My employer was jerked onto his feet, and Achemalas towered over him. "And what do you have to say for yourself, slave?"

Doctor Phinagler cleared his throat. "On behalf of the Great College of Collegium, the loftiest institution of learning in this latterday world, may I say what a tremendous honour it is to stand before such an exalted individual as yourself. I have devoted my life to learning of the most distant past, convinced that it contained wonders not guessed at by my peers back home, and now I feel my studies and my travels are all validated in the most magnificent way. I cánnot express how happy I am to be here, in your presence. I am, of course, yours to do with as you will, but if I could have my fondest wish, I would sit at your feet and learn even the least scraps of your deeds and ways, and this would make my life complete." There was nothing in his confident tone that suggested he was half-painted by Brandt's blood.

My employer has always had a way with foreign diplomacy.

Achemalas regarded him lop-sidedly, and then turned left and right to his servants. I saw it then: precisely what they cowered from. "This one speaks well," the Master decided. "I shall keep him, for now."

"No!" Ethiganos spat. "When a slave raises his hand against his master, he must be punished! This is no safe creature to keep to do your bidding! Let me serve you, as the Moths have ever served! Teach *me* your secrets, Great Lord –"

"The Moths," Achemalas said flatly, cutting him off. "I remember the Moths."

"Yes, Great Lord!" because apparently Ethiganos could not read the giant's tone of voice at all. Perhaps, like Brandt, he was too absorbed in his own made up histories,.

"Always prying and sneaking," the Master went on. "Always wheedling after power and learning they had not earned. Yes, I remember the Moths."

And at last Ethiganos heard what he was saying, but too late. Even as he opened his mouth to protest, Achemalas was looming over him.

"I take my mark from you," the giant declared, and I was thinking, *Well, how's he going to do that?* when one great hand descended and clutched at the Moth's head, fingers crushing in with effortless strength.

Ethiganos shrieked, collapsing to his knees with his hands to the torn wound that had been his face. Then the Sun Spider-kinden had him in their barbed grip, and they tore him apart, just one great yank between them to unseam robe and skin,

Achemalas turned back to the others, and the rising sun gleamed on the pattern of glyphs picked out in gold on his chest.

"I shall keep this one. He speaks with the proper respect," he decided. "But, for the rest, make an end to them."

And I liked Saveta, and I saw one of the other soldiers was Smer, who despite his amusing name had seemed a good, honest man. And so it came down to me, as it so often does.

I streaked from my hiding place, across the heads of Those Who Race The Sun. In my hand was my knife. I want you to think about that, for a moment: a knife fit for a Fly-kinden against a twelve-foot giant not inconvenienced by the loss of half a head.

I was shouting a war-cry, too, although only Doctor Phinagler would know it. In retrospect, "Clock!" is not really something to strike terror into the hearts of the mighty, but for any aficionado of the duelling at the Prowess Forum it sets the heart racing like nothing else.

I attacked Achemalas like a… well, like a fly. My knife tore into his chest, hacking furiously away as swiftly as I could, and I evaded his grasp for five long heartbeats before he caught me up.

The look on his half-face was one of derisory amusement. "Another little thief," he pronounced. "And see, you have not even drawn blood."

Given the state of his head, I was not at all sure there was any blood to draw, but what I said was, "I wasn't trying to."

He transfixed me with half a frown, and I added, "Sorry about your clothes, Great Lord. I reckon your city's short of tailors these days."

He looked down. I had slashed the front of his regalia to ribbons. I had hacked through gold thread and priceless ornament. Most of all, I had rendered unrecognisable the glyph of glyphs, the single figure that all the golden sigils had made together. The commanding image that all his servants' eyes had been fixed on.

He did not understand, at first. He was still lost in the dream of his own greatness that the desert had parched and blown away a thousand years before. But then one of the Sun Spiders stood, hulking up to match Achemalas, height for height.

"Master," said Rurat, but he was looking the broken giant in the eye.

"How dare you address me? Down in the earth with you," Achemalas hissed.

Rurat took a step forwards, tentatively, waiting for some unseen barrier to halt him.

"Cast this slave down!" the Master demanded, gesturing furiously. What he gestured with was me, and my teeth rattled so hard I nearly lost consciousness and missed the rest.

The other guardians of the city were slowly rising from their knees and haunches, though, like men long chained who suddenly find their limbs free. They made no move towards Rurat. They stared with their deep-set, narrow eyes at their Master.

A mere approximation of that glyph had sufficed to protect me from them. It had given them the choice of what to do with me. What they had done was listen.

They were waiting now, to see if the simple fact of Achemalas's kinden and history would strike them down with some new bondage. He was one of the Masters, the people who had enslaved them back at the dawn of time. Or had that ancient bargain been eroded away by the passage of the years and the sands of the desert? Had it been just that deep-ingrained sigil holding them back?

Rurat stood before Achemalas and took me from the Master's grip. When Achemalas tried to prevent him, he broke those beringed fingers.

There should have been a great knell sounding across the sky at that moment. There should have been a thunderous retort go through the desert like an earthquake. Perhaps, to senses other than mine, there was.

Achemalas looked at his hand. Not pain, but something that cut far deeper was in his remaining eye: it was the horror of the master whose slaves say 'no'.

Rurat set me down, almost tenderly, and then returned his attention to Achemalas.

"No Masters," he grunted. For a moment there was silence, but then another voice echoed him – Meret perhaps – and then another and another.

I scurried back, then, and set myself to untangling the chains that held the others. I did not look, as Those Who Race The Sun gathered together and descended on the one who tried to command them. I did not see that mote of history annihilated, like so much else of the past. I am, in the final analysis, not that dedicated a scholar.

When Chirnemeg came back, she found us – those of us who had survived – camped well outside the city's boundaries. She asked few questions, simply assuring us that we were profoundly lucky to have escaped our comrades' fate. The cities, she said, were places of death, watched over by dreadful guardians. All this we heartily agreed.

But I have seen the streets of Teshemes begin to live again. I have seen Those Who Race The Sun abroad by daylight, rediscovering what it is to be free human beings, and not monsters from an Inapt bedtime story. And perhaps they will go from city to city, spreading the creed of liberation, of no more Masters. And perhaps a terrible thing has come back into the world, that would be better locked away, but I am a true child of Collegium, and I cannot mourn the unlocking of shackles, no matter what might be released.

# Masters of the Spire

*Being an account of Doctor Ludweg Phinagler's expedition to the Exalsee and the Forest Aleth, and what he found there, as told by his amanuensis, Fosse.*

I will confess I have been approached more than once by concerned readers asking me if the regular incidents of extreme peril I encounter in the employ of Doctor Ludweg Phinagler are really compensated by any financial or educational remuneration I receive. These well-wishers, being generally of my own kinden, are quick to lay these episodes of danger to life and limb at the larger feet of my employer, and in many cases this distribution of blame is sadly accurate. However, I am nothing if not a diligent recorder of the truth, no matter how much scepticism my accounts may breed amongst College masters and similar luminaries. I must therefore confess that on occasion my own desires set in motion events that lead inexorably towards unpleasantness. This is one such case.

I will go farther, in fact. My regular readers will be familiar with a variety of unpleasantnesses that I have endured while serving the good Doctor as loyal amanuensis. Perhaps you are even now considering what we found as Lake Limnia, or our brief stint as slaves in Everis, or even – I shiver to recall – being hunted by the Mantis-kinden for defiling their sacred isle of Parasyal. I will grant that the Doctor and I have been faced with a remarkable number of horrors in his search for the unknown, but they pale in comparison to the terrible revelations I am, at least, about to reveal. Of all our adventurers, all our hard-won knowledge (no matter now scoffed at by the literati of the College), I would undo and unlearn this, if I could. But knowledge is like midges in a bottle: good luck getting them back in once the stopper is removed. In this case, I judge it best to lay the truth out for others in the hope that nobody will unwittingly retrace our steps to that ghastly place.

Adrian Tchaikovsky

My fault, small as it may seem, lies in a long-standing desire to see what might be considered an innocuous location in the world, namely the lakeside city of Solarno. Little more than a name until a few years previously, Solarno had become renowned as a restful and pleasant destination for well-heeled Collegiates to go and take the air. It was a Spider city without the politics, a Beetle city without the pressing concerns of industry, and most importantly it was a Fly city where my kinden were properly appreciated. Or that was the general word, and obviously I was most anxious to experience this prodigy for myself. Unfortunately, what Solarno was not noted for was plentiful remains of some past civilization, which was the only thing for which Doctor Phinagler might have borrowed the funds to travel there. We almost visited on our way to the Nem, but instead ended up at Ostrander, a small, suspicious and remarkably unwelcoming Ant town built around some rather surprising structures the Doctor had shown some interest in. I did not want to go back to Ostrander. I most certainly did not want to go back there to see my employer executed by some xenophobic Ants, because while his eccentric career was surely going to get him killed at some point, that would be a lamentably mundane end for such a remarkable man.

Now, I am but a poor servant and travelling companion, it is true, but association with Doctor Phinagler has put me in some fairly well known academic shadows, and most of those have had servants with whom I sometimes correspond. In the absence of any late-discovered ancient Solarnese ruins, and on discovering fresh sketches of the Ostranden spires in my employer's notebook, I knew I had to plant some seeds in his mind. Avoiding the direct approach, that would be guaranteed to send him off at a tangent of his own, I began to talk about certain rivals of his who were invited to all the best conferences in Helleron and Sarn, events that had inexplicably omitted to invite The Leading Authority on the ancient world. What should a gifted and influential academic do, I mused. If only he could call on a few like-minded fellows and hold his *own* gathering of the minds somewhere.

Then it just remained for me to start dropping names – individuals of similar bent likewise excluded from the Collegiate orthodoxy and none of them local to Collegium. I mentioned Domina Hastella from out of the Spiderlands who had written to the Doctor so keenly after his Nemean expedition, or what about Colonel Shendric who had been investigating (for which read: pillaging) some of the ruined castles of the occupied Commonweal (for which read: not ruined before he and his artillery arrived). And there was such and such and so and so, all names that the Doctor considered fine scholars, or at least scholars who had yet to raise a dissenting opinion on one of his theories. But so wide a spread of them! Where could such elder statesfolk of history meet in comfort! If only there was a town renowned for its congeniality that was situated equally between Lowlands, Empire and Spiderlands!

Well, perhaps I simplify just how I went about it, but for once it all worked perfectly, and in due course we took airship for Solarno. If the airship itself was a tatty little tramp freighter, and if our purse meant that we would be sampling the actual delights of Solarno on a shoestring budget, that just couldn't be helped.

Solarno itself was all I could have hoped for. Even living in Collegium, to which I always return with a light heart, one underestimates the benefit of a visit to a truly beautiful place. The Exalsee spread out from its shores in turquoise abandon, dotted by lushly forested islands one could reach with a little boat or a taxing flight. The architecture was a perfect balance between Spider elegance and Beetle practicality, and the people were friendly and enthusiastic and entertaining. There was always music, or perhaps there would be aerobatics out over the water or some remarkably energetic duelling in the street, which was always worth a spectate. The local cuisine was heavier on the aquatic than we were used to, but only made us realise what opportunities the chefs of Collegium are missing. After dark, the town seemed alive with tavernas and hostelries where one would never want for a game of cards or some understanding company.

The one thing Solarno was missing, in fact, was like-minded academics to hold the Doctor's attention. He himself is notoriously task-focused, and was not minded to simply sun himself before the lake or go and admire the Spider-kinden etchings, but got progressively more agitated when the various other scholars failed to put in an appearance by the appointed day. At first he fretted that they had entered into a worldwide conspiracy to snub him, and then, because such a fear could not long survive his great self-regard, that I had failed to properly send the invitations. The latter I hotly refuted, and indeed I had been counting on my employer being fully occupied while I took in the sights of Solarno. At the time it was all a vexing mystery.

What had actually happened, of course, is that they all knew something we didn't, and I'm sure you, with the benefit of hindsight, can guess exactly what that was. But more of that later.

The next day I caught the Doctor packing his bags with the air of a man who has made a decision. I asked timorously if we were returning to Collegium, but no, it was worse. Ostrander, the Doctor said, was just down the coast after all, and while we were here…

Seeing that everything was already falling to ruin, I hastily offered to arrange passage to the place, then left him with the intention of doing anything but. I confess, a few days of truly being able to enjoy myself had somewhat loosened my usually absolute obedience to my employer's wishes.

The problem was, surely, that we were in Civilization which, much as it is to be desired as a state, is essentially the polar opposite of the places Doctor Phinagler is usually interested in. The cities of the Exalsee are either urbane, or alternatively savage but still well within the traditions of the cultures we are familiar with – say, Ostrander or those Princep Exilla Dragonflies who seem so full of themselves. I didn't think the Doctor would want a tour of the cabbage-packing plants of Dirovashni, or the low dives of Chasme (for all the thought of a city of rogues and pirates gave me something of a frisson.)

So I went to the tavernas of the waterfront and started asking some urgent questions about what a bored academic might stick his nose into around the shores of the Exalsee. And that, right there, is how I opened the door to so much.

Late in the day, having worked my way down the ladder of establishments from sophisticated through to adequate to the genuinely rough dives where the working Solarnese go, I fell in with an aviatrix named Teela. Or, more properly te Seela Baro-Halle. I confess that my kinden in Solarno were inclined to put on airs and never so much as in their names, but she didn't insist on it, and so I ended up calling her what the local Beetles did. Teela ran supplies north and south across the lake, which sounds humdrum until you recall that there is a whole city of air-pirates out there who like supplies but dislike being restricted by the legal title of others. Moreover Teela (who I suspect may have been one of those pirates, from time to time) did not just run to Dirovashni or Porta Mavralis, but instead supplied a handful of little trading posts along the Exalsee's southern shore, hard against the possibly endless expanse of the Forest Aleth.

The Forest Aleth is huge – you could, I suspect, lose most of the Lowlands in it. It forms the south-Western border of the Spiderlands, and just extends south and west as far as anybody cares. Probably the Spiders have mapped a great deal of it, but they are no aviators, nor do they readily share their knowledge. Hence, as far as any of you, my readers, will be concerned, the place is simply of unknown extent, and almost entirely unmapped.

Aleth itself could mean the forest, or the Alethi Ant-kinden who were its most widespread inhabitants (from whom arose the hostile Ostranden, but I wouldn't hold that against them), or – as in this case – a little trading post that Teela was talking about, and was just about to go and deliver a shipment. As well as the usual comestibles, she had a private contract to drop off some gear for a special customer, she explained to me. An explorer, a Beetle-kinden, a man whose business was uncovering ruins.

I took this as the purest good luck, more fool me. After making provisional arrangements with Teela I ran back to the good Doctor and explained the spontaneous meeting I had just had, and would Doctor Phinagler fancy a jaunt across the Exalsee to listen to tales of far venture by a bona fide explorer? Surely that would be preferable to being arrested by angry Ant-kinden for getting too close to their special rocks.

I had a whole battery of inveiglements lined up to talk him round, but his eyes lit up suspiciously quickly.

"Aleth, you say?" he asked me. "Why, I was just reading about that the other day. Some fascinating rumours about the place."

Any sign of enthusiasm from Doctor Phinagler would normally set off alarms all through my brain, but it wasn't as if we were going *into* the Forest Aleth, after all. We were hardly prepared for any kind of expedition. We were just going to *talk* to this explorer fellow, and then perhaps I could return to Solarno and have another few days of happy hedonism while the Doctor and his new friend swapped stories and compared notes. Oh foolish me, you say, but I really *liked* Solarno. Which makes what happened afterwards so very bitter, almost personal.

Teela was tapping her foot at the airstrip when we arrived. A sketch: she was taller than me, with that sandy skin that Solarnese Beetles and Flies both have, though little of it visible right then. She wore leather reinforced with chitin plates, and looked quite the warrior, for all she was only planning to do battle with the elements. Her goggles were already down, and had a little clockwork box alongside that unfogged them in poor weather – her own invention, I learned, for every Exalsee pilot is advised to be her own artificer. She looked the Doctor up and down as though wondering if she would have to jettison some ballast to get airborne with him on board, but then nodded companionably enough and led us over to her orthopter, named *Happy Parasite*. I had expected a tub of a thing, the winged equivalent of the airship we arrived in, but it was a sleek, muscular machine, four wings standing straight up as it waited for us, its prow and cockpit hooked forwards, its abdomen – the cargo hold – held canted upwards higher off the ground. A pair of repeating ballistas was mounted beneath the cockpit like hungry mouthparts, the bolt heads heavy and cross-sectioned. I have never been a great devotee of flying or flying machines – the talk of those ground-bound air aficionados at Collegium had always seemed a special language full of 'well-actually and I-think-you'll-find' designed to exclude the unenlightened. However, I think I fell a bit in love with the *Happy Parasite*. He (Teela called the vessel 'he' after the Spider manner for ships) was a beautiful conveyance.

Inside was another matter. Teela sat forwards, with the controls and the view, and the Doctor and I were relegated to the hold, sitting at the front of a stack of crates all held in place by fraying ropes, and some containing live crickets that kept up a constant strident complaint about their living conditions, as indeed did my employer. I am not fond of being trapped in cramped environs, and my mind was full of air-pirates and similar terrors that might result in the *Happy Parasite* ending up a sunken wreck with the Doctor and I trapped inside. I will confess, our escapades over and under Lake Limnia have left me with something of a horror of ending up beneath the waves.

To listen to the raconteurs on the Solarno waterfront, it was impossible to go any distance over the Exalsee without being attacked by corsairs or Dragonfly raiders or some sort of monster, but as it happened Teela skipped over the azure waters without incident, taking us all the way to the little outpost of Aleth without even mild peril, so that the discomfort of our berth was the greatest danger we encountered. She even commented as we set down about the unusually uneventful nature of the journey, as though disappointed she had not been able to show off her piloting skills. So it was that we crawled out from the close confines of the *Parasite* and beheld Aleth, and behind it the forest of the same name.

There were a few permanent buildings, most of which were concerned with the storage of goods, but one of which was a taverna of sorts, run by a formidably ugly Thorn Bug-kinden named Chudi. Beyond those rude walls was only the forest: a wall of green that loured over land and water both, putting all the works of human hands in its shadow. I took wing to see how far the canopy extended. In truth the distance was obscured by a rising mist, or perhaps steam, from the trees, but there was no end to it, just as the stories said. The horizon and drifting curtains of rain might limit how much of the Forest Aleth I could see, but I had no doubt that the expanse I laid eyes on was not even half of it. It was sobering, that vast extent of green. I was a city girl, after all, and born into a culture where such cities are the rule, and the space between them of little concern save for travel or agriculture. The Lowlands have their forests, though the Mantids tend to make them something of an exclusive prospect, but nothing like the Aleth. So much nature all in one place can make one feel insignificant. What is a College education or a good crossbow to all that green?

Of course, Doctor Phinagler had brought more than a crossbow, and his earthbound perspective remained resolutely centred on himself. He took one look at the wall of greenery and nodded in that proprietorial way that Beetles have, as if asking it to wait its turn before being exhaustively catalogued and dissertated upon.

I was rather quiet when I dropped back to his side, though possibly he did not notice. Mostly it was the great shadows I had seen, out across that green sea. I had been to Ostrander, as I say. I had a strong suspicion I knew what I was spying, and I made a decision not to encourage the Doctor's curiosity which, as it turned out, was spitting into the academic hurricane.

"Just in time, too," Teela remarked to me, apropos of nothing. "I thought your Beetle there was going to cost me, the time it took to get him settled."

She nodded, and I saw that the Aleth Post I had seen was being expanded on even as we arrived. The forest verge was alive with movement – human movement. For a moment all I saw was the bustle, but then I identified a kinden behind it. The trees were swarming with Ants.

They were not the short, compact breed of the Lowlands, but tall and rangy, with a greenish caste to their skin. I had seen their kin before in Ostrander, but the Ostranden were playing at being the Ants they had doubtless met from the Empire or points west. The Alethi seemed of a very different temperament. At first, seeing dozens of Ants swarming from the trees, I had thought we were all going to get our throats cut in short order. Ants on the move in quantity usually means war where I come from. As we were to discover intimately, for these Ants being on the move was the natural state of affairs, and they had come to the post for trading, not fighting. As I watched, they began to assemble a camp with that faultless division of labour their Art permits them. Some went to the lakeside for water, others set fires or brought wrapped burdens out into the open. Still more worked with the trees themselves, using ropes and ingenuity to bend them this way and that, interlacing branches and tensioning trunks until they had constructed a great palace, it almost seemed, from the living wood. This was then layered over with waxed fabric, and abruptly the Ants had a new home and the trading post had increased its population and area by a factor of ten.

I saw that this was not merely a war party – there were Ants of all ages here, from elder stateswomen down to children in arms. There were far fewer of them than might be found in the city of Sarn or Tark, say, but this was nonetheless an entire Ant community.

"There are dozens of them in the interior," Teela explained, as she supervised a pack of villains from the taverna in unloading the *Happy Parasite*. "They run the place, as much as anyone does." She shrugged. "I guess they just wander about, and they fight each other if they meet. If any warlord ever brings them together then this half of the Exalsee is screwed, I reckon."

I looked over at the Alethi. There were certainly warriors amongst them. I saw chitin armour, spears and bows – and a scattering of metal crossbows and mail as well. Unlike their cousins from Ostrander, though, they were not staring at every non-Ant as though waiting for the order to kill us. Possibly it was a forbearance that came of not regarding this land, or any land, as exclusively *theirs*.

Teela had brought up tools and finished goods, practical machine-made goods the Alethi could use but not manufacture themselves. They had a little smithing, she said, but only what they had learned from visitors, and either they didn't mine or the forest was short on mineral wealth. The Ants themselves traded meat, chitin and some striking shell jewellery, which I was rather taken with. Negotiations were just beginning and we headed into the tavern for a bowl of something.

Teela had come in with a long, lean Ant who was their chief trader, and was plainly keen to get down to cases. Before she did, though, she had an introduction to make.

"This," she said, "is Corvaris Blaze."

The taverna held a wide variety of reprobates who had collected on the southern shore of the Exalsee for want of anywhere else that would have them. I saw Solarnese Beetles, Spiders, Scorpions, Dragonflies, and most of them probably murderers or flesh-traders when those trades were in season. I paid them little heed, though, because my eyes had already found Corvaris Blaze and he was a very striking figure indeed.

Regular readers will be aware that the wild and the physical are traits I have been known to find untowardly attractive, irrespective of kinden or social standing. Blaze was wild. Blaze was physical. Most remarkably he was wild and physical and also a Beetle-kinden. I hope I offend none of my Collegiate readers when I say that the people of my home city are a calm, considered and sophisticated breed, who value fine words and learning, and these are all of course traits to be desired. Yet one can grow a little jaded with propriety and good manners.

Blaze saw Teela across the room and gave us a smile bright as the full moon. He shouldered his way through the murderers and flesh-traders and dropped down across the table from us, nodding cordially to my employer but his gaze resting a little longer, I fancied, on myself. A sketch, then, of Corvaris Blaze: a broad-shouldered, athletic man, with a waist somewhat trimmer than is fashionable in a Collegiate Beetle, and a head fuller of hair to boot. He sported a neat beard in the Spider fashion, and the dark skin of his shoulders (displayed by his sleeveless leather vest) had been tattooed in intricate geometrical patterns using metallic violet inks. He had a strong jaw but eyes that glittered with humour as though everything in the world had the potential to yield him some amusement. He wore a broad belt set with many pouches, with a satchel slung over his shoulder to rest on one hip, balanced by a small axe and long knife on the other. He moved with an assurance I had never seen in any of his kinden before – something more belonging to the Mantids, or perhaps to some dangerous jungle predator.

"How is my beautiful water-fly?" he asked Teela, beaming at her. He had a touch of an accent – that Spiderlands drawl that lets the speaker play with their words as though with an orchestra.

"Busy," she told him, utterly proof against his charms. "But I've brought you a distraction. This is Fosse, from Collegium, and That's Doctor Fingle-something, They're here for the book-learning you're so fond of."

Blaze raised an eyebrow. "Scholars south of the Exalsee? Now that is interesting." For just a moment, because of the manner of our introduction, his gaze was fixed on me, and he leant forwards and took my hand, touching it to his lips as though I was a Spider Arista and he my humble servant. "I will always value the company of a fellow quester after knowledge," he said. I admit that I fumbled any attempt at a proper first impression and just squeaked at him as though I were a girl at my first dance.

Then my employer was rising to the occasion, hand thrust out and rattling off his name and credentials, utterly assured that the Great College would carry weight even out here, and Blaze was clasping fingers, identifying himself as a member of the Planten League of Exploration, and I was once again in the shadow of Doctor Phinagler. I swear Teela gave me a sympathetic look before she went off to take care of business. I just sat there, musing wistfully on the hidden joys of academia.

And then he said, "So, I'm sure you've seen Ostrander," and for a moment I thought that it had all been an artfully baited trap, and that by morning we'd be back in bloody Ostrander getting the side-eye from the Ant-kinden there. The bottom fell out of my world as Doctor Phinagler launched into an enthusiastic confirmation that of *course* we had seen Ostrander and how very interesting it all was.

"It's nothing," Blaze told us, grinning mischief. "Just dust. The real business is out there." His hand took in the expanse of the Forest Aleth beyond the walls of the taverna. "But by all means, tell me what you made of the Ostrander Spire."

I suppose I will need to elaborate, and to summarise my employer's response, for those readers fortunate enough never to have heard of the structures. Ostrander is dominated by a single enormous featurethat dwarfs the Ants and all their huts and shacks. A spire is one way of describing it. I would have said a mound, save that it reaches well over a hundred feet into the air and its sides are almost sheer. It is not quite regular – the surfaces lumpen and a bit craggy, with openings here and there, some small and high enough that I wondered if my kinden had some hand in its crafting. Its actual substance appeared to be simply brown-red earth, cemented somehow into that towering form.

The Ostranden did not build it, for certain. I do not believe they even took it from its builders. They came out of the Aleth generations ago and turfed out whatever squatters had been making free with the place, and from then on it was Ostrander and theirs. The architects themselves remained a mystery.

When we had passed through, Doctor Phinagler had been in pursuit of a different quarry and his interest had been more towards the pictograms still visible on the spire's weathered lower reaches, which the Ostranden had objected strongly to him examining. Corvaris Blaze was interested in the hands that had made the huge dwelling, hands that, he claimed, were still living out in the forest. And of course I had seen the distant shadow of just such a thing, out on the horizon, when I went aloft.

You might think that this was where it started, and that by nightfall we would be hacking our way through the undergrowth in the wake of Corvaris Blaze. Certainly Doctor Phinagler ran long on his own academic credentials, angling for just such an invitation. We had already learned that the arrival of Teela's shipments and the Alethi themselves were what Blaze had been waiting for, and that he planned to talk his way into the Ant-kinden's company to head into the interior. When Doctor Phinagler expressed his enthusiasm for such an expedition, though, Blaze made a variety of easy excuses about how the Ants might take such an intrusion. It was quite fascinating watching the two of them talk round each other. Despite the marked difference in appearances, they were very plainly fruit from the same bush when it came to carrying out their academic duties. I suspected that the Planten League of Exploration had only the loosest idea of where their errant son was, and were probably also scratching their heads over certain financial irregularities, given that Blaze was plainly not short of funds for his expedition.

And of course I chose my moment to pipe up and express my great admiration for such a man of learning and his visible academic credentials, despite Doctor P's sidelong frown at me. I was, of course, only trying to advance my employer's interests.

However, by the time Teela was ready to leave, neither of us had inveigled an invitation from Corvaris Blaze. He parted from us very warmly, promising the Doctor he would share his discoveries upon his return, and then touching my fingertips to his tongue in parting, a Spider pleasantry that sent a shiver down my spine. It reflects a subordinate showing absolute trust in his mistress, they tell me, presumably because in the Spiderlands everyone's so very fond of poisonings.

Doctor Phinagler was somewhat subdued when we got back into the *Happy Parasite*. In truth, so was I, and Teela laughed at us, not unkindly.

"Our Professor Blaze can have that effect on people," she confirmed. It was a Spider title, and seemed to be redolent of adventure and mystery.

So, you will expect us to return to Solarno and, if I get my way, spent some days enjoying the waters, or if my employer (as is more likely) gets his, end up in Ostrander nailed to a board by angry Ants. In fact neither eventuality befell us, because when we came within sight of Solarno it became apparent that events had moved on without any of our knowledge, and that the city was now on fire.

Not the whole city, of course, but quite a lot of it. The air was full of fighting orthophers, a great many of them bearing the black and yellow, and the harbour was filled with troop ships flying the many colourful flags of the Aldanrael and their dependants, and it became immediately clear that Teela had chosen a good day not to be at home. This was, of course, the first shot of the second Imperial war, and the combined Wasp-Spider forces would be marching their way up the coast into the Lowlands soon enough, while the bombs would start to fall on our own home of Collegium. Right then we knew nothing of the wider geopolitical implications of what we were seeing, though, and it just seemed a remarkably long way for the world to go to inconvenience us.

There followed some interesting minutes, because an Imperial Spearflight orthopter decided to make the *Happy Parasite* a good deal less happy. Teela was, thankfully, all the pilot she had claimed, and moreover had no intention of going dragon-fighting against the whole of the Imperial Air Corps. She slung us about the sky until the Doctor and I were black and blue down in the hold, and got far south enough that the Imperial craft broke off to attack Solarno again, preferring a larger target less able to evade its shot. Our pilot was very quiet as she retraced our aerial steps. Only once the southern shore was in sight did she ask, "Where do I drop you?"

The Doctor and I exchanged glances.

"I'm for Chasme," she said. "I need to get the engine wound, and I've some friends there. It's not to everyone's tastes, though. Dirovashni's tamer."

Doctor Phinagler bristled, entirely wasted as Teela had her back to him. "Drop us off at Aleth," he said. "I need to see a man about an expedition."

Teela spent as much time at Aleth Post as it took Doctor Phinagler and I to drop from the belly of the *Happy Parasite*, not even sparing the clockwork it would have taken to land and take off again. I spared a last glance for her orthopter as it wheeled across the sky seeking a more technically convenient harbour, before turning my attention to the camp.

The camp, it turned out, was in chaos, or at least everyone there was doing their level best to abandon it as quickly as possible. A number of boats had turned up, from Chasme and Dirovashni, and the crew were clearing out the store-huts there with the obvious consent of Chudi, the Thorn Bug who ran the taverna. It appeared that news of what was going on across the water had been swift to reach the little post.

"But why do they care what's going on in Solarno?" the good Doctor asked, baffled. In truth it was obvious to me. The political stability of the Exalsee had just taken a serious knock, and the people who did business along the southern shore probably had plenty of enemies in high places. Even as I thought it, someone shouted out a warning and pointed across the water. There were sails out there, a little flotilla just coming into view. That said *Spiderlands* rather than *Empire* to me, and it seemed very likely that one of the innumerable Spider factions was taking the chance to settle old scores.

The Alethi Ants were plainly just as keen to retreat to their forest haunts. Their great tent-hut-thing had been dismantled and they were loading themselves up with boxes and bags of the things they had traded for, and in their midst was Corvaris Blaze, looking as eager to be gone as any of them.

He spotted the Doctor striding over and I saw his eyes widen.

"No! Absolutely not!" he shouted at us. "Under no circumstances are you coming with me!"

"My dear fellow," protested my employer, "news has obviously reached you – our lodgings, our luggage, our every connection to this part of the world just went up in smoke. Under normal circumstances I would of course respect your wishes, but as a fellow academic, I beg of you, surely you can't abandon us on this desert shore?"

It was far from a desert shore, but Doctor Phinagler has a peculiar power with words. I often thought he should have taken to the stage. His eyes were moist with tears, his lip quivered, sincerity bloomed like a fungus in every word of his voice.

"You are a man of my kinden, a fellow devotee of learning," he added, heartfelt. "I throw myself upon your mercy."

Spoken with such passion, few mercies could have withstood the bulk of Doctor Phinagler being thrown on them. However, the one audience routinely immune to my employer's rhetoric was fellow academics, and I saw Blaze wrestle with his conscience and pin it two times out of three.

"Absolutely not," he said. "I'm sure the Spider-kinden will treat you kindly, Doctor Phin."

I had been watching his face carefully – and not just because it had chiselled cheekbones and a pleasingly strong jaw. I saw the look he cast towards those sails, and it was cousin enough to looks my employer had worn in the past for me to parse it.

"Fear not!" I declared, leaping forwards to hover in between them. "If we are taken, we shall not say you were here nor tell them where you went." For there was that element of the furtive to Blaze. He was a man skipping town ahead of his creditors – most likely creditors who had funded one too many unprofitable expeditions. As I say, Blaze and the Doctor really did have a lot in common.

I had brought the proverbial crossbow to a knife fight with those words. If I had misjudged the man's character, or his influence over the Alethi, then things might have gone badly indeed. I did not peg Corvaris Blaze for a murderer, though, nor the Ants for his servants. Instead of anger or even indecision, he just threw me a marvellously wounded look and then flung his arms wide. "Well of course you must come, kinsman!" he cried with a faked sincerity to match my employer's. "But swiftly, for we must be out of sight amongst the trees before they send scouts overhead, or we're all screwed." He turned and called out to the lean Alethi leader. "Barteyn, I'm bringing my assistants."

The Ant-kinden's eyes flicked from him to us and back, but of course their faces give away precious little of what they think at the best of times. At last she shrugged.

When one thinks of Ant-kinden, the Lowlander sort anyway, one imagines a plodding, inexorable advance – men and women in a great heavy load of mail with big shields just tramping forwards in silence. The silence was the only thing that image had in common with the Alethi. Their progress through the forest was swift enough to test my employer's stamina until he was dragging at the end of the column, wheezing and relying on the charity of passing Ants to help him along. Nor did they simply cover distance. The Alethi were constantly at work, parties of them ranging ahead and on either side, hunting and harvesting everything the forest had to offer. I thought at first that they must be a kind of plague, stripping the trees bare of everything but the leaves and leaving a denuded desert behind them. After a day's progress I realised that they were not raiders but a curious breed of farmers, the whole forest their plantation. They chose precise paths, going where no Ant column had passed in sufficient time for the fruit and game to regenerate, and they took precisely as much as they required. I even had the sense that they planted seeds behind them, shaping what the forest would turn into so that, next time around, there would be more of use to them. They cut timber as well, and gathered vines for weaving. They shelled game for chitin and hide, and all without letting up their progress.

Doctor Phinagler, as I say, was rather left behind by all this fierce industry, and might actually have ended up devoured by something if the Ants had left anything in their wake large enough to devour him. In truth, I think they kept an eye on him, and the returning foraging parties kept lending him a shoulder to boost him along. For a people who lived on a rope stretched over the unpredictable jaws of nature this seemed remarkably charitable to me, but Corvaris Blaze explained it thus: "They are masters of this place not because of their strength or their ferocity, but because of their community. Each looks out for the rest and, because we travel with them, we come somewhat under their protection. Of course, we don't mesh minds like they do, so they will forget about us from time to time, but they make good hosts. They have cousins all the way south, ranging over most of the forest and beyond. A frontier the

Spider-kinden's vaunted diplomacy has never managed to breach, because we have little they need, and because they are very many."

"I wonder that they don't turn up in force at someone's gates," I mused.

"Perhaps one day, but they're not like city-dwelling Ant-kinden. Lacking a permanent home that needs constant defence, they don't see everyone as enemies in the same way. And lucky for us."

Now that our presence on his expedition was accomplished, Blaze was all smiles again. He had no difficulty keeping up with the Ants, of course, and my wings could carry me quite happily along at any pace they cared to set, so the two of us spent much time together.

Each night, the Ants constructed their great tent-fortress around their camp every entrance manned with watchers. Fires were lit, meals cooked, and I had the impression of a vast and complex social life happening invisibly between the heads of our hosts. The first evening, the good Doctor crashed down into instant slumber, quite worn out, and Blaze and I were able to become acquainted quietly over a shared cup of some fiery spirits he had somehow found room to bring along with him. The Alethi, for their part, did not drink liquor at all, he explained, though they were quite able to drive hard bargains against drunken city-dwellers.

By the second night, Blaze had warmed to Doctor Phinagler enough to try to impress him with tales of past exploits. That, fortunately, was a game my employer could play just as well, and so he used Ostrander as a springboard to talk about our dealings in the Nem and all the unpleasantness we found there. A certain wary rapport soon arose between the two men, although I suspected that the first whiff of a genuine discovery and they would be at each other's throats. Nonetheless, the ice had thawed sufficiently – and we were far enough from civilization – that Blaze explained the object of his expedition.

"Whatever people built that spire the Ostranden have pirated, they built more deep in the Aleth," he explained. "And we've known about these things forever – you can dig as deep as you like in the stacks of the Egreppe Conservatoire and you'll find academics speculating about the civilization that raised them. Was it Art, was it an early flowering of Artifice, was it mystic power, you know. Except nobody does know. A lot of them decide it was the Ants, but the Ants are pretty adamant it wasn't. And last year I ran into a Fly-kinden who'd gone some ways into the Aleth, and he'd caught stories that if you go far enough, they're *still there*, the builders. Some place in the heart of the forest, where the spires are still the domain of the hands that raised them. When I bring the truth of that back, I'll be able to name my own price in gold and tenure."

"Unless the truth of it is that it isn't true," Doctor Phinagler opined, but Blaze shrugged that off.

"They're out there, believe me," he assured us.

"Don't the Ants know?" I asked. "If they're sharing a forest with some great spire-building civilization, after all."

"They say they don't. This lot's regular round doesn't go there, certainly, but we're heading to some great meeting place where Alethi columns get together to trade. Someone there must know," Blaze declared, with an absolute confidence all too familiar to me.

The next day, Blaze and I – running ahead with the Ant vanguard – got to see a hunt. The quarry was a magnificent beast, a beetle as big as the taverna building back at the post with a single curved horn jutting from its snout. It was fierce in its defence and remarkably swift, charging at any threat and quite capable of knocking whole trees down with the impact. The Alethi used nets and spears and impeccable coordination to bring it down, and by the time the column's end had passed the site the great creature had been entirely dismantled into shell and fibre and meat. After the kill, though, Blaze went aloft into the trees, his Art letting him vault up the trunks with a speed and sure-handedness I was unused to in his kinden. I joined him up in the canopy, where he was taking advantage of the gap opened up by the horned beast's frenzy. There, across the green sea of foliage and partially obscured by sheets of onrushing rain, stood the striking bulk of a spire, looming to an impossible height above the trees. There, according to Blaze, was our destination.

"So what happened to them, the builders?" I asked.

"As I said, they're still about."

"But they're not at Ostrander any more, and this place ahead, that's an Alethi camp now, you said. So whatever they are now, it's less than they were," I pointed out.

He grinned at me, appreciating an intelligent question. "You're wasted in Phinagler's company, you know that?"

Even back with my feet on the earth, I didn't quite feel that I had come down. I will confess, with the advantage of hindsight, that I suffered something of a failure of the scholar's impartial eye, when it came to Corvaris Blaze. I will even go so far as to say that I followed him about like a lovesick felbling. In my defence – that smile, that voice! That mind and that body, so unlike the scholars back home. That he was a Beetle-kinden, and certainly not the good Collegiate my mother would approve of, mattered not a jot. I was, I felt, somewhat in love.

The Alethi spire sat in a clearing – not one kept clear by the axe, I felt, but one where the trees simply no longer grew. Standing close to its base was an invitation to neck pain – the spire just went up and up as though a diligent climber could have reached the moon by it. I took wing and went up above the canopy for some perspective, and even then it reared higher than the tallest roof in Collegium. And yet it was less than the Ostranden spire because this was only a stump. Time or calamity had brought it down from perhaps the midpoint, leaving a jagged, honeycombed break that time had smoothed over and filled in. When whole, the structure must have been insanely tall, far higher than any man-made structure should be, as though its architects had woken one day with a terrible yearning for mountains.

The Alethi were gathered in great numbers at the spire's base – two whole columns of them, each as large as the one we travelled with. I thought that would be trouble, because Ants so seldom get on with Ants, but the Alethi had things well worked out. One column was already packing to leave as we arrived, and our Ants slotted into their place with an order that showed they must all be in each others' minds. That was quite a thought: Ants of rival cities cannot touch their Arts together to speak, but these Alethi – however many columns there were making their intricately planned paths about the forest – were all of a kinship. Each column had far fewer Ants than might be found in Sarn, say, or Vek, but all together there must have been a fearsome number of them. The world is very lucky that they seem, for now, content with their lot. If so many at once decided to go to war I'm not sure all the armies of the Empire could even have slowed them down.

Blaze and the good Doctor were quick to descend on the spire for study. Unlike the suspicious Ostranden, the Alethi just let us get on with it, and the Beetles took measurements and samples and even went some way into the guts of the thing. We discovered a maze of tunnels and chambers there, and even with thread and lamps we didn't venture far into the interior. The Ants themselves had commandeered the nearest chambers to store perishables in, for there was a constant rush of air within the lightless halls that kept everything cool and fresh. Beyond that, we saw galleries that reached vertically a hundred feet or more, and others that plunged into the ground where the structure evidently continued, far vaster even than its outward appearance would indicate. But we did not go far. There were hostile beasts dwelling in the more distal reaches of the place, we were told – whip scorpions and centipedes and blind, carnivorous crickets. Also, it was all very bare, lacking even the Khanaphir glyphs we had seen in Ostrander. We did not see a single artefact or carving, and I had the bizarre sense that the artistry in the place lay in the construction itself, all those weird little rooms and twisting passageways making up some grand picture appreciable only in the minds of its builders. Mostly we did not wander, though, because of a sense of utter desolation. The ruins of the Nem at least retain the image of their makers, but whoever had raised this spire had gone some place where even history could not reach. The Alethi seemed to know nothing about them – they had stories about how they had come to this place, and some claimed they had driven the builders into the earth, or away into the forest, but others – which I felt were the more true – spoke only of empty halls and vanished makers. I could hear Blaze's teeth grinding at the utter lack of clues.

He and the Doctor discussed their options, and more and more I heard them talking about striking off into the trees. There were other spires out in the forest, after all. Perhaps there would be more significant trace of the builders at the next.

Leaving them to their talk, I went out and tried to scare up some information from the Alethi. They were very much at their ease at that spire – the whole place seemed to be their festival ground as much as anything. As usual, most of what they were about passed silently between their heads, but I saw plenty of games and contests: wrestling, foot races, the throwing of various objects martial and non-. What they were not there to do, apparently, was talk to me, especially about any neighbouring spires we might go and examine. After a while I began to get a very uneasy feeling about the whole business, because those Ants were not just too busy for me. The topic of other spires made them shut up like a clam and pretend not to have understood me in the first place. This told me three things: yes, there were other spires out there; no, they weren't just more stops on the great Alethi pilgrimage; yes, there was a good reason for that.

Their unified refusal to discuss the subject was maddening, because I knew that once one of them had come to that decision, they'd all follow suit. I spent half a day at my wits end, feeling every informational door closed to me, before realising that there were other visitors there besides the Ants.

They were not, of course, the spire builders, although for a handful of seconds I thought I might have just solved the entire enigma. Nor were they instantly attacked by the Ants, although the Alethi plainly kept an eye on them, just as they no doubt did on us. I saw quite a variety of travellers walk into that huge camp to trade or talk or even entertain. There were some scorpions who were barely taller than I, and some hairy, robust Spider cousins whom I knew for Tarantula-kinden from an encounter in Everis. I spent more than an hour watching a Butterfly-kinden man dance for the Ants' entertainment, a performance of such a candid nature I had difficulty in ordering my thoughts for some time after – and who even knew that Butterflies lived anywhere outside the Commonweal, let alone somewhere as wild and primal as the Forest Aleth? There were others, too. I saw a small-framed woman with velvety grey skin sweating glue from the palms of her hands, which she traded with the Ants for food and hides, and after her came a trio of Beetles.

This was as much a surprise as the Butterfly, because although there were Beetles in Khanaphes and a different breed in Solarno, the Collegiates were always very keen to keep track of their distant relatives, and nobody had any idea that a whole tribe of them lived in the Aleth. They were quite distinct from the artisans and scholars of Collegium too, more suited to a life of fast movement and sudden strife. Two women and a man had come out of the trees to haggle with the Ants, and the least of them was a head taller than Blaze or the Doctor. Their brown skins were streaked and striped with paler slashes, so that when they stood in the shadow of the canopy, even my Fly eyes had difficulty keeping track of them. Most of all, they moved very differently to a Lowlander. I got to see one of them fight a mock duel with some of the Ants, and the forest Beetles had some Art that let them rush about with great force and swiftness, so swift it was hard to follow them. All in all they seemed a very dangerous prospect, and I was rather hoping the Doctor wouldn't spot them.

And he didn't, and he wouldn't have done, except the next morning I turned around and found one of them right behind me, having crept up on me with terrifying ease.

It was one of their women, tall and rangy and in only a hide wrap that left her long limbs bare. I stared at her and she dropped instantly into a crouch to bring her more to my level. Her face was hard to read, her expression broken up by the mottled stripes and at least one old scar.

"Little person," she said, and I saw that her piercing teeth were far larger than they had any right to be, curving down like sharp mandibles until it was a marvel she could close her lips around them. "Little person from the city-lands. Have you brought toys of metal here to trade?"

I stammered some denial and tried to back off, but she had me by the wrist with the sort of effortless swiftness one looks for in Mantis-kinden, She had my fingers to her mouth in the next heartbeat and I thought she would just chew down on them as if live Fly-kinden was a delicacy where she came from. Those fierce teeth came out, but she just bit at my ring, deforming it and popping the stone from its socket to be lost in the dust.

"Fffr," the woman spat, and even as I tried to reclaim my hand she had my knife from my belt, examining the blade keenly. "More like it. I will trade you for this, and more like it. Toys of metal are always useful."

"It's not for trade!" I shouted. That ring had been cheap and ill-made, I admit, but it had also been a present from a young man I had once been fond of, and now it was trash. And I valued the knife, too.

"It is for trade," the Beetle woman told me, still with that iron grip about my wrist. I tried to catch the eyes of the passing Ants but they plainly considered it none of their business. "You will trade it for knowledge, for that is what you are here for."

"What?" I squeaked, and she stood abruptly, absent-mindedly yoinking me off the ground entirely.

"The Ants tell me," she explained. "They say you are asking questions you should not." She jabbed up at the heights of the spire with my knife. "All these things, your men ask questions of. What, why, who made?"

"You know who built them?" I asked her, my peril and possessions forgotten.

"Trade, and I will show you," she said.

"The other spires, there are artifacts there?" I pressed. "The builders left something behind?"

She laughed then, showing me far more than I wanted to see of her wicked dentition. "They left themselves behind, little person. I will show you to them and you can ask them yourself."

And oh, this was dangerous stuff, and I knew even then that the Ants had good reason not to go chasing off after spire-builders, but at the same time all I could think was how Blaze would look at me, when I brought him this gem.

At the time this woman – her name was Tchotte or something like it – seemed everything the civilized Lowlander might expect in a savage from distant lands, far more so than the eminently organised Alethi. Likewise her proffering her services seemed simple opportunism from someone who seldom got the chance to snag manufactured goods. In retrospect, however, I honestly wonder at the convenience of it all, and I wonder just what ears were listening when the Doctor and Corvaris Blaze asked their questions about the spire-builders. Or perhaps it was just Tchotte putting on an act to make herself seem simpler than she was, to improve her bargaining position. Or she genuinely was just one of those energetic, fierce people who take joy in life and think little for tomorrow, and I have met enough of those in the Lowlands that to find them in wilder places should be no surprise.

Anyway, whether I was being played or not, I made the introductions according to plan, and Tchotte duly impressed her two distant kinsmen, both with what she was offering and with her very presence. I had a sudden moment of dismay when I thought that Blaze must surely be very taken with her – despite the teeth and stripes (or because of them?) She cut a remarkable figure, and if I was honest with myself, I would confess that her lean, athletic physique was very much in vogue back home at times. (If I had the time I would write about a friend of mine, to remain nameless, who spent nine months trying to woo the Mantis Akkestrae back home based on just such aesthetics, which ended up as something of a costly lesson in when not to press your affections.)

Blaze was wary and businesslike, though, and I had cause to wonder just how things were in the Spiderlands for a man trying to make his way with only his wits. He must have got into plenty of embroilments with Spider-kinden Aristas in the past, and to him Tchotte was just one more potentially useful source of information. Doctor Phinagler, in stark contrast, found the forest Beetle quite the spectacle.

Blaze did most of the talking at first, hammering out what Tchotte was offering. She was coy with it, if a seven-foot woman with fangs can reasonably be said to be coy, but she was willing to lead us to where more spires were, and she swore the kinden that lived there was the same that had, in the remote past, raised them. Despite this falling exactly into line with his plans, Blaze was trying for scepticism. He asided to the Doctor that probably it was just some successor kinden, or at best some time-distanced shadow of the builders who had forgotten everything they ever knew about their ancestors. Still, I could see the flame of academic excitement lit in both of them. Blaze, at least, had the goodness to thank me, and I spent that evening cuddled up beside him at an Alethi fire, feeling warm and useful and thinking inappropriate thoughts. Doctor Phinagler spent the evening talking to Tchotte, who not only failed to murder him, but somehow got on with him very well, so that I remember looking over and seeing him regale her with some anecdote or other that made her laugh uproariously with every other word, sharp teeth flashing in the firelight. Possibly it was just that he had finally gone far enough from home that he'd found an audience for whom his tales were actually fresh, but I am being mean-spirited by saying so. In truth, as I have oft remarked, Doctor Phinagler has a remarkable ability to get on with absolutely everyone except for his peers, and Tchotte was no exception. As I was 'little person' to her, so the Doctor was 'Soft One', and I am still not sure if it was insult or term of affection.

The next morning we packed up what we had left, gave most of it to Tchotte in trade and then set off on our fateful journey to meet the masters of the spires. We each felt ourselves very much the daring explorer, cutting through the dense undergrowth of the Forest Aleth, further and further from any of our homes, following in the tracks of as barbaric a guide as anyone could wish. In truth we had no idea what we were getting ourselves into. I heartily recommend the hospitality of the Alethi, if you can get it, but there are good reasons for their prohibitions, and the deep interior of the Forest Aleth is a place we all should have shunned.

Travel with Tchotte was eventful, and the first thing we found was that we were leaving the Alethi sphere of influence, or perhaps I should say corridor. The Ant columns cut intricate, geometrical patterns across the forest, that must have been worked out between all the different bands so as not to over-hunt and farm any one section. They were the undisputed masters of wherever they were, but there was a living to be made in their wake, or keeping ahead of them, or simply in those triangular regions of forest that their routes bordered but did not cross. The Alethi were good neighbours unless trifled with, and Tchotte said that any other people who took too much ahead of a column would be driven off or even exterminated without compunction. Tchotte revealed that her own people were also nomadic, mostly moving in small bands across the forest, hunting game and terrorising anyone except the Alethi whom they might come across – she was very proud of this last and I had the impression that her Tiger Beetle-kinden were very much the bully-boys of the Aleth when the Ants weren't around. What that appellation meant was made plain to us two days into our trek when we had the misfortune to meet one of her totem. I had never seen the breed before, and I barely saw it even as it attacked – only Tchotte's bark of warning saved us. A blurred green and white shadow bolted from between the trees at us – I had a glimpse of huge round eyes and mandibles like curved swords. Blaze had leapt aside, and I was in the air even as the alarm rang out, but Doctor Phinagler would have been scissored in half had Tchotte not shoved him. She herself also jumped, but only up, so that she came down on the beast's back. I had a brief chance to look at it then: a beetle half again as long as a man, high off the ground on slender legs. The speed of its charge had been swifter than an automotive at full throttle, but on finding itself with empty jaws it just stopped in utter bafflement, seeming almost embarrassed. Tchotte took the opportunity to ram her knife – that had been my knife – in between its wing cases, enough to prick the creature, and it flared its wings, forcing her to leap off. Instantly the two of them rounded on each other. Tchotte was grinning with wicked concentration, knife in one hand and a flint-studded club in the other. She said later that hunting these predators – the inspiration for her kinden's Art – was something of a rite of passage amongst her people.

This time around, she did not have to prove her prowess. There was a sharp snap, and a hole pierced the beetle's thorax, oozing yellow goo from within. It recoiled from us, then snapped at Tchotte, seeing her as the threat. That gave my employer a chance to reload his snapbow and loose again, this time clipping the top of the beast's head. I heard him curse at the poor shot and fumble for another bolt, but the tiger beetle was plainly aware that something uncanny was up, because it whirled around and bolted for the trees.

Tchotte ambled over, eyeing the Doctor with a rather different appreciation. "What is your toy, Soft One?" she asked, which meant our expedition was halted while Doctor Phinagler showed off Collegiate engineering, or in this case Imperial engineering, this particular weapon having been left behind by the Seventh Army after the Battle of the Rails, along with most of the rest of the Seventh Army.

Yes, we had brought a snapbow. My employer had acquired one from a returning veteran, and had been practising with it back home, in that way he has of suddenly deciding to acquire a new skill. Being able to shoot had enjoyed a brief fashion in Collegium in the aftermath of the fight with the Empire, before it was overtaken by everyone talking about the latest twirls to come out of the Seldis Grand Ballet, but the Doctor had kept up his practice, hence the presence of the bow amongst his effects. All that practice added up to only a mediocre ability to actually hit anything, but the beetle had proved a cooperatively large target and Tchotte was duly impressed. That evening, I suspect she made some fairly extravagant offers for the weapon, but the Doctor managed to hang on to it, though he did let her loose off a few of his remaining bolts to try it out.

And there were other escapades I will gloss over: rivers to cross on precarious rope bridges that, of course, were no terror to me whatsoever. We were attacked by Tarantula-kinden once and had to make a run for it as their javelins split the foliage around us. Another time, the good Doctor fell into the hungry jaws of what turned out to be some kind of carnivorous plant, unknown to science, and had to be hurriedly cut out from between its toothed leaves. But all of this is sideshow, for Tchotte was as good (or as bad) as her word. One evening, she bid us climb high enough to have sight over the canopy, and even my employer ended up perched on a branch and staring, wide eyed and struck silent for once, at the sight.

We were close to three of the spires, raised close enough together that they might have shared a single subterranean base. Once we were able to see the sky, we found ourselves virtually in their shadow, rearing up towards the stars. The Ostranden relic, the stump of the Alethi, these had only a blunted mystique in comparison, domesticated as they were by the latecomer Ants. These spires were the Unknown, off the track and undetailed in any books, hence the ambition that had drawn the two Beetles and I into their orbit. To discover, to be the first to *know*.

And they were inhabited, in a way quite different to the temporary occupation of the Ants. We saw smoke against the darkening sky, venting from some of the high apertures. We saw the dim glimmer of fires lighting other irregular windows orange-red, and the sky about the whole seemed to shimmer with ghostly currents of heat and cool.

"Tomorrow," Tchotte promised, and she hugged Doctor Phinagler to her, hard enough to whuff the breath from him. "Heart's desires tomorrow, Soft One." And then, soberly, "Make the most out of tonight."

In the morning, we crept to the edge of the treeline – as with the Alethi spire, there was a great ring of clear ground around these three where the forest simply didn't happen. I don't know what my Beetle companions were expecting to see, but I was assuming there would just be more Ants here, perhaps of a different colour. I was right and wrong.

Tchotte had, presumably by design, brought us by a path that avoided the locals, for there were indeed locals and they were heading out into the forest in orderly little lines, while others clambered about the outside of the spire or dragged rubbish and rubble out from the interior. I saw at once they weren't Ants. They had something of the same compact frame, but they were taller and lacked the physicality that Ant-kinden have; it certainly took more of them to move anything heavy. They were pallid, too, their skins so white I half-expected to see organs pulsing within. They wore knee-length smocks, with what looked like tools hanging from their simple belts, and some had a little armour, mostly about the head and shoulders. Overall, I thought they looked more like Roach kinden, or perhaps even Mantids, but all the same there was a definite Ant-ness about them for they exchanged not a word with one another. The entire sprawl of pale people moved in utter silence, yet were plainly coordinating with one another, linked mind to mind just as Ants were. Well, it wasn't a uniquely Ant Art, but few other kinden possessed it to the extent that whole communities could simply get on without any audible direction.

They did not look warlike, but there were a lot of them and I was considering how Ants really didn't like visitors, and how the Alethi were keen enough to avoid this place that they wouldn't even name it.

"The trees around here are all cultivated," Blaze noted. "They must cut them back constantly for the wood. They're different breeds from the rest of the forest too."

"I wonder if they're new hybrids cultivated by the builders," Doctor Phinagler murmured back, "or some old stock lost to the rest of the Aleth."

"You're that sure they're the builders then?" Blaze obviously felt these pallid Ant-like people lacked some of the splendour he had been hoping for.

"Look, they're up there maintaining the things." My employer pointed to the locals who had scaled the outer walls. It could have been what they were doing.

Blaze sat back, rubbing at a little scar on his chin (from a duel, he had told me, with a Spider Aristo). "Well this is going to be a tricky business," he remarked to me. "It doesn't look as though they're keeping up the sort of keen watch the Alethi were, but one sees, all see. And Tchotte was saying they just keep this up all night, and probably they see in the dark way better than we do, even you, Fosse. But we've got to grab a look inside somehow…" He glanced around, as if seeing whether we could somehow rappel across from the closest trees.

"You want to sneak in?" I asked him. Of course I could have done so easily – none of the locals appeared to have wings and the spire had plenty of high openings. It was just that such a mode of entrance was not what I was used to.

Blaze grinned at me. "Well surely. How else would we go about it?"

"Well," I started, and became aware that Doctor Phinagler was not participating in the conversation. Instead, he was already out in the open and striding towards the spire, smoothing down his robes and then flinging his hands out in welcome.

"I say!" his voice came to us. "Would you mind awfully taking us to your leaders?"

Blaze and I froze, staring at each other. We were awaiting the ululating howls of rage at a trespass onto sacred ground. Surely a horde of these pale denizens would flood from the bowels of the spires and tear Doctor Phinagler apart or carry him off for some dreadful Inapt ritual. I realised, in that split second, that he had simply never been around when the Alethi had been asked about the spires and been so obviously evasive. My employer had been making his own enquiries, and apparently these had not yielded such results as to suggest to him that these lands were forbidden to outsiders and that even the fearsome Alethi didn't go there. And so there he was, waving serenely at the host of this unknown kinden.

Nothing happened.

By which I don't mean that no such thing happened, but that no thing happened at all. Doctor Phinagler's wave slowed and then stopped, and all around him the pale people continued at their jobs in silent concentration and spared him not a glance. In fact, as he called out again and was similarly blanked, it reminded me of nothing more than the Founder's Day Grand Revel a few years back to which he had not been invited but somehow arrived at anyway, and had stood there asking which seat was his while everyone did their best not to look at him. What had been rather ungracious behaviour in the Masters of the College was frankly uncanny in so great a throng of busy workers. Doctor Phinagler stepped slowly forwards until he was well in their midst, and they carried on as if he simply didn't exist to them.

Blaze and I exchanged a look of a different character, and we stepped forwards carefully, ready to bolt just in case there was a material difference to these people between one intruder and a trio. We were as roundly ignored as the Doctor, however, and at first it was a very eerie business indeed, as though we were surrounded by the ghosts the Inapt go on about, or perhaps as though we ourselves were those ghosts. We reached Doctor Phinagler's side, as he turned slowly on the spot looking out at all that heedless activity, and he spread his arms at us and shrugged.

"Seems rather rude, to be honest, but an unparalleled opportunity for research I suppose," He suggested. "Have you seen their tools?" He directed us to a nearby quartet of pale people who were sawing up timber hauled in by their fellows. The saws were finely formed, the teeth as regular as a machined piece from the Helleron factories, and yet they were not metal. As our dealings with Tchotte had shown, the Forest Aleth was short on mines and forges.

(It was around this point that I realised Tchotte had not come out with us. In fact, as we would discover, she had simply left, her work done in bringing us that far. I do not know, I really do not know, whether she was simply a pragmatist, or whether she had some other paymaster than us, but the idea of guiding us *out* was apparently not on her agenda. At the time we did not mark it much, and later events were sufficiently in the foreground of our thoughts that her desertion did not strike us.)

We all gathered around to look at the white dwellers cutting wood with a sawblade coloured brown-black. I thought it was wood itself, at first, toughened by Art or artifice, but then I saw the fine residue sloughing off it, mixed in with the sawdust. It was like sand, and the saw itself was… earth, somehow. Just dirt sealed together into that elegantly effective shape. I caught Blaze glancing from the saw to the spires that had us in their shadow, and followed his thinking.

"A whole technology at variance with our own," Doctor Phinagler murmured. *That* had some bad memories surfacing, of our sojourn beneath Lake Limnia, and in truth I should have taken the hint and left.

"There's a lot here to study," Blaze agreed. "As you say, though they're apparently going to be ideal subjects. I wonder just how far one can go within, before they deign to take notice of us…" Another little clue I missed at the time, but Spiderlands academia is quite a different beast to that of the Lowlands. Their researchers have rather distinct priorities.

Something caught my eye, just the merest flicker. An expression had come briefly to the face of one of the sawyers. Abruptly we were out of the realm of the uncanny and right back at that Founder's Day Revel, for what I'd seen was undisputable one of them signalling one of the others with a wide-eyed look of *They aren't going away!* so profound that even a Mindlink couldn't contain it. With that revelation, I realised that this whole wordless host of busy workers was *not* locked in some telepathic communion so strong that even the advent of strangers could not break it, but was just being terribly terribly polite in the misplaced hope that we clumsy offcomers would leave.

But that jig was well and truly up, as our words had indicated, and abruptly they all stopped working, a universal downing of tools that would have done credit to any Worker's Assembly back home. And they stared. A couple of hundred people so pale they'd make the Tarkesh look sunburned, just staring at us without any particular emotion – meaning that they could erupt into any particular (read: negative) emotion without warning.

Then more of them were coming out, though thankfully not the murderous host I feared, but just a handful, and then just one making a straight line for us. He was dressed in a longer smock than the others, bore a straight staff of grey wood, and there were some lines of coloured beads across the front of it which suggested that he was someone in authority. Apparently the Doctor had got his wish by sheer persistence. As usual.

My employer shot a distinctly pleased-with-himself look back at Blaze and myself and then prepared to receive this embassy from a lost world. He threw out his arms again and declared, "Greetings from the Assembly of Collegium!" for all the world as though he was an official ambassador.

There was a moment when it was plainly going to go wrong. The pale leader was anything but welcoming as he approached, even shaking his head pointedly, eyes fixed on the Doctor. I didn't think about it at the time, but you don't see Ants shaking their heads amongst themselves. They don't have all those little mannerisms because it goes on invisibly between them. These pale folk were not quite so impassive as Ants, but they had a touch of it and that head-shaking was very heavily telegraphed. It was a message to us, if we had only been sharp enough to read it.

And there was a moment when the chief was going to turn Doctor Phinagler away. He hurried up almost furtively, raised his staff as if about to enact some decree of banishment or execution, and then stopped still. They were all still, as if Doctor Phinagler was the only mobile thing left in that whole huge clearing. Even the pale people halfway up the sheer walls of the spires were fixed in place.

Now I have dealt with Ants a bit in my time. One of the things you learn is that it's no use noting where they look. There's always a pair of eyes in every direction, when there's enough of them, and they share what they see. So where the one *you're* talking to is looking at means nothing at all. But when you have a lot of them, you can sometimes work out what they're interested in by a sort of current of attention through the whole throng. Right then, I became acutely aware of where all those pallid people were *not* looking.

My eyes scaled the nearest spire until I found an opening that seemed more balcony than vent, and there I saw them, the masters of the spires.

They were robed from head to foot in elaborately folded cloth, faces nothing but shadows within their cowls. I have seen Moth Skryres, and once an eccentric gentleman who claimed to be a Mosquito-kinden with an appetite for human blood (we were tied up at the time and the blood he had his eye on was ours), but for sheer mysterious presence, those three shrouded figures beat the rest. My blood went cold with the sight and my mind flooded with thoughts of the Bad Old Days when charlatan magicians held sway over all the world, and held the power of life or death over such as we.

But then they were gone, stepped backwards into the darkness of the spire, and the headman or chief or whatever he was, he of the beaded apron, brought the end of his staff down onto the earth with a thud.

"Welcome, travellers from distant lands," he declared, as though the words choked him. "To what do we owe the honour of your presence, we who have so few visitors?"

Blaze broke in before the Doctor could claim the whole culture for the Lowlands. "We are but simple seekers after truth, who have come following rumours of the splendour of your people." He tried his best smile.

"And your seeking shall be rewarded," the headman said. "You are tired, you are hungry. You must come in and be our guests, and we shall talk, and you will learn much."

Really, I can't think of words better calculated to put the Doctor at his ease: knowledge *and* a meal. And of course he has that facility with strangers by which they open up to him and grant him some measure of respect even if they are, by nature, cruel or indifferent people. I have seen my employer in the good graces of Rekef officers, Scorpion brigands, and there was even that Spider-kinden torturer who spent a tenday only pretending to rack the good Doctor to keep up appearances, whilst sharing a bottle of wine with him each evening. And so when these pale dwellers were instantly welcoming, he took it as his due, and Blaze was obviously used to his charm getting instant results. I think only I found it all a little convenient.

But they were shepherding us towards the spires now – those vast structures that had been the start of all of this. And I had my qualms, I can tell you. I pictured cannibal kitchens, appalling rituals of the elder days, sacrificial altars, or even such mundane fates as a cut throat or a cell within the buried bowels of the place, but the two Beetles were going in, and if they had decided not to, the pale people were present in sufficient profusion to press their invitation beyond the possibility of declining. I could have flown off, I suppose. I didn't see so much as a sling amongst them that could have brought me down, even if they could hit me. But that would mean abandoning both my employer and Corvaris Blaze, with whom I remained rather infatuated. And so I went in and trusted that, if need be, my wings would suffice to give me the freedom of the place. Small chance of that, doubtless, for a structure wormed through with little tunnels and chambers, except that when we actually got within the spire, the sight was quite different to what I expected.

The abandoned spire the Alethi had taken over had been in bad repair, the collapse of the upper sections resulting in a fair amount of rubble below, and only small, solidly-walled chambers surviving near the entrance for the Doctor and Blaze to examine. What greeted us now was something quite different. We stepped into a space neither cramped nor even dark. Past the earthen walls, the chamber soared high into the innards of the place, a great buttressed space that echoed back every scuff and shuffle of our feet. The walls were not regular, nor yet naturally random, but formed of a sequence of folds and creases and thin intrusions that led upwards as far as the eye could see. Probably the chamber's height was only a fraction of the whole spire, but it was awe-inspiring, the tallest single interior room I had ever been in. The air was grey and dancing with dust, light coming to us through a dozen hidden shafts that seemed to highlight the gloom rather than dispel it, and higher up we saw a constellation of some kind of lamps, gleaming in the artificial firmament and illuminating nothing but themselves.

The pale people were everywhere, both on the ground around us and climbing up and down the walls with their Art, evidently cleaning and maintaining their home. I saw insects too, mostly arising from and descending to buried levels – they were as pale as their people, seeming soft as pupae save for their heads, which were brown as corn kernels and armed with ferocious sickle-shaped mandibles. Still, there seemed no harm in them, and they were as obliviously industrious as the humans around them. Several seemed weirdly swollen, as though about to push out a huge clutch of eggs, and these beasts worked only erratically, often just standing still and twitching for prolonged periods. It's odd what you notice at these times.

Faced with such a remarkable vista, both my Beetle academics were inordinately concerned with the walls. Doctor Phinagler was examining the pristine finish – very different to the weathered ruin the Alethi had co-opted. "They must maintain this all the time," he murmured. "Some manner of Art, surely…" For his part, Blaze had a glass out and was trying to peer into the gloom above us at the vanes and ripples of the upper reaches. "Do you see something gleaming up there?" he asked me.

I took flight a little, no more than head height to a Beetle, and let my better eyes resolve the shapes up there. I definitely descried a pattern of brighter patches and threads set into the earth, as though some huge mural was mouldering away in darkness up there, and some of the actual vanes – like big fins sticking ten feet out into space and ascending for thirty feet or more – seemed constituted of the same stuff. Was it metallic? I thought it might be. In fact, it had a lustre even in the dimness that seemed like one metal in particular.

"But surely it can't be gold," I said. "Not so much of it."

Blaze waggled his eyebrows at me, as if to say that cities of gold were no unusual thing to a seasoned explorer, but then our guide, the leader of the pale people, spoke up.

"It is gold that you see," he confirmed mournfully, as though having an Arista's ransom of precious metal hanging above his head was a dreadful bore. "For its thermal properties."

On the subject of things we note, but fail to give inappropriate weight to, I will mention here the spark that lit in Blaze's eye at the confirmation.

He hid it quickly, though, and turned his easy smile on the chief pale person. "So, are you the Aristo here?" Seeing the man's unfamiliarity with the term, he went on, "or king, monarch, emperor perhaps? You lead?"

"My name is Laiko," the man said softly. "I am a foreman, tasked to ensure that you lack for no comforts in your visit here. We so seldom meet with travellers who have come so far."

"Foreman?" I burst out, for it was such a familiar term. It made sense of his simple attire, though, save for the beads.

"Don't forget Khanaphes," the Doctor murmured. That city, after all, was run by 'Ministers' paying lip service to masters who had been extinct for centuries (though not, as we had cause to know, as extinct as they ought to be). "So when might we meet the fellows at the top?"

"Oh, they are most eager to meet you," Laiko told us, and again I felt that the words and the vestiges of expression about his face were at variance. By then, though, the music had started. I say music. It was not the Siennis Grand Opera. It was not even the Collegium amateur opera scene (amongst whom I was then persona non grata after some reviews that were not as anonymous as I had believed). Mostly it was percussion, as a line of children filed out to stand before us and hit hollow blocks of various sizes with sticks. Then there were some horns, which were bizarrely twisted and made of the same stuff as the saws outside. The overall effect was rigidly rhythmic and yet unmelodious, but apparently this was meant as an impromptu honour, and so we stood there and endured it until it was done, by which time more pale people had arrived offering to convey us to chambers. The spires' true masters would send for us, Laiko explained.

Our chambers were spacious and half-lit in the same manner, light reaching us through angled shafts from high above. Blaze was the first to point out that the builders must be a dab hand at mirrors, for the shafts came from all angles and could not possibly have gone straight to the exterior. Doctor Phinagler was once again examining the walls.

"Founder's Mark, look at this!" he exclaimed. He had found a line of roughness running up the side of the room. "This was more than one chamber, and recently I'd wager. I think all that caterwauling was to give them time to convert a room for us.

There were beds in that room – in the sense of shapeless mattresses far softer than anything any of us were used to. There was also running water that came in via a hole in the wall and flowed along a spiral channel in the floor before vanishing down another opening. Everything had a faint rough edge to it that supported the Doctor's contention.

"Shaping this stuff must be effortless to them," he murmured. "And there's a breeze – cool air, and dry, not the forest air from outside. It must be a property of the spire's structure."

"So how long do we wait?" Blaze asked us.

"Until?" Doctor Phinagler blinked at him.

"Until they've settled enough for us to explore." He looked from me to my employer. "How else will we learn anything?"

"Well." The good Doctor made vague gestures. "You know, talk, getting to know them."

"That's how you do things in the Lowlands?"

"That's not how you do things in the Spiderlands?"

"Oh *talk*, certainly, but there's always a point when the talk won't get you any further. There's always something they won't say, after all. So you have to go dig," Blaze explained.

I reflected that, usually, the point at which talk doesn't work was imposed on us externally and sometimes with extreme prejudice.

"How about we at least try talking as a first resort?" Doctor Phinagler asked, nettled, and Blaze held his hands up, mollifying. Whatever he might have said next was bitten back because our hosts had returned, Laiko in front nervously playing with his beads.

"I hope this meets with your approval," the foreman said.

"Could do with a little more light," Blaze replied promptly, and politeness be damned. He came from a culture with a lot of servants, however, and was far easier speaking to them as such.

Laiko took the criticism as his due. "It shall be attended to," he confirmed humbly. "In the meantime, I am asked to convey you to my masters."

It sometimes seems that, outside Collegium, the whole world is divided into masters and servants. Or masters and slaves.

We were escorted through three more halls, and I don't mind telling you I started losing track of how *big* the place was supposed to be. None of the poky little rooms I had expected, but each chamber as soaring as the last, with just a few handfuls of the pale people cleaning and trimming. We got a brief glimpse of their Art on the way, and they were just building up sand and earth and fixing it in place as though they sweated cement. The spires had been raised from the very dust, one grain at a time.

And then we were led up a ramp by Laiko, its surface gritty where everything else had been smooth, so that I wondered if that, too, had been fashioned only now, for our convenience. At the top was a perfect arch into a chamber of more modest dimensions. Beams of light struck straight down from the ceiling, not diffusing into the grey air but somehow remaining sharp-edged. Doctor Phinagler ran up to peer into one, squinting against the radiance to see where it came from. It was left for me to tug at his sleeve to indicate that we were not alone. We had indeed been brought into the presence of Laiko's superiors.

"Ah, ahem." My employer addressed the folds of his robe to ensure all was hanging properly, and then fixed the darkness beyond the beams with a sunny smile. Blaze lounged closer to the door, and I saw one hand no great distance from his hatchet should matters fall out badly.

My eyes being better, I could see three robed figures awaiting us on a dais at the back of the chamber. They seemed slighter than most of Laiko's people, but with all that swathing it was hard to know. They were presumably waiting for Doctor Phinagler to introduce himself, but he was squinting blindly at them, unsure who if anyone was there, and so I took hold of the awkward silence and decided to play the majordomo.

"May I present Doctor Ludweg Phinagler, ambassador without portfolio for the Historical Anthropology Department of the Great

College of Collegium, and Master Corvaris Blaze of the Planten League of Exploration!"

The echoes of my little voice scuffled murmuringly about the room and then let themselves out by the arch. For a moment I thought that was it, and we'd just be bundled out, never again to lay eyes on the mysterious robed figures again, but then one of them stepped forwards until it stood within one of the beams. Thus illuminated, it reached up and pulled back its cowl.

I ended up almost back through the door, and even Doctor Phinagler took a step backwards in shock. Blaze was the only one unmoved, but that was because the Empire never really made many inroads into the Spiderlands.

The man was a Wasp.

Oh true, he was smaller than men of the Empire usually are, and without their imposing physical threat, but the features were Wasp nonetheless, and he was just as pale as they generally are (some way short of the albinism of Laiko's White Ant kinden). What was especially strange was seeing a Wasp of any stripe got up in such a way, robed like the grandest of Moth mystics and fairly exuding the mystery of ancient days and lost places.

This prodigy observed our surprise with a mild smile that was condescending but within the bounds of politeness, the sort of expression one sometimes finds on the faces of senior College Masters about to explain to my employer why his request for grant money is regrettably being denied.

"I observe familiarity. Do I understand my kinden is known to you?" His voice was soft, oddly sexless, a world away from the habitual warrior bark of the Imperial Wasp.

"Indeed it is," the good Doctor confirmed. "Do you know of the Empire? Some way north of here the Wasp-kinden have quite the martial reputation."

The Wasp smiled a little more, as at the foolishness of children. "Who would have thought we had such fierce cousins! You must tell us all about them." He made no gesture, but abruptly there were servants of the pale Ant-like kinden bustling in, pressing earthenware goblets into our hands and proffering platters. Others came in and made furniture. I am afraid we became rather poor guests in that moment, because it was a sight to behold. They just raised stools up from the cemented earth of the floor, shaping the flow of the dry grains and fixing them in place with application of their singular Art. At the end, Doctor Phinagler was on his knees examining, with all his scholar's focus, what had been intended purely as a convenience. Blaze, somewhat more leery of *faux pas*, had to tap him forcibly on the shoulder.

"So," I said, to plug the silence, "you're not the fighting kind of Wasp, then?"

The robed figure regarded me curiously. I had seen none of my stature in the Aleth so maybe that puzzled him, or perhaps he was as unused to having his attention drawn to servants as the Doctor was to furniture.

"We do not fight," he confirmed. "Our sole concern is our greater understanding of the underlying forces of the world. We are pursuers of learning, as we understand you are, too."

"A prodigy." The Doctor straightened up, muttering to me, "Wasps that won't fight." To our hosts, who had most certainly overheard him, he added. "In my culture, Masters, learning is also our highest pursuit. My own home city is built around and named for its institution of scholarship, and…" Here he paused generously to let Blaze fill in his own credentials, but to my surprise Corvaris was content to stand back and let the Doctor make the running,.

"Alas, our learning is likely of a very different order to your 'underlying forces'," the Doctor added. "Not that I'd object to hearing of them, of course, but you may find I can't tell the head from the abdomen, unfortunately." He sat down on the now complete stool and accepted a goblet, sniffing and then sipping appreciatively. "Oh, this is fine," he added, upon finding what I had already discovered, that it was a very pleasant honeydew. The food, which I thought was sweet, doughy bread, was revealed after to be a kind of fungus, and more of that later, as well as many other things that would have better remained in darkness.

"The secret paths of the universe are not for all," the Wasp agreed placidly. "But we would hear of your own studies, the lore of your people. So few can penetrate the forest barriers that surround us, the barbarous Ants, the predators and the sheer distance. Such great travellers must surely be prodigiously learned."

Doctor Phinagler glanced at Blaze again, as if expecting the man to jump in, but in the Spiderlands they are decidedly more cagey with their learning than in my own generous home, and I think Blaze was not going to give for free what might be offered in trade. It is widely noted across the Lowlands, however, that Collegium is the one topic of conversation that Collegiates abroad never tire of.

And so we got the potted history of my home city, or at least my employer's take on it. The Doctor was trying to be diplomatic, faced with an Inapt magnate whose own field was the mysteries of the universe. Hence he did his best to bring the Inapt kinden into his history without dwelling too much on, say, the revolution. Did the Wasp know of the Moth-kinden? he asked. No, our host had not heard of them (and how that would gall them if they knew, I thought!). What about Khanaphes and its mysterious Masters? Yes, there were ancient tales that named such a place. The Wasp seemed wary of mentioning it, and something in his terse response struck me as odd, for any contact must surely have been centuries before and yet the caution he evinced seemed almost personal. Perhaps, I mused, that was just their way, that they took on themselves the deeds of their distant ancestors. That seemed an Inapt sort of thing to do, after all.

It is shameful to report, in retrospect, but at that meeting we learned almost nothing about our hosts, but instead the Doctor told them a great deal. Their spokesperson was a subtle questioner, and my employer's enthusiasm for the virtues of our home was enough to more than meet it halfway. In the end, when the robed Wasp stood to indicate the interview was over, Blaze had to put in, "Forgive me, but may I ask your name, Aristos?, And that of this place and your people?"

The Wasp regarded him with that smile, which by now seemed to me to be concealing a world-full of secrets, worse even than a Moth's. "Why, we know this place as the Colony of Tirimach. I am Prospectin Jagon, and you are very welcome guests of the Ichneumon."

We retired to our lodgings, surrounded by a constant patter of servants – those who were not 'Ichneumon' but instead called by Jagon 'Termite-kinden'. The precise relationship between them, and why the Termites laboured to support the studies of the Ichneumon, had not been delved into, although I was already determining to make a thorough interrogation of one of the Termites when I got the chance.

We were overheard every moment, I have no doubt, but still the Doctor and Blaze set to discussing somewhat forcefully just what we had learned. My employer was buoyant, convinced that we had made a fine impression and that he had played his self-bestowed ambassadorial role to the hilt. Blaze was more dour about the whole business, pointing out that we knew practically nothing. He had been very quiet returning to our chambers, and was plainly hiding some concerns he did not trouble the Doctor with. When we finally retired, however, I took the chance to flit over and talk a little more, softly so the Doctor (and hopefully our hosts) would not overhear. He was evasive with me at first, but after I had kneaded some tension out of his broad shoulders and back, he let me prop my head on his chest and whispered to me.

"That name, Ichneumon, it's not new to me. There are old Spider accounts where it features – accounts I was never meant to see, for the Spider-kinden hate others to know what they fear."

I frowned. "I wouldn't class Jagon as particularly fearsome." I was thinking of other 'masters' we had been guests of. The androgynous Wasp seemed no more threat than any other Inapt charlatan full of pretensions of mystic wisdom.

"And yet there must have been a time when these Ichneumon were the world's prime terror for the Spider-kinden," Blaze revealed. "I don't even know if I can safely spread the word that they're still here. It's the sort of knowledge the Spiders might want to scrub away all trace of, including the messenger that brought it."

"I though the Spider-kinden valued learning?"

"They value the having of it, but like most things, to them, such having is devalued when others have it too. But perhaps these latter-day Ichneumon are nothing but the name. It's hard to see how they can still be some great threat to the world."

"So what did they do that was so bad?" I asked, and he shrugged. Spider-kinden accounts were maddeningly elliptical at the best of time, just like most Inapt histories.

The next morning, I woke to the twin revelations that, first, I had never got round to returning to my own bed, and secondly, I had Blaze's bed to myself, because he was gone.

Naturally I was at the Doctor immediately, and at first he tried to bluster it out because, I think, he didn't want yet another research trip to have turned into a deathtrap. "I'm sure he's just gone for a stroll," he tried, or, "You know those Spiderlands fellows, always fond of creeping about the place." But I wouldn't have it, and I was sufficiently upset that at last he sat back down on his bed and murmured, "Well yes, but I'm not sure what we can *do* exactly, right now. I appear to be getting along famously with their chief shaman, or whatever a Prospectin actually is, but if they have done something villainous to poor Blaze, I don't think my just asking about it over a bowl of wine is going to shake loose any answers."

Which was a fair point. And, as my employer pointed out, we were right in the midst of their 'colony' as they called it. They could have disappeared the lot of us, but instead only Blaze had been vanished away. I remembered him talking about the Ichneumon and relayed the information to the Doctor in the barest whisper. "Basically, they're some secret enemy of the Spiders from way back when, and the Spiders don't like to talk about them, and now I guess the Ichneumon don't like people talking about it either."

"So we won't. I will meet up with our friend the Prospectin and tell him some yarns about Collegium and the Empire – he seemed dashed interested in it all. And you... Why don't you try and broach that fellow Laiko. He's a majordomo or steward or something; that means he probably knows most of what's going on, and he didn't appear unfriendly."

That seemed a sound plan, but one thing stuck in my throat a bit. "Why do you think Jagon is so interested, exactly?"

My employer shrugged, even as we heard the soft shuffle of bare feet approaching. "He probably imagines we're right next door to the Aleth, and dreams of a second Wasp Empire. You know these Inapt types – no grasp of cartography. And let's face it, most of what I say's going to go over his mystic head, isn't it?"

Laiko and some others arrived then to politely invite the Doctor to resume his conversation, which he accepted with great jollity. I was eyeing the foreman narrowly, because if he was the majordomo that Doctor Phinagler suggested then he could be responsible for most of what was going on, as well as just knowing about it. He was glancing around our room, though, and even through his lack of expression I could almost see the words, *Didn't there used to be three of you?* on his face. One thing about Ants and similar linked minds, they lie terribly, in word or action. Laiko didn't know what had happened to Blaze, and so it was presumably the direct work of his Ichneumon masters and whatever Rekef-like agents they used to make people vanish.

The Doctor took up his pack, all the better to impress the locals with some trinkets and toys of Collegiate artifice, and I trailed at a safe distance, every bit the demure servant. Jagon and a couple of his peers were waiting for us, just as before, and my employer gave them a hearty greeting. He tried a few questions about their own pedigree at first, perhaps aware that he had been more an exporter of information to date, and their answers were vague, yet maddeningly suggestive. Jagon revealed that they had come to "bless the Termite-kinden" many centuries before, and I wondered if this was when they had lost their struggle with the Spiders. He seemed to take it as an article of faith that there were other colonies of his kinden elsewhere, though he waved away their importance: Tirimach was the current centre of the Ichneumon world, as far as he was concerned. That told me that the 'colony' referred only to his people's presence in the spires. The spires themselves predated their coming, and had thus been colon*ised*.

After that, talk was deftly turned towards my home and its wonders, and Doctor Phinagler settled down to blind our hosts with science, talking about all manner of commonplace marvels such as plumbing and counterweight doors. Jagon took in each word but gave away no indication of his ignorance. The occasional polite comment he made related to the effect of such progress rather than the mechanism by which it was brought about, and showed that the spires possessed at least some innovations to allow the throughflow of clean air, for example, and the disposal of waste.

"I am sure they are very cleverly shaped," agreed the Doctor. "I have noted the freshness, and that it is neither hot nor cold anywhere here. It's a wonder what can be done even without moving parts."

I thought condescension was going to be his downfall then, but Jagon took it all without offence and continued to ask his questions. Did his cousins in the Empire have these magics? Was there strife between cities? How was Collegium governed? This latter seemed to him far harder to understand than plumbing or the Doctor's steel lighter, but then to tyrants, our Lots will always be a wonder beyond even the scope of magic to bring about.

As they had plainly settled in, I stole out and found Laiko, who was loitering just a chamber away, perhaps awaiting his masters' call.

I was trying to think of a way to broach him rather than just storming in and demanding we upend the whole spire searching for our lost companion. He was looking at me almost fearfully, and I saw his pale hands fiddling with the coloured beads across his apron. In a sudden flash of inspiration I realised it was not a badge of rank at all, but an abacus, which put the architectural marvels around me in a new light:

raised with Art, yes, but Art not driven by the mindless force of Inapt prophecy, but good Apt mathematics. That commonality gave me the courage to break in on his reverie.

"So you can obviously count," I said. "So you've noticed we're a man light this morning. Where did they take him?"

His eyes went wide in horror at my direct approach and he retreated until his back was against a wall, his hands frantically calculating the odds that I would just go away, which turned out to be infinitesimal.

I followed up, but he was clearly very frightened, eyes straying to the other Termites working close by, as though any one might be a spy for the Ichneumon – and perhaps it was so. Certainly in the Empire one is never more than ten feet from a Rekef informer at any time, or so the saying runs.

But at least he was frightened, and someone frightened of Fosse the Fly-kinden is unlikely to be a dreadful enemy. As his back was at the wall I flitted up with my wings and hissed in his ear, "Take us somewhere we *can* talk then! Surely there are empty store-rooms, forest clearings, somesuch?"

He shook his head a little. *There is nowhere.* And I could see he was too on edge to risk himself for some strange foreigner, so I dropped down again. "Well that's fine," I said loudly, as though we had been discussing something entirely different. "In that case, I'll just talk. Let whoever overhear it. My employer is currently telling your masters all about our home, so I'll do the same for you fellows and, if word spreads up and down the spire, no doubt another perspective will not be unwelcome to the men in the robes."

Laiko continued to regard me with extreme doubt, and everyone else was just working away, but I had a sense of open ears at least, and so I sat on the ground and just let my mouth run. Those who know me will not be very surprised to hear that I could fill a silence even the size of the spire's interior, lackingany other voice to contradict me. The ill-educated ascribe it as a fault, but I prefer to think of it as one of my charming eccentricities. Anyway, I talked, and they had little choice but to listen: the best kind of audience.

I actually got a bit tearful and nostalgic going on about Collegium. We had been away quite a while, what with all the hacking through the Forest Aleth, and I suddenly remembered I'd missed the poetry reading at the Egalitarian Pride that I'd been looking forward to, and that they'd have broached a new year's brewing of beer in the cellars of Fiko's. I had meant to talk about how Collegiate culture is the best in the world, the Lots, the Assembly, the College, all the usual things one is expected to brag about to annoy foreigners, but instead I'm afraid I just rambled on about all sort of inconsequential things and somewhat forgot why I was doing it. I am not normally given to homesickness – thankfully, considering my employer's love-hate relationship with Collegium – but I caught a bolt of it right through the liver just then.

When I finally choked to a stop, and saw Laiko still just staring at me like a doorstop, I felt emptied out. "Well I know, what's it to you?" I asked him roughly. "I'm sure you've got it made here, with your stupid big towers and your sandcastle Art and your masters who know best, eh?"

Laiko was without expression, as usual, so he caught me completely by surprise when he lunged forwards and caught my arm. I yelped and tried to break free with my wings, but he was stronger than he looked and he marched off through the tunnels with me bobbling about on the end of his arm like an uncooperative balloon. We went down, mostly, and after I stopped my fruitless fighting I felt us pass from pressure to pressure, different levels and chambers of the spire seeming to have their own isolated currents of air. One possible purpose for this was made plain when we stepped into a large, deep-buried room where the air was pure ordural stink.

I gagged and gasped, and all around me Termites were tending great gardens of bloated white fungus that was very plainly growing on a diet of nothing but the massed bodily waste of the spire's inhabitants. I started fighting again with a will, because I saw there a most offensive demise for one of my refined sensibilities. Was this what had happened to poor Corvaris Blaze? Was my fate to be nothing more than part of the Tirimach food chain?

Then Laiko popped me down on my feet, still not letting go. There was a terrible tension in his face but it was not murderous. Despite the raw sewage reek about us, that my nose was not getting used to any time soon, I calmed.

"We can talk now," Laiko told me. "They will not come here."

"None of these fellows are spies?" Perhaps sewage worker was too lowly a thing for the Ichneumon's informers.

Laiko shook his head agitatedly. "They will not come *here*." And he tapped his own brow. "Always they can be watching, listening. They are within us all, hearing our thoughts. But here, they must also smell *this*, and so they do not like to, and they will be out of my head until I am elsewhere."

"You're Mindlinked with them?" I asked him. "But you're not the same kinden, even!"

"They are in us, and know our thoughts as soon as they ask for them," Laiko confirmed. "We are not in them. Their minds are their own."

"But… there must be thousands of you across the spires. How can they ever keep control of you? How many of them even are there?"

Laiko stared at me. "They are eight," he said. At the time I assumed he meant a ruling council of eight – eight men if they were like the Wasps we knew – over a population much larger.

"I don't mean to tell you your business," I said, "But you should just go wall them up somewhere and be rid of them."

An expression of agonised fear gripped him – and you must remember, all these expressions I describe were the merest tip of his actual feelings, given how little the Termite faces showed. "We can never!" he gasped. "No hand can be raised against the masters. We may as well stab ourselves in the heart! But you, you must leave! Alone, or with your big friend, leave. You have told us of your beautiful city, with its freedoms and its kindnesses. Of course you must return to it, return and never leave. But go from here while you still can, before the masters take a true interest in you. Go, and leave all thought of this place far behind you!"

"Well I'd love to," I said, "but where is my other friend? Where did your masters vanish him off to? He was taken from our room!"

"He was not," Laiko said flatly. "But he is taken now."

I didn't quite understand the distinction – that would come later – but even as I opened my mouth (while holding my nose) to query him, Laiko jumped like a guilty cricket.

"They seek me," he gasped, and hauled me out of there as quickly as he had dragged me in, rattling me through the tunnels and chambers of the place until he was back near where we had been. Then he stopped, and I swear I saw him empty his mind of all that had been said, adopt the persona of the meek servant so that his masters would find nothing offensive in his mind.

We strolled into the presence of Prospectin Jagon and his friends to find the Doctor in full flow. He was, in fact, demonstrating the very latest marvel to come out of the world of artifice. He was shooting things with his snapbow. His target was a statue, or at least a manlike form raised from the earth by the Termites, and at the enclosed range I'd have thought his ricochets were more dangerous to anyone than the shots themselves. He was enjoying himself, though, with that engaging enthusiasm he gets in him, which tends to drive out any more serious concerns. The statue was definitely the worse for wear from his demonstration.

"This is a remarkable harnessing of the universal forces," Jagon was saying as we came in, sounding mightily impressed. "Pray explain how you make it perform."

Doctor Phinagler chuckled jovially and, as we waited, demonstrated the air battery workings that give the snapbow such power, phrasing each stage of the operation in such technical terms that I confess I could barely follow it myself. To the Inapt, his lecture might as well have been the buzzing of a bee for all the information it conveyed, but Jagon's eyes followed his hands and the man made a great show of being impressed with the cleverness of it all. The Doctor even went so far as to catch my gaze and roll his eyes theatrically.

"You have given us much to think on, Doctor," Jagon said when he was done, and he did look very thoughtful indeed. "But here is our servant to take you to your repast. Perhaps we shall talk again before nightfall."

As we walked away from the Ichneumon I murmured to my employer, "Do you think that was wise?"

"Perhaps I got a little carried away," Doctor Phinagler said dismissively, "but really, with neither mechanical understanding nor a source of good grade steel, what's the harm?"

I had a chance to talk with the Doctor then, and appraise him of my discoveries by whispering them. Firstly, that the Ichneumon were apparently able to tap into the Mindlink of the Termites, meaning that wherever their servants were, so might their attention be. Secondly, that the Termites were not wholly dominated by them, for ruses such as Laiko's taking me to the stinking mushroom farm showed that they practised some quiet form of rebellion, though they seemed terrified of their masters' displeasure beyond all reason. I think my employer and I were both wondering why the revolution of Apt against Inapt had not come to this place a long time before. I also confirmed that Blaze had apparently met with some sort of fate, about which I was wretchedly fretting, with no means of finding him. After that, and a light repast the taste of which was coloured from my having smelled the source, Doctor Phinagler went back before Prospectin Jagon in a more sober mood. I think he had been enjoying showing off the marvels of Aptitude to his hosts and had forgotten that, once, his ancestors were slaves like the Termites.

I tried to find Laiko again, but he had made himself scarce. Certainly I had detected a sympathy in him and a willingness to act against his masters if he could do so in safety. No doubt he felt the edge of that safety had been reached, for surely he was avoiding me. I was forced to buzz about our little chamber in impotent worry. Eventually, the Doctor came back, and we talked a bit about what we could do. He had tried to raise the subject of Blaze with the Ichneumon but Jagon, he said, had seemed not to hear him, or had dismissed the subject as not worthy of comment. I turned in to sleep with a very bad feeling in my gut.

And yet I could not sleep. My bed, which had sufficed before, was now intolerably uneven. I should explain how it was made: a bowl-like depression in the floor was home to a springy mattress of wicker, marvellously woven – they could have sold them at a profit on Woodmarket Row, believe me. Except suddenly even my small weight seemed to be driving parts of the floor into me wherever I rested. After an hour of this, with the melodious snores of my employer rumbling about the room, I lost patience and dragged the mattress out of its bowl with an eye to reshaping it.

There I discovered the problem.

The floor of the bowl, that had been marvellously smooth when I first investigated it, was now creased and lumped and grooved as though a thousand minute rivers had weathered a topography into it. In the dim light that still descended from above I stared at the wrinkles and spidery lines, wondering if this was a Termite practical joke. Then something flipped in my perception and my heart leapt. It was a map. Laiko, unwilling to pledge his help openly, had nonetheless left me a gift.

It was a complex business because it was mapping a three-dimensional space, but it had been so elegantly crafted by the Termite Art that I swiftly came to comprehension. Too complex to memorise, and of course I could not carry it with me, I ended up taking all the paper I could get and making a rubbing of it, working with feverish speed. When I was satisfied I had not missed off any errant escape route or useful ductwork, I knew it was time to move. There was a circle that corresponded to our sleeping chamber, and elsewhere Laiko had provided a triangle, an arrowhead indicating a destination: Blaze, I hoped, or else his mortal remains. They were deep within the spire, far below ground level, and I had no great wish to go spelunking in this grim place, but Blaze needed me. Or at least, I hoped he would agree that he needed me once I had freed him from whatever peril he was in. With such thoughts to warm me I crept off into the tunnels of the spire.

I am as light on my feet as any of my kinden, and the Termites were not used to intruders who could fly and fit through narrow gaps. I knew I had to avoid as many of them as possible – not because they would raise an alarm, but because any hint of me in their thoughts might be communicated to their sinister masters.

So, picture me if you will, creeping through the halls of the Termite-kinden, hearing their industry on all sides. They did not sleep, or not as a people, one shift taking over from the next in those sunless halls: harvesting, going out, bringing back and always the ceaseless maintenance of the spire itself, reshaping it room by room to the desires of their rulers. I had an unhappy feeling my map would not be current for very long.

And I expected pitch darkness as I descended, which would be a problem. I guessed the Termites could see in the utter dark like Moth-kinden, and while my eyes are good I need yet a little light to see, Anyone who has been forced to such stealthy exertions (and it was not my first time) will know that nothing draws trouble quicker than light in a lightless place.

But there was light, even as I descended. It was all very dim and gloomy, but everywhere there was some shaft or other giving out a radiance that I knew now could not just be sunlight, unless the Termites or their masters had mirrors or glasses that could somehow trap the sun. In the day, the natural light conducted to the upper chambers had fooled me into thinking it was mere architecture that kept the place illuminated. Now, past midnight and deep underground, it was plain that those shafts had something other than the open air at their apexes. The quality of the light was strange: golden and yet with an acidic tint that distinguished it from the solar. To my eyes it seemed to flicker, so fast it was at the very edge of noticing, and probably a Beetle or a Wasp would not have told it at all. And sometimes they dimmed, all together, guttering weakly like candles but then snapping back to their former illumination with an unnatural suddenness.

I almost shinned up one of the shafts to take a look, but I had more at stake than my scholarly curiosity. I was following the path to Corvaris Blaze, and the sands were running in the glass.

The road down to the bowels of the spire was not a straight one. Often I took a wrong turn and had to compare the map with the orientation of the tunnels around me. Had Laiko simply drawn the sort of map of convenience I might have used to guide someone through the streets of Collegium, I would have been lost. He was nothing if not exact in his workmanship, though. He must have had a perfect picture of the spire's current interior within his mind, or else he canvassed all his kin and together they made one that was astoundingly accurate in miniature. And armed with that, the spire's innards were a Fly-kinden's playground, a maze of little passageways and shafts that I, with my wings and slight frame, could navigate more easily even than its builders.

As I went further downwards, wondering just how far into the earth these chambers descended, the quality of the air became, not a problem but a feature. There were stenches, I will say that. As well as the ripe stink of the mushroom farms there were other distinct vilenesses upon the air, including that of massed human sweat. I picked up also the scent of burning more than once, and sometimes the sharp smell one sometimes gets before a spring storm. What was remarkable was the way the air moved – the foul scents coursing outwards, fresh air moving in, so that the place was thoroughly ventilated and liveable no matter what pungent doings went on. At the time I attributed this to heat differentiation and cunning design, and certainly there was a great deal of that going on – the Termite-kinden are ingenious architects whose design could teach us a lot, their buildings changing daily to fit their function to the prevailing conditions outside and the needs of the community within. And yet there were things going on that required such design to be helped along its way, and that was the secret at the heart of the place, I believe Laiko plotted my course so that I would uncover all the clues to it. It is not his fault I was a slow student that night.

Certainly, one particularly acrid route took me past a chamber more brightly lit than the rest, and there I cowered back because the occupants were not only Termite-kinden, but two of the robed Ichneumon lording it over them, I almost gave myself away with a gasp when I saw what they were doing. Their servants were moving about the components of some great artwork or idol, I first thought: bulbous containers formed of the same refined stuff the sawblade had been made of, connected by ducts and mysterious tubes. I watched, bewildered, until something in my head shifted, and I saw it was not ritual they were about, but alchemy, reacting and mixing unknown elixirs and discussing each result in whispers between themselves. One of their servants was caught by a splash of the resulting vitriol, searing a long blackened streak up the Termite's pale skin. The afflicted man dropped to his knees, head bowed and his body rigid with agony. The Ichneumon's response was to tut in annoyance at this interruption to their studies. The injured Termite was not permitted to go tend his wounds, but another rushed in a moment later to take his place, unwittingly almost trampling me in the process.

I watched longer than I should, because alchemy is one of those odd antique fields much in vogue at the College. Evidence from the Commonweal (where it is still practised) suggests that there is some Apt sense in the study, and yet it also suits the wild mystical minds of the Inapt, so that both, using separate logics, can arrive at the same result. Some say alchemy is the crucible where the first Apt minds were forged.

And so the Ichneumon liked their alchemy. I mentally shrugged and drove myself onwards and downwards until I came to the chasm.

I don't know how far down it went – possibly it was a natural feature of the earth that the Termites had discovered and worked around, but if so its edges had been smoothed and made regular. Probably it served some function in the airflow of the place, and certainly the breath that rose from its depths was hot and sharp in the nostrils. It had been marked on my map, though I'd not understood the notation and, besides, what was a chasm to me?

The chambers on either side were many, and I could only locate the route I needed by finding a bridge that had been marked on my map as something decidedly temporary. There were few stone arches down here, and I had the impression that the living work of the spire required regular remodelling. Then I saw the bridge, a weirdly irregular, skeletal structure against the faint light seeping down. And of course I just flew over it, and so it was only when I touched down on the far side that I realised what it was built from.

Perhaps there would be a permanent earthen span across the chasm here some time soon, but for now the bridge had been constructed from a more fragile building material. It was built from bodies, live for the most part. I could hear them breathing, and just occasionally a tight-lipped groan of discontent. They were Termites, of course, locked together hand to ankle, hand to wrist, even hand to neck. Some of them seemed to be dead, but some instant rigor mortis had seized them in place within the structure. I wondered if they would all die before they could build something more permanent. I wondered if that something more permanent would be constructed *around* their rigid bodies.

Horribly, the analytical part of my brain was already telling me how structurally sound the whole venture was, how artfully designed.

I must have known the truth then, but I shouldered it aside because I had a handsome Beetle explorer to save. Perhaps I told myself that the Termites did this to themselves, sacrificing themselves for the weal of the whole like an Ant battle line making that final charge for their city. We forget, sometimes, that the Mindlinked are individuals too.

And then I was tracking down a low hallway even darker than usual, deep in the earth, and there I found Corvaris Blaze and – I had begun to doubt it – he was still alive.

They had taken him with something of a struggle, or so his bruises suggested, and he was secured direct to the wall with earthen manacles. He saw me only when I was right before him, and his eyes widened, teeth flashing in a heartwarming smile.

"What happened to you?" I hissed, already racking my brains to think of some way to free him.

"Our hosts are surprisingly negative about scholarly curiosity," he told me. "Have you a knife to pick this stuff away?"

"Our hosts are going to sacrifice you or test their acids on your body," I told him. "Our hosts are slave-owners of the worst kind and not nice people." I picked at the hardened earth about his wrists, and my blade skidded off and almost opened his arteries.

"Slave owners." His trapped hands made an equivocating gesture, and of course the Spiderlands has no corner where people cannot buy and sell one another, and perhaps the cruellest of the Aristoi are as bad to their slaves as the Ichneumon were to theirs. But still I had a bad feeling about our current hosts that overshadowed any mere Spider decadence or excess.

My knife was getting nowhere but, a short hunt away, I found a stack of tools of that hard, glassy substance the Termites made. My employer had enquired, and apparently this was annealed out of regular dirt when they were required to work at materials they could not simply shape. Perhaps there was some hard rock down here that had needed clearing, but I wondered if Laiko had sent word to have the implements placed for my use.

Whatever the cause, I set to work with a will, using one of their saws that cut through the cemented earth with agonising slowness, especially in my too-small hands. Blaze had proof of my efforts in a score of nicks and cuts before I was finally able to free one of his wrists, after which he made short work himself of the other.

"Right," he declared, bouncing to his feet with remarkable energy. "How much of night remains to us?"

"I'm not sure it matters," I pointed out.

He grinned that damnable grin at me, melting parts that should have been thoroughly tempered by life experience. "Mistress Fosse, you are invaluable. I invite you to share the next part of my adventure with me."

"Would that be escape from the caves of horror, because I have to go fetch the Doctor…" I started, but he was shaking his head.

"Escape is only a part of it. Escape empty-handed? What would that serve, without any proof to bring back home?"

"Proof of…?"

"This lost civilization, of course," Blaze told me, ratcheting up his grin.

"Well in Collegium we generally rely on meticulously written accounts," I started, although to be truthful my own such accounts were very seldom taken as proof of anything.

"We know better in the Spiderlands," Blaze explained. "Any traveller can tell tall tales, after all, but in the best Conservatoires and the parlours of the Aristoi, one needs hard proof. And hard proof means treasure."

I stared at him.

"You know, golden idols, statuettes, plates of precious metal with vanished histories inscribed thereon, votive jewellery, sceptres, crowns…"

"Have you seen the Termites? They're not exactly decked out in barbaric splendour," I pointed out.

"Well I don't know how flash you lot usually are in Collegium, but in my experience the stuff I'm looking for isn't exactly for day-wear. They'll have a vault somewhere, some deep chamber with treasure in it." He cocked his head. "However did you even find me, little saviour?"

I gave him a potted history of Laiko's help, and he raised his eyebrows. "Splendid. Once we've got the loot, you can guide us back."

"I am not going *stealing* with you," I insisted, somewhat weakly because the daring of the proposition – in his company – was working on me. "I'm not that kind of Fly."

"It's not theft, it's scholarship. These things belong in an institution where they can be properly appreciated." And he flashed that smile at me. "Fosse, I could go alone, you know I could, but I'd rather share the prestige with someone bold enough to deserve it. Imagine what they'd say back at your College if you bring them the bejewelled death-mask of Termite the Third for their collection, eh?"

As a loyal daughter of Collegium, I liked to think that they would tell me to take any such item right back and repatriate it with its proper owners, but part of me suggested the response might vary depending on exactly how bejewelled the notional death-mask was, and besides, here was Corvaris Blaze offering me very nearly an equal partnership, and not insisting on dictating *anything*.

Reader, I said yes. One of my many regrets, but then things were never going to go well in that terrible place, and sometimes it is best to jump into trouble feet first.

Blaze led the way – for a Beetle he had good eyes, solid Climbing Art and a nimbleness even I could learn something from. He was going downwards – not into the hot chasm but down side passages he must have noted before, and marking quick sigils into the wall with one of the tools I had found, to aid in the return. He had a plan, and I think something of the layout had suggested where some treasure trove might be. Did I believe in the buried treasure of the Termite-kinden? I can't say. I was caught up in the dreams of Corvaris Blaze, with no room for my own speculation.

The air currents were stronger here, foul air being expelled through some shafts, sweet through others, to counteract the natural stagnation of any underground chambers with only a tortuous access to the surface. I think I even muttered something about approaching the lungs of the place.

Well, soon after, we came out into a great cavern, lit patchily here and there, but not from shafts above. I saw at last, there, the vessels the light came from. They seemed to be transparent crystals or perhaps jars, set high in the wall, many of them at the mouths of shafts descending still further down into who knew what abyssal depths. I had the sense of a great confusion of movement, and then my senses began to inform me that it was a regular motion, and not just the chaotic bustle, and therefore surely was not made by a mass of Termites as I had thought.

Blaze was already skulking off at a brisk pace, and I followed after, keeping to the chamber edge. The movement – rising and falling and vast complexities spinning about and above us – was a constant nag at my mind until at last I grabbed Blaze's belt and hissed, "Machines!"

He looked at me, and his face was a little haunted. "Yes. Of a sort," he said tightly, and I realised that he could see in the dark better than me, perhaps even as well as the Moths themselves, with that Art some rare Beetles have, and he knew exactly what was around us.

And I had to know, so I stopped and would not be budged until my eyes had parsed what I was seeing, and what it was that moved.

I had been right first time. There was a mass of Termites in the chamber. Or perhaps not a mass, for that implies disorganisation. The Termites were… arranged, as that temporary bridge had been, but these were not simply clinging to one another as scaffolding.

There were great wheels there, and pulleys and levers, joints and complex cogs, and they were none of them made of metal, nor even of the hard stuff the Termites fashioned tools of. They were made of bodies, clasped to each other, or else in constant motion to allow a human form to perform the work of a component. I hear some Assemblers complain that factory lines turn artisans into mere repetitive stampers-out of pieces; I hear agitators claim that each Wasp soldier is no more valued than a cog within a greater machine. These mere metaphors were, within the spire, made flesh. We were seeing a vast machine of a hundred moving parts, and all the parts were men and women, groaning and gasping, and some of them dying and still performing their infinitely menial part of the whole. There were spent bodies on the floor, we saw, and a constant drip of new blood came to replace them, taking up station uncomplainingly within the great arching human device. This was not the pump that powered the air, I saw instantly, though no doubt there were chambers where elaborate assemblages of bodies performed just such a function. I could not even fathom what the host of interconnected bodies was about, until three or so all dropped from exhaustion at once and, in the heartbeats before they were replaced, all the light-jars guttered like dying candles, only to flare up once more as the great generating machine spun up to speed once more.

"We have to go," I told Blaze in a flat voice.

"When we have something worth having had to see this," he told me, and went on scouring the place, looking into each side-chamber, peering up and down where shafts sprang off. And at one of these he paused at last, squinting past a swift-flickering crystal lantern and peering into the depths.

"I see it," he hissed. He tried to get an arm into the hole, but he was too brawny to fit far. "Fosse, come here, can you make it down?"

I never got the chance to try. I never saw what he had glimpsed. Perhaps it was treasure, perhaps just some mirror showing back to him his brilliant smile.

All around us a sound started up, and it came from the living machinery. Every component of that incomprehensible engine was moaning, very softly in their throats, but the combined effect buzzed in my ears and rattled my bones. It was a sound of dread, of recognition. Someone was coming that they feared more than anything, these who you'd think had no worse fate to fear.

"Blaze, we have to go," I hissed, but he was still after his treasure, pushing his arm into the shaft to the shoulder and snarling with frustration.

They could see us, of course. I was guilty of the slavemaster's vice. I had seen them employed as mere mechanism, and had dismissed them as no more than that. But they were lives, they were minds and pairs of eyes, and those minds and eyes were the playthings for their masters. We had been observed.

I should absolutely have taken off then and left Blaze to his fate. I dragged at his tunic collar but he shook me off, and I could see him making new plans frantically in his head, and coming up with one that I knew I wouldn't like. Then it was too late, because in the inconstant light we could see a robed figure coming towards us.

One of the Ichneumon, yes, and quite alone – a small-framed Wasp in a voluminous gown, his face pale and unhealthy in the light. He had no weapons, and though Wasps are surely never unarmed he did not even have a hand directed towards us to unleash their stinging Art. Perhaps, I thought with sudden hope, this stunted offshoot of their race lacked the power that made Imperial soldiers so feared. Perhaps they had lived in mastery of their absurdly abject slaves for so long that they had no idea how dangerous an outsider could be.

And even as he advanced I boggled at that servitude, the utter fear all the Termites seemed to have of these feeble-seeming rulers. How many Ichneumon even were there, compared to what must have been thousands of Termite-kinden?

The Wasp stopped, smiling at Blaze – I had flown a little way off, a little way up, either overlooked or dismissed out of hand.

"You are making quite the nuisance of yourself," the Ichneumon observed pleasantly. "We must discuss how you became free."

"Some other time, perhaps," Blaze suggested, tense as a drawn wire.

"Later, then," the Ichneumon agreed equably. "I suppose we will have to find some more permanent means of stopping you wandering about where you are not wanted, Master Blaze."

Blaze rolled his shoulders. He was grinning too, as though they were old friends passing the time. "I'm afraid I'm a nuisance to the bone, Master…?"

"Intendin Pregon," the Wasp introduced himself. The very cordiality was scraping my nerves like nails on a teacher's board.

"Well, Pregon, it's like this," Blaze said with a shrug. "You've got secrets here, that's fine. I know I wouldn't want the Spiderlands to get a whiff of me here, if I were you. That's not a problem, I can pass them off with some vague nothing about your Termite fellows here, but only if I have something else to distract them. Some keepsake, to remind me that you fellows wanted me to direct my peers away from this little principality of yours."

Pregon frowned, smiling all the while. "You are suggesting we persuade you to go away with gifts?"

Blaze spread his hands disarmingly. "It's practically the Spiderlands way to give gifts to your enemies. Or I'll just keep on being a nuisance."

Pregon took a few more steps towards him, close enough now to be fighting if either man had a spear. "I don't really think we want you to go, Master Blaze. We have discussed the probabilities and we do not believe we will endure a plague of visitors from the Spiderlands, and nor do the Spiderlands interest us. We find them backwards. Your fellow visitor interests us considerably more, both with his generosity of wisdom, and his more tolerable behaviour as a guest. You, alas, are just a nuisance."

It was the first time anyone had ever referred to Doctor Phinagler's 'generosity of wisdom' to my knowledge.

"Like I said, it's in my bones." Blaze was shuffling nearer, toe-length by toe-length.

"We may have to remove your bones," Pregon said, as though this was an unfortunate contingency Blaze had proposed, and he was regretfully concurring.

"I didn't think you were the fighting type of Wasp." And Blaze moved very swiftly, one hand coming up from behind his back and holding the saw I had used to free him, so that its furthest teeth were at Pregon's throat, drawing beads of blood.

The Ichneumon's smile did not falter. "Master Blaze, is this truly your next resort after requesting a bribe?"

"I might have skipped a few on the way." Blaze was very still, utterly poised.

Pregon sighed, a lament at human stubbornness, and then everything disintegrated around us.

Not everything, not actually, but it seemed like that to me. Abruptly all those bodies, which had been in preordained and regular motion, were loosing hold of each other, the entire convoluted mechanism breaking up. I fled for the ceiling to be out of the way of falling bodies and flying limbs, and then all the light died, because that which had generated it was no more.

Everything below was very quiet after that, and I stifled the sound of my own breath as much as I could and clung to the earth above. After perhaps thirty of my hammering heartbeats the light began to return, the crystals flickering dully and then sending out their stuttering amber radiance across the chamber as some other horrible living engine took up the slack.

They were all around him, the Termites that had just been human cogs a moment before. A great mob of them had formed a circle with Blaze at its centre, keeping a wary distance only because he had grabbed the Ichneumon and was holding his saw-blade to Pregon's throat.

"You'll have them step lively now," Blaze told his captive. "You and me are going for a walk."

"Kill him," Pregon said flatly, and I saw Blaze's arm tense, and a shudder go through that pallid crowd. Every movement of the saw drew a horrified inhalation from them. It was not love for their master, of that I was sure. It was not reverence or awe, but the thought of Pregon coming to harm woke some deep dread in them that kept them paralysed, acceding to neither party's demands.

"I said kill him!" Pregon snapped, smile gone at last and frustrated with these fallible instruments of his will, and Blaze overlapped with, "I'll kill him!" and the Termites shuffled and swayed and whimpered and would not move.

The impasse could never have lasted. I was already trying to come up with some plan to sow chaos and give Blaze a chance to escape, but I was not the only one working on the problem. Pregon himself sighed in exasperation, just like a College master with a slow student. "Just tear him apart," he told his people, the sawblade jagged at his throat. "He's not important like the other one." Then he reached up and put a hand on Blaze's own.

I flinched, waiting for the flash of a sting, but instead he pushed. Blaze was tensed to keep him from dragging the saw away from his flesh, but that was not Pregon's plan. Instead his force, and Blaze's instinctive pulling back, sufficed to tear the blade across the Wasp's ready throat, ripping giving him a second fatal smile and showering the assembled Termites with their master's blood.

There was a horrified pause in which Corvaris and the Termites all stared at what Pregon had wrought, and then it was all up for Blaze. They tore him apart, and neither his smile nor his swiftness could save him. They went at him in a berserk throng, and it was not hate or rage that moved them, but grief. Not for their lost master, either, but for themselves, as though Pregon's death presaged some dreadful fate that they would have to bear.

Or perhaps I am filling in the details after the fact, given what I now know.

Anyway, I fled. I shed a tear for Corvaris Blaze but perhaps not so much as I might have done the day before. While I have on occasion found ruthlessness to be an attractive characteristic despite my better judgment, avarice is never pleasant to see, and my respect for Spiderlands scholarship was left rather tarnished.

I spent rather longer than I wanted ascending through the tangled halls of the spire. I had to find my way back to some assemblage of rooms and tunnels that fit the map, and I had a horror of the whole place shifting about me, thousands of Termite hands reshaping the speleology of the place even as I was clawing for the surface, of passages just closing up ahead and behind me, emtombing me forever as part of the nightmarish place.

Then I was at the chasm, with the living bridge twisting and writhing slowly below me – or at least I could only trust it was the same bridge – the same *chasm* even, for I had the impression of the underground reaches of the spire being infinite, just stacked layers of ghastly sights all the way down. But I trusted my rubbing of Laiko's map and followed it up, up towards the air, up towards the light, for some shafts were now definitely delivering an illumination more wholesome than the jittery yellow light of the crystal jars. I had been lost in the bowels of the place for the whole night, and morning came down to meet me even as I fought my way up towards it.

I exploded into our sleeping chamber, uncomfortably aware of the number of Termites that must have seen me in the last stretch, and found

Doctor Phinagler already awake and dressed. His initial cheery grin fell off somewhat when he saw the state I was in.

Surely the call would come in soon to fetch him to Prospectin Jagon, and I didn't want to think of the sequel. One of the vaunted Ichneumon had *died* and I was sure that would be enough to have us both flayed or buried alive or whatever they did for judicial fun around there. So I vomited out a great tangled mess of exposition for the Doctor, trying and failing to encapsulate all the night's nefarious doings into a single sentence: the lights, the living machines, Blaze's death. I gabbled and babbled and, in the end, the Doctor was left looking at me with mild concern.

"My dear Fosse," he said, "I don't mean to call your accuracy into question but this sounds positively hypnagogic."

"I didn't imagine it," I insisted. Even then, perhaps doubts were creeping in. I'd been below ground a long time, which is no great favourite experience of mine. And yet the images were so clear and Blaze was definitely absent. "We have to get out of here!"

"I would ask," a new voice broke in, "that you avail yourself of our hospitality a little longer, Doctor." Prospectin Jagon was in the doorway, Laiko and some other Termites behind him. "I wanted to show you something, actually, and ask your educated opinion." He seemed very pleased with himself. I kept expecting him to send a look my way, to gloat over Blaze's death, but I was beneath his notice, and I realised that he genuinely wanted to show my employer something he was proud of. That enthusiasm was the most human thing I ever saw him show.

"Well, ah, of course, yes," Doctor Phinagler said weakly, and Jagon stepped into the room.

"There has been much talk of having something tangible to take back to your scholars at home," the Wasp said, with no look to me, so the echoing of Blaze's demands could have been entirely incidental. "Your words, and especially your demonstrations, have convinced us that your people in Collegium are indeed advanced and worthy of our time. We will have some more dealings, you and I, and when you are properly prepared as an ambassador, you must return to your people with our words of greeting."

I saw Laiko stiffen at that, going from despondent to rigidly tense. Some subtext of Jagon's speech had passed me by.

"Look here," the Ichneumon said, and one of the other Termites brought forward something. It was a long device, perhaps four feet, most of the length being a slender cylinder, hollow at one end and bloating out into a bulky casing at the other. It looked like a mace crafted by a madman and was entirely of the hard semi-translucent stuff the Termites used for tools.

There was one oddly familiar part of it, though: set into the casing was a little crank handle that was the near cousin of the one on the Doctor's snapbow, that charged the air battery.

Doctor Phinagler stared at the artefact. "In truth, I'm not sure what I'm looking at."

"It is a first attempt," Jagon admitted mournfully. "We have much to learn, obviously, but see." And he took it from the Termite bearer and pointed the tube part at me while energetically turning the crank.

I was still full of the Ichneumon as mystical overlords and the artifice coming from the shackled termites. I was almost too late to see the meaning in that simple turning of a handle. Only the incomparable reflexes of my kind saved me.

The device spat a dart that cut neatly through the air I had been occupying and buried itself in the wall. After a demonstration and a look at the workings, the Ichneumon and their slaves had duplicated a very effective snapbow without access to even basic metallurgy.

His face admitting to no attempt to murder me, Jagon smiled at the Doctor with childhood enthusiasm. "We have some way to go, but I think a closer relationship with your people would be very profitable." And I knew, I just *knew*, that he meant the sort of close relationship they had with the Termites, however their supremacy there was maintained.

Doctor Phinagler wrung his hands. "Well obviously we would be happy to carry your best wishes, but if we're do to that, we really ought to be making a move, vagaries of travel through the forest and the like…"

"Our best wishes, yes." Jagon's smile was now wide enough that I was waiting for his head to fall off. "We would very much like you to carry our best wishes to your Collegium. We think our best wishes would find fertile ground there."

Just as with Blaze, the weird politeness of the exchange was paralysing, as though to take action to save our lives from a fate worse than death would just be unthinkably rude. However, abruptly there were Termites at the Doctor's elbows, not quite manhandling him but ready to escort him firmly somewhere.

"We must prepare you, Doctor," Jagon said happily. "We must bring you into our mystery."

"I'm not sure I want to be brought into –" the Doctor started and then abruptly I was done with being polite. I, little Fosse, was taking a stand, which is a hard thing to do when you're in the air.

I basically just bowled into them in a pretty artless way, knocking my employer and the two Termites in all directions, and then I was gripping the Doctor's sleeve and dragging, as though we could simply have walked out of their past every enslaved Termite in the place. I was shouting, though, and it was Laiko I was shouting at.

"There are only a few of them!" I yelled. "One less since last night, and you must know it! Why do you let them rule you?" It was not exactly the most sophisticated piece of democratic rhetoric, but I didn't have time to get down to cases.

"Enough," Jagon said with quiet authority. At last he deigned to look at me. "You ridiculous little creature," he said. "You are becoming a nuisance." And I remembered from Pregon's conversation with Blaze that a nuisance was the one thing the Ichneumon would not tolerate.

He had more orders then. I saw them on the tip of his tongue. I was for the vats or to fertilise the mushrooms, whatever the custom was. And then Laiko hit him.

The implement was a spade, with wooden haft and a head of that fused earth compound, but the Termites were strong and the edge was sharp, and Laiko just about took Jagon's head off with it.

Utter silence descended. The other Termites were looking with horror at Laiko – and pity too, I thought. Doctor Phinagler was also somewhat taken aback, and a spattering of Jagon's last cut-short utterance was streaked across his robes. Laiko himself was not triumphant, the start of nobody's vengeful revolution. Instead he looked absolutely sick, a man who has put himself under the shadow of some terrible fate.

Only I had the sense I was born with, in that moment. "We move, Doctor, right now!"

Laiko's head snapped up. "I will lead you."

"What?"

"I will take you from here. I will take you as far as I can. Within sight of where the Ant columns move, if I can, before…" The muscles of his face jumped, but there was no word for the expression he was trying to form, and he was too unpractised at them.

But he was good as his word, and he hurried us through the tunnels as though somewhere the sands were hissing through the glass. Other Termites we passed were ostentatiously looking away from us, giving their masters as few cues as possible to track our progress.

"Why?" I hissed, flying at Laiko's ear level. "Why would you do that for us? You owe us nothing."

"You are free," he said simply. "You, especially: free to fly, free to think your thoughts, and from a place where you say everyone is free. The masters will take it all from you, if they can: your thoughts, your words, your home, none of it your own."

"You need to rise up and throw them out," I insisted. "It can happen. It happened in Collegium."

He gave me only a haunted look. "You don't understand," he said. "You can't know how it is. Better you never find out. Just get far from here and never come back."

I had the sense that things were stirring up a treat behind us, but Laiko kept pushing on, and I suspect his kin kept dragging their heels about any plan the Ichneumon might have to recapture us. With daylight visible ahead – an actual exit large enough for Doctor Phinagler to squeeze through – I finally said, "I don't understand. You can plainly resist them, disobey them, even kill them. You just need to kick them out!"

But Laiko just looked at me sadly and said, "Yes, you do not understand."

We escaped into the forest, cutting swiftly across the cleared area around the spires and then dodging away between the trees, heading for... out. We weren't going back the way we came, although we didn't realise that at the time. Instead, Laiko was just doing his best to put distance between us and his home as rapidly as possible.

Towards the evening he collapsed for the first time. It was only momentary, but I saw his eyes wandering, staring at me and the Doctor in bewilderment as though everything was strange to him. Then he was back with us, but by then we were all exhausted, and ended up lighting a fire and sleeping without even keeping a decent watch. Perhaps the fire kept the beasts away, or perhaps it was some other scent we could not detect but that spoke directly to the common sense of the average nocturnal predator.

The next day Laiko was sick – almost greenish in hue and with veins broken in his eyes and cheeks. He insisted on leading us, though, setting such a fierce pace that I thought he was going to kill himself. The spires were only visible in the distance if I flitted up past the canopy, by then, and we had seen no trace of pursuit, yet Laiko pushed us as though the hunters were at our very heels.

As the first shrouds of evening were cloaking the eastern sky (showing that we had in fact been heading due east, rather than north towards the Exalsee shore) Laiko dropped to his knees.

"What is it?" I demanded. "Is there some drug they give you, that you can't do without?" My mind had been working on the nut of the Termites' helpless enslavement, and that seemed to fit.

Laiko shook his head, though. "We would go far, if our masters bade us," he wheezed. The skin about his lips was cracked, with a yellowish liquid seeping there. "If the Alethi did not know our masters for what they are, and were not always on their guard for any unfamiliar thought that came to them, we might have been sent many places. The Alethi are strong, but you have found a toy that might make our masters stronger in time."

I shivered, thinking of the snapbow, and Doctor Phinagler obviously had similar thoughts.

"How was I to know they were *Apt?*" he grumbled, but his expression showed he knew how foolish a question it was. He had made an assumption, and it had been ill-founded. A scholar should have known better and he could not bluster his way out of that one.

And even so, even throwing Aptitude into the mix, who could have thought that the Ichneumon would be able to manufacture a functioning ersatz snapbow so swiftly? What did that say about the scope of their ingenuity?

And none of this answered the question of why Laiko seemed to be dying. If we were Inapt, perhaps we would be talking of curses, but the whole problem was that *nobody* in that spire had been Inapt.

He was shivering and whimpering when we lit our fire, and I asked over and over if I could do anything to make him more comfortable. From the look in his eyes, he must have known that we would not speak again.

In the morning, I stretched and woke, piecing together my recent past as one does. Ah yes, the Aleth, Blaze, the spires – and the Ichneumon! Blaze, dead! Laiko-! And I gasped and sat up and found I was the last to wake. Doctor Phinagler was sitting up, clutching his snapbow to him, though with no intent to use it, his eyes fixed on Laiko. Or what Laiko had been.

I took one look and lost what little remained in my stomach. Laiko's body had bloated out as though he had been in the river for a tenday, but his skin had gone hard as chitin. Hard, and indeed translucent, so that we could see the thing inside.

At first I thought it was some squirming grub, all crushed up within that distended humanoid prison, but then I began to make out discernible features: hands pressing at the inside of the brittle casing, twisted limbs that straightened as I watched, as a butterfly's wings will do when it is out of the cocoon. And features, all skewed within the clear mask of Laiko's agonised face.

With a sharp retort, Laiko split open and, writhing bonelessly, the thing within him shrugged its way out into the air and took a breath. Bright eyes regarded us, and that new-formed mouth pulled up into a pleasant, genial smile.

"As I was saying," Prospectin Jagon told us, "we had hoped to prepare you properly to carry our true message into Collegium, but alas that will not be possible, thanks to deficiencies within our servants." He looked down at his naked, sexless body wryly. "However, please do tender our fond greetings to your colleagues, Doctor. We are delighted to have uncovered such an oasis of enlightenment in the world, and when circumstances permit we will of course arrange a proper visit." He stood, already steady on legs where the residual gore of Laiko was still drying. "Such a serendipitous meeting, Doctor. Such a shame it was cut short."

I expected threats then, or some other demonstration of abominable Art, but Jagon had said his piece and just strolled off into the Forest Aleth, heading unerringly, no doubt, for the spire where his fellows held court. I wondered then how many there truly were of them – perhaps it was just a handful after all, but a handful who lived over and over, body after body, planting their seeds in each generation of the Termites just as they had been going to in Ludweg Phinagler. And even now I shudder, because who knows how that Art of theirs was effected, and whether they had not already started the work on both of us. There might be some germ of Ichneumon in me even now.

I will be brief about the rest: how we came out in the Spiderlands and had a merry time of it evading becoming slaves, wooing Aristoi, offending Spider-kinden academics. I had no wish to end my days chatting expansively with a professional interrogator, but I left written word for after we departed, naming the Ichneumon prominently therein. Perhaps the Spider-kinden's old familiarity with the breed will mean they have some means of countering the reincarnating Art of the masters of the spires.

Eventually we came to Siennis, where old acquaintances aided us to escape to Sarn, as Collegium was even then in fierce dispute with the Empire and some parts of the Spiderlands. It was a poor time to be a scholar, and people were far more interested in the threats of the here and now, than those from the depths of history.

But I have my account, now, for my modest following, and a copy for the College library should that institution be accepting books any time soon. And I will most certainly have a copy for any bold explorer proposing to brave the Forest Aleth seeking lost civilizations, because sometimes they are lost for a reason.

# For Love of Distant Shores

*Being an account of Doctor Ludweg Phinagler's expedition past the western ocean and to the furthest extents of the world, and what he found there, as told by his amanuensis, Fosse.*

Frequent readers of the exploits of Doctor Ludweg Phinagler will no doubt assume, when I say that we were guests of the city-state of Tsen, that my employer had committed yet another grievous *faux pas* back in our home of Collegium; that he had insulted the wrong Assembler, said something incautiously positive about the Wasp Empire or got into an argument with an academic of greater standing and credibility.

It will doubtless surprise you, my familiars, when I say that in this case we were present in that far state for no other reason than that we had been invited. For once, we had left behind neither professional rivals nor any of my own usual detractors, vis jealous wives and sore losers at the gaming tables. It was that brief and rosy time immediately after the Wasp wars had ended – properly ended, rather than that wistful interbellum after the death of Alvdan II which had so much promise and ended so precipitately. Rather, now that the fighting was genuinely over, it was a time of hope and outreach. Collegium was becoming the true centre of the diplomatic world, and there were ambassadors on the streets from places nobody had dreamt of before the war – or at least nobody who had not read my accounts of the Doctor's escapades. I had quite a nasty turn when I arrived early for a liaison at the College and came face to wide-mouthed face with one of the Lake Beetle-kinden from beneath Limnia, a breed mostly unknown to the wider world, and which had attempted to have me vivisected a while before.

The war had widened the world. Whether that was worth the attendant pain and property damage is a matter for the philosophers, but it is quite true that Tsen had previously been too far away to have much

to do with Collegium. As a city-state, we always imagined it as a barren
little place clinging to the rocks of the Atoll Coast. Certainly it was far
enough that even the other Ant city-states didn't trouble it much, save
for some maritime scrapping with Vek.

After the invitation, the Doctor had us pack immediately and even
found the wherewithal to book seats on a flight to the Ant city, rather
than go the long way by ship. I should give a sketch of my employer at
this point, or at least update the image you may have of him.

I look at him now with the eyes of memory, which are never as keen
as the actual. Like most Beetle academics, he came from a College
education and a reasonable store of family money. Unlike most, he had
never been keen on serving out a long apprenticeship being dragged
along on others' coat-tails. He espoused a variety of ideas not shared by
his fellows, and the fact that many of these turned out to be halfway true
had been no salve for his reputation. Every so often he would enjoy a
brief moment when a new crop of students took aboard his teaching and
made him fashionable, but disinfatuation would set in relatively soon.
Somehow, however, he always found the next opportunity, and the next.
He always had a new paper or book on the go when at home, and
whenever home tired of him there was always another expedition. The
academic acclaim he so yearned for never settled upon his shoulders,
though, and I will remark that by the end of the second war he was not
a young man any more, though still robust and energetic as most Beetles
in their middle years manage to be.

As for myself, I am still Fosse, and I was always the Doctor's junior
by some several years. I confess I remain winsome and trim of waist, a
detail I include specifically to answer some of the more alarmingly
personal letters I have received in connection with my writings on the
Doctor's behalf. It is content that he would no doubt decry as being
irrelevant to the business at hand, but he is not here now to edit, and so
I modestly confirm myself still in possession of those charms that have
attended me throughout these journeys.

Vis the Doctor's career, however, and its failure to quite reach the heights that he always imagined, you will appreciate his excitement on discovering that his next expedition would not be some shoestring adventure of his own but that a place had been reserved for him on something that seemed far grander. I myself, having perused the missive, was not convinced that the upshot would actually be that much grander than the journeys he had orchestrated himself, but such was his excitement that there was really no talking to him about it. The truth, in fact, lay somewhere between our diverging expectations.

We flew to Tsen, as I say, and in a hybrid fixed-wing/orthopter based on the Imperial Farsphex machines that had been such a terror to the Collegiates in the early stages of the second war. Instead of bombs, however, this expanded vessel carried us and our modest luggage, together with a pair of Collegiate engineers off to study Tseni engine casings and a Spider-kinden woman with a colossal amount of baggage who was intending a fairly epic fishing holiday.

Tsen itself was not the barren little clutch of huts of popular Collegiate imagination – or perhaps I should say pre-war imagination, because the Tseni had started making quite a showing in the city after the first war, with the upshot that, firstly, everyone became aware that their artificers could match the College's best in many fields, and secondly that their ambassadors were almost always coldly beautiful women who were well aware that flustered male Beetles made lots of mistakes. It was not the sort of underhand tactic one expected from Ant-kinden.

Tsen – as became apparent when we came in to land – was smaller than most of the Ant city-states Collegium was used to dealing with, though. The landward side of the Atoll Coast was indeed rocky, and became practically a desert when you got away from the coastline itself. The city was built on a strip of land that seemed more vertical than flat, resulting in it being less tediously orderly than most Ant domains. Flying over Tsen, I felt as though someone had taken a regular city and pushed it down a cliff. That all the buildings boasted pearlescent domed tops rather than the flat roofs of home also gave the secondary impression of a profusion of mushrooms.

The airfield was on the sea, which was alarmingly novel. There were great floating platforms of wood – not even piers because they were held up with bladders rather than finding footing in the sloping sea-bed. For a regular fixed-wing the landing would have been impossible, but our pilot had the option of switching the orientation of the wings and coming down in a hover. Even then, I thought we would end up in the drink, and the edge of the platform was very close when we disembarked.

I was sorely in need of a wash and a sit down on something that wasn't vibrating with the grumble of a badly tuned engine right then, but Doctor Phinagler was looking out towards the sea, and the reason that part of the world had its name.

Beyond the harbour of Tsen, and making an alarming hazard to shipping for any ship's master unfamiliar with the place (such as invading Vekken navies for example), the sea's implacable reach was ruffled with arcs and points of islands. When the sun struck the waves from the right angle, one could see this was the least of it. The waters beyond Tsen were a maze of structures hanging ghostly beneath the waves until they were lost in the depths beyond. And 'structures' is the correct term, my more pedantic readers should acknowledge, for these were no works of mere geology or weather. Everything we saw was, or had been, living, built up from little cells no larger than my fist. It was as though another city were out there, greater in size than Tsen itself, drowned under the waves, but it was a city architected by and of coral.

Of course, after events in the second war, everyone was aware that cities of coral may be more than mere natural wonders, and in this we were only just catching up with the knowledge of the Tseni. Some distance offshore from Collegium, and at great depth, is a place named Hermatyre, they tell me, and the further sea is dotted with such colonies where kinden like and unlike ourselves live out their bizarre underwater lives and have their own differences of opinion which only seldom intersect with ours. Little did I know that it was our new accommodation with the Sea-kinden that had given rise to the invitation Doctor Phinagler was looking to accept.

Stepping onto firm land, we were greeted with a remarkable profusion of different kinden around the Tseni docks. Like most Ant-kinden, the locals were generally opposed to foreigners, but simultaneously aware of the fiscal opportunities they represented, and while Tsen did not trade much with its eastern neighbours, mostly because there were hostile Ant cities in the way, there was a rich interchange of goods and ideas up and down the Atoll Coast that had grown up almost entirely independently of Collegium's sphere of influence. We saw plenty of other Atollers there – Bee-kinden and Grasshoppers, and a remarkable number of Skaters who brought back all sorts of bad memories of Jerez. There is a marshy town called Cerrith, I am told, in the coast's northern reaches, and the locals just walk the waves to Tsen whenever they wish. At the time, though, we didn't have much inclination to stare at them, because we were staring at the Sea-kinden.

There are frankly dozens of different kinden under the water, with a complex and hierarchical nomenclature that no Land-kinden can be expected to understand. Many of them plainly share common ancestry with drier lineages, and so we could see some who seemed kin to Spiders, others who were like pale Grasshoppers, still more who could be of my kinden save that they were hairless and earthbound. And then there were the Greatclaws, of course – anyone present in Collegium during the liberation will remember them, tall as a Scorpion and twice as broad, lumbering about in their colossal suits of armour. There were Greatclaw merchants in Tsen, if you can believe it, and I discovered then that the armour barely exaggerates their size. I saw them counting the odd bone-looking Tseni coins with their outsize hands, the jutting claws of their Art making even that activity look like a prelude to evisceration.

Before we could get lost in the throng, and probably murdered for our teeth, we were met by the Doctor's correspondent. She turned out to be a rounded Beetle woman of comparable years to my employer, with a well-favoured face only enhanced, in my opinion, by the touch of iron in her hair. She wore Tseni fashions, which were quite elaborate for Ants just then – they had a love of wide-sleeved tunics that went to the knee and had quite a lot of ornamentation at the hems. They liked complex fastenings and buttons, too; hers were of interlocking gears that served little mechanical purpose but were pleasantly decorative.

"Doctor Phinagler! Delighted to make your acquaintance," she called as she approached. "Haile Millern, at your service."

The good Doctor put on one of his broadest smiles, the sort that seemed a bit careworn around the edges these days. He had come in his full Collegiate robes – struggling into them in the confines of the orthopter cabin had involved some interesting gymnastics – and I could not help but note that they had seen better days, too, too much darning and too many stains that hadn't come out. Even so, he drew himself to his full height and mustered that erratic and unreliable charm that has got him – and me – into and out of so many scrapes.

Haile Millern clasped his hand enthusiastically. "Are you up to meeting people so soon after your journey? Only everyone's here and Master Aratean is already provisioning the ship. I'm sure they'd have waited, but it's good you're actually here so quickly. I'd like to introduce you to them, and explain why I want you along."

The Doctor's enthusiastic progress through the crowd slowed so abruptly that he almost got a Greatclaw spike through the back of his head.

"I was given to understand in your letter," he said, "that my place on this voyage was assured." He uttered the words with great dignity, but his eyes flicked sidelong to me, and I knew that he was anticipating trouble. After so many years and expeditions, even Doctor Phnagler was starting to admit that the course of his life so seldom ran as smoothly as it might.

Haile was all assurances, though, and she had with her a pair of impassive Tseni who went off with our baggage, or at least one of them did and the other one just trailed after her looking a little let down by our lack of worldly accoutrements. We ourselves were hustled off and up the incline of Tsen, which to Doctor Phinagler's relief was accomplished by a counterweighted funicular rather than trekking up the steep paths. Indeed, we could see that a great deal of the everyday traffic of the city was so automated, and that the counterweight to our upward journey was a similar weight of Tseni and their goods heading downwards. Tsen as a city made up for its lesser size with considerable sophistication and ingenuity.

Soon after, we were within one of the dome-roofed buildings being introduced to our co-conspirators in this latest and most ambitious voyage. Haile took us into a room unusually decorated, for the Spartan Ant-kinden. The owner had decked it out with charts, taxidermied lobsters and fish, and pieces of ship, as though to remind himself each morning that, yes, he was in fact a man of the sea.

This owner and mariner was Master Aratean – and in Tsen 'Master' doesn't just mean 'someone of any reasonable significance or social standing', but referred to matters naval. Aratean had a ship and a crew, which was important because we were going on the voyage to end all voyages. As noted, the Tseni knew what they were about with boats, and Aratean had invested heavily in artifice to ensure that he had something fit for a very specialist purpose indeed, to wit a long open ocean crossing.

No doubt my readers are lifting their eyebrows even at those words, but humour me, and let me tell the tale my own way. The purpose of this little gathering had been entirely clandestine, and even my employer, who has been known to be over-frank about any given venture he is associated with, had been close-lipped about it. To be sure, this was more because the ridicule of his peers had at last begun to sting through even his emotional carapace, but silence was silence nonetheless. I have a feeling that even Aratean was, insofar as any Ant can, keeping the details from his own people.

Aratean, then, a sketch: a sharp-featured man, taller than most Ants, very lean of face, with that blue-white colouring the Tseni have. He wore the loose clothing Tseni sailors preferred, that could be swum in or go under armour with equal ease, but on the table before him was a remarkable hat, with a peak to shade the eyes, and a high crown decorated with spray of glittering dragonfly wings. This was because only about four in ten of his crew were actually Tseni, and he wanted to be very sure those sailors not linked with him mind to mind could find him in an instant. I assumed this was standard practice at the time, but an examination of other ships on our departure from the harbour showed that in fact it was a conceit of Aratean alone. He was, I will say now, rather fond of himself.

Aratean and Haile jostled elbows a lot over who should be doing most of the talking, but at the time I paid him relatively little heed because of the man standing next to him.

This man looked mostly like a Spider-kinden, but by then I knew the differences to look for – the curly hair, the shape of the ears and the like – so I could tell him for Sea-kinden. I had seen plenty after the liberation, but I'd never been this close to one; at the time native caution had kept me out of the way of their Greatclaws and other martial showing, just in case the liberation was a new conquest in disguise. Anyway, Aratean's friend was Sea-kinden, and he showed the world a visage sufficiently pleasing to the eye that I am afraid I had to reconstruct a lot of what was said from memory and guesswork, when I came to write up the meeting for the Doctor's notes, because my attention was most unprofessionally distracted from the business at hand.

Xerixes was his name, or at least what it sounded like. I eventually, stammeringly, asked him how to spell it, and his response baffled me entirely because the Sea-kinden don't write like we do. They speak like us, of course – it was long-accepted academic doctrine that language is an innate facility that will always develop along set lines, and so the Sea-kinden simply had something of an accent that lent Xerixes an additional exotic attraction. Writing, apparently, was by no means innate to the human mind, and his characters had nothing in common with these letters. Hence you must make do with my spelling or go find your own.

Xerixes was very pale of skin, his hair almost blue-black and his eyes violet. He wore a great shawl about his shoulders, and when he went out into the sun he would bundle himself up until only his eyes were showing, to stop that skin of his from peeling red in the heat. In that room, though, he had it thrown back, and open down his bare chest as well because Sea-kinden have no sense of modesty. He was not too lean, not too muscled, a perfect counterbalance of physique such as a Collegiate sculptor would ache for in a model. When I was, belatedly, introduced to everyone, he smiled at me with teeth white as the moon. He looked, I thought, like the sort of pirate who turned up in certain works of literature that I patronised and of which the Doctor strongly disapproved.

There was another there, Jaq, but to be honest what with Xerixes present, and Aratean going on about the voyage, I didn't really notice him at the time. More about him later.

And Aratean had indeed got a map out. My mind still full of pirates, I half expected it to show lost islands and secluded pleasure palaces, but it was a formal maritime chart and so mostly showed shoals and currents.

"In a handful of days we will set off on a journey that will render this chart obsolete," he proclaimed, which made me wonder why he'd bothered to unroll it in the first place. Still, the sentiment was true, and I will confess to a little frisson of excitement. Doctor Phinagler was contriving to be the calm and reasoning man of letters, but I could see his knuckles standing out where he clutched his robe. Haile Millern then spoiled his pose still further by yanking on his arm like a little girl.

Master Aratean then went on with quite a speech about the venture and his own role in it, and how only Tsen could possibly have produced such a man as he to conceive of the project, but you will be glad to hear that my general distraction vis the members of the group my attention was most drawn to meant I cannot now regurgitate his words wholesale. I will instead summarise and, if we ever meet, you may thank me.

We were sailing west, that was the thing. The thought may not strike my Collegiate readers as it would a local from the Atoll Coast. Let me ask you, what is west? The standard answer on the streets of my city would be, 'Tsen'. So let me ask you again, what is west of Tsen? The sea, only the sea, without end.

Except all things must end, both in time and geographically.

Aratean's curiosity had been piqued years before when he had read the account of an Imperial explorer who had left the Empire's eastern edges and travelled for many months. I vaguely recalled a version of the tale as being fashionable in Collegium between the wars, full of the barbarous practices of Scorpion-kinden, discoveries of lost civilisations and hitherto unguessed-of kinden, just the sort of nonsense that everyone laughs at and never credits. The Tseni were of a more credulous nature, however, for Aratean had swallowed the account whole. Moreover, he had been much taken with the final chapter where the Wasp hero finds the eastern edge of the world, beyond which is sea, only the sea.

The world is round, of course, and Aratean leapt initially to the conclusion that one might put out from Tsen and sail west until one reached the kingdoms and republics the Wasp wrote of, should they in fact exist. The fact that those states were written of as being vastly wealthy doubtless came a distant second to academic interest to him. Now, of course, enter professional cartographers such as Haile Millern, already a student of naval charts and who met with Aratean after chartering her own voyage to Tsen. Millern and her peers found the prospect of such a huge open space of sea a threat to the intricacies of their profession, for the distances were considerably greater than Aratean had supposed. However, they dug up some truly ancient accounts from long before the revolution, wherein Spider-kinden mariners told tall tales about a land to the west they had reached somehow (navigating, of course, by 'magic', if you can believe!).

To simply set out westwards and hope, to those of us not assisted by non-existent supernatural forces, would of course be suicide. The sea off the Atoll Coast, beyond the effective sea-wall the coral creates, is notorious for its ill weather. In the old days, any ship reliant on sail would be turned back or destroyed, and there are records of several that met just such a fate. In more modern times, where a good strong engine might be relied on to shoulder aside the weather, there was the matter of supplies. Ships must carry water, at least, even if it were possible to sustain oneself on the ocean's bounty alone. One cannot drink the sea.

Aratean's innovation came from a long association with the Sea-kinden, having been liaison with their offshore cities for some years. Everyone knew they could breathe the sea through their Art, but I think even the Tseni assumed they could, indeed, drink it. However, imbibing salt water is near as toxic to them as to us, it turns out. They just have some remarkable transformative Art at their fingertips which can do all manner of things, including transmute the salt out of water to leave it potable. A voyage with a willing Sea-kinden would simply draw up barrels of sea-water every morning and have enough for everyone to drink. Living off fish and vitamin tonic, such a ship could go about its business practically forever. Certainly long enough to cross the western ocean, storms and all.

This was also where our guide came in, and I became belatedly aware of Jaq's presence. At first I will say I was not much taken with him, certainly not when he came to stand alongside Xerixes. Jaq was a Skater-kinden from the northern coastal marshes of Cerrith. Just as with the Skaters of Jerez, he had a head and body fit for a Fly-kinden on limbs that set him as tall as Doctor Phinagler, or they would have been if he didn't skulk about with such a crouch to him. Even in the relative stuffiness of Aratean's study he was wearing a coat down to his knees and a curious hat, peaked at the front and worn long down his neck to his shoulders at the back, and the whole of it made of black fishskin the texture of sandpaper.

I did wonder, at the look of him, what service Jaq would be providing for us, and it transpired that he was a hunter. The Skaters of Cerrith were apparently sea-wanderers of note, and Jaq would lead our efforts to secure fish, and scout ahead of the ship when needed. I wondered just how slow the ship would be moving for this to be possible, but Jaq himself didn't seem to find the proposition problematic. I took all of this with extreme scepticism at the time, though a look at Jaq's face began to bring me round. His features were thin and pointy like most Skaters, but they were weatherbeaten and tanned, and he grinned like a man who has known storms and adversity, and triumphed over all of them.

This, then, was our company, and Haile was tasked with securing our place in it. She herself would be the chart-maker of course, but I could not see exactly what service my employer might be providing to the venture. Looking into Arakean's beaky face I had a sinking feeling that Doctor Phinagler was about to take yet another knock at the hands of polite society.

But then Haile spoke up, and she began to tell Aratean all about Collegium's pre-eminent explorer.

I listened, open-mouthed, as she recounted the various adventures of Doctor Ludweg Phinagler, famed seeker after distant lands. She built a picture of a man of intense scholarly curiosity, great erudition, resourcefulness and, above all, a man respected and honoured by his fellow Collegiates, whose account of our voyage would be widely publicised and read by all the intelligentsia. I was most taken by the fact that, from her repeating certain exaggerations and fancies of mine, she had plainly taken most of her knowledge of my employer from my *own* accounts. Later I discovered that she read voraciously when travelling between Collegium and Tsen, and that my work had been some of her favourite fayre.

Looking back on that now, I do wonder if one can be too successful in one's craft.

However, this was enough for Aratean. As noted, it had been just such a tale of travels that had set him on this path, and he clasped Doctor Phinagler's wrist and welcomed him to the expedition. For his part, the Doctor took it all with genuine humility, because I think he had never heard himself described in such glowing terms, or indeed in terms of any luminosity whatsoever, and was somewhat dumbstruck.

As with Aratean's speeches, I will spare you the next two tendays, because maritime expeditions take considerable planning even for the efficient Ant-kinden. The Doctor himself hung about Haile and the ship's Master, and I think he was somewhat surprised at the idea of actually planning something like that ahead of time. For myself, on the reasonable basis that posterity would not want a blow by blow account of precisely how much salted grasshopper meat and how many barrels of honey we laid in, I was left to twiddle my thumbs and acquaint myself with the bustle of the port. I had wanted to better acquaint myself with Xerixes, but he was busy beneath the waves making his own arrangements. The one member of our fellowship I did catch up with was Jaq.

I saw him strolling along a pier, and for a moment I thought he had, so to speak, jumped ship and was going off with someone else's expedition. I flew down to him, which surprised most of the dockworkers there, because in Tsen even the Bees don't fly much, and certainly not as nimbly as I. Jaq just gave me that windblown grin and tilted his hat back a little.

"Off to visit the weather," he told me, with a stronger Atoll accent than anyone else I'd heard, the words blurring and burring into each other. He had a wickerwork coracle on his back, but other than that he seemed woefully underequipped to visit a maiden aunt, let alone anything as abstract as the weather. At the pier's end he even took his sandals off and strung them around his neck.

"That's a very small boat," I told him, rather archly I confess.

"It is not," he said. "It is a very small bed." Again that grin, showing teeth that looked too big for his face.

I stared at him. "How can it be a bed?"

"What else to sleep on when I'm tired, ja da?" He waggled his eyebrows, which made the brim of his hat dance as well. "Be gone two, three days. Back for setting out time, don't you worry."

"I wasn't worried," I told him, being very aloof, and then spoiling it by saying, "but what about the fish, or sea monsters or something. Won't they eat you? Or won't you get just... washed away."

He crouched down and looked at the water. This was a thing he did, I saw it several times. Following his gaze, all I saw was the somewhat oil-slicked harbour waves breaking against the stanchions of the pier. Jaq saw lots of things in water, though. I knew a Mantis once, who could go through a forest and tell you everything that had passed that way, everything about the trees. Jaq was like that with the sea, somehow.

He fished out a fist-sized lump of iron held in a cradle of rope, which seemed to be attached to his coracle. "See?" he asked, and I understood it was by way of a sea anchor, that would provide enough drag to stop him getting too lost overnight. As for the monsters, he just grinned again, and I had to assume that wickerwork was particularly unappetising to the denizens of the deep.

True to his word, he was back in time for our embarkation, though only just, appearing from nowhere and hopping bare-footed up the gangplank even as Aratean's men were drawing it up. He nodded to me with more of his damnable grinning and then folded himself up in the front of the boat, which I was just learning to call the bow.

Aratean was quite the disciplinarian on board, and I was profoundly glad to be little more than a passenger. Doctor Phinagler, Haile and I got to watch the Tseni Master stalking about the deck snapping out orders and condemnation at the non-Ant crew, and no doubt giving his own kinden a similar lambasting within the privacy of their own skulls. I anticipated a mutiny the moment we got underway, but apparently this was all business as usual for boats, and everyone just knuckled down and got to work.

The ship was named the *Tessius* after some Tseni hero whose story I never did uncover. The crew compliment was forty three, of whom seventeen were Tseni, including the engineers. Of the balance, twenty were Bee-kinden from Seym, north up the coast from Tsen, who performed the bulk of the work aboard ship – cleaning, fixing, cooking and the like. The rest were a grab-bag of Inapt, some Spiders, some Dragonflies and Grasshoppers down from the Commonweal. They were no help with the engines, of course, and even had problems with the hatches, but the *Tessius* had sails as well as a propeller, and when the wind was favourable and the weather not too harsh, Aratean would order the mast raised and we would conserve our fuel and run before the wind, with the Inapt up in the rigging. The Tseni and Seymish could sail if they needed to, of course, but it seemed to be received wisdom on the waves that the Inapt simply had a better feel for such things, and that was worth the trouble of occasionally having to let them in or out of rooms.

I will say that the crew was not delighted about the voyage. This was in part because Aratean had not told them where we were going. They discovered fairly soon in that we were about an epic journey of discovery, mostly because a certain Fly-kinden amanuensis happened to let it slip because she hadn't realised it was a secret. This then resulted in a delegation of the non-Tseni crew coming together to beard Aratean in his cabin, and I genuinely thought the entire venture would end in bloodshed there and then, especially as even the Tseni crew were pointedly just standing back and not intervening.

Aratean tried to brazen it out, telling them things they probably already knew about how wonderful the *Tessius* was, and mocking their fears. When his charming personal manner unaccountably failed to win them over, he let Xerixes out from belowdecks to speak. Xerixes didn't like the sunlight on his delicate skin, and he arrived wrapped up like some walking corpse from an Inapt ghost story. It was plain that the mariners had a great deal of time for the Sea-kinden, though, and he explained to them how the water would work, and that every man of them would be famous when we got back to port. He spoke well; his voice was as admirable as the rest of him, in fact, and he won them with honey where all Aratean's vinegar would catch nothing. Soon enough everyone was back to work and happy about it, and the venture was not lost after all. There were plenty there who would follow just from infatuation with the man, I thought. Certainly my own native caution had gone completely to the winds.

Aware of that competition, I went to find Xerixes belowdecks, but it was a very different man who confronted me. He was tucked in with the water barrels in the hold, and everything about his posture suggested abject misery. I dropped down beside him instantly – giving him quite a scare because flight is, of course, unknown below the waves – and was properly solicitous, which I admit involved kneading the soft skin of his hands and looking into his violet eyes.

"I'm sorry," he whispered. "You're very kind. I'm sorry." That collected, confident man from abovedecks was absolutely gone, leaving only sheer vulnerability.

"What's the matter?" I asked him.

"This voyage is a terrible mistake," he said in a very small voice. "Aratean has me. I must do as he bids. But nobody should go where we're going."

My heart and other organs sank, because this was all sounding bleakly familiar from so many of Doctor Phinagler's escapades. "Why?" I asked.

His tortured eyes suggested there was a great deal he wanted to say but could not. "Stories," was all he would tell me just then. "The oldest stories, the oldest enemies."

Then I could hear the Doctor calling for me, of all the luck, and it was cursed hard to grab a moment alone with Xerixes after that.

We weighed anchor at some small islands out beyond the first reaches of the atolls, and if we had not been planning so much of a more ambitious voyage I think the Doctor would have wanted to spend more time there. They were a scattered archipelago of hunched backs breaking out of the waves, each with its own colony of lush foliage and the larger ones with the work of human hands still visible, albeit only ruins. Haile explained that they were widely reckoned to be Spider-kinden work from a very distant time ago, back when certain Spiderlands families maintained some manner of wide-ranging sea empire long fallen into obscurity. They had stocked these islands with beetles and crickets so that any mariner could find fresh meat in these waters, and we took advantage of their antique generosity as generations of sailors had done before us.

Past those islands the open sea stretched to the far horizon and beyond.

I got to see Jaq's scouting soon after, which I had so scoffed about. He would climb down the side of the pitching ship and stand on the waves, riding them as if they were an unruly animal whose ways he knew. He had his coracle-bed on his back and, of all things, a kite in his hands, practically as big as he was. He would hurl this into the gale and hold to the string, and the wind would whip him off faster than the *Tessius* could possibly follow, his Art giving his bare feet a marvellous frictionless quality, with no draft below the watermark to drag him back.

We had many days of long voyage ahead of us before the sea would throw a serious obstacle in our way and despite all those pirate romances, life aboard ship can be terribly dull. I found some small duties to divert myself in keeping watch from the mast-top when the sails were out, though in truth there was nothing to watch *for*. Also, the weather grew fouler and fouler as we made headway westwards so that more often than not we were labouring against the wind with engines only, the mast folded down and stowed.

We did have Xerixes, of course, and he was quite diversion enough. In truth I was not the only one with eyes on him, and several of the younger Tseni hands made their blunt overtures and were rebuffed, along with a Spider-kinden woman who took his affrontery very ill indeed. Xerixes was a curious character. When the weather was overcast, as it was more and more, he would come out on deck in nothing but a pair of pantaloons, with an utter innocence of the havoc he was wreaking on tender hearts. Or else, when the seas were calmer, he would strip to his very loincloth and plunge into the water, holding on to a rope let out behind the ship and enjoying a brief return to his element. Much of his time was spent in the hold with the water barrels, however, transmuting the salt to fresh, and it was there I usually sought him out.

I made sure I was there with some ostensible purpose of my own, usually taking a lamp and making a great show of writing up the Doctor's adventures. I would snort and smirk over various passages of our previous travelogues, and eventually even Xerixes would be forced to ask precisely what was so funny. He was not, after all, made of stone. For my part, I noted how he avoided anyone who had made outright overtures to him, and so let our acquaintance grow like a trained vine, rather than wither like a plucked flower.

After about a tenday of this he would stay to listen to snippets of my past escapades – selected to be amusing and not downright horrifying as so many of the Doctor's expeditions turned out to be, and soon after that I had him talking about himself. What, I wondered, was the hold that crusty old Aratean had on him?

The answer completely flabberghasted me.

"I'm his slave," he explained.

Now, I'd seen the Tseni had slaves, though not so many as you might find in Vek or Tark, say. In my mind, the Sea-kinden were the epitome of freedom, though. I speculated about what mischance could have caused such servitude – perhaps he was a prince cast onto the land by his evil uncle (this was something of what had happened offshore from Collegium, and a hundred variants on the theme were in print all over the city). Or perhaps he had been taken by some sea-floor raiders and dragged up to the markets of Tsen, never to see his kin again… I was getting quite absorbed in my own fictions when I saw him shaking his head sadly.

"Money," he told me. "Just money. My family is poor; those we owe are rich. I was sold to the Edmir of Gorgonis and his officers sold me in turn to the Tseni."

"Sea-kinden have money?"

He frowned at me. "Of course we have money. How else could we trade with the land?"

I racked my brains for reliable information on the undersea people. "You know, we have a sea colony off the coast of my city, called Hermatyre, and I don't think they have money or debts or slaves. They didn't even have anything to do with us land-dwellers until recently." In fact, I recalled that the Sea-kinden's apparently unlimited ability to conjure pure gold from the seawater was causing considerable worries over at the Department of Economics. "And *we* don't have slaves at all." Always the proud Collegiate boast.

He regarded me thoughtfully.

Aside from me, the only individual Xerixes seemed comfortable with was Jaq. He would usually come out to watch the Skater set off on his kite-drawn scouting errands, and he would be there when Jaq came back with lines of fish, some almost as large as he was, to distract the palates of the crew from salt cricket and dried beans. Jaq himself would spend his easy grin on Xerixes, although I will say he directed it more at me, if I was around to be grinned at. When he had time to spend on board I found him stealing up on me like a hunter trying not to spook his quarry, manufacturing odd times to stumble upon me so he could talk of the sea and get me speaking of Collegium. I realised far too late in the voyage that he was stalking me in exactly the same way that I was stalking Xerixes.

I managed to sneak some time with the Sea-kinden every other day or so, while also dancing attendance on the Doctor as he, Haile and Araten sat in the master's cabin and discussed what they might find on that far shore. Aratean reckoned it would be Spiders as far as the eye can see, since they were the great seafarers of the elder age and had constantly been splintering into factions, any one of which might have made the unthinkable crossing rather than remaining to fall prey to internecine struggles. Haile was all for speculating about new lands, terrain that had never known the cartographer's gaze, mountains and rivers to name. She reckoned this land would be uninhabited, too far from familiar shores to know a kinden's tread. My employer's preference was for a country ideally devoid of thriving cities, Spider or otherwise, but marked with the ruins and traces of ancient civilizations, the artifacts and knowledge of which would finally make his name back in Collegium. So the three of them dreamed away the voyage, until the day came that Jaq returned early from one of his scouting rounds with news that the way ahead was blocked.

How could it be blocked? Aratean demanded as Jaq hauled himself hand over hand onto the deck. "It's the *sea*," the Tseni pointed out reasonably.

But soon enough the lookout was shouting, and the call was *Land!* For a glorious moment it looked as though the entire point of our venture would be accomplished in double time and we'd all be heroes.

But the lookout's next call had a querying tone to it, and Jaq was already making plain that what lay ahead of us was anything but firm land. By then the keener eyed among us, such as myself, could already see the shadow on the edge of the waters: a low, flat expanse that ran plain across the horizon, unbroken.

"What is it then?" Aratean demanded, getting his own glass out.

"It is the ship-taker," Jaq said darkly, "the weed."

There followed a slow motion dance of wind, wave and engine as Aratean tried to keep clear of the colossal obstruction ahead of us. *The weed*, Jaq had said, and in its simplest form that was all there was. The currents of the ocean moved in such a way as to congregate here a vast continent of greenish-black seaweed, buoyant upon the surface by virtue of the fist-sized bladders that sprouted from it like unhealthy fruit. It was not just a shallow layer upon the water, either, but great mounds and hills of the stuff reaching greedily for the sun, piled up by the random action of the wash until it was thick enough in many places for a heavy man to stand supported. As we would see.

The same currents that had assembled so great a living colony of flotsam were also determined that the *Tessius* should conjoin with it, and though our engine could keep us clear, fuel was the one commodity which we lacked in infinite supply. For three days Aratean ordered us to push straight north against wind and the prevailing waters in the hope that a far edge might be sighted, and the obstacle circumnavigated. Jaq went out on jaunts ahead of us, although the weather meant that he ended up crossing the actual weed more than the water. He reported no far shore to the weed, and more, he told us that the weed itself was far from being mere a vegetable obstruction. The sea life beneath, he said, was rife and voracious, as might be expected from so great a body of organic matter in the barren desert of the sea. That life extended to the top of the weed, too, and I sat with the others one night and listened to him describe his life or death struggle with a great crab that had tried to make a meal of him. It might have been taken as mere traveller's fancy, save that the pincer he had brought back – and cooked with rare skill – gave substance to his words.

Xerixes was sitting with me to hear out the tale, and his eyes seldom left Jaq, with a kind of wary fascination. I had learned soon into our association that the Sea-kinden was not a warlike or even an adventurous man, but one who liked comforts and pleasant conversation. Jaq made a kind of shadow to his brightness, and there is always a certain attraction in opposites.

"We'll keep north," Aratean decided, then his eyes lost focus and I knew he was hearing out one of the other Tseni among the crew. It turned out to have been one of the engineers, because he grimaced and shrugged – deliberately, for our benefit – and told us, "We need more material for the furnaces. They're omnivores. I had 'em made so. They'll burn fish bones and excrement if they have to, but they'll certainly burn weed well enough. The cursed sea's determined for us to make that place's acquaintance but we'll do it on our terms. Then we'll burn its cursed green flesh until we're clear of it and can switch to the regular fuel."

Docking safely with the weed was no easy matter, for it had no hard boundaries like a landmass, but instead simply dissipated into random fronds the further out one came from its main body. Hoisting sail would have driven us willy nilly into the tangle of it, and the propeller was constantly being fouled by the sinewy strands, so that eventually the crew took turns in the *Tessius*'s two oarboats, rowing into the weed and hauling the ship after.

The weed itself was not, of course, some animate vegetable monster that preyed on ships, but one could be forgiven for the suspicion, for the fronds seemed apt to curl about anything they touched so that, once we were in a position Aratean was happy with, moored precariously to a great knot of weed, there was almost constant activity at the waterline to stop us becoming a permanent fixture. Meanwhile other crew were off hacking away at the substance of the place and sending bushels of stinking, slimy tendrils to be dried out and readied for the furnace.

It stank, my readers, it stank to the ends of the earth. The weed that had lain out of the water any length of time was decomposing, crawling with various maritime species of mite and hopper and overcast with a pall of flies for which I felt no congenial affection whatsoever. I would have been perfecly happy to spend the entire sorry event below decks with Xerixes, save that Aratean had him in the water almost constantly, watching for marine predators that might want to make off with the work details. Which predators, I might add, were most certainly present. Also, of course, my employer decided he wanted to explore.

I tried to put my foot down, but in this case the weed lacked solid purchase for it. Aratean was also highly condemnatory of the venture, saying that with all the work details he could not provide an adequate guard. Jaq promptly volunteered, however, and Haile Millern was apparently coming as well, and reluctantly the Master detailed a Spider-kinden woman named Jandra and a Tseni named Charkus to go with us.

Doctor Phinagler and Haile Millern, strolling over the uneven and slippery surface of the weed, made a very odd sight. He had put on, if not his College whites, then at least a long tunic of that hue which would be hopelessly filthy in moments. Haile wore the loose, sun-shading clothes the Tseni preferred, which meant she sweated a good deal less, though the pair of them were fine candidates for heatstroke in my book. I myself borrowed a broad-brimmed hat from one of the crew, and also flew as much as possible because the spongy, giving feel of the weed beneath me was nauseating.

We nearly lost the Doctor within two minutes, as he wandered left and promptly vanished through what had seemed a solid floor of the weed. Jaq must already have been lunging for him, for he caught my employer's collar, at first nearly strangling him and then nearly denuding him in his efforts to land the floundering Beetle. Despite the prodigious catches he had come back with, I hadn't appreciated just how *strong* Jaq was – those long limbs gave an impression of awkward frailty, but he braced himself like a derrick and hauled Doctor Phinagler back onto more solid footing almost single-handedly.

"Where I walk, ja da?" he advised everyone, and then shot his lean grin straight at me, as though all his heroics had been entirely for my benefit, and otherwise he wouldn't have bothered.

I ended up beside him as he went ahead, watching him test the weed, pushing at it with all his force so that he could be sure a pair of Beetles would not be too much for it to bear. I could hear my employer and Haile talking over the academic mischief of the day behind me, as if they were simply doing a turn of the quad back home.

"So this is you, this business? Or is it just 'im?" Jaq asked me in his barbarous accent. Seeing my expression, that grin came back. "A woman for the horizons, ja da? A love of distant shores?"

"I go where my employer goes," I told him somewhat standoffishly. "If it were me, I'd be curled up at home with a book, thank you very much."

He raised his eyebrows until they were lost beneath the brim of his hat. "I don't believe it."

"That's very forward of you," I told him, attempting to emphasise the social distance between a passenger and a mere hireling of the crew, but then remembering that I was only a hireling myself, truth be told. "You've never seen Collegium, I'd wager." At the shake of his head I continued, "Well then you'd not know how beautiful it is and how nobody in their right mind would ever want to leave it."

He laughed at that, and it was a profoundly aggravating laugh. His cocked eye at my employer made me realise I'd just written off the Doctor and Haile as lunatics.

"Except for purpose of academic research, of course," I added hastily, but then the Doctor exclaimed and was calling for Jaq.

"There, we must go there!" he cried.

I squinted in the direction he was pointing and, for the longest time, could see nothing to distinguish one mound of weed from the others. True, this one appeared a little more angular than most, but that was no doubt the rocks the weed was draped over...

Except there were no rocks, of course. Everything we saw was afloat in the heart of the ocean. Then my eyes re-evaluated what I was seeing and I began to see something resembling a structure, but all made of the weed itself.

"Impossible!" I declared. "Nobody could live in this place, surely." It was more a plea to the universe than to anyone present, though. The Doctor and I had found people thriving, if that is the word, in some very unlikely environments in the past.

"Some castaways, perhaps," Haile said, as Jaq found us a path there.

"Melancholy thought," the Doctor considered, giving her his hand to help her up a treacherous slope of mounded vegetable putrescence. I watched that human contact with some suspicion, for he was not a man given to such gestures by nature. *Has he conceived an affection for her?* I wondered, falling immediately into the parlance of the romances I so like to read. *How very unprofessional.* I would have said that she was not his type, too, but if asked what his type was, my mind generally flitted to a colossal Scorpion woman he shared a tent with out in the Nem desert, and she probably did not constitute a representative sample for the purposes of academic study.

What we discovered there was almost a building. It had walls and a roof, all held up by finely crafted pillars. There were even rooms inside, and a descent into a reeking, flooded cellar space which nobody much felt like exploring. But it was made of the weed, only the weed – and not even weed cut and treated like timber, say, but just the living weed as it lay there, plaited and folded until it made the odd semblance of a meeting hall or something, some weird vegetal Amphiophos for an Assembly of crabs and sandflies. Despite all the indications, I could have been persuaded that some fluke of nature had led to it being there. Certainly it was not the work of castaways from a civilized shore, who would not have thought to build in such a fashion.

"Perhaps there was some ancient kinden who found this place in numbers, Spider refugees maybe," the Doctor mused. "They came, they built, but alas they became extinct, leaving only their relics…"

"Permit me to disagree," said Haile, sounding distinctly nervous. "Ludweg, everything here rots. This place is rotting around us as we stand here."

Doctor Phinagler blinked at her. "Your point...?" he started to ask and then the understanding hit him. This place was nobody's ancient ruin. It would be sludge in under a tenday. Someone had raised it recently.

Jaq had been circling round the doorway, ill at ease, and now he leapt as though stung and shouted, "Out! Get out, all of you," and Charkus the Tseni, who had also stayed outside, began shouting as well. I bolted straight outside, wings ablur, and saw the weed all around us rippling and moving, as though the entire slimy expanse was coming alive.

"Go!" Jaq shouted, and Charkus needed no encouragement, leaping and slipping over the weed back towards the *Tessius*, still distantly visible. I hung in the air, waiting for my employer to emerge.

I saw Jandra at the doorway, a blade in her hand, but she ducked back in despite Jaq's shouts. The weed was shivering and shuddering everywhere, and then I saw it was breaking into separate parts, individual clumps of it scuttling forward on thin limbs, a grotesque melange of human and plant. They had weapons, though: I saw spears with bone heads and there were blowpipes lifted to recesses within the slimy green that might contain lips.

The Doctor and the others were still holed up within the structure, but the Weed-kinden were undaunted – they simply seemed to flow through the walls, parting the woven strands without slowing, and then there were shouts and cries from within. Jaq bared his teeth and cursed, and then he was off and away from the temple – I found I was thinking of it as such, and our presence as some desecration that had attracted primitive ire. I buzzed about his shoulders shouting for him to go back, then saw he was running to help Charkus, who had run into his own difficulties. Some tentacled thing had half-emerged from the water to snare him as he ran, and Jaq reached him moments before he would have vanished entirely into the depths. A broad-bladed knife came out and the

Skater hacked brutally at the suckered whips that had Charkus by the legs, sending a shudder through the monster, which released its prey and disappeared into the frond-clouded murk. That left the three of us some way from the temple, which was the centre of considerable activity.

I got my little glass out and peered that way, desperate for any sight of my employer. I found him soon enough, being hauled out from the temple by a great host of the monstrous plant-people along with Haile and Jandra. Except that, beneath the glass eye of artifice, the attackers were revealed to be less abominable than I had thought, though plainly just as hostile. I saw enough pallid bare skin, enough recognisable hands and feet, to understand that they were indeed kinden, and that the weed constituted a camouflage they had donned and not a skin they had been born with.

Jandra and my employer were both limp, but I could descry no blood on them, and I thought they had simply been rendered helpless by some drug or perhaps a solid beating. Haile Millern was still very much awake, and her voice reached us, desperately entreating their captors, as the three of them were marched off.

"Back to the ship, the two of you," Jaq ordered, watching the retreating mass of Weed-kinden and their captives.

"And you?" I asked him.

"I will see where they go." There was on his long face an expression of utter determination. "I will leave markers, for a safe path. You get Aratean to put together some fighters and follow after, ja da?"

"Ja da," I agreed, because that was apparently a Cerrith way of saying things, and I was caught up in the moment. Worry for my employer took up a great deal of my mind, but enough remained to be struck by just how calm the Skater was, despite being about to go up against locals who were plainly very much the masters of their weedy domain.

Charkus and I did make it back to the ship, though mostly because, by the time we had picked up sufficient of a trail of hungry crabs, Charkus was close enough to call for help mind to mind. Aratean led the rescue party that sallied forth, and the marauding crustaceans were driven off, so that we could relate what had befallen the two Beetle-kinden.

It turned out that things had not exactly been roses and honeydew for the shipboard party either. In our absence there had been an attack by some manner of sea monster – something like a long swimming woodlouse with a single pincer-headed tentacle and an improbable number of eyes, according to witnesses. Which would all have been so much diversion had not one of the crew been snatched by it. Worse, Xerixes had gone missing during the attack. He had been in the water, and crew consensus was that another such monster had plucked him down into the depths and made a meal of him.

I knew I was in trouble then, because the news hit me like a forge-hammer. I stopped, and then I denied the possibility, then I started babbling, and in the end I think I actually threatened to cut Aratean's throat if he did not detail the crew to start trawling the whole ocean for Xerixes or his mortal remains. For his part, Aratean ignored me for as long as possible and then slapped me across the face, which stopped my demands, though it also deepened the considerable dislike I had already developed for him. He was, after all, Xerixes's *owner*. The loss to him was one of property. The loss to me was… Well, I had not realised how much until I felt it.

By then the crew was organised into two parties, one that Aratean would head, to go and fetch back the Beetles and Jandra; the other to stay cutting weed at the ship. The Tseni contingent would all be with Aratean to best employ their link, and he was plainly unhappy with such a division in case the Bees, Spiders and the rest suddenly decided to have it away with the ship, but there was little for it and time was pressing.

I was able to lead everyone more than ably, flitting before them and guiding them as best I could, although there were several nasty moments of sailors plunging through seemingly solid weed into the monster-ridden water beneath.

I got them to the weed temple, though, everyone with swords and snapbows at the ready, watching every hump of weed in case it would turn into one of the locals. The structure was looking lopsided already, deliquescing into the mire.

"Well?" Aratean demanded of me, at which point Jaq popped up from precisely nowhere, nobly sparing me the admission that I had no idea.

"They 'ave taken them to some kind of village," Jaq explained. "They were making a place to keep them, last I saw – or perhaps it was a court, to try them."

"Making?" Aratean asked him.

"Just folding it up out of the weed. Quite the craft they 'ave 'ere," he explained. "They need some place for business or pleasure, they just twist the weed about until they 'ave it."

"If they're going to that effort, they're not about to just kill them out of hand," I put forward.

"Maybe they're making an abbatoir," Aratean said darkly, displaying the limits of his dingy imagination. "How far?"

"Some ways, quite a trek," Jaq admitted. "For me, not long. For you, I will 'ave to find the winding path, ja da?"

"Just lead," Aratean growled.

Jaq set off, and it was plain to see what he meant about the timing. His Art let him skip over the weed whether it was solid or not, and he was constantly ranging ahead and back, guiding us to where the massed weed was solid enough to support Ant-kinden feet, or away from where some monstrous denizen was lurking.

"Who are they, Jaq? What monsters live in such a place?" I had the chance to ask him as we clambered over a particularly solid tumour of knotted fronds.

He gave me a sour look much at odds with his usual grin. "Unfortunately I find that they are of my own kinden."

I stared at him, but only for a moment. It made a lot of sense, when I thought about it.

"I 'ad never 'eard of such a thing," Jaq explained. "But there must 'ave been some band of my folk swept far out to sea, long ago. Probably they 'ave no memories of my 'ome, or any other kinden. This is their world now."

I told him about Xerixes and he hung his head and squeezed my shoulder sympathetically. "That is a poor thing, Fosse, a very poor thing. But for now, we must remember those we can save, ja da?"

So I resolved, and even cadged a dagger from one of the Tseni, determined in my grief to put it to good use. In this belligerent frame of mind, we came within sight of the weed village.

Whatever I had been expecting – and mostly that was squalid drudgery – this was not it. I've mentioned that the weed continent as a whole remained afloat by the presence of ubiquitous air bladders, hand-sized or smaller. Here we had evidence that they could be made much larger by some applications of aquaculture unknown, and made rigid too, even when the pressure of air within was released, for that was what these Sea Skater-kinden used for dwellings. We beheld a fearful number of then, a hundred house-sized bladders at least, scattered in a broad-ranging polis all about the weed. In shape the community was a ring, and in its centre a kind of amphitheatre where one of their temple-like buildings had been raised. That, Jaq said, was where the captives were being held.

Aratean's eyes flicked over the panorama and then his people were on the move, fanning out to make a line, and most with snapbows to hand, an innovation that the weed people would have no familiarity with. I think his plan – not shared with those who couldn't read his mind – was probably to drive away the locals for long enough to effect a rescue. Jaq was murmuring in his ear, long fingers sketching out angles of attack and patches of safe ground. So prepared, we advanced with Aratean holding the leashes of his countrymen and adjusting their lengths based on Jaq's advice.

We were never going to achieve a surprise attack, and as we approached there was a sudden flurry of motion about the town. We saw thin-limbed figures casting spidery shadows from within the bladders, and then there were Skater-kinden issuing out, armed with their spears and blowpipes – and some of those spears were bone and shell, but others looked to have bronze heads, which should have set me thinking save that I was wound far too tight by Xerixes's loss. Not clad in camouflage, they seemed less strange and less savage – smaller than Jaq (though most Skaters were smaller than he) but with the same disproportionate limbs and pallid skin, mostly shaded by garments like hooded shawls that fell to their bony knees.

Aratean did not falter, which meant his people didn't either. He formed them into a shooting line, snapbows at the ready and drawn swords at either end. Jaq had a pair of hatchets out, ready to wreak all the havoc that long arms and mechanical advantage can deal, and I had my dagger clutched so tight my knuckles were pale as a sick Wasp. Violence was strung taut between us, waiting to see who would draw first blood.

"You have something of ours," Aratean called out.

"You are trespassers on our land," one of the called, an older-looking Skater woman wielding a hook-ended polearm.

"Tsen goes where it will," Aratean declared contemptuously. I forebore to add, *So long as the Vekken aren't already there, or someone else with better soldiers.* The heat of my anger was cooling somewhat, seeing all those lean, pale faces and sharp spear-points, and also my opinion of Aratean, as a warmonger frustrated with a lack of enablement by the current Tseni establishment, was becoming more firmly cemented. Tseni foreign policy was more ruled by the diplomat than the tactician, after all, and perhaps Aratean had grown up on dreams of martial achievement that had soured with middle age.

"They're coming," Jaq said, quiet but clear. The Sea Skaters were indeed bunching together for a charge, and the snapbows would kill a lot of them, and then hopefully they would break and run away or we would be in trouble.

At this point Doctor Phinagler walked jauntily out from the central building, clad in nothing but a weed-woven towel somewhat low-slung about his hips, and stopped, mouth open a little, standing directly between the battle lines.

"Um," he said. "Hello."

The Tseni shooting line shuffled awkwardly, which I took to be the sign of some internal apoplexy on the part of Aratean. At last the Tseni master snapped out, "Get over here, man! They'll kill you!"

The Doctor peered a little myopically at all the spears being directed past him at us. "I wouldn't have thought so." Then he frowned at the snapbows being directed past him at the locals. "Haile, something's going on!"

Haile Millern and the Spider Jandra also emerged. Haile was similarly hastily draped in wrappings that left little to the imagination. Jandra was still in her grimy, weed-stained sailor's greys, and she had her sword at her belt.

Jaq strode forwards hastily, before Aratean could decide that it would be a shame to waste a perfectly good shooting line no matter what the facts. The locals eyed him curiously, seeing a man of their own kinden amongst our number.

"It is good to see you well," Jaq called, for everyone's benefit. "Plainly there 'as been a misunderstanding. We 'ad thought you in mortal danger, given the manner of your accepting their... 'ospitality." He cast a sharp look back at Aratean, and the sailors slowly lowered their snapbows, though they kept them ready and to hand.

"Well I suppose that's to be expected," the Doctor said mildly. "They were a little angry at first, but we talked a bit and now we're getting on famously."

"Then what were you doing?" Aratean demanded. "Why didn't you come back to the ship to let us know?"

"Well the ship, yes, exactly," Doctor Phinagler said, so vaguely that I thought Aratean would convene a new shooting line just for him. Thankfully Haile stepped in to clarify, saying "We knew the *Tessius* needed to get through the weed, and we were just negotiating with the Argyrin here for safe passage." The Argyrin apparently being the locals, which made this township Argyre by my reckoning.

*That* at last got through Aratean's frustrated pugnaciousness. "There's a way through the weed?" he asked, because it seemed almost impossible.

"They can open one," Haile explained. "Or rather, *they* can't, but their allies can." Seeing our blank looks, she smiled. "Sea-kinden, Master. This is the sea, after all. There are several colonies of them on the sea floor below. This isn't just some lone village or," and here she cast a fondly exasperated look at the Doctor, "lost civilization. There's a whole federation of different city-states here, the Saragassum, they call it."

More Skaters were coming out of the central building, some clad and others as impromptu as the two Beetles. I discovered later that the Skaters of Saragassum talked matters of state in the bath, or at least in weed pools that they heated by some alchemy we never learned. Doctor Phinagler was full of praise for the idea and proposed recommending it to the Assembly, but I managed to talk him out of it.

And you will have guessed the sequel, for when we arrived back at the *Tessius*, there were the Sea-kinden, already half clued-in on what was happening. Some were what they call the Onychoi, meaning both the huge Greatclaw types in their colossal shell armour and also the little Fly-kinden-sized variety (rather demeaningly called 'Smallclaw' I understand), but most were the Spider-looking sort, known as Krakind or some similar appellation, and amongst them, having brought them to the aid of our ship, was Xerixes.

I flung myself into his arms, I confess. Right there, before everyone. He was very busy accepting a multitude of congratulations but he spared the time to hug me back, before going on to throw his arms around Jaq for, I felt, slightly longer.

The Sea-kinden could make a channel through the weed, it appeared. We had to trade quite a lot of what we had on board to both them and the Skaters – mostly things they hadn't seen before, wooden barrels, one of my notebooks, some furniture from Aratean's cabin, all manner of things strange to them but commonplace to us. One of the crew tried to barter with metal tools and found himself laughed to scorn because the Sea-kinden could manufacture far finer, by some means of their own that never saw a forge. The Skater elders were a shrewd bunch who knew just how stuck we'd be without their help, and drove us hard in negotiations.

Still, mostly through the easygoing mediation of the Beetles, it was all resolved without Aratean storming off too many times. Soon enough we were back aboard the *Tessius* and it was being towed by a huge octopus through a kind of canal opened up in the weed.

Xerixes had gone back to his duties belowdeck, applying his Sea-kinden Art to barrels of salt water. I went down, full of good humour, in the hope of an exchange of adventures, and discovered him very melancholy indeed.

"Fosse," he said quietly. "I can talk to you, can't I?"

I assured him he could, and we checked to ensure nobody was eavesdropping.

"I hate myself," he told me. "I'm such a coward."

I didn't understand, and said so.

"There are cities below," he told me. "Cities of shell and coral. There are Pelagists who travel to a hundred other places, north and south. The clutch of my home and its debts doesn't reach here. I could have found a place."

"And not be a slave," I realised.

He nodded miserably. "I ran away. I found my people. I was going to stay, but... but I didn't know how it would be. I have no family here, no place. What if it was just one type of slavery for another? I was... I was scared, Fosse. I know how hard my people can be, Why should these be different?"

"So you came and saved us," I said, putting as bright a gloss on it as I could.

"You'd already saved yourselves," he told me dispiritedly.

"That's not how people see it. That's not how I see it." I took my heart in my hands. "Or him."

The ray of sunshine that came to his face felt like a knife wound, but all the same he was happier, suddenly. Surely that was worth dashing a girl's dreams.

"He's only got eyes for you, though," Xerixes said, still smiling though.

"Nonsense." Although Jaq's cursed grin did pop into my head right then. He cast it about a lot, certainly, but perhaps I was the beneficiary more than most.

I broke out a flask of some kind of cherry spirits that Aratean didn't realise was missing from his cabin yet, and Xerixes and I solemnly toasted the idiocies of the human heart, whether on land or sea.

From there, once the weed was behind us, it was open sea for more days than I care to count. We did not starve nor die of drought, thanks to Xerixes and Jaq and the better fishermen of the crew, but dying of boredom was certainly a danger. Doctor Phinagler spent much time up on deck with Haile Millern, conducting what I reckoned was an affair so academically dry it probably came with footnotes. Certainly their discussion, when I loitered close enough to overhear, was entirely on matters scholarly, discussing diaspora patterns of the different kinden and whose footprints we might find in the new land, should we ever see it. Haile was still confident we'd find none, that nobody in history had ever travelled as far as the *Tessius*, but in this I reckon the Doctor had the more experience. People would find a way to live anywhere, he said, as the Saragassum behind us evidenced.

Xerixes was growing more and more jittery the further west we got, and eventually I had to beard him about it. Apparently the Saragassum Sea-kinden'd had Things To Say about the direction we were planning on travelling. Specifically, they didn't go far towards that point of the compass, not even the 'Pelagists' who were apparently their great travellers. North and south, deeper into trenches of the ocean, all of that, but westwards was a direction laden with bad stories, for them. They said that way belonged to sea monsters. I laughed at that, because sea monsters to me were the everyday livestock of the Sea-kinden, but Xerixes was not laughing.

"There are things in the ocean that hate us," he told me soberly.

"Us meaning your kinden? Or all Sea-kinden?"

"I think all kinden, all of us," he told me. "They are our enemies, from birth. They kill us where they find us, or we kill them."

"What are you talking about?" I demanded. "Crabs? Giant squid?"

*That* made him laugh, though weakly, and after all what is a crab but a tail-less scorpion of the sea? What is an octopus but a slug with hands? They were the cousins of familiar land-beasts that I might see anywhere in the known and settled world.

"Menfish," Xerixes said, which gave me a very curious picture of some bizarre and uncomfortable halfbreed.

"If it's dangerous, have you told Aratean?"

He nodded sourly. "He said to say nothing."

A little spark lit in me, that he would take me into his confidence despite the prohibition, and yet I was frowning at the circumstances of it. "Xerixes, does Aratean... *beat* you?" Because he seemed to shrink from the name whenever I uttered it.

"No, no, it's just... I was in a poor way, when he bought me. I remember... they kept us in filthy water. We were the dregs, those nobody cared about. Sold onto the land was the worst fate for anyone. It's so dry your skin cracks, your eyes hurt. It's too hot, it's too cold. You're always thirsty, never comfortable. When he got me, I had... sores, worms," His eyes were fixed on me, waiting for the revulsion, and I held my face very steady. It was hard to credit, in all honesty. He was such a feast for the eyes. Yet it must have been true and, in admitting it to me, he was as vulnerable as anyone I ever knew.

"He beat me a little, at the start, so I wouldn't just sit there," he explained. "But I made sure I gave him no cause, after that. And he's not a bad master, now. He values me. I've a place with him. If I went back... it would be worse. And probably it would be worse at Saragassum. It must be, for someone with no kin, no place, no skills. I'd die there. I would."

I listened to him brick himself back into servitude, telling himself any alternative would be worse. Probably it would be kinder to leave him like that, but the Collegiate in me kicked my sense of social right, and I said, "He's not a good master."

Xerixes looked at me sidelong.

"He might be a better master than others, but there are no good masters," I explained. "Because the act of owning another human being is bad, as a matter of fact. Any slave owner, even the kindest, commits a grievous wrong every day by not releasing their slaves. If they need their work, then pay them as servants. No exceptions, no excuses."

From his wondering look, I could tell that Collegiate philosophy would be as poorly received in his aquatic home as in Tsen.

A few days after that conversation we sighted the islands. Little did we know it, but we had reached the edge of our world.

They called it the Ikerisen Nauarchate, a tiny state of perhaps a thousand people split over a string of sixteen islands seemingly almost close enough to step from one to another. The wind was apposite so they saw our sails long before we arrived; I suspect they didn't know what they were looking at, but we found them waiting with good natured curiosity, lining the golden beaches of their home, with the trees of their orchards waving gently in the background. We could see little nests of buildings scattered all over the islands – low structures of cemented sand, elaborately worked with abstract shapes of land and sea on every surface, as though their artistic expression was pressing at the boundaries of the limited space they had.

I don't know if Aratean had harboured any thoughts of waving a snapbow around and taking things by force. Since the face-off with Argyre he had seemed like a frustrated man spoiling for a fight. At the time, an amicable arrangement with the Skaters and their Sea-kinden had been the obvious right choice, but I'd heard him muttering about it later, saying that our superior weapons would have prevailed and we could have got more from them for less, for all that what we gave away was commonplace to us. Now here was a more conventional community and surely he had a thought of playing the conqueror with them? However, a good look through the glass at the calibre of the locals must have dissuaded him long before we dropped anchor.

They were Greatclaw Sea-kinden. Not a one of them there was under eight feet tall, and many seemed almost as broad. They were not in their suits of armour, but that just let us note their vastly powerful physiques and the Art claws that curved forwards from their knuckles.

They had received no visitors in living memory, or even in their stories. They welcomed us relatively calmly, given that, but they could not imagine who we were. They had tales of coming to the islands from elsewhere, but those tales themselves had become hopelessly corrupted. They did not talk about seabound ancestors, but placed those precursors on some other islands to the east, seeing the whole world as a reflection of their little territory, islands all the way down. When we told them stories of the continent we had left, its cities and kinden, they nodded and plainly took it all with a great pinch of sea salt. Their belief in *us* seemed limited to the brief span we stood before them, and I could imagine a great tide of scepticism sweeping all memory of us away the moment we left them.

When Xerixes spoke of their actual kin on the Atoll Coast and across the floor of the sea, they laughed openly, taking it as a joke. We were at a feast, at this point – guests of the Nauarch, a huge, hearty woman whose laughter shook the curved, carved ceiling. They fed us with twenty kinds of fruit, nine of which we had no names for and all of which were delicious. They fed us fish and shellfish too, though all shallow-water varieties by Doctor Phinagler's estimation.

Xerixes, standing, looked about at the Greatclaw, frowning. "But surely you have colonies off your shores?" he asked, and I could hear the echo, *Surely this isn't it?*

Now they weren't laughing any more. The Nauarch leant forwards imperiously. "We know the water is death," she said, "and you are fortunate to have reached our Nauarchate without mishap. Any vessel that sets out beyond the shoals is marked for destruction."

Xerixes teased the truth of the situation out of them slowly, more slowly still because he could hardly believe what he was hearing. They had no great ships like the *Tessius*, these Sea-kinden, but it was not because they had better methods of traversing the ocean. They had only small boats to cross between their islands, journeys of a single step that seemed to them to be a great and perilous undertaking. They did not seem to have the Art that would let them breathe the water, that had once been their birthright.

They did not even *swim*.

Aratean, somewhat sozzled on bowls of their excellent fruit liquor, announced that he would split the western horizon in his search for the true land that must be out there. The Nauarch and her people were horrified. It was not fear for themselves that made them protest – they kept their feet dry, so there was nothing we would stir up that could come back to bite them. They took his declaration as a suicide's note, though. There were beasts in the western ocean that would destroy any boat, devour any man. They had been placed there as guardians to keep people from islands beyond, where the monsters' masters dwelled.

It all sounded like Inapt twaddle to us, and even the Inapt amongst the crew like Jandra found it all very quaint. None of us listened as well as we might.

We stayed as guests of the Nauarchate for two nights, by which time it was plain that we would be exhausting their hospitality and supplies should we impose on them further. The Nauarch and her people had continued to try and dissuade Aratean from his course of action, and, finding him resolute, on the night before the morning of our departure they held a remarkable ceremony. Specifically, they held a funeral for our ship's master, which he had the unusual opportunity to attend in person. They made a small boat out of the great flat leaves of the local trees – a toy, really, too small for a real body – and launched it out to where the current and wind would take it westwards, and then one of them used a sling to send a hot ember out over the dark, calm water until it struck the boat, which was soon burning fiercely upon the waves. The whole event was a weirdly magical experience, which is not a word I would use lightly. The water was very calm, almost like a mirror for the stars to look at themselves in, so that the red eye of the flying ember was doubled, and the flames that reached for the sky were simultaneously reaching down for the depths. And then Aratean and the rest of us were dead to them, a lost cause given up on, and we spent that night aboard ship and none of them turned out to see us off at dawn. Inapt twaddle, as I say, but I think most of us felt a little trepidation as we set our course westwards. Xerixes, who really was Inapt, was convinced we were all to die.

His mood was not improved when the Menfish began to make a showing.

My lurid imaginings aside, when they first showed up none of the sailors paid them any heed because they did *not* have the bodies of men and the tails of fish. I had been influenced, I suspect, by carvings I'd seen in Khanaphir and the Nem, of fantastical creatures with the lower parts of centipedes and scorpions and the like, and the upper halves of loyal Beetle servants to the ancient Masters of those places. But Menfish looked like fish, mostly. Only when Xerixes came on deck and declaimed them for pure evil did anyone start looking at them more closely.

There were quite a few of them following the *Tessius* by then, apparently in shifts, keeping up effortlessly with our labouring engine. They were the size of a human, sleek grey fish with a curious twist to their mouths that made them seem to be smiling cheerfully at us. They made odd sounds, too, in a manner that actual fish themselves are not known to do. The sounds were complex enough that sometimes I almost fancied they were talking to one another in some unthinkable language all their own.

They would not take baited hooks nor let themselves be snared in nets, but simply swam alongside the ship for hours at a time, coursing along the surface of the water with such bounding energy I half expected them to take wing (as some fish do, the sailors say). Soon enough, the novelty of their presence had worn off and the sailors ignored them. Only Xerixes could not, and he grew more and more upset at their continuous companionship. He would not go into the water for any money, and swore that the creatures somehow intended us harm. I did not laugh, and nor did Jaq, but a great many of the crew did. The Menfish were down there, after all, and we were up here on deck. What were they going to do?

Then one night they did something.

I woke from my hammock, an innovation which I found delightful and which the Doctor, with whom I shared the cabin, fell out from at least once a night. I thought it was just such a disturbance that had startled me from sleep, but instead I found him still hammock-bound, his head cocked as he listened. There was some manner of commotion from up above, unsual in a ship with so many Ant-kinden.

Then we both heard it, the high, clear cry of the Spider woman on lookout. "Land! Sighting land! Reefs and shoals!"

"Impossible," the Doctor muttered, but he rolled from the hammock onto the floor and struggled into yesterday's robe. I was already in the air, belting on a tunic. Together we burst out onto deck along with Haile and Xerixes into a rain-lashed night, the ship pitched at an alarming angle by wind and wave.

Aratean was already on deck and bellowing over the squall at the lookout. "What land? Where?"

"I saw a reef ahead, or an island," came her voice. The mast was down, so she was standing on the very prow, trusting to her Art to cling to the bowsprit as she kept watch. No doubt Aratean would have preferred one of his kinden, who could have shown him exactly what had been seen, mind to mind. Ant eyes were poor in the dark, though – worse than Spiders', worse than mine.

"I see none!" came a shout from one of the Dragonflies, and moments later Jaq's rough voice echoed it.

The ship was coming about, though, so doubtless Aratean had decided to be safe and called down to the engine room to turn. Even as he did so, though, Jaq was calling out, "Land! Island ho!" and leaping to the rail at quite a different quarter.

Aratean stomped up to him. "What land? We're in mid-ocean!" A moment later he cast about, and one of the Tseni sailors started letting out a weighted line into the water for a sounding. Everyone clung to the rails as we waited, and I saw Jaq grind his teeth in frustration for no others had seen his supposed island. For myself, I stayed in the air, riding the wind and making it my servant, clawing for a higher vantage to watch out for reefs.

"Just a wave," Aratean decided, informed by his crewman. "The sounding doesn't touch bottom at all. Too deep here for islands or reefs."

Jaq was about to answer, and none too politely, when his eyes went wide and he was pointing again. "There!" he cried. "Land, as I am living…"

I was quick enough to follow his gaze, and I saw there a great rounded rock that seemed to roll against the surf breaking about it. In another moment the waters had covered it, and our keel was making swift progress for where it had been. I added my voice to Jaq's, and for a moment even the keening wind could not be heard above our arguing over where the rocks were and how they could be there.

Xerixes was trying to tell us, but we were all bellowing over the wind and he was a poor shouter. Only when I saw his mouth wide as it would go, trying to yell in Aratean's ear, did I realise his voice underlay all of ours and he alone knew what was going on.

"It's not rocks!" he finally made us hear. "It's the Menfish!"

"Don't be ridiculous!" Aratean snapped at him, batting him away, but even as he did so I saw that great black bulk surface, not thirty feet out from the rail. I saw spray gout from it, and then it ducked down and vanished into the sightless depths, and Founder's Mark, it was as big as the *Tessius*, an emperor of Menfish beside which the rest were just minnows.

I came down quickly, tripping over my own words as I tried to back Xerixes up. Aratean was having none of it, angrier and angrier as neither of us would just go away. Then the bottom of the ship ground against something, just as though we had passed narrowly over a sandbank, and everyone was abruptly silent, listening to the groan of the riveted hull.

Then there was nothing but the wind and wave, and I saw everyone there start to relax, everyone save Xerixes.

I made my decision, dropping down beside my employer.

"Get below," I told him. "You too," to Haile Millern. I could see a near future where clumsy, well-meaning Beetle-kinden would be tumbling over the rails into a hungry ocean.

"I really don't think…" the Doctor started, and then the ship shuddered again as something shoved against the port side, just an inquisitive nudge really, but it made every plate and timber moan.

"We really should," Haile Millern decided briskly. "Ludweg, perhaps you'd accompany me?"

"Perhaps I will," he agreed. "Fosse…?"

"I can be more use up here," I told him.

"Be safe." Haile was already dragging him to the hatch. "Be careful, Fosse! No heroics!"

Aratean had his people on deck now: Tseni armed with snapbows standing at the rail, staring into the obscuring immensity of the sea, that could hold all manner of monsters. I saw plenty of the little Menfish now, leaping and dancing on the surface of the ocean, grinning implacably at us.

"What is it?" Aratean demanded of Xerixes. "It can't be a *fish*."

"It is," the Sea-kinden insisted, and surely he ought to know. "The greatest of all fish, and it hates us, Master. It hates all of us, just for being."

Jaq bundled past me. I saw he had his cap on, and a fistful of spears. There was a speculative look on his face as he crouched at the rail.

"You can't," I told him, coming down too fast just as the sea was shoving the deck up, and ending up almost biting my own tongue off.

"You care?" He grinned again.

"Enough not to want you to die."

"But this is what we do, ja da? We make the sea work, if it wants to have us."

Then the Manfish hit the *Tessius* amidships and the time for pleasant conversation was most definitely done.

I had just been lifting off into the wind, and so the great hammerblow the ship took didn't touch me. It was as if the world had suddenly shifted beneath me, as abrupt and surreal as a dream-change. The *Tessius* went from upright to heeling over at a truly alarming angle, and I saw men and ropes and a scatter of loose objects bounce along the deck. Several of the crew ended up in the water and I was only glad I'd got the Beetles belowdecks before they too had gone to meet the Menfish.

I think a wooden vessel might have caved at that blow. I think the Manfish got a rude surprise as it encountered the reinforced steel of our hull. Nonetheless we nearly capsized entirely, and that would have been the end for every one of us because we were too far from land for even my wings to rescue me.

And yet the physics of buoyancy asserted themselves and I saw the far rail, which had vanished beneath the clawing waves, re-establish itself in the air as the ship found its balance. I zipped out over the water, looking for our crew, and caught sight of Jandra, the Spider who'd been caught by the Argyrin. She was striking out for the ship, where ropes were already being flung out into the water, but she was a ways out, and I saw the rounded backs of Menfish surface and vanish near her, with a brief glimpse of their unkind smiles and cold eyes.

I do not like the water. I did not like deep water long before the Doctor dragged me to Lake Limnia and I loved it far less after, and Limnia was like a cup of spit compared to that ocean. Horror was crawling in me, telling me to get back to the ship where I might find some cupboard to hide in, and yet be safe.

Sometimes there really is nowhere safe.

I dived for her, and she saw me and thrust up an arm. I could not have carried her above the water, but I could speed her through it, and I clasped her hand in both of mine and threw all the strength I had into my wings, hauling her towards safety. I saw one of the Tseni, further out still and floundering, suddenly cry out and thrash the water – dark and growing darker all around him. He was crying out for help, and there is precious little to make an Ant call aloud. Then he was gone, yanked down beneath the waves, and there were only the fins of the Menfish, like curved blades quartering the water where he had been.

I looked down into Jandra's eyes. We were almost at the *Tessius*'s side but I think neither of us believed we would make it.

Then the great Manfish surfaced right beneath me, so that for a moment I was standing on its black, lumpy hide, scrabbling for footing with Jandra a weight at the end of my arm. She was fighting for purchase, trying, I think, to use her Art to scale the beast's side. I saw her skin raw and bloody from the shells and barnacles that studded the thing. The Manfish had learned its lesson about a direct strike against the *Tessius* but now it was shouldering up out of the water, trying to lean against the ship's side to upset it. I could not hear the snapbows over the wind but I saw random divots of red spring from the monster as the crew took what shots they could. I was busy dragging Jandra up to the apex of the beast's back but some of those bolts came perilously close to making an end of me. The Tseni were shooting into the dark, and they knew where *they* were. The rest of the crew, not linked to their minds, had to take their chances.

The *Tessius* shuddered and groaned as if it, too, were some vast thing of the deeps, grievously wounded. I swear I heard rivets popping from their sockets, plates parting company with their neighbours as the Manfish brought its colossal weight to bear.

Jaq took his moment, then. I saw him skip up the sea-beast's vast flank, spear couched and seeking some vulnerable place across the great leathery desert of its skin. A moment later his hunter's eyes had found his quarry for he lunged forwards and drove his lance to half its length into the monster's flesh. Now it was the Manfish's turn to groan and shiver, and abruptly it was falling back into the sea's embrace, and so were we.

I hauled until I felt my wings would tear from my back and go whirling to destruction in the storm. Jaq had skidded off down the monster's flank but I saw him running for us, first on its hide and then on the very sea itself, feet knifing atop the water and cutting glittering lines of spray.

For a moment Jandra was kicking towards the *Tessius*, maddeningly close. Then she screamed and was yanked downwards by the grip of some unseen jaw. I felt my arm nearly part from my socket but would not let go of her, striving against air and ocean to drag her back. A moment later I was down to my shoulder in the water, with the next swell about to eclipse me entirely, and it was *she* who would not let go of me, no matter how I fought. One of the smaller Menfish surfaced beside me, parting the water like a sword's point slides clear of a man's back when he's stabbed. I saw its amused eye note me, its toothy maw gape a little in mirth. Then it plunged back into the water and I felt Jandra shudder. A moment later, her clasp still iron, she had dragged me beneath,

I screamed, which was stupid as I was underwater. A moment later I felt Jaq's clutching grasp snag my belt and pull, his heels no doubt braced on nothing but the sea itself. There was a colossal thrash from Jandra, enough that I felt muscle and bone begin to part company in my elbow. Then I was free, or rather the weight in my hand was no longer enough to speak of a whole body, or even a whole arm.

I exploded out into the air, still screaming when I could and hacking up sea water when I couldn't. Jaq practically bundled me under one gangling arm and I stared at Jandra's be-ringed hand and half her forearm, all that was left to me of her.

"Now fly!" Jaq shouted in my ear. "The air is safe, ja da? Or safer!"

"Can't!" I was too weighed down with water, too clutched by cold.

Jaq cursed, and then he was skittering back across the water as one of the Menfish lunged up from beneath him. Its teeth closed on air and he rammed one of his spears into it, deep behind the eye. It shrilled like a child before its voice travelled so high I could barely hear the whine of it; a blink later it was gone to the sea in a bubbling wash of red.

Jaq ran for the *Tessius*, carrying me like a bedroll wedged into his armpit. I saw the Tseni crew still mostly there with snapbows, and a handful of the others with crossbows and bows.

"Fly a little!" Jaq shouted at me. "I will throw you up. You must do the rest yourself."

"What about you?"

He brought me round so I could see his face, his grin. "So, you do care, ja da?"

"This is not the time, *ja da?*"

"Of course." Still that grin wouldn't go. He glanced up, and we were abruptly in the shadow of something vast pitching down at us. I am afraid I screamed rather more, because I thought it was the giant Manfish, but instead it was the *Tessius,* battling the storm.

"On three," Jaq announced, and then changed his mind and just slung me straight up, utterly unprepared and howling at the unfairness as though it was a test I'd be marked on later. I fought for my wings, felt them flare into being and catch the air, then stutter as my Art failed me. A Fly, failed by her flight! What a curse to have on your lips as the sea claims you!

And yet I didn't fall, because someone had lunged from the rail to snag me, yanking agonisingly on that same arm Jandra had almost taken with her into the depths. I looked up into the panicking face of Xerixes.

He was no man of action, my Xerixes. He had me, but he lacked the strength to land even so small a fish as I. He wouldn't abandon me, though, and so I dangled at the end of his weakening arm as he called for aid and the crew ignored him, concentrating rather on the huge sea-beast that was on its way back to us.

Hanging above that busy ocean I had a better view of it than I would ever have wished. Its great blunt head broke the waves like a battering ram, scarred and encrusted and almost devoid of feature. Was that a tiny human-like eye set into the side of it, like a worm burrow in a great stone wall? Did I glimpse beneath the water a jaw the size of a rail automotive gaping wide?

It surged on, not head to head but aiming itself like a siege engine to strike the *Tessius* another bludgeoning blow along the side, where the plates were already dented out of true. Xerixes had named the monsters well for I could see the calculation in its angle of attack, how it would employ its thunderous momentum to greatest use.

In its path was Jaq.

He was a hunter of monsters by trade, so he had been introduced, but I think he had never encountered such a thing as this. He did not let that slow him. As the monster built its speed towards us, so Jaq flashed directly beneath me, a lance held under his arm and his feet skimming over the roiling deep, held perfectly at the maddened line between air and water, no matter where waves and weather took it.

In the face of the Manfish, he was a mote, a dust-speck, mere flotsam before the living mountain of the depths.

It did not even notice him, seeing only its quarry, the *Tessius*. In the instant before they met I drew my limbs in, trying to brace myself against who knew what. But I could not look away.

He leapt as he struck, kicking off from the water to arc through the air the last of the distance, long limbs unfolding like the sudden arms of a trap to drive that spear deep into the monster's flesh. Was it the eye he had struck? Or had he buried the shaft in the monster's gums or the roof of its mouth. Whichever, there was barely a stub of the harpoon left in sight, and nothing at all of Jaq. Of the monster itself, it spasmed away from the *Tessius*, its hide blistering with the narrow wounds of snapbow bolts. That spear was the final argument it had to bow to, though. Instead of unseaming our ship it plunged into the depths, and I saw the shadow of it fill all the sea beneath me as it fled.

"Ha –" I managed before the flukes of its tail gave the *Tessius* a final parting slap, and abruptly I was loose in the air once more, and Xerixes beside me, the pair of us hurtling down to a sea not lacking for danger even if its greatest son had abandoned the fight.

I fought for my wings again, but this time they did not even flicker and I struck the water as hard as if it were a board. For a moment I couldn't even flail, the breath beaten from my by the impact. Then Xerixes had me and at least he could swim like a native. I saw a Manfish surface close by, though, malice in its glower, and remembered how frightened he had been of them.

For a moment the monster considered us, and I had a sense of connection one seldom does with beasts – I felt that rage and loathing Xerixes had vouchsafed in them, not hunger or territory, but a deep desire to kill us for some ancient, forgotten wrong. Then it had vanished, and I braced myself for the scything underwater rush of its jaws.

Instead I got Jaq erupting from the water, cap lost, spears used up, but grappling to take both Xerixes and I into the protective compass of his long arms.

"Up!" he sputtered.

"Can't!" I shouted in his face, but he didn't mean fly, he meant climb. The *Tessius* was right there, and at least some of the ropes trailing in the water were for our benefit, rather than the detritus of damage.

I could barely climb, by then, but I didn't weigh much and there were strong arms up top. Xerixes and Jaq followed me, and the three of us ended up in a sodden cluster beneath the rail, stripping away our ruined clothes without any room left for propriety and struggling into whatever dry garments could be found.

Seven of the crew had been lost, including Jandra. Aside from us, few others had survived a meeting with the water. The Menfish had been hungry.

The *Tessius* itself was limping, by then. At least the Menfish had not been Apt, and so had not thought to cripple the propellor, but the pumps below were operating at full, and though the crew were caulking and whatnot as best they could, we could not effect proper repairs here on the open ocean. It was touch and go whether we could even reach the Nauarchate again.

All this washed over me in the babble between Aratean and his crew. I was nestled into Xerixes's armpit with my legs draped over Jaq's lap. My arm hurt abominably and the core of me was still freezing, no matter what hot infusions or dry cloaks were on hand. And I was happy, in a curious way. I was happy to be alive today, even if death would wait like a polite bailiff for tomorrow to come around.

I shook my head at Jaq. "You are ridiculous, ja da?"

"I try." His grin was tired, but still sporting on his face like an aphid nymph. Then he turned the expression on Xerixes, who was regarding him somewhat dreamily. And then, before I could get jealous, our Sea-kinden turned the same regard on me, and I hugged the pair of them and had rather un-Collegiate thoughts about how things might be if we ever survived any of this.

My reverie was interrupted by one of the crew crying out, "Land! Sighting land!"

Everyone had the same thought at that, and the crew instantly rushed to the rails with weapons to hand, waiting for a new Manfish to rise up from the deep and finish us off. But it was not an attack. We had well and truly made ourselves too expensive a prize for the sea monsters to take. Instead Aratean was consulting with the keener-eyed members of our crew, peering over the rail through his glass and cursing the night and the storm.

But it was land, true land: not weed, not mere rocks but a great swathe of land just proud of the western horizon. Land: the land we were seeking, for even the western ocean had edges, and we had found the most distant of shores.

What we couldn't do was just *go* there, of course, because boats are difficult and sailing is unexpectedly procedural. Apparently turning up in a half-sinking boat on an unknown shore full of rocks in the dark is more than the most modern of shiphandling can bear, and so we shuddered and rocked out the night with the pumps eating our fuel until the sun finally lit up the sea behind us, reaching past us towards our long-sought prize.

It didn't actually look amazing, as promised lands go. We did see a lot of rocks and then a lot of mountains not far beyond the rugged beaches, suggesting that the interior of this place was likely to remain a mystery for a while. Aratean was busy with his instruments trying to get an idea of where we were, and his best guess was that, between our efforts to circumnavigate Saragassum and the night's festivities we were far north of where we'd planned. That was mostly a problem for the return journey, though. After all, this was the unknown shore. It didn't really matter *where* we made landfall.

And so we limped southward, looking for a bay where we might bring the *Tessius* up for what repairs we could enact. The pumps had begun to sound more laboured, and we were all very aware that getting here was quite literally only half the journey. Nobody wanted to become a resident of that forbidding shore just yet.

There were things in the water. Doctor Phinagler pointed them out: round-bodied monsters with huge eyes above a muzzle bristling with whiskers. These were not Menfish, but perhaps they were cousins of them, and certainly they stared with alarm at the *Tessius*'s encroachment on their waters. Ahead, at the beach we were steering for, a great host of them sloughed from the gravel into the water and fled us, for which we were all grateful. Nobody fancied getting out into waist-deep water while such beasts might be around to make us regret it.

We crept in towards the rocks with two sailors taking soundings every minute or so, and with Xerixes out in the water, unhappily, as additional insurance. Even so we had a few tortuous-sounding scrapes with the rocks before coarse sand was crunching beneath the keel. The crew were casting worried eyes at the sky, because another storm might well drive the ship all the way up onto land and scuttle it. After the tempest we had endured, though, the skies were passably clear.

The Tseni leapt out at Aratean's unspoken command, putting their Ant strength to good use as they stabilised the ship, a quarter out of the water, and with anchors set to keep it there. After that they began their work, and patently didn't need much instruction from their master. Aratean's kin were setting up a mobile forge to try and hammer the plates back into some semblance of shape while the Inapt and the Bee-kinden minded to the wood beneath and boiled up some cauldrons of ill-smelling waterproofage to slap over everything when the repairs were done.

Which left the land to us.

Upslope of the beach were shallow foothills, the mere heralds of the greater mountains we could see beyond. They were cloaked in trees, a variety I'd never seen before, slender and tall with narrow, angled branches, and leaves thin as awls, so meagre one wondered why the forest had even bothered. They grew thick, though, enough so that noon beneath the boughs was like twilight.

"How long for the repairs?" was my employer's question.

Aratean paused to get a best-guess estimate direct from his people, then said, "Three days, maybe." He was eyeing the forest too. "Do I take it you want to go on another scholarly jaunt, Doctor?"

"Well we're here," Haile put in, leaning past my employer. "We might as well."

"And if you're going to throw the Saragassum business in our faces," Doctor Phinagler added, "I'd point out that worked fairly well for us, all in all."

But Aratean wasn't about to slap them down. "You're right. And we need to know what's out there. We'll need to fell a fair amount of timber to get us back and running, and to fuel the furnace. And here we are."

"Yes," Haile echoed. The three of them stared into that dark forest thoughtfully.

"If we were home, staring at a place like that, you'd think what?" Haile asked them.

"Mantis-kinden," the Doctor said promptly. "Just their sort of place."

"The Commonweal's got forests like that," Aratean added. "Mantids, Dragonflies, stranger kinden too."

"Is that what you think we'll find, though?" Haile pressed, and they both shook their heads.

"The air's different," she said softly. "The ground's different. And listen…"

There was a not-quite-silence about the place. What isolated sounds we heard were utterly alien, high shrills and cackles, but nothing loud and nothing close. We heard no crickets, no lazy buzz of big wings as some beetle took flight. The new world was holding its breath for us.

"I will take an expedition into the trees, to see what might threaten our wood-cutters," Aratean announced. "I will lead it myself. They can manage here. But you will come with me, you Beetles. I will be the first, here, and you will record my story. I want you there to witness it."

Doctor Phinagler was looking put out, and I wondered if he might ask me to record a slightly skewed variant that gave him a little more pre-eminence, but the sheer lure of all that unknown was a voice loud enough to drown out his pride.

I had somehow assumed Xerixes and Jaq would come with us, but food and water remained a pressing concern and the crew needed both their talents. Instead it was Aratean and the two academics, yours truly and a half dozen of the crew, all that could be spared. We loaded our packs with provisions and tools, and Aratean left the ship under the command of one of his kin, with strict instructions to set a watch.

We passed into the quiet of the forest with barely a clink of a buckle. I still wonder what might have happened had Jaq been with us – a hunter of the sea he might have been, but doubtless wiser to the ways of the land than any of us there. I have a great fear that we did a terrible thing through ignorance and vainglory, when we set out into that land, and only histories yet unwritten will vindicate or vilify us.

I have known forests. The Doctor and I once had cause to penetrate incautiously far into the interior of Parasyal, and the Mantis-kinden nearly ended up wearing our skins for cloaks (or, in my case, a modest shawl). We went into the Forest Aleth, and discovered exactly what unpleasantness made that such an unhealthy place to visit. We even ended north of the Empire one time, in the great rotting jungle-swamp the Woodlouse-kinden call home, and perhaps some time I will break my vows and spill their secrets, but not today.

The forest across the sea, the forest past the end of the world, was unlike all of these. Quiet, as I have remarked, and those sounds we heard all dreadfully unfamiliar. Cold, too, like the Commonweal is said to be, with mist writhing between the trunks like ghostly centipedes.

Quiet, yet not untenanted. The Spider-kinden man we had with us had a little woodsy lore, and he began pointing out tracks, not human but not of any familiar beasts either. Some seemed a little like horses, though small and sharp. Others resembled nothing we had ever seen. One was as big around as my head, like a huge blunt hand with sharp nails. We began to see smaller denizens of the forest too. The Doctor and Haile managed to maintain their academic curiosity in the face of these prodigies. For my part, my skin was crawling after the first sighting. I had been flying but came down fast when I saw what I shared the air with. Their bright colours had made me think them butterflies or wasps, but they flew in quite a different manner, their wings beating slowly and often just gliding like a novice pilot's orthopter. They had sharp mouths and skin covered with scutes like the scales from a moth's wing, but larger. Also up in the trees we saw little russet things that looked a little too human for comfort, staring at us as their horrible gnawing teeth made short work of the nuts and seeds held in their disturbingly prehensile hands.

Haile tried to sketch some of them, though she did them little justice. Doctor Phinagler was muttering something about ancient dig sites and bones he had read about, and the carvings in the restricted collection of the College cellars, that he had once broken into. He did not regale us with his theories, though. Perhaps he was disappointed that we had found no ruined cities to pick over. That other continent should have been the very perfect place to hide the mother of all lost civilizations.

"We should shoot something," Aratean said, apparently on general Tseni principles, but then he qualified, "to take home the pelt or skull. Nobody will believe we have seen such things."

"We should find ourselves a spot and be quiet and still," Haile offered. "We're blundering about here like a three-beetle wagon." She conferred with the Spider-kinden who showed us what he claimed was a game trail, and we followed it until we found water. There, within sight of a silver stream that wound its way between the trees, we made camp and let the natives come to us.

We waited most of that afternoon, long stretches of which were entirely uneventful. Every time Aratean or the Doctor began to get fractious, however, some new prodigy would be drawn to the water to drink as we watched with horrified fascination.

We saw no insects larger than a finger's length. There were no grand webs in the canopy, no cuts in the bark where ants had collected the sap, but the forest was alive with an entirely alien form of life. A herd of slender-limbed horse-like beasts came first, the largest seeming almost as though we could have thrown a saddle over them to ride. Save that those same largest each sported from their brows an arcing pair of antlers, the mimic of similar adornments carried by certain male beetles to fight and wrestle over females. Perhaps these horse-kin used theirs the same way. After them came a handful of sleek grey shapes that stopped on the far bank and snarled at us, a sound that chilled us to the marrow. They were long-limbed and swift, shown as killers by their sharp teeth. Doctor Phinagler decided they were analogous to those spiders that chase down their prey rather than wait in webs. He and Haile were trying to build up a picture of the ecology, in the endearing assumption that such a benighted place would have to make sense. In this their efforts were fatally compromised by Aratean and his crew, because the ship's Master decided that a hairy little tree hopper was insufficient trophy, and instead he must have something grander.

He took down some of the antlered things, killing several and then sawing the tines from the one dead beast that actually sported them. He killed some of the grey spider-slinkers too, and hacked a head off to have boiled down for its skull. After that it was mostly fruitless waiting, for word got around quite swiftly between the animals that a Tseni explorer was looking to take parts of them as evidence of his greatness.

"We'll extend our stay a few days," Aratean decided. "I'll post a reward amongst the crew, for the best pieces." The killing had quite invigorated him and his hands were messy with the creatures' blood, which looked worryingly human – though of course goats and horses will bleed red as well.

Towards dusk there came a monster larger than all the rest, and thankfully once again on the far side of the stream. It was huge and rounded, lumbering on four limbs that sported claws like hooked knives. Still, there was an odd clumsiness to it, a ponderous fumbling in the way it moved that reminded me like nothing so much as a tardigrade, those comical water-beasts that are so hard to kill. Seeing a monster of such size and strength drained all the comedy from the moment, though, and while Aratean raised his snapbow to his shoulder, he somehow never mustered the courage to shoot, blaming the late hour. It was only a shadow of the great Manfish in size, but I think we all doubted the stopping power of a snapbow bolt against so large a monster.

By then the dimness beneath the trees was being replaced by full night, and Aratean had his people build a fire, for the cold was getting to all of us. I think he felt obscurely defeated that we had met no humans to whom he could proclaim himself the great navigator, to whom he could tell stories of the glorious achievements of his home city. But how could there be kinden here, when there were no beasts to be kinden *of*, only these misbegotten monsters?

We passed a chill and uncomfortable night, pressed close to the fire for its meagre warmth, and changing watch often. There were eyes out in that dark gleaming back our fire at us. There were the calls and cries of unseen horrors that sometimes sounded just an inch off human.

"Could they have a kinden, these beasts?" I asked the Beetles. They had no certain answer, but we all felt in our hearts it could not be. Even as they were deliberating, though, Aratean poked me in the shoulder, specifically the injured one.

"You'll go scouting tomorrow," he told me. "You're the one with wings. Go find us some herds of these beasts. There was one I saw with horns half again as great as these." And he kicked his own trophy disdainfully. "There are larger as well, I'd wager. Come dawn, I want you in the air."

I was not feeling up to any prolonged flights just then, but the firelight caught Aratean's eye with a bit of a mad gleam and I decided not to argue. After that, he monopolised the fire with talk of how Tsen would receive him. "You will make a good tale of it," he emphasised to the three of us. "Make sure your historians know how my name is written." And then he threw his hands up to encapsulate a title, as though trying to leap the image from his imagination direct to ours. "Conqueror of the new world!" he declaimed.

I looked beyond our firelight at the dark, still woods and reckoned they looked fairly unconquered to me.

The next morning I was roused from a remarkably spicy dream of both Xerixes and Jaq by the toe of Aratean's boot, specifically as it intruded into my ribs.

"Sun's up," he told me. "So should you be." He grinned, and it was a far less pleasant thing that Jaq's habitual expression, too many teeth and too much hunger.

The upness of the sun was debatable, given the gloom made by the interlocking of all those upthrust, needled branches. The two Beetles were still slumbering, for certain, and Aratean's sailors seemed half asleep on their feet. No such courtesies were extended to me, alas, and besides, getting out of boot-reach of Aratean seemed a worthy end in itself. I let my wings flower from my back and buzzed myself off with the general aim of letting the poor monsters be and just finding a comfortable tree to nap in.

I wove my way up past the treetops, reflecting that it was just as well I was a Fly, as any larger airborne contingent would have found themselves barred behind a wooden cage. Up in the open air at last – and bitterly regretting it because of the freezing wind coming at my back off the sea – I had a chance to take my bearings.

I will be sufficiently un-Collegiate as to say that it was beautiful, that land. I know it is out of fashion to elegy about the wonders of a wild landscape – very *Inapt*, they say – but I found it so. Stark, yes; forbidding also, and yet those high, purple mountains capped with snow that seemed to blaze in the dawn light, the great expanse of black-green forest, serried like an infinity of spearmen on guard… It was a wonder, and it was only mine. Haile would never sketch this, the groundbound Tseni would never share the image one to another.

And I was wide awake by then, shocked into it by the immensity of the sight, the far distance to the horizon on my left and right, the sheer daunting altitude above me. What lay beyond those peaks? Were there the Doctor's lost cities, or just more dark forest that went forever until the sea reasserted its sovereignty? I flitted over the canopy, forgetting my mission and my companions, resting in treetops where I startled away a host of the little ragged fliers each time. I felt like the only human being in the world, and I might even have just lost myself in it, all that unbounded wilderness, had it not been for the smoke.

Well, I was embarrassed, I can tell you. I had thought myself heading into the wilderness but instead I had just made a circle and come back to our fire again. Perhaps, I thought, some part of me was less adventurous than I wished, and had guided my wings back to the relative security of the camp. With a sigh I descended to check with my employer and confirm to Aratean that I had seen no new monsters for him to murder.

My error was immediately apparent.

It was not the camp. I had come down by a stream – the very same, as it turned out, but closer to the source – and there, where a dozen trees had been felled, was a house. Had I been looking properly I would have seen it from above, but I'd had eyes only for the horizon, and my nose had just said *home* when the smoke reached me. Smoke that came from a hole in the dwelling's roof.

My first impression was that this was a terribly primitive place, less ambitious even than the weed temples the Argyrin had raised, that lasted mere days before they rotted. A closer look corrected me, though. The place was built of logs plastered with mud, and there was a precise art to it, a care and forethought that spoke of a craft that had been perfected over generations. It was a house stripped down to just what was needed in this cold, damp place, with monster hides hung in layers over the door and stretched, translucent, across window holes. And the smoke kept rising, and at last I appreciated that was probably because the house-builder was still resident.

I went very still. For an absurdly long time I had seen the house as an artefact in a museum, nothing that remained relevant and used. But if there was a house, that meant the work of human hands. Or something like human. I had images of those hybrid things from Khanaphes – human in part, perhaps, yet with the heads and legs of the hairy monsters. And I had a small knife, of course, and no other weapons.

I became aware, by way of my Art and the nameless senses we all possess, that I was being watched. Very slowly, holding my wings ready to fling me up past the treetops, I turned.

I was facing someone of my own stature, just about. She was human; she was female, her skin close to the tan of a Sarnesh Ant, her hair dark and long, bound back with twin beaded braids. She wore a kind of animal-skin smock, and like the house it all looked very crude until you noticed the details – how neat and intricate the stitching, how elegant the fringed edges, how her little belt was made of interlocking seashells painstakingly chosen for regularity of size.

She was a child, that I could see. The house had not been built for kinden of my size, and this incautious creature was only the builder's offspring.

I raised an open hand cautiously. "Hello!"

She stared at me,

"My name's Fosse." I wondered if she'd seen a Fly-kinden before, whether she thought I was another child. She did not seem afraid but she was staring at me as though I was some prodigy, not a perfectly reasonable human being.

"Can you talk?" I wondered if she was simple, or else if the children of these parts came late to speech. "I won't hurt you."

I stepped closer, and that was too much for her. She bolted, but not far, because her parents had arrived.

I swallowed, wide-eyed. They had crept up so softly that, if they had been more belligerent, I'd have an axe in my chest to prove it. I saw a man and a woman, similar in look to the girl-child. They wore hide, and over it fur – monster, not the bee fur that's such an expensive luxury in Collegium. The woman had a knife with a flint blade, but the head of the man's small axe looked to be bronze, and I reckoned it was for fighting and not for wood.

There was something to them that marked them out from the people I knew. A fullness, was it? An energy within them, even as they just stood there. Some strange quality. I'm glad I'm not Inapt. I might come up with all manner of stupid theories.

"Greetings from beyond the sea," I tried, spreading my hands out and smiling. "My name is Fosse of the great city of Collegium," because, to the pits with Tsen, frankly, "and I say good day to you. I have travelled a long way to meet you."

They stared at me as though I'd grown an extra head, trying to exchange glances without taking an eye off me. The woman tapped the child on the shoulder with a quick word and the girl dashed off into the forest, presumably to some pre-arranged hiding place.

"Well yes, I appreciate your caution. I'm not really armed." I showed them the knife in my belt, and then held my hands out. "Tell me of yourselves, friends. What do you call this place?"

The man squinted down at me. The pair of them were regarding me with what I can best characterise as horrified fascination, almost seeming to stare *into* me rather than at me.

"Come on, now, you can't be frightened of so small a thing as me," I tried with a slightly forced laugh.

At last the man stepped forwards, his axe still half raised to ward me off. He spoke.

I couldn't understand him.

My readers will find this hard to appreciate. It was not that he mumbled. It was not that he had some strong accent, as indeed I might expect. I have travelled more than most, from Khanaphes to the Atoll Coast, Jerez to Aleth. I know accents. This man spoke loud and clear – indeed quite slowly, perhaps exaggerating his words for my benefit. Except they were not words. They went up and down like speech, and there was a lift at the end that suggested a question, but what came to me was more like "bar bar mow mow mow?" than speech.

I laughed. It was undiplomatic but I couldn't help it, and he actually laughed a little back, against gritted teeth. We had that in common, at least. Then he said it again, or something else that sounded the same. "Bar bar mow mow bar bar bar?" and a gesture that could have meant anything.

I was very frightened all of a sudden. Speech is speech. There is nowhere you can go without finding people who say the same words, even if they write them down wrong like the Sea-kinden do. When I say 'beetle' it is, so say the academics, because it is precisely that sound that most naturally calls the concept of a beetle to the mind. Indeed there is evidence from the oldest of written records that our words have only grown more uniform over time, no matter the distances and isolation involved.

And yet: "Bar bar mow mow bar!" and I just spread my hands and smiled helplessly.

"I don't understand. I'm Fosse. I've come from over the sea." And I jabbed a finger in the direction of the coast. It seemed to confirm all their worst fears, from the way they reacted. They were growing more and more afraid of me, and it was definitely mutual. It was not the axe I feared, it was the difference, the weird, word-like sounds they made which were so alien to the ear.

"Just talk to me!" I demanded, and I let my wings carry me closer in a flurry of Art. The man yelled out and leapt back, axe raised high, and the woman was shrieking, pouring out her nonsense sounds, terrified by what I had done.

"I'm sorry! I'm sorry!" They didn't know that Art. Perhaps they didn't know any Art. I wanted to reach out to them, but plainly they wanted me no closer than I was, and the axe would have something to say about it if I tried. I so badly wanted to try. I didn't want them to be afraid of me. Nobody has ever been afraid of me. My kinden doesn't tend to elicit that kind of a response in people.

And then I heard a familiar voice bellow, "I'm coming, Fosse!" and splashing from downstream, and It happened.

This is what nobody will hear. This, that I set down for you, is my honest evidence, from my own eyes. The Doctor would not have it. None of them would, but I saw.

They became monsters, the two of them. They went from man and woman to lean, grey beasts snarling in my face with their fang-filled jaws. The clothes, the axe, all became part of their new shapes. It happened in the blink of an eye, but I didn't blink; I saw it happen.

Doctor Phinagler arrived then, soaked to the waist and waving a snapbow, calling my name and yelling at me to get clear. I was yelling right back for him to go away, that he mustn't, that he *mustn't*…

Even as I shouted it, I heard the percussive retort of a snapbow and one of the monsters leapt up onto its hind legs with a terrible whimper and collapsed onto its side. Onto *his* side. I think it was the man who was shot. The other, the woman, fled instantly, lost in the trees.

Aratean came stomping proudly from the woods, fitting a new bolt to his weapon. "How's that for a shot?" he demanded, and then stopped, staring at the house. "What's this?"

Doctor Phinagler was goggling at it, too. "But then there *are* people here!" he gasped. "But where are they? Did the monsters drive them away?"

I tried to tell them. I was tripping over my own words, I was so desperate to tell them what I had seen. I didn't quite believe myself, even as I garbled the story of it. I was trying to revise my own memories so that they could be something other than they were. Of course they didn't change their shapes. Of course the people weren't the monsters. That would mean the monsters we'd spent yesterday killing might have been people, and where would that leave us…?

But they didn't listen. When they finally understood me, they thought I was hysterical. The Doctor and Haile were sympathetic, but everyone started talking about the beating I'd had with the Menfish, and how I was obviously spooked by how alone I'd been out here. Plainly the monsters hadn't built this place. They had no *thumbs*...

The two Beetles were pushing inside the house, remarking at how incredible it was – as though the owners had just stepped out. Most of the sailors went with them, perhaps to snag some souvenirs. Aratean was already putting a knife to the dead beast he'd shot, to take a trophy.

"Remarkable," he muttered. "Its teeth are like bronze!"

I felt sick. I will be honest with you, I also felt weak and every part of me ached, and soon enough I would have something of a fever (and Xerixes would care for me, which almost made it all worthwhile). Perhaps you will take this as evidence that I didn't see what I know I saw. All I can do is swear that I saw it, and right then I felt sick not from the cold or my injuries but because of what had just happened, and because I was having no more success communicating its import to my fellows than the locals had speaking to me.

And Aratean was hacking away at the dead monster's neck, saying how he reckoned it was smaller than the head he'd already taken, so probably he'd just throw it away, but he might as well take it to compare...

I saw the eyes glint between the trees. I met that furious, mute gaze. Vengeance needs no language to make itself understood. And I was a bad chronicler in the end. I took sides, and I took what most of my readers will probably say was the wrong side. I just stepped away and said nothing.

The other beast – the female, the *woman* – exploded from the trees and rammed into Aratean, hurling him off the body of her mate. He got an arm in the way and she savaged it to the bone, even as his people were piling out of the little house. With a great surge of his Ant-kinden strength he flung the monster off him, but with only one good arm she didn't go far, landing almost at his feet.

This happened next. I saw this. I swear it. She became the woman again, the human woman, opening him up from navel to neck with her knife, and then, the next eyeblink, the monster, lunging for his throat and ripping it clean out so that the bones of his neck were visible through the blood.

The sailors were retaliating even then – I saw one snapbow bolt plunge into Aratean's lower back, and that would probably have killed him if he wasn't already dead. Another bolt ploughed into the beast as she turned away, alongside the Spider-kinden's arrow. She keened as she fell, thrashing against the wounds. She was trying to reach the shadow of the trees, even though there couldn't have been much life left in her. I have gone back through these words of mine. I have changed 'it' to 'she' each time. I know what I saw.

The Tseni crewmen hacked her to death, heedless of trophies. They cut her apart with their shortswords, furious at the loss of their master. By that time the Beetle-kinden were out of the house, blinking bewilderedly at Aratean's body.

They still wanted to stay, of course; academic curiosity knows no bounds. The sailors were having none of it, though. They took the body of Aratean and they forced the Beetles to move, practically at sword-point. And they demanded I come with them, even though I was weeping and looking frantically about the dark of the forest in the hope that I might spot the child, the girl I had first seen, because she was out there, and she was an orphan now, and what would happen to her, out here in this monstrous, terrible place?

I tell myself she had aunts, uncles, cousins. I tell myself she had somewhere safe, where someone would take care of her. I tell myself these things because they make me feel better, not because they are at all likely.

And in the end I left with them, because they would have abandoned me otherwise, and that land was no fit place for any of us to be.

Back at the *Tessius*, with repairs having proceeded apace, I did my best to describe what I had seen to Jaq and to Xerixes. They gave me more credit than the others at least, but then the Inapt will believe all sorts of things.

With Aratean dead, none of the crew wanted to prolong our stay there, despite the Beetles' requests. Haile and the Doctor had only sketches, Aratean's trophies and a few keepsakes from the house to evidence what we had found. It would not be quite enough to set the academic world of Collegium on fire, but word would get around and reach interested ears.

Of our return voyage, what is there to say? The Menfish did not impede us, and the people of the Nauarchate did not know what to do with us, back from the dead as we were. We parted the Saragassum as before, and paid for our passage with stories of what we had found to the west, that they were mightily entertained by but did not believe. I was asked to tell my share of those tales, and I declined.

There was a time, when I was very young. I broke my aunt's crystal vase, that she had all the way from the Spiderlands. There was a period between my breaking of it and her discovering the loss that remains acute in my memory, knowing I had done a terrible thing and waiting for the inevitable sequel. Sailing back from the western lands I felt the same way, and I have not entirely shaken the feeling even now. We went somewhere we should never have been, somewhere things work differently. How will we survive that place on our return? How will it survive us?

For there will be a return. A new expedition is planned, part-funded by the College, partly by other interests. They will take a far grander ship, they tell me, and an airship as well, Imperial war surplus. Further Imperial war surplus will be the Wasp-kinden soldiers who will serve as pioneers and guards to the various academics and prospectors. They are men who find the new Wasp Republic not so much to their liking, and have tired of the wars in the Spiderlands. They are not who I would choose to take to a new land, nor yet the host of itinerant adventurers and opportunists that have sprung up around the venture, let alone the weird interest shown by some of the Inapt. But I do not get a say, of course.

Doctor Phinagler and Haile Millern are going. They have what they wanted: sufficient academic credibility to get such a grand venture off the ground. I've never seen my employer happier about his prospects.

I sat him down and told him again exactly what I saw, sparing no words and refusing to salve his incredulity. At the end, I think he believed me a little, perhaps enough to keep an open mind

"You'll come with us, of course," he said, not really needing an answer.

I gave him one anyway. "Actually, Doctor, I would like to hand in my notice."

He stared at me, genuinely hurt. "But Fosse..."

"I do not want to go back there, but that's not it," I explained, as kindly as I could. "I've enjoyed being your amanuensis, Doctor, but the time's come for me to try my hand at the expedition game myself. I have a different voyage lined up."

"I... hm? Where?" It was quite endearing to see how bamboozled he was by the news.

"Hermatyre," I told him, letting the exotic name roll off my tongue with relish.

"But that's... under the sea, isn't it?"

"It is," I confirmed.

"But you don't like the sea."

I was touched. The history of our association didn't support the idea that he had kept track of my likes and dislikes. "Even so," I agreed. "And yet even I can come round to something, given enough incentive. And there's a permanent embassy there, as of last month, and I've found a submersible master named Wys who will take us down there, for a little wherewithal."

"We? Fosse, I'm going back west," he complained. "I really can't... Wait, who's 'we'?"

"Me, and Xerixes, and Jaq," I said firmly. "Xeri's sick of living in the dry, and it sounds like Hermatyre's a friendlier place than the one he comes from. And I want to be with him, and Jaq wants to see it for himself. And be with me."

"Oh. Oh, my." The Doctor's eyebrows virtually disappeared over the top of his head but he hauled them back down. "How very... cosmopolitan. Well. Well, well, well." And then he pulled himself together and went on, "Well, that's grand, Fosse. That's grand." He blinked rapidly. "I don't mind saying, it won't be the same without you, but you should be happy."

Or maybe he raged and railed and promised me his firstborn if only I would commit to one more doomed venture of his. Perhaps he broke crockery and cursed my name. Let it be whichever you prefer.

He has gone now, anyway, the expedition departed from good old Collegium harbour, and I write this looking out over the docks at the nautilus-shell submersible that Wys holds ready for us. She is one of the Smallclaw Sea-kinden, a sharp-featured bald woman an inch or so taller than I, who keeps her much larger crew in line with a tongue like a razor. I like her a great deal. I like Xerixes more, and he and Jaq and I appear to have reached an unorthodox but perfectly comfortable arrangement. And I will live beneath the waves for a little while, and dress scandalously, like the Sea-kinden, and talk fondly of Collegium with the other submarine expatriates until I feel the need to travel, whether it is home, or further out.

And one day I will hear of the fate of Doctor Phinagler and how the west was won, or lost, or both.

# Afterword from the Author

Doctor Phinagler first came about, in name only, in a blog post entitled "Doctor Phinagler's Amazing World of the Ignorant", nothing to do with the insect-kinden at all, but just me ranting at the supercut videos people put up on Youtube, headlined as wonders of the unexplained and featuring entirely mundane animals. The name bobbed about in my mind for a while until I came to write *Heirs of the Blade*, which was originally conceived as having an early subplot involving the Lake-kinden coming after Sef, all of which got cut. I was left with a desire to go visit the denizens of Limnia and no regular avenue for it, hence *Cities of Silver*, where Doctor Phinagler became embodied as an unlikely hero of the kinden's version of pulp adventures, accompanied (Phileas Fogg style) by his (semi-)faithful assistant.

Phinagler became my gateway to explore those parts of the kinden's world that I knew were out there, but that the main narrative – and even most of my other short story protagonists like Gaved or Dal Arche – would never visit. Making them first person narratives through the somewhat ascerbic voice of Fosse also gave me room for all manner of little games played entirely for my own amusement. Following on from the conceit that these are actually published stories written by and for Collegiates, the text becomes a guide to an educated Collegiate's view on the world, including the political events of the main series. Phinagler's adventures here neatly cover from before *Empire* to after *Worm*, with *Sand* fitting immediately before *Scarab Path* and *Spires* coming right in the middle of *Air War*. Phinagler and Fosse bumble their way through the entire history of the two Imperial wars, very occasionally referencing existing characters, but mostly giving an everyman counterpoint to the grand sweep of epic history the novels provide.

They are also unashamedly Pulps, of course. I've had fun in the past taking other genres and kindenising them – see for example *Alicaea's Children* and *Fallen Heroes* in the *A Time for Grief* collection, a detective noir and a western respectively. The Phinagler stories are riffs on traditional Pulps, right down to kinden versions of the tropes in those stories, though hopefully with something of a more modern take on, say, attitudes to native people and similar prejudices often found therein. *Cities of Silver* is my Verne/Wells story, probably more *First Men in the Moon* than *20,000 Leagues Under the Sea*, and that would make *Written in Sand* and *Masters of the Spires* falling somewhere between H Rider Haggard and Indiana Jones, with the Wasp-kinden, Brandt, as ersatz Nazi mystical/historical revisionist, and Corvaris Blaze looking like Doctor Jones himself but turning out, in the end, to be more of a Belloq. *Distant Shores* has its brush with Melville in the middle, and even a bit of a nod to the 1968 film *The Lost Continent* and Hope Hodgson's *The Boats of the "Glen Carrig"*, but it is more its own beast, as I'll come to below.

Of the individual stories' significance in the kinden canon, *Cities of Silver* expands the setting of Jerez and Lake Limnia by finally giving a view below the surface of the remarkably unpleasant world of the Water Beetle-kinden (if only Achaeos or Tisamon had read it before their own journey there). *Written in Sand* presents the Solifugid-kinden mentioned in *Scarab Path* and briefly encountered in *Heirs of the Blade*. Their hostile relationship with the Wasp military arises out of the bizarre reputation solifugids seem to have amongst US/Western soldiers serving in the Middle East, where they are supposedly reckoned to be able to kill a camel unaided. *Masters of the Spires*, whilst it does give me a chance to give the Alethi Army Ant-kinden a decent look-see, is mostly a plunge into a whole ecosystem that I never got to play with properly, with especial reference to perhaps the nastiest Art in the entire Insect-kinden world.

And then we have *For Love of Distant Shores* (which, no matter how I slice it, is a title that owes a great deal to Ursula le Guin). This linking narrative was always planned, although it wasn't always going to be Doctor Phinagler on the kinden's first fateful voyage west. For those who have read both *Shadows of the Apt* and *Echoes of the Fall*, and have made the connections that are optional, but there to be made, this is it. "Bones", the short story featured in *A Time for Grief*, is the far past of the kinden's world, and *Shores* is where the kinden and their long-estranged relatives/enemies finally intersect once more, with tragic consequences that then play out through the *Echoes of the Fall* novels.

# TALES OF THE APT

## Adrian Tchaikovsky

**Tales of the Apt** is a companion series to the best-selling decalogy *Shadows of the Apt* (Tor UK) by 2016 Arthur C. Clarke Award winning author Adrian Tchaikovsky.

Tales gathers together short stories from disparate places and supplements them with a wealth of new material written especially for the series. Together, they combine to provide a different perspective, an alternative history that parallels and unfolds alongside the familiar one, filling in the gaps and revealing intriguing backstories for established characters. A must read for any fan of the *Shadows of the Apt* books, where epic fantasy meets steampunk and so much more.

"The whole Shadows of the Apt series has been one of the most original creations in modern fantasy" – *Upcoming4.me*

"Tchaikovsky makes a good and enjoyable mix between a medieval-looking world and the presence of technology" – *Starburst Magazine*

### Spoils of War
### A Time for Grief

Available now from NewCon Press: www.newconpress.co.uk

# Feast and Famine

**Adrian Tchaikovsky**'s first ever short story collection

Contents:

A solicitor by profession, scientist by education, and historical martial arts hobbyist by choice, Adrian Tchaikovsky is best known for his *Shadows of the Apt* series – epic fantasy laced with steampunk and other influences. In *Feast and Famine* he delivers one of the most ambitious and varied collections of stories NewCon Press have yet published. Ranging from the deep space hard SF of the title story to the high fantasy of "The Sun in the Morning" (a *Shadows of the Apt* tale), from the Peter S Beagle influenced "The Roar of the Crowd" to the supernatural Holmes-esque intrigue of "The Dissipation Club", Adrian delivers a dazzling array of quality short stories that traverse genre. Ten stories in all, five of which appear here for the very first time.

Released as part of the *Imaginings* series, ***Feast and Famine*** is available as a signed limited edition hardback and an eBook.

www.newconpress.co.uk

# Origamy

## Rachel Armstrong

"*Origamy* is a magnificent, glittering explosion of a book: a meditation on creation, the poetry of science and the insane beauty of everything. You're going to need this." **– Warren Ellis**

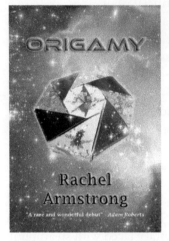

Mobius knows she isn't a novice weaver, but it seems she must re-learn the art of manipulating spacetime all over again. Encouraged by her parents, Newton and Shelley, she starts to experiment, and is soon traveling far and wide across the galaxy, encountering a dazzling array of bizarre cultures and races along the way. Yet all is not well, and it soon becomes clear that a dark menace is gathering, one that could threaten the very fabric of time and space and will require all weavers to unite if the universe is to stand any chance of surviving.

**Rachel Armstrong** is Professor of Experimental Architecture at Newcastle University and a 2010 Senior TED Fellow. A former medical doctor, she now designs experiments that explore the transition between inert and living matter and considers their implications for life beyond our solar system.

"*Origamy* crackles with a strange and brilliant energy, and folds the conventions of SF into beautiful new shapes. A rare and wonderful debut."
**– Adam Roberts**

"Perhaps the most astonishing and original piece of SF I've read in a long, long while." **– Adrian Tchaikovsky**

"A visionary masterpiece. Science Fiction, Fantasy, science and poetry combine to create a lyric on life and death that spans the whole of creation. Delightful and mind-expanding. If you miss it you have missed one of the finest examples of literary art." **– Justina Robson**

# IMMANION PRESS

Purveyors of Speculative Fiction

## Madame Two Swords by Tanith Lee

An unnamed narrator, in the French city of Troy, finds an old book of the writings of the revolutionary, Lucien de Ceppays, who lived and died in the city two centuries before. She feels a strange bond to the life and thoughts of this long-dead man – what is the mysterious truth behind her obsession? Perhaps she did not find the book at all – perhaps it found her. Some years later, impoverished after the death of her mother, the narrator – in a state of desperation – finds herself inexorably guided to meet the peculiar and unnerving Madame Two Swords, an old woman with a history, and her own enduring bonds to Lucien – as well as the book. For the narrator, reality seems to unravel, as she begins to penetrate just how intimately she is connected with Madame Two Swords and Lucien. Previously only available as a limited-edition hardback in 1988, the long-awaited new edition of this vintage-Tanith novella includes illustrations by Jarod Mills. ISBN 978-1-907737-81-7 £11.99, $15.50 pbk

## Salty Kiss Island by Rhys Hughes

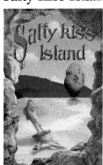

What is a fantastical love story? It isn't quite the same as an ordinary love story. The events that take place are stranger, more extreme, full of the passion of originality, invention and magic, as well as an intensification of emotional love. The stories in Salty Kiss Island are set in this world and others, spanning the spectrum of possible and impossible experiences, the uncharted territories of yearning, the depths and shoals of the heart, mind and soul. A love of language runs through them, parallel to the love that motivates their characters to feats of preposterous heroism, luminous lunacy and grandiose gesture. They include tales of minstrels and their catastrophic serenades, dreamers sinking into sequences of ever-deeper dreams, goddesses and mermaids, sailors and devils, messages in bottles that can think and speak but never be read, shadows with an independent life and voyagers of distant galaxies who are already at their destinations before they arrive.
ISBN: 978-1-907737-77-0, £11.99, $15.50 pbk

## A Raven Bound with Lilies by Storm Constantine

 Androgynous, and stronger in mind and body than humans, sometimes deadly, and often possessing unearthly beauty, the Wraeththu have captivated readers since Storm Constantine's first novel, The Enchantments of Flesh and Spirit, was published in 1988, regarded as ground-breaking in its treatment of gender and sexuality. This anthology of 15 tales collects all her published Wraeththu short stories into one volume, and also includes extra material, including the author's first explorations of the androgynous race. The tales range from the 'creation story' Paragenesis, through the bloody, brutal rise of the earliest tribes, and on into a future, where strange mutations are starting to emerge from hidden corners of the earth. With illustrations by official Wraeththu artist Ruby, as well as pictures from Danielle Lainton and the author herself, A Raven Bound with Lilies is a must for any Wraeththu enthusiast and is also a comprehensive introduction to the mythos for those who are new to it. ISBN: 978-1-907737-80-0 £11.99, $15.50

## The Lightbearer by Alan Richardson

 Michael Horsett parachutes into Occupied France before the D-Day Invasion. He is dropped in the wrong place, miles from the action, badly injured, and totally alone. He falls prey to two Thelemist women who have awaited the Hawk God's coming, attracts a group of First World War veterans who rally to what they imagine is his cause, is hunted by a troop of German Field Police who are desperate to find him, and has a climactic encounter with a mutilated priest who believes that Lucifer Incarnate has arrived…The Lightbearer is a unique gnostic thriller, dealing with the themes of Light and Darkness, Good and Evil, Matter and Spirit.

"The Lightbearer is another shining example of Alan Richardson's talent as a story-teller. He uses his wide esoteric knowledge to produce a story that thrills, chills and startles the reader as it radiates pure magical energy. An unusual and gripping war story with more facets than a star sapphire." – Mélusine Draco, author of "Aubry's Dog".

**info@immanion-press.com**
**www.immanion-press.com**